ONE
WRONG
MOVE

Books by Shannon McKenna

FATAL STRIKE

ONE WRONG MOVE

BLOOD AND FIRE

FADE TO MIDNIGHT

TASTING FEAR

ULTIMATE WEAPON

BADDEST BAD BOYS

EXTREME DANGER

EDGE OF MIDNIGHT

ALL ABOUT MEN

HOT NIGHT

OUT OF CONTROL

RETURN TO ME

STANDING IN THE SHADOWS

BEHIND CLOSED DOORS

BAD BOYS NEXT EXIT

I BRAKE FOR BAD BOYS

ALL THROUGH THE NIGHT

SHANNON McKENNA

ONE WRONG MOVE

ZEBRA BOOKS
KENSINGTON PUBLISHING CORP.
http://www.kensingtonbooks.com

ZEBRA BOOKS are published by

Kensington Publishing Corp.
119 West 40th Street
New York, NY 10018

All Kensington titles, imprints, and distributed lines are available at special quantity discounts for bulk purchases for sales promotion, premiums, fund-raising, educational, or institutional use.

Special book excerpts or customized printings can also be created to fit specific needs. For details, write or phone the office of the Kensington Sales Manager: Attn.: Sales Department. Kensington Publishing Corp., 119 West 40th Street, New York, NY 10018. Phone: 1-800-221-2647.

Zebra and the Z logo Reg. U.S. Pat. & TM Off.

First Kensington Books Trade Paperback Printing: October 2012
First Zebra Books Mass-Market Paperback Printing: July 2013
ISBN-13: 978-1-4201-4239-6
ISBN-10: 1-4201-4239-9

10 9 8 7 6 5 4 3 2

Printed in the United States of America

1

Sheepshead Bay, Brooklyn, NYC
5:41 a.m. Thursday morning

Nina looked back. Her heart jolted up into her throat. That car was following her. It wasn't nerves, or paranoia. She'd slipped into the all-night supermarket for a few minutes to talk herself down, sip some weak coffee from the deli counter, get over the crawling sense of being stalked. It didn't seem possible. It was so very obvious that she had nothing worthwhile to steal. She made a point of that. She dressed down to the point of vanishing. She'd made it into a high art.

And yet, that car had parked somewhere and waited for her while she dawdled in the supermarket. And now, it was crawling steadily along behind her once again. A Lincoln Town Car, nondescript beige color. She noted the plate number as her nervous, fast walk quickened into a trot. She wished she hadn't drunk the nasty coffee. It roiled in her chilled guts like acid slush. She punched 911 into her cell with the useless, scolding rant blaring through her head, how she should have trusted her instincts, stayed in the store, called the police from there, yada yada. No running back to the supermarket now. The car was between her and it, and all the businesses on the street were deserted this early in the morning. Across the street were apartment complexes, lots of shadowy lawn and shrubbery to sprint through. She'd never get anyone's attention in time. She couldn't have picked a worse spot to be at this hour if she tried. *Shit*. Brain-dead *idiot*, thinking she could walk to work at this hour. Idiot, for agreeing to man the hotline this early in the morning, for not getting the car fixed in time, for not calling a cab.

The engine revved. The car was gaining on her. A squirt of raw panic jolted her even faster, rubber-soled sandaled feet thudding as the 911 operator squawked into her ear. "I'm being followed by a beige Lincoln Town Car," she panted back into the phone, and gabbled out the plate number. "I'm on Lamson, just turned off Avenue Y—"

The car screeched to a stop right behind her, and a door popped open. "Nina? Nina!"

What the *hell*? It was a woman's voice, thin and shaking. Nina teetered as she twisted to look. Her breath rasped in her chest. She thumbed the speakerphone button on. As if that could help.

A wraith stumbled out of the backseat and onto the side-walk. A woman, older, graying. Skeletal. Bloodshot eyes, sunken into sallow, shadowy pits. Blood dripped from her nose, and from a cut lip. Her clothes hung on her, and her hair was a snarled black-and-gray mess.

The woman lurched closer. "Nina?" Her voice sounded beseeching.

Nina skittered back, her hackles rising. A feeling was growing, almost like recognition, but not quite. More like dread.

"Excuse me?" she asked cautiously. "Do I know you?"

Tears streamed down over the woman's sallow, caved-in

cheeks. Words burst out of her, in a language Nina did not recognize. And she was coming forward way too fast.

Nina backed up. "How do you know my name?"

Another impassioned outburst, and Nina did not understand a goddamn word of it. She continued backing up. "Look, I don't know who you are or what you want, but stay away from me," she said. "Just keep your distance."

Thud. Her back hit the newsstand. The woman came on with unnerving swiftness. Her gibberish had a pleading tone. She grabbed Nina's phone out of her hand, and clicked at it, still babbling.

"Hey! Give me that!" Nina lunged to get her phone back. The phone dropped to the ground, spinning, as the woman grabbed her arm, snake-fast. Nina twisted, squirming to get free, but the woman's icy hand was horribly strong. Her other hand flashed out.

Nina screamed as a hypodermic needle stabbed into her forearm. It burned like a wasp's sting.

The woman let go. The syringe dropped, rolled into the gutter.

Nina's back hit the newsstand again, with a jarring thud. She stared into the other woman's haggard face. Gasping for air, but she had no place to put it. Her lungs were clenched in a huge, cold fist.

Recognition finally kicked in, with a shuddering prickle over her entire body. "Helga," she croaked. "Oh, God. Helga?"

The woman raised her hands, flapping them in mute apology. She bent down, and scooped up Nina's phone.

"What was—wha—why did you do that?" Nina's voice no longer felt like it came from her own body. It floated, small and tinny and disembodied. "Wha—what the fuck was in that needle?" She tried to sound tough. Hard to do while sliding down a wall, flat onto one's ass.

Helga's face hung over her, grotesque with its mask of smeared and dripping blood. She was still talking desperately. A man's face joined her. Chubby, stubbled, anxious, smelling of cigarettes and beer. The driver of the car. Nina did not recognize him. He was yelling at Helga, in that same unknown language. His raspy voice shook, like he was afraid. Helga was weeping, yelling. Tears mixed with blood.

They slapped her face, yelled her name, but she no longer felt particularly attached to her face, or her name.

Her limp body twisted, flopped. She was being hoisted, dragged. Bundled into the car. Shoved over the slippery leather seat. She smelled cigarettes. Helga slid in beside her, babbling. Still clutching her phone.

Helga hung over her, pleading. She could not hear, did not care.

She just kept falling.

Alex Aaro strode through the churning mass of humanity on the JFK concourse. Everyone in his path who glimpsed his face scuttled out of his way. The end result was like the parting of the Red Sea.

"No, I don't have time. No, it's not convenient," Aaro growled into his cell phone. "I can't do what you're asking of me. I'm busy."

"What would it cost you?" Bruno's voice had lost its coaxing tone a while back, and had moved on to righteously pissed-off. "You're in New York already. The plane has landed. You're right there. What's so hard about a short delay in your personal agenda for the day? Just translate that recording from Nina's phone. They think it's in Ukrainian, but nobody there has gotten around to translating it yet. So you're up, dude. You're the one."

Aaro ground his teeth. "I can't do it now."

"I'm looking at a Google map right now. Twenty-five

minutes gets you to the hospital. You translate the recording of whatever the needle-stabbing hag said, hang out with Lily's bestest bud for an hour or so, just keep her company until we can get a guy we trust in place to watch her. When the new guard takes over, you're out of there. Piece of cake."

Cake, his hairy ass. Any sort of involvement in the affairs of the McClouds or their associates inevitably turned into a monster goatfuck. It never failed. He'd experienced the phenomenon on several occasions in the past. Davy McCloud had roped him into helping out some years ago, on the basis of their old Army Ranger connection. That crazy adventure had involved a ring of ruthless organ pirates.

And it had been straight downhill from there. One of the latest episodes had resulted in the total firebombed destruction of Aaro's residence, and all of his motor vehicles. But the worst one had happened about six months before. Bruno was jerking him around because he could. All because of Aaro's massive fuckup, the one that had practically cost Bruno's and Lily's lives. Bruno was flailing him with the lash of guilt. *Whoosh, smack.*

It worked, too. Aaro hated guilt. It made his guts twitch. And even so, he couldn't comply, not this time. "I'm busy," Aaro muttered.

"Busy with what? With fucking *work*, Aaro? Haven't scored enough cash yet with your cyber-counterattack service? Miles told me you guys were raking it in. Push the lunch meeting with the fat cats up a couple hours! You can stop at the goddamn hospital to help out Lily's friend! Your balls are big enough, man. You have the clout."

"I'm not having lunch. I'm—"

"I don't care, Aaro. Seriously, Nina's terrified. She got zapped by a drug that knocked her out, and the crazy bitch that did it is in a coma now, so nobody can say what the junk is. She's scared. She needs support. Preferably armed support. It would make us all feel better."

"You think someone might attack her?"

"Who knows? We don't know what that woman said to her! This situation needs you, Alex Aaro, personally and specifically! Come on, Lily's beside herself. It's not good for her to be upset right now."

"Don't start," Aaro snarled. "I wasn't the one who got your lady friend pregnant. Her delicate hormonal condition is not my problem."

"Dude. You're biting my ass. With big yellow fangs."

"I'm not good at holding hands, Bruno. This is me. You know me. This chick needs a trauma therapist, or a social worker, or—"

"Nina *is* a social worker, bonehead!"

Aaro winced. Worse and worse. Social worker. Christ on a crutch.

"Look at it this way." Bruno's voice was a nail gun, punching the words in deep. "It's a babysitting job. You don't have to be sensitive or touchy-feely. You don't even have to be polite. Be your own assholic self. Grunt, fart, scratch your balls, I don't care. Just translate the recording, and stay in the same room with her. Davy's got a guy in Philly who's on his way. Old army buddy. An hour and twenty, and you're free. Last favor I'll ever ask of you, I swear to God."

Aaro hesitated. *I'm racing to the Mercer Street Hospice to say good-bye before my dying aunt croaks.*

Nope. He couldn't say it, even though it was true. Playing the pity card just wasn't his style. "No," he said. "Can't."

"You *asshole*. What the hell is so important . . ."

Aaro turned the squawking down to white noise and focused on keeping the guilt-twitches to a minimum. Deep breathing. Clenched belly. Helped a little. He picked up speed as he neared the baggage claim, anxious to have his bag in his possession. He hated checking weapons into cargo. Being separated from his guns made him more than usually bad-tempered. Knowing that Aunt Tonya was lingering at death's door made him feel sick. And the thought of facing his family of origin ratcheted his stress level up to the stratosphere.

Fielding Bruno and Lily's batshit request was the final ass-kick.

"Aaro, it's not that big of a deal." Bruno's voice came back into focus. He'd stopped bellowing, was trying sweet reason again. The guy was like a pit bull.

"There are tens of thousands of people in New York City who could translate that recording for her," Aaro said. "Find one."

"They're not six foot four and armed to the teeth and meaner than a rattlesnake with PMS. Yeah, Lil, that's right. He's too busy." Bruno's voice was muffled now, directed toward his soon-to-be wife, Lily, who was evidently in the room with him. There was a shrill response. "Lily wants to talk to you now." Bruno's voice took on a sly edge. "Soon as she's off the phone with Nina. Brace yourself, man."

"Do *not* put me on the phone with her," Aaro said curtly.

"I swear, I will," Bruno threatened. "Nina needs somebody there. She hasn't got family, and there's no husband or boyfriend to—"

"Are you trying to fix me up?" The irritated nerve from Aaro's teeth-grinding problem throbbed, nastily. "Don't even think about it, man."

"No way," Bruno assured him hastily. "We wouldn't wish you on our worst enemy. Just translate the recording, then stand around with her looking intimidating until somebody spells you. You're good at that."

Aaro yanked his bag off the carousel. He couldn't even count all the things there were to hate about this scenario. A terrified woman on the streets of Brooklyn, babbling Ukrainian, torn blouse, bleeding face, needle full of junk. Why even ask? Another hard-luck story. Violence, rape, betrayal. It drove the woman to drugs, insanity, and finally into a fucking coma.

And they wanted him to translate all the gory details for them. Great. Just great.

He did his Red Sea routine again, in the direction of the rental car counters. He didn't want to translate this pathetic tale of woe. It was going to suck ass, and there was nothing he could do to help. He needed to stay far away from women like Lily's unlucky pal Nina. Bleeding heart do-gooder at her battered women's shelter. She tried to help the huddled masses and the wretched refuse, and this was the thanks she got. What a total clusterfuck.

No, he would drive hundreds of miles out of his way to avoid Lily's friend, and her big-ass problems. Let someone else hoist up that cross.

"Lily's giving Nina your cell, right now," Bruno informed him. "I'm sending you the audio file. Be looking for it."

Aaro's breath hissed through his teeth. "Goddamnit, Bruno—"

"Then Nina will call you. Tell her to her face you don't give a shit. That you just can't be bothered. Go ahead, say that to the scared, traumatized, crying girl. I wish I could be there to watch the show."

Aaro hung up on him, and got in line at the rental car counter, rubbing his thumb over the hot, sickening red throb in his forehead.

He would be worse than useless to this woman, standing around in a hospital room with his guns, taking up air and space. Helpless and stupid, like a big dumb rock. What good would that do her? He'd just make her uncomfortable. Like she didn't have enough problems.

God, he hated flying. His guts hurt like fingernails were poking into them. And he hadn't slept since he'd heard about Aunt Tonya.

Weird, this reaction. Hadn't seen his aunt in decades. Hadn't spoken to her since he broke contact with his family.

There was no way to maintain contact with Tonya and stay clear of the rest of them, so he'd cut ties. *Snip, snip.* Ruthless bastard with the bolt cutters, that was him. He hadn't thought of Tonya in so long. He'd put an insulating mental fuzz between him and his past, disturbed only by the biannual reports he got from the P.I. who kept the Arbatov clan under surveillance. He paid the guy well for that service. Watching Arbatovs was dangerous work.

It was from the latest report, received three days ago, that he'd heard about Tonya being in the hospice. He'd hacked into the hospice computer for details. Feeding tube. Respirator. Dialysis. Morphine.

Tonya was dying. And with that realization, the memories amassed behind the retaining wall burst through.

It had wiped him out. Oh, man. *Tonya.*

Tonya was the youngest sister of Aaro's father, Oleg Arbatov. Like Aaro himself, she did not belong in the Arbatov family. Dreamy, absent, never learned English worth a damn. Never married, despite being beautiful in her youth and having many suitors. Aaro's mother had died of cancer when Aaro was five and his sister, Julie, only two. Tonya had come to live with them to take care of the children. That arrangement had lasted five years, until Oleg got married to the poisonous hell-bitch Rita, who was barely nine years older than Alex himself.

Rita had run Tonya out. Things had gone pretty much to hell, from then on.

Tonya was . . . well, different. She'd spent more than half of her adult life in the nuthouse. She saw things no one else saw, talked to people no one could see. She made people nervous. It had comforted them to label her crazy. But she'd never seemed crazy to Aaro. He'd loved hearing her dreams, her stories, her visions. Aunt Tonya had read his palm, his face, his eyes. Said he was destined for great things. Fame, fortune, travel, true love. Huh. So much for her precognitive abilities, but he appreciated the thought. Julie had loved her, too.

When Aaro was thirteen, Oleg had gotten violently frustrated with his son, as had often happened. He'd broken Aaro's arm, ribs. Bruises, contusions, ripped cartilage. Tonya had rebelled, surprising everyone. She stole Rita's jewelry to pawn, snatched Alex and Julie, and ran with them. That took guts. He hadn't appreciated how much at the time.

They'd taken a bus to the Jersey Shore, and spent almost a month there before they'd been dragged back. His arm and ribs healed slowly and itchily, while he and Tonya and Julie took long, shivering walks on the beach, picnicked on sodden sand under the deserted boardwalk as if it were high summer, watching seagulls squawk over garbage washed up by the surf. They giggled over dumb TV programs on the grainy old set in their motel room, ate greasy food in the diner, went to the movies, played cards. Tonya had told them stories. Fables, from the Ukraine.

None of them had ever been so happy.

It couldn't last. All of them had known that. The pawned jewelry had eventually betrayed them. Tonya had been sent back to the nuthouse, and he and Julie—well. No point even thinking about that.

That brief taste of freedom had stuck in his mind ever since. It hung there in his head. Like a star. Always out of reach.

He batted the unhelpful thought away. It pissed him off, this nagging, sucking feeling, of something slipping away from him. Like he'd ever really had Tonya, after not seeing her for almost twenty years. What was he losing that he hadn't already lost, decades ago?

And why did he feel guilty? Like he could have helped her.

She'd helped him. She'd been there for him. It cost her big.

He flinched away from that. He couldn't help Tonya. He'd failed utterly at helping Julie. He'd run away. Saved his own skin.

His life would be worth nothing if the remaining members of his family ever came to know his whereabouts. He did not appreciate being held hostage by guilt, from a past he'd done everything to bury. God, when was it enough? His heart had been thudding double time for days. He could not even fucking breathe.

Voilà, enter Bruno and Lily with their sobbing social worker. Fresh guilt, poured over old guilt. Like fudge sauce on a sundae.

He reached the head of the line at the car rental counter. A perky, snub-nosed girl directed a flirtatious smile into his bloodshot eyes—and it stuck there a moment, a frozen grimace, before fading. Like a rabbit hypnotized by a snake. Chick was smarter than she looked.

They got through the paperwork with gratifying swiftness, and he headed out to the lot. The headache sucked rocks. A hard, rhythmic *thwack* with each beat of his heart. He wanted to punish the headache for existing. To kick the shit out of it. But, whoops, it was inside his own brain tissue. Bummer, that. Yeah, he was Oleg Arbatov's son. A real chip off the old block. For Oleg, it was all about punishment. Since he was on the theme of punishment, his phone beeped. A multimedia message. The 911 call. The hard luck suck-ass story, for his enjoyment.

Aaro got into the 2011 Lincoln Navigator. Dug into his duffel. The knives, first. Kershaw in his left jacket pocket, Gerber in his right, the all-purpose onto the belt sheath. He groped around in his clothes for the holsters, the gun cases. FNP-45 in the waistband side holster, the .357 snubbie S&W tucked into the boot grip. Yeah. That let a little more air into his lungs. He pulled out the Saiga shotgun case, laid it on the seat, and just sat there, sucking in more badly needed oxygen.

When the woman called, he'd tell her no. Let them all hate his guts if that's what they needed to do. Then off to Tonya, for his next dose of guilt. He'd call Nina back after, if he was still functioning. Ask her if she still needed help. Best he could do. Hell, it was all he could do. With any luck at all, she'd tell him to fuck off, and he'd be free.

Bruno would be disgusted with him. Lily, too. But he'd withstood massive, prolonged doses of toxic disgust before.

Come to think of it, he was uniquely trained to tolerate it.

2

"So, Ben? Can I count on your support for my campaign?" Harold Rudd sipped his coffee while exerting a precise, delicate pressure on the stress points in Benjamin Stillman's decision-making process.

He did not enjoy the surgical approach to compulsion nearly as much as his usual style, which was somewhat rougher. It was more satisfying to clobber the bastards with his psi talent. Watch them crawl and gibber, pleading for mercy. He liked that. It gave him a buzz that lasted hours. Sometimes even outlasting the effects of the psi-max.

But reducing Senator Stillman to crawling and gibbering on the floor of the exclusive dining club would not advance Rudd's cause, however enjoyable it might be in the short term. He needed the man fit and forceful and articulate on Rudd's behalf, throwing all his political muscle behind Rudd's upcoming campaign for governor. Not drugged up in a private clinic, being treated for a nervous breakdown.

Self-control. Rudd was a practical man. *Smile at the bastard.*

"I don't know, Harold." Stillman shoveled a chunk of

brunch omelet into his mouth, shoved a triangle of toast after it. The man's flabby cheeks distended as he chewed. "You don't really have the kind of experience that I think is necessary for the . . . for the . . ." Stillman stopped, choking and coughing.

His face reddened. His eyes darted, confused. He'd lost his train of thought. People in Rudd's vicinity tended to lose trains of thought that did not further Rudd's own ends. That trick gave Rudd no end of entertainent. Rudd pushed. Hard enough to confuse the man. Then a little more, hard enough to hurt.

He released Stillman. The man coughed into his napkin.

Rudd patted his back. "Ben? Are you all right? Should I call someone? Do you need medication?"

Stillman shrugged him off. "No," he gasped. "I'm not taking any goddamn medication. I just . . . ah . . . had a moment there."

"We all do, now and then." Rudd poured the man a glass of water. Yes, one did. Particularly when one had brunch with Harold Rudd. But Stillman would never make that connection. He could count on the man's antiquated worldview the way he could count on the sun rising. Rudd's secret talent would never show up on Stillman's radar.

He recommenced delicate pressure as Stillman gulped water. Being taken down a peg had softened him slightly, but there was still a wall. Shoveling horseshit back in his youth had been easier than this. He pitied the senator's wife. The guy must be a dominating asshole at home. Perhaps the senator had a bit of latent psi power of his own.

Or perhaps Rudd himself was the problem. He was due for another hit of the precious psi-max to bring his talent of compulsion back up to full strength, but he'd been making a painful effort to pace himself. He had a supply, but it was not bottomless. And that business with the Kasyanov bitch making a run for it made him frantic. He needed her to produce more. Develop the perfect formula. He was so close to the big time. So much power to be grasped, if he did it all just right. Everyone had to be on board. Everyone had to be *good*.

When he got his hands on Kasyanov, she would pay for defying him. Without incapacitating her, of course. Kasyanov was the only one who could cook up a stable dose of psi-max. Rudd had funded labs full of useless eggheads who had been trying to duplicate her formula for eighteen months, but their efforts had all fallen short. Yes, Kasyanov had been holding out on them for a while. Lying hag.

He tried again, harder. Ben Stillman shoved a wad of egg and smoked salmon into his mouth and frowned out as he chewed, at the dark wood paneling, white tablecloths, white china. *Come on, bastard. Give it up.* Rudd bore down. A little bit more . . . almost there . . .

"Sir?"

Rudd whipped his head around, concentration broken, and Stillman grunted, shaking his head like a dog shaking off water. The moment was lost. *Shit.* Rudd glared at his aide, who blinked apologetically with his big puppy dog eyes. Fucking *idiot,* interrupting him at the worst possible moment. He smiled benignly. "Yes, John?"

"Sir, Roy is here to see you," John murmured, eyes darting nervously toward the door. "He said it was urgent. I just thought I'd, ah, to be on the safe side—"

"I understand." Rudd's hound, Roy, had intimidated John into soiling himself.

Rudd glanced at the door. Yes, there was his problematic henchman, Roy Lester, slouching in the dining room where anyone could see him. Idiot.

Roy could wait. Rudd fumbled for contact with Stillman's mind. It was easier to find this time. When he had it, he locked eyes with Anabel, who was sipping soda water at a nearby table. He smiled, as if only just noticing her, and gestured her over.

Stillman turned to look, and did a double take. He dabbed with his napkin at his purplish, discolored lips.

Time for the big guns. Which was to say, Anabel's tits and ass. She used them the way a terrorist used a fertilizer bomb. No mercy.

Anabel's face brightened. Her finger flutter said *Oh, goodie! What a coincidence!* She jumped up and headed toward them, weaving gracefully between tables. Beaming. Shining. For the love of God, she'd dosed up, the naughty slut, and after he'd expressly ordered her to wait. His teeth ground. Her psi-max-enhanced glamour had taken hold. Rudd winced, as heads turned all over the club. *Don't overdo it, you vain, whorish bitch. It's just Stillman. You don't have to fuck the whole room.*

Too late. Slim, curvy, blond Anabel was lovely enough to turn heads even without a psi-max-fueled push, but there was nothing she liked better than starting to sparkle, watching men trip over their feet, forget that they were arm in arm with their own wives. Anabel had been known to cause car accidents when she sparkled at peak dose. And that was on top of telepathy, her primary talent. She stopped at the table, and bent to give Rudd a peck on the cheek. "Hi, Uncle Harold!"

He beamed at the self-indulgent slut. "Anabel, this is Senator Ben Stillman. This is Anabel Marshall, the daughter of a family friend," he explained to a transfixed Stillman. "She's working on my campaign, and she's a pearl beyond price, so don't even think of trying to steal her!"

The two men chuckled. Anabel blushed. Stillman eyed her jutting bosom, beautifully showcased in the tight black ribbed turtleneck. Anabel preened and posed and sparkled, extravagantly beautiful. In that unguarded moment, Rudd gave the final, tipping shove . . .

. . . and Stillman's decision clicked into place, covered by Anabel's tinkling laugh, her chatty bubbling. Stillman's support was his. *Yes.*

He smiled at her. "My dear, would you be kind enough to entertain Senator Stillman for a few minutes while I go see what Roy needs? We shouldn't be more than ten minutes or so in the suite."

Anabel knew just what to do. "My pleasure," she cooed.

Rudd made his way to the door, allowing his disapproval to flagellate Roy's sullen, unresponsive mind, as soon as he was close enough to make it really sting. "Let's find a private place," he hissed.

Roy was cowed on the ride up to the suite where Anabel would soon bring Stillman. The senator was in his pocket, yes, but a sweaty bout with Anabel with the cameras running would not be a bad addition to the archives. Rudd had an extensive video collection of Anabel's exploits. Political figures, judges, corporate heads. Men, women, young or old, Anabel wasn't fussy. She would do anything for her dose.

Rudd followed Roy into the suite and slammed the door. "What the hell do you think you're doing here? I told you to stay away!"

Roy reeled as the punishing energy of Rudd's compulsion battered his mind, stumbling into the architectural model that dominated the room. The costly model his staff had painstakingly finished putting together just that morning. "You idiot!" Rudd bellowed. "Get away from that! Do you have any idea how much that thing cost?"

Roy jerked away, bouncing off the wall, and thudded down onto the king-sized bed, cringing. "Don't," he pleaded. "Stop."

Rudd strode over to inspect the model of the future Greaves

Institute, to make sure nothing had been broken. "You knocked off four trees. Clumsy idiot. This just arrived today! I need to have it delivered to the Convention Center at Spruce Ridge before Saturday, so if you could avoid crushing it to splinters, I would appreciate it!"

"Uh, yeah." Roy rubbed the mottled, purplish burn scar that covered his entire neck, extending up under his chin like a turtleneck sweater. Rudd found the man's nervous habit intensely annoying.

"What on earth are you doing here?" Rudd hissed. "You should not be near me in public! We had this talk! I am in the public eye! It was not a gentle suggestion to stay away, you idiot, it was an order!"

"Stop whaling on me! I can't fucking think when you do that!"

"You have trouble with that in the best of circumstances," Rudd snapped, but he scaled back his attack. Roy sagged, panting. "And watch your language," he added, as an afterthought. "Family values."

"My ass," Roy spat out. "Hypocrite."

Rudd was unoffended. It was impossible to hide one's true nature from employees who were enhanced with psi-max, but he knew the ugly secrets squirming in Anabel's and Roy's minds just as they knew his. It balanced out into an uneasy partnership, if he managed to control them. Between the heads Roy had broken and the dicks Anabel had sucked, the two might soon become a liability for his shining future.

But that was an issue for another day. "So what's the crisis?"

"It's Kasyanov, boss." Roy wouldn't meet his eyes. "I lost her."

Rudd's guts chilled at the implications. "Lost her?" he repeated. "How is that possible? You can follow a target at a mile or more! You said you couldn't lose her frequency if you wanted to!"

Roy's high, balding forehead was shiny with sweat. Rudd suddenly noticed the purplish knot on the side of his head. "She was at this house, out in Brooklyn. Anabel told me she was planning on trying to get to JFK or LaGuardia today, so I was going to take her when she came out to get in her cab. And she, uh . . . she got me."

"Got me," Rudd repeated, his voice like stone. "Define 'got me.'"

Roy squirmed as Rudd battered at him, using his psi on Roy the way a lion trainer used a whip. Roy's jaw shook. "It was the drug," he choked out. "The new one, Psi-Max 48. Stop it, boss, if you want me to tell you, 'cause I'm gonna puke, right here on the bed, I swear."

An odorous mess would be inconvenient for Anabel and Stillman, so Rudd grudgingly released the pressure. Roy sagged, wheezing.

"Fucking asshole," he gasped out. "Cut that shit out!"

"Just tell me," Rudd said, with chilly patience.

"Like I was trying to say! It was the formula you shot into the doctor's arm last weekend, up at the lab! Remember that tantrum, Mr. Fucking Family Values? When you got into a snit, and decided to conduct your own little private medical experiment?"

A snap of the mental lash made Roy grunt and twitch. "Do not presume to scold me," Rudd said. "Just tell me what happened."

"I had her pinned, in Brooklyn. But . . ." He trailed off. "It must have been the drug. She made me see things. It was . . ." He shook his head, speechless. His eyes looked haunted.

Rudd folded his arms over his chest. "What did she make you see? Come on. You know telepathy isn't my thing. Tell me."

Roy's reddened eyes flicked away.

Rudd laughed. "Oh, something personal? Mean Mommy, coming into your bedroom to put the nightly clothespin on your dick? Straight pins to the testicles? Something sadistic and incestuous?"

"Fuck off," Roy muttered.

"Interesting," Rudd mused. "So the enhanced formula gave Kasyanov a brand-new talent. How would you characterize it, Roy? Illusion? Invasive telepathy, like Anabel?"

"Worse," Roy blurted. "Deeper. A mix, maybe. She pulls it from your head, and then she throws it back at you. Sick, crazy bitch."

"Enterprising of her," Rudd murmured. "But what I don't understand is how she got away. No matter what she hit you with, on ten mg's of psi-max, you should have been able to narrow in on her frequency afterwards, from miles away! How the hell did you lose her?"

Roy's eyes slid down. "I was unconscious," he muttered. "When I came to, she was out of range. No trace at all. Just gone."

"You fainted?" Rudd started to laugh. "Scrawny Helga Kasyanov, scared you unconscious? Roy. I'm disillusioned."

"I hit my head when I fell down," Roy protested, gingerly prodding the lump on his pate. "And when I came to, I—"

"Shut up, Roy. The details of your failure are not interesting to me. So you have no leads?"

"Not exactly. Our guy in the NYPD checked out the nine-one-one calls. A guy at a corner grocery on Fourth Avenue in Brooklyn called an ambulance for a woman found lying on the sidewalk only fifteen blocks from the house where I lost Kasyanov. She was gone by the time the ambulance arrived, though. A car service driver stopped, some guy who spoke Ukrainian. He took her away in his car."

"And . . . ?"

"The clerk gave me the number of the car service." Roy looked pleased with himself. "I called the dispatcher, described the guy, told her I'd left a briefcase in his car. She gave me the guy's name and cell, just like that. Such a nice girl. So sweet and helpful."

"People are such idiots," Rudd said, with dark satisfaction.

"Yeah. Yuri Marchuk. Came from Odessa fifteen years ago. One divorced daughter. Preschool-age grandson. Apartment on Avenue B."

Rudd pondered that for a moment, rubbing his chin.

"Well, boss? How far should I go with this Yuri character?"

"As far as necessary. We don't want tales told, do we?"

"You want me to outsource this one?"

"What, Roy? Lost your nerve?" Rudd taunted.

Roy waved that jab away. "I have contacts in Brighton Beach who can communicate with this clown in his native language," he said. "Dmitri Arbatov is good. And in my experience, once the hedge clippers come out, people tend to revert to the mother tongue."

Rudd considered that. "Fine, but Anabel should be there when this guy talks, no matter what language or what methods of persuasion you use. Your telepathy's not strong enough. You're only good for long-range surveillance. You're a tracker, Roy. Nothing more."

Roy looked stung. "My talent's been plenty useful to you so far."

"Not today," Rudd murmured, pointedly.

Roy shrugged, defensively. "So I bring Anabel with me."

"She'll be busy fucking the senator this morning. Which can't wait."

"Neither can this. Ah, boss? One more thing you should know."

Rudd braced himself, eyes closing. "Yes, Roy?"

"Arbatov could be our telepath for this job," Roy said cautiously. "He's good. As good as Anabel."

Fury rose in Rudd's head like a red fog. "You've been passing psi-max around to your *friends?*"

Rudd's outrage battered Roy down onto the bed and pinned him there, writhing. But at this rate, he would have to completely remake the bed for Anabel's impending exploits with Stillman. He let Roy go.

Roy struggled up. "Sorry, boss." His voice burbled with snot. "I was actually trying to kill the guy. I figured, he'd be like the others, the ones we tested back at Karstow! I thought he'd go bonkers, and his brains would pop! I'd used him for a job, and I was cleaning house. Figured I'd flush him that way, so I wouldn't risk his uncle Oleg coming after me. But, uh . . . he didn't die. He, uh, went telepath."

"And you've been supplying him with psi-max? Behind my back?"

Roy nodded sheepishly. "It was that or kill him."

"You should have killed him. No wonder you're always short." He drummed his fingers on the table. "All right, Roy. If you say you can vouch for your Arbatov friend's ability, I will authorize this. But only today. Are you sure you can control him?"

"If I have psi-max for him, I can," Roy said. "He'll do anything."

Rudd rolled his eyes. "Well, then. Go to the supply site, get whatever you need, drugs, paraphernalia. When you get the information from him, have your mafiya friend do the honors. A drug deal gone wrong. One thing." Rudd's voice hardened. "Being linked to this would not enhance my tough-on-drugs platform, so explain to me why we couldn't discuss this on the dedicated, encrypted phone."

Roy hemmed and hawed. Rudd stuck his hands in his pockets and waited for it.

"I'm low," Roy admitted. "I used two hits to power up while I was going after Kasyanov, and if I supply Arbatov, I won't have enough—"

"You idiot," Rudd snapped. "You can't eat it like candy! Kasyanov was the only one who could cook it up properly, and you lost her, Roy, along with the last two known doses of Psi-Max 48 that exist! I take it you didn't find out whether it's true? About the new formula stabilizing the psi? Or is that just another one of Helga's lies?"

"Kasyanov didn't talk, boss, and Anabel wasn't there to read her."

Kasyanov had made a big deal about the enhanced formula, promising that it would render their psi powers permanent, and much stronger. Kasyanov was hard to read, heavily shielded, but Anabel had still sniffed out the stink of a half-truth, so Rudd had deemed it prudent to try out Psi-Max 48 on the good doctor herself, in case it was a trap. Figuring that he'd see for himself just how well it functioned upon her.

Well, hell. The drug made her strong enough to escape from the lab where they had been holding her for three years, ever since they faked her death at the research facility fire. Strong enough to fell a vicious thug like Roy. Psi-Max 48 was strong stuff. He wanted it.

"Get on this, fast," he said curtly. "We lose Kasyanov, we lose Psi-Max 48 permanently."

"If you want me to catch her frequency, I'm going to need more hits," Roy said. "Give me twenty, at least. Thirty would be better."

Rudd pulled out a stoppered tube, and shook some small red pills out of it. "I'll give you ten." He passed them to Roy.

"I'll need ten for Arbatov, too," Roy reminded him.

"Eight," Rudd said sternly, measuring out more. "But you want the magic pills? Do your job. And keep Arbatov under control. If you fuck this up, the well goes dry, and you're just any old worthless schlub again, my friend, like in the bad old days. You want to go back to that?"

Roy's Adam's apple bobbed beneath the red scar tissue

that covered his throat, swallowing saliva at the sight of the pills. Junkie trash.

"Wait, Roy," Rudd said, in a warning voice. "Wait 'til you need it."

Roy poured the pills into a vial that hung on a chain around his neck. "You know what, boss?"

Rudd spun at the door. "What, Roy?"

"You're such an asshole, you might just make a pretty good governor," Roy said. "If you get Psi-Max 48, and it makes you as strong as the freak doctor, you could be fucking president."

Roy was just brownnosing, now that he'd topped up his stash. But even so, Rudd felt a pleased smile twitch his lips.

"Clever boy, Roy," he said. "You've found me out."

3

"No! You don't understand," Nina told the doctor. "Helga Kasyanov was like an aunt to me. She was my mother's best friend. They did research together, at Columbia. Helga was in psychiatric pharmacology, I think. I babysat her daughter, Lara, when I was in high school. I didn't recognize her at first this morning, because it's been years, and she was so thin, and she'd been beaten. But she had nothing against me. She had no reason to hurt me. She was my friend!"

The tall, elegant black woman doctor whose name tag read DR. TULLY harrumphed, clearly not counting on that. "In any case, we'll still cover all our bases with the testing. But it'll be a few weeks before we can have definitive results for the HIV test."

Nina couldn't stop shaking her head. "It wasn't like that. I can't explain. It wasn't like she was holding a needle on me demanding money or anything like that. She would never do that."

"How can you be sure of that, Ms. Christie? Didn't you

tell us yourself that you couldn't understand a word she said?"

Nina couldn't articulate it, but she couldn't stop shaking her head. Sticking her with a dirty needle on the street, it was so base, so squalid, so nasty. So not the Helga Kasyanov she remembered. Helga had been elegant, brilliant, confident. Mom had leaned on her back then, a lot. But then again, Mom had tended to lean. After too many years with Stan, she couldn't stay upright on her own for long.

No, there had to be another explanation. She just couldn't imagine what it might be. "She spoke English when I knew her," she repeated stubbornly. "Perfectly, with no accent. Plus seven or eight other languages. Maybe she had some brain trauma to her language center?"

Dr. Tully harrumphed again. "Why don't you concentrate on your own problems, Ms. Christie, and don't concern yourself with—"

"Her problems *are* my problems at this point," Nina snapped, and then bit her tongue. "Sorry," she muttered. "I'm very tense. And the fact that she recorded what she was saying means she was at least trying to communicate with me. I have to get that translated. How long will it be before the tests give you some idea of what that stuff might do to me?"

"Not long." Dr. Tully frowned. "You're not showing any symptoms at the moment, and the fainting could be attributed to shock. But you'll need to stay a while longer under observation before I can let you go."

Nina let out a careful breath. "How is Helga now? Has she woken up? Has she said anything?"

Dr. Tully shook her head. "Still unconscious."

"Well, the driver, then. Maybe he can—"

"The cab driver dumped both of you at the Urgent Care and fled the scene," Tully said, her voice hard. "He won't be of any help to you."

"I have his plate number, and my friend's ex-FBI buddy

got someone to run his plates, so I know his name and address!" she said triumphantly. "His name is Yuri Marchuk, and he lives on Avenue B, in the East Village. I've been trying to find Helga's daughter, Lara. She could translate the recording, and if I can find the driver—"

"You're agitating yourself." Dr. Tully's brow creased. "Try to stay calm. We'll talk later when we have more information."

"Information is exactly what I'm trying to get," Nina said, through gritted teeth. "Look, if she wakes up and starts to talk, tell me, OK?"

"Certainly." Dr. Tully's voice was cool. "Later, then."

Nina let out a jerky breath as the door to the examining room clicked closed. Agitating herself, her ass. Talk about understatement. Every part of her jiggled and clattered against every other part. She slid off the examining table, her phone rattling in her shaking fingers. Her friend Lily's number was still up on the display.

Thank God for Lily. She and Bruno and all their super-tough, macho McCloud friends had leaped right into emergency mode on her behalf, and she hadn't even met them yet. Awesome people. She loved them already. Lily had already called her three times from Portland. They were the ones who had procured the address of the cab driver, in record time. Lily had even threatened to fly to New York, though her guy, Bruno, and Nina had both instantly vetoed that idea. Lily was in the eighth month of a problematic pregnancy, was taking anti-spasmodics, and was currently admitted at OHSU for observation. No way was she getting on an airplane. But it was great having a friend who cared enough to want to come.

Nina missed Lily so badly, it hurt. All those late-night takeout dinners they used to have in her Upper West Side apartment, giggling and gabbing and just being together. It had been wonderful to have Lily nearby. A college roommate who had become the sister she never had. They'd counted on each other to fill the place of family, for years.

It was Lily's moving out to Portland that had finally prodded Nina to break the lease on her Upper West Side studio and move back into the house out in Mill Basin that she'd inherited from her stepfather. The family she'd rented it to had recently moved away, and New Dawn, the battered women's shelter for which she worked, was in Sheepshead Bay, so her commute to work was far shorter from there.

She had mixed feelings about that house, bad memories, but years had gone by. The past was dead and gone. So was Stan. She was not that damaged person anymore, and a house was a house, for God's sake. She was damn lucky to own one.

To think she'd thought that ditching her two-hour commute and being able to walk to work would improve her quality of life. Hah.

With Lily gone, there was no reason to stay on in Manhattan. Lily was in Portland, three time zones away. Madly in love.

Nina was happy for her friend. Really. Lily deserved to be adored the way Bruno adored her. After years of backbreaking work, Lily had finally gotten lucky. Bruno was smart, sexy, tough. A good dad, too. He'd demonstrated the dad skills with the toddler twins that he'd recently adopted. Lily was part of a big extended family now.

So it was all good. Good for Lily. Yay. Hurray.

And the sad, flat silence that followed that statement forced the comparison with her own arid life. Her own more-or-less shit luck.

Goddamnit, she didn't even want thoughts like that to cross her mind. She didn't want to feel lessened by someone else's good fortune, particularly not that of someone she loved so much. It felt hateful, small, and pathetic. It made her angry at herself. God, she missed Lily.

Damn, girl. You have bigger problems than loneliness and envy right now. Like dying from some mysterious poison, for instance.

She stared at the phone number that Lily had texted to her. The number of this guy named Aaro, an army buddy of one of Bruno's adopted brothers. The one who spoke Ukrainian and various other Slavic languages. The phone jiggled in her fingers like a live thing. It had been twenty minutes since she'd last spoken to them. Bruno had been talking to Aaro while Nina spoke to Lily. He'd sent the file already. Aaro knew how urgently she needed this information. He might have already listened to it. He might know, at this moment, some crucial fact that Nina's doctors needed. Something that could save her life, or her sanity, or her liver.

So why was he sitting on it? Why the *hell* wasn't he calling her?

"Shit," she muttered, and hit "call." If he thought she was a freaked-out head case, so what? He'd be right. So?

The phone rang four times before the line clicked open. *Yes.* She sucked in badly needed air, and opened her mouth—

"What?" a deep voice barked. As if she were bugging him.

Her heart rate spiked. It took a stammering couple of seconds to frame a coherent phrase. "Ah . . . ah, is this Alex Aaro?"

"Who wants to know?"

"I'm Nina Christie, and I—"

"I know who you are," the guy snapped.

Nina's raw nerves jangled at his brusque tone. Her response popped right out. "If you already know, why the hell did you ask me?"

Dead silence. The guy had no good answer? Fine. She'd give him one herself. "Is it a verbal tic?" she asked tartly. "Something you say automatically? To put anyone who speaks to you on the defensive? Very slick, Aaro. I bet that wins you lots of friends and admirers."

There was a shocked pause. He cleared his throat. "I'm not interviewing for friends," he said. "And I don't need admiration."

"Damn lucky for you, considering," she retorted.

He harrumphed. "Had a tough morning, lady?"

Her spine prickled up, like an affronted cat. Smart-assed son of a *bitch*. "You could say that," she said, enunciating very carefully. "Bruno briefed you about my tough morning, am I right?"

"Yeah." His voice was cautious. "Hell of a thing."

"Good. Then you know already that I have no time for bullshit. Have you listened to the recording yet?"

"No," he said.

The flatness of his "no" was disconcerting. "I wish you would hurry up with that. Shall I call you back after you—"

"No," he said again.

She floundered. "What . . . but . . . did you not get the message with the audio file? Should I resend? I urgently need to know what—"

"I can't translate for you right now. I'm on the Belt Parkway right now, heading to Brighton Beach. There's something I need to do out there before I can help you. It's urgent."

Urgent? "But I . . . but this drug . . . my doctor needs to know if—"

"Contact the Ukrainian embassy. Ask someone there to help. You'll find the number online. Come to think of it, there are probably residents right at the hospital who are Ukrainian. Ask around. You'll find someone. I've got something to do, and it's time sensitive."

"More time sensitive than this?" Her voice cracked.

"Yes," he said, with all the flatness of utter finality.

Yes? Her head wagged, in mute denial. How dare he? How

could he? Of course, she had no reason to assume this guy would feel obligated to help her, except that Lily and Bruno had assured her that he would. Warring impulses locked swords. She wanted to beg him to just listen to the file. She wanted to plead, to babble, to implore.

She also wanted to tell him to fuck off and die.

She tried again. "But . . . but Lily and Bruno said you could—"

"I don't know what Lily and Bruno told you, lady."

"They told me you could translate that file." It burst out with explosive force. "What they didn't tell me was that you are an asshole!"

"I'm sorry," he said, sounding anything but. "When I'm done, I'll call you back, and if you still need me to—"

"Don't trouble yourself. Really. And with all my heart, fuck you, too. Have a nice afternoon." She hung up on him, and burst into tears.

Oh, God, how she hated crying. She hated Aaro even more, for driving her to it. As soon as the weeping had died down, she grabbed the phone and clicked around in the menu until she puzzled out how to block the jerk's number. She'd never bothered learning that function before, but it was the only spiteful, petulant thing she could think of to do. Nyah, nyah. As if he'd ever call her now, after her snit fit.

"Ms. Christie?"

She jumped at the voice. "What?"

A tall, balding, red-faced man in a white doctor's coat peered into the examining room. "I'm so sorry. I didn't mean to startle you."

"Um, do you need the room? I'm sorry," Nina said shakily. "I . . . I got distracted. But I was just leaving."

"Don't worry. I was looking for you, Ms. Christie. I'm glad I caught you. I'm Dr. Granger. This is Dr. Woodrow, my associate." He walked in. He was tall, huge shoulders. Grinning so his gums showed. He had a disfiguring burn scar that covered his neck. A beautiful blonde followed him in, giving Nina a dazzling smile. All that manic smiling. It was eerie.

She couldn't smile back if she wanted to. "Um, yes?" Her voice felt thin and wobbly.

"We need you to come with us to the lab upstairs." Dr. Woodrow's perfect teeth glowed like they were lit up from inside. "There are some tests we need to run."

"Really?" Nina pressed her hand against a cramp in her belly. "Did you discuss them with Dr. Tully? She gave me the impression that we'd covered everything."

The two doctors exchanged speaking glances. "Well, about that," the male doctor said. "There's a lot of talk, about your case. Everyone has strong opinions about it."

"Dr. Woodrow and I feel that the tests that Dr. Tully ordered left out a few important possibilities that need to be ruled out," the blond doctor said. "There's no time to lose."

"Ah. Well." The pain intensified, getting bigger, wider. "The thing is, I don't want for the right hand not to know what the left is doing." She forced the words out with difficulty. "Since Dr. Tully is handling my care, I'd rather you discuss it with her. Preferably with me present."

Dr. Granger's eyes flicked to his colleague. "Of course," he said smoothly. "I admit, this is irregular, but, well . . . there's no way to put this delicately. I've worked with Dr. Tully for years. She's a capable doctor, but strictly by-the-book. Even, well, plodding. Though I hate to criticize a colleague. A situation like yours, with so much at stake, calls for outside-the-box thinking. Are you going to risk your health, maybe your life, out of politeness?"

Nina gasped for breath as the pain squeezed harder. "I— I, ah—"

"If the tests we run help, Dr. Tully will probably think she ordered them herself," Dr. Granger said. "If they do not, I

will accept all the blame for any improper professional behavior. Your life and your future is worth it to me, Ms.
Christie. Is it worth it to you?"

Cold sweat pooled on Nina's forehead. The doctors' puzzled faces swam in her vision. "I . . . I don't feel well," she
squeaked.

"I'm not surprised." Dr. Woodrow took Nina's hand.
"Please, Ms. Christie. Come with us upstairs. We also want
to know everything this woman who attacked you with the
needle said to you. Every single word. We want to help you.
Help us help you."

Her hand felt so . . . cold. Even with the squeeze.

Like a corpse.

The thought flitted through Nina's head. Her head swam.
The room spun. Her blood pressure plummeted. Her stomach flopped. . . .

"Excuse me." She lunged for the connecting bathroom,
got there just in time. There wasn't much inside her, just coffee, but it went on and on. The blond doctor sidled in, making sympathetic sounds. She stroked wisps off Nina's sweaty
forehead, and patted her back.

Her hand was cold, even through the layers of Nina's
blouse and her loose over-dress, as if it were sucking out
Nina's vital warmth.

"These new symptoms are all the more reason to move
fast." The doctor dampened a paper towel in the sink and
passed it to Nina.

Nina straightened, mopping her face. Her stomach still
twitched, though there was nothing left to toss. She pressed
the towel against hot eyes, and tightened her belly against
that free-falling feeling.

Was it a panic attack? The drug Aunt Helga had attacked
her with, finally taking hold? Oh, God. She was so scared.
She did not want to die. Yes, she'd go to that lab, and do

more tests. Hell, yes. She'd do anything. She needed all the help she could get. She let the towel drop, looked in the mirror, into her pallid face, her red, blinking eyes—

A corpse stood behind her. A skull, with rotting flesh and peeling skin. The hand on Nina's shoulder was a skeletal claw.

She flinched away with a shriek, cowering back in the corner—

And Dr. Woodrow was abruptly normal again. Her beautiful face was fresh, pink, and blooming; her blue eyes were soft with concern.

"Ms. Christie?" she asked. "Are you all right?"

"I . . . but you . . ." She panted, gulped. "I must have had . . . a hallucination. I thought I saw . . ." She glanced back at the mirror. Dr. Woodrow was normal in the reflection, now. Nina's heart galloped.

"What?" Dr. Woodrow's voice was sharp. "What did you see? Tell me!"

"I, um . . . I . . ." Nina floundered. The doctor advanced upon her, her gaze intensely focused. "Try to relax," Dr. Woodrow crooned. "Just breathe. What did you see? Picture it in your head. Describe it to me."

Nina cowered back. No one touched her, yet she felt . . . groped. A rough hand pinching and prodding, but not her body. *In her mind.*

She clenched her teeth, and generated a burst of mental energy. Imagined swatting the offending, prurient hand away.

The sensation eased. Dr. Woodrow blinked, frowning. "Roy!" she called. "Get in here! I think she's going into shock."

The two doctors muscled her out of the bathroom, seizing her by the elbows and hustling her along and out the door of the medical suite.

What the hell? Did she have a hallucinogen in her system? The rotting corpse image had been bad enough, but the sensation of groping in her mind made her feel violated, unclean. She wanted to bathe.

Lights reflected off the floor in a blinding streak that made her eyes sting. She coughed. "Didn't you say that your lab was upstairs?"

"Yes, it is," Dr. Granger said.

Nina craned her neck as the doctors muscled her along, pulling her almost off her feet. "But the elevators are in the other direction."

"Oh." Dr. Woodrow's laugh tinkled like out-of-tune bells. "The elevators are out of order. We'll take the stairwell. It's quicker."

Nina had left her glasses on the bedside table, but through the myopic fog, she could see people walking into elevators, others walking out. These people were lying to her.

She twisted out of their grasp. "Just a second. Let me run back to my room. I feel naked without my glasses. And my phone. And purse. I'm expecting a call. An important one. It can't wait."

"I'll get them." Dr. Granger's deep voice made shivers ripple up her spine. His pale eyes were laser pinpoints. "Wait here."

She took off. "No, I'll do it!"

She sprinted back, the soles of her sandals squeaking as she spun around the doorjamb, and lunged for her glasses, phone, and purse. She shoved the glasses onto her face with hands that shook violently. When she burst out, the doctors were closer, and oh God, both were corpses now, rotting skull faces contrasting grotesquely with their spotless white doctors' coats. Orange nylon ribbons with name tags hung around necks with peeling skin, decaying flesh, exposed tendons. The smaller corpse had straw-like tufts of blond hair adhered to her red-smeared, discolored skull. "Ms. Christie? Are you all right?"

The bell-like feminine voice issuing from that skeletal maw was the final jolt that set Nina sprinting, a blur of raw panic. Thrumming heartbeat, pounding legs. People veered out of her path if they were lucky. Many weren't. She plowed into several, veered around rolling gurneys. Narrowly missed running down an old man tottering on crutches. The corpses gave chase, calling to her. She sacrificed a fraction of a second to check how close they'd gotten when she neared the elevator. About four yards behind her, human again, but the feral glint in their eyes was as chilling as the festering ghoul faces had been.

Who the hell were they? *What* were they?

She timed her pounding progress toward the elevator. People filing out, now in . . . the click, the hum, door starting to close—*now!*

Suck in the gut. Slide in sideways. Yelling faces, thudding feet, bore down on her as it closed. They pounded the door, from the outside.

Nina fell against the door, panting. Sweat ran down her back. Her raw, whooping gasps filled the silent elevator. All eyes were on her.

She wanted to beg for help. But no one had seen those walking corpses but her. That was her own private hallucination, and the medical personnel here would stick a needle in her arm and tie her down to a gurney if she started babbling about it. And who could blame them.

She stabbed at the button for two floors below, and caught sight of herself in the shiny panel. She looked crazy. Sweaty, white-faced. Staring, shadowed eyes; wild, tousled hair. Rasping pants, gulping for air. Hell, she *was* crazy. Zombies? What the *hell* was that about?

Didn't matter. She could lecture herself all she wanted. She had no control over the urge to flee. She'd keep going until whatever drove her allowed her to stop. She sidled out of the elevator, and bolted down the hospital corridor. Heads turned, eyes on her. . . . *You OK?* . . . *need help?* She activated her trick. The one she'd used back in the bad old days, when Stan was in one of his moods. When not being noticed meant not getting screamed at, or hit, or kicked. Or worse.

She'd learned to disappear. She'd learned it so damn well, in fact, that she'd been chipping doggedly away at unlearning it ever since. For her entire adult life. For all the good it had done her. And check her out. After years of therapy, her disappearing trick was still in perfect working order. All that careful, systematic dismantling of "outdated survival mechanisms." Hah. She slipped so smoothly into the familiar pattern. *Nobody here. Nobody here.* She locked on to the frequency, made it strong and steady. It throbbed off her while she gathered herself inside, tucking in everything that stuck out, everything that fluttered or glinted. She tucked it up tight, hiding it behind a thick, soft, gray fuzz of no thoughts, blank mind. *Nothing at all. Nobody here.*

She forced herself to walk normally. Inquiries just stopped. Heads stopped turning. No eyes snagged on her. People walked on by, intent upon their own business. *Nothing to see. Nobody here. Nothing to see.*

She zigzagged to the stairwell on the opposite end of the building. Three floors up. Then the elevator again. Four floors down. Hoping the random pattern would be in her favor. She found a stairwell, reached the ground floor. *Nobody here. Nobody here.* Slunk out the entrance onto Ocean Parkway, feeling horribly exposed. *Nobody here. Nobody here.* The sidewalk was hot. Her knees wobbled. Car horns blared, but the sound was muffled by the fuzzy blur of *nobody here.* She had to dodge people. They did not see her. She ran across Ocean Parkway, dodging cars. A couple of heart-stopping near misses got her across the road. She ducked up the first residential street she found, squeezing her brains to orient herself. This was a part of Brooklyn she didn't know well, but she thought there was an F-train stop on Avenue X. Fifteen minutes, ten if she sprinted. *Nobody here, nobody here.*

She didn't want to wait in line for a MetroCard with her heart thudding like that, so she used a trick she'd learned as a teenager when she was short on cash. A guy with two huge suitcases was being buzzed through the service gate, so she just followed him through, using her invisible trick. *Nobody here. Nobody here.* No one saw. Not the subway attendant, or even the suitcase guy himself, though he walked backward facing her, red-faced and cursing as he dragged his bags up the staircase onto the elevated platform. Once there, one of his suitcases spun and fell on its top-loaded front, *plop.*

. . . sweating like a pig, gonna smell like a dead dog on the plane . . . should've taken a goddamn cab . . . transfer at Atlantic Avenue going to kill me . . . just to save fifty measly bucks . . . old man could just open his damn wallet, help me out for once in his life, but no way, not him . . .

Nina reeled back, disoriented, at the voice blaring in her head.

But the man was not speaking. His mouth was a hyphen, sealed and tense. He dragged his suitcases toward the edge of the platform. The nattering hum of old, toxic anger subsided as the distance widened.

What the hell? She stared at the guy's hunched back, gulping, but her mouth was dry as sand. Had she just heard . . . no, that was absurd. The train roared into the station. Her heart thudded, fluttered. She was hallucinating again. Yes, that had to be it. That was all it was.

Even so, she kept as much distance as humanly possible between herself and everyone else as she boarded the train.

4

"Lost her?" Rudd's voice over the cell phone was glacial. "You lost this one, *too?*"

"I don't know what happened! We were taking her into the stairwell, and suddenly she freaks and bolts—"

"And you just let her run away?"

"We were in a crowded hospital corridor! It's not like I could tackle her! I was grabbing her, and she ducks into an elevator!"

"And your tracking skills? Why do you think I wasted eighteen hits of our precious dwindling store of psi-max on you?"

Roy spun, staring up and down Ocean Parkway, groping for the woman's elusive frequency. "I don't know what happened! She winked out of existence! She was in the fucking building! I should have felt her! I should feel her now, anywhere in Brooklyn! She winked out on me!"

"You're slipping, Roy."

Rudd's gentle tone was the most chilling thing Roy had ever heard, and after six years of working for the guy, that was saying a lot. "No, boss. Kasyanov shot her up with Psi-

Max 48. The drug made her strong, and she blocked me, that's all. I'm not slipping!"

"Two hours after initial dose?" Rudd snorted. "Get real. She has no idea what's happening to her. She can't control the psi at this point. She's on the roller coaster, remember? The spikes, the hallucinations? You were a maniac yourself, as I recall. We had to confine you physically. You wore restraints for twelve hours."

"That was normal psi-max! This is the new stuff, and it's—"

"Even stronger, yes. So the spikes should be stronger, too. She'll be experiencing all kinds of phenomena before she settles, and it will be even harder for her to control them than it was for us. You know how long that learning curve is, Roy. It takes years. She doesn't even have the benefit of knowing what's happening to her. Even normal psi-max drives most people batshit. Before they die."

Roy bit his fist to keep from screaming as he cast his feelers wide, wider, wider than he'd ever tried to feel. Still. Nothing. "It's that bitch's trick," he snarled. "I'm not slipping. She's blocking me."

"Come on, Roy, just accept it." That gentle voice made his guts loosen. "There's a point of diminishing returns with this stuff. You need to start thinking about retirement, my friend. You've had a good run."

The image formed in Roy's mind, as if Rudd had sent it there telepathically. Himself, with a bullet hole between his eyebrows.

"No way. I'm in great form," he said hastily. "I'll find her, boss. I'll get her. It's not me. Who knows what this bitch will be able to do, if Kasyanov dosed her with the new shit? Could be anything!"

"The real question is, Roy, who *else* will soon know what she can do if she isn't stopped? I don't have time to listen to your excuses. Was Anabel with you when you spoke to her? What did she get?"

"Nothing, boss!" he burst out eagerly. "She blocked Anabel, too! She said it was like getting whapped in the face! It pissed her off."

"I can well imagine. A double failure, then. Where is Anabel now?"

"She went to the ICU to see what she could get out of Kasyanov."

"You've covered her workplace? Her house? Nina Christie's wandering the streets of Brooklyn somewhere, Roy. She doesn't know what's happening to her, so she'll probably end up in a psych ward, and once she's in an institution, it will be more complicated to do what needs to be done."

Roy felt compulsion flailing his mind, though he knew it was just conditioning. Rudd couldn't do his badass juju over the phone, only in person. "You want me to off her?"

Rudd sighed. "I always have to spell it out for you. Do you want to read about the amazing effects of psi-max in *Time* and *Newsweek*? What would that do to our edge? Have your Arbatov friend and his thugs help you if your balls aren't hairy enough. If you can make her tell what she knows, so much the better. Everything Kasyanov told her. Who else knows. If there are any doses of the new formula left. Where they are. But after she spills, she dies. Have I made myself clear?"

"I'm on it," Roy said hoarsely.

He broke the connection. His head throbbed. He got the headache often these days. The more psi-max he used, the more it hurt. It was so worth it, though. He reached into his shirt, clutched the vial. Out of eighteen pills, he'd taken one and given six to Dmitri, in exchange for his backup and his personnel. Only eleven left. Fucking shit.

It drove him nuts, that the bitch could block him. He was

not slipping! He was red-hot! A super-hound. Loyal like a hound, too, though all he got for his loyalty was abuse and contempt.

If Kasyanov's fairy tale of stabilizing the psi was true, oh God it would be sweet. To be able to use his gift without having to scramble for a dose, to beg and plead and bargain. No headaches. No side effects.

And no Rudd, either.

If he didn't need the drug, he wouldn't need Rudd. In fact, if he were free, he would start making some careful plans for Rudd. Plans that involved large amounts of C-4 and det cord. Yeah, that's right. *Boom.* Suck my dick, boss. President, his ass. Psi-Max 48 was too good to be true. He hadn't believed in Santa Claus and the tooth fairy for some time now, but just look what this Nina Christie chick could do. Blocking him and Anabel both, just two hours after initial dose. And look what Kasyanov had done to him that morning.

The memory still made him shudder, swallowing bile. He rubbed the old scar on his neck. It itched, uncomfortably.

Too good to be true. But a guy could dream.

A sense of desperate urgency prodded Helga from below. *Wake up.*

She resisted. Nothing awaited her up there but pain and terror. She wanted to let go and fall back, arms out. Like she had into the water of the lake, as a child, long ago. Letting the cool dark catch her, embrace her. She'd been dreaming of that deep lake. So cold. So clean.

Lara. Nina. Not yet. Not yet!

She rose up, by slow, agonizing increments, as the black turned to angry, pounding red. Every part of her hurt, but paradoxically, her senses were very keen. She heard the breathing of the woman in the next bed, every word spoken in surrounding rooms, wheels on the gurney a hundred yards away. Every *beep* and *whir* of monitoring machinery. She was in a hospital. It hardly mattered. She was dying. Day five. The process could not be arrested now. Too late. She was just a corpse that still breathed. Just a matter of time. And not much time.

She should be dead already. Deserved to be, certainly, after what she had been forced to do. She'd lasted longer, now, than any of her unfortunate test subjects. It tormented her, that it had been she herself who had identified all those wretched people, gathered their names and addresses into a database in the course of her studies. Before she knew what Rudd was. Before she knew what he would make her do to them. Her own original parapsychological talent was in identifying people with enough latent psi to survive pharmacological enhancement.

And she'd done nothing but kill with it.

Her victims' eyes haunted her. Looking up at her, strapped down to the gurneys, hooked up to the machines. She wondered if they would all be waiting for her when she stepped across the threshold. Their eyes, reproaching her for all eternity. But she could not worry about eternity.

Lara was still alive. Still captive. And Rudd still needed to die.

No time for guilt, but still it twisted, like a blade inside her. She should not have involved Nina, either, but the girl was the only person she could think of that had enough intrinsic control of her psi to handle the effects of the drug, even if she had never recognized her abilities for what they were. Helga wished she'd been able to explain, but after four days, the A dose of the Psi-Max 48 had disintegrated the language center in her brain. Everything broken down, mixed up. It was up to Nina to figure it out for herself. God help her. And help Lara. *Please.*

She'd been watching Nina since she was a child. Lovely

girl. So gifted and kind. Lara had always been so happy when Nina had come to sit for her, on those evenings when Helga had needed to go out.

Nina had deserved better than that hellhole she'd been forced to exist in, but Helga had never succeeded in convincing Helen, Nina's mother, to leave Nina's stepfather. That bastard pervert Stan had destroyed his wife, but Nina seemed to have come through the fire intact. Subdued, but whole. The stress of her family life had caused the child's talents to develop naturally, in sheer self-defense. As a result of that, the Psi-Max 48 would not crush her. Or so Helga fervently hoped. Assuming the girl got the B dose in time. *Oh, please, God. Please. Not another death on her hands.*

She pushed away the guilt. Any woman would be driven to desperation by what she had been through. They had faked her death, enslaved her, forced her to do cruel, unspeakable things. Things that made her hate herself. And they had done it so easily. By constantly reminding her of what they would do to Lara if she did not comply.

She should have known from the start. The research that led her to psi-max, upon which all her work had been based, was tainted by horror and cruelty. She'd distanced herself from the madman Osterman years ago, and his twisted applications of the formula. She had tried to create something good. Something pure from what was once evil.

She might have known such a thing would be impossible.

She'd tried to escape four months ago, but her shield had not been strong enough. Anabel had caught a tail, followed it back. *Busted.* The American slang term drifted up from the garbage heap of her brain. Before she'd been injected, she had been fluent in eight languages. They were a jumbled mess, databases dissolved. All that was left was the dialect of Ukrainian she'd spoken in her infancy, and that was slipping, too. A dose of Psi-Max 48 dissolved barriers. All barriers. Even blood vessels, in the end. Unless the B dose was injected in time.

They had taken Lara to punish her. Mounted a video camera in Lara's cell so that Helga could watch her daughter's captivity, minute by minute. It had driven her mad, shaken her down into her composite pieces, to watch her daughter sleep, stare into space, weep. Exercise, meditate. Eat the small, bland meals they gave her. Vomit them up, more often than not. Week after week. Thinner and paler every day. Enduring it, completely alone, never even knowing why. Lara thought her mother had died in that research facility fire three years ago.

Then Helga caught the frequency, the way one caught a bad smell. Anabel's bright, toxic mental sparkle. She was sending out questing tendrils to the limits of her range, about twenty feet. Anabel was enhanced, at peak dose. There was no evading her. And Helga could not move anyway. She heard footsteps. Smelled Anabel's perfume, sensed her body heat. Helga forced her eyes to open. The lids were so heavy, like lead. Her own frail body barely made a bump in the sheet.

Anabel was dressed like a health care professional. White coat, ID badge. Hair swirled in a neat updo. Smiling, pleased with herself.

"Helga," Anabel murmured. "At last. We missed you."

"Go to hell," she whispered, in Ukrainian, but with a telepath, it hardly mattered.

Helga gathered thoughts, feelings, with their vaporous dangling tails. Stuffed them into that still, calm place inside where no air moved.

"You were injected five days ago, Helga," Anabel went on cheerfully. "And you do not look good. This suggests to me that maybe you weren't being completely honest with us about the effects of Psi-Max 48. Maybe you were trying to poison us? Oh, Helga." Anabel looked hurt. "How could you? After all we've been to each other."

Helga gasped and twitched as the mental probe sank in, like a heavy hook thrown into her flesh. The woman didn't bother to be gentle. It was breaking and entering, poking, jabbing, knocking things over.

"Don't think you can play your new illusion trick, Helga, like you did on Roy," Anabel whispered. "I am so on to you. Roy's just a dog."

Helga stayed calm while Anabel ravaged. Stillness surrounding her secrets. Floating separate, apart from the ransacking invader.

"Roy and his Arbatov thugs killed Yuri," Anabel said. "But not before they dragged every last detail out of his thick brain that would stick. Let's see . . . Joseph, right? Your ex-husband? And the B dose?"

Anabel felt the jolt of alarm in Helga's mind. She tittered. "You can't block me. You made Psi-Max 48 a binary drug, hmm? Naughty, naughty! You thought you'd inject us, and then be able to control us by withholding the B dose? You thought you could cut us a deal, Helga?"

I had to try. Helga whimpered, writhing. Blood trickled from her nose into her throat, making her cough.

"Nina!" Anabel crooned, triumphantly, at the goodies she pried out of Helga's mind. "Nina Christie. The New Dawn Shelter. We've got her already. Yuri gave her to us. She's meat, Helga. And we'll get Joseph, too. They'll tell me everything. They always do."

Helga tried to stop the tail as it flicked out of control—

But Anabel caught it, with her lightning mental reflexes, and followed it down to the source. "Oh!" she whispered. "You're still fussed about Lara? A little late to worry about her now. You've signed her death sentence, you dumb cow. Some mother you are. We'll tell her how badly you handled everything . . . before we kill her."

Helga writhed, arching in the bed. Anabel stared down, bright blue eyes white-rimmed and burning, face contracted in a feral snarl.

"Tell me now, Helga," she hissed. "Tell me where the B dose is, and maybe Lara's death will be a little quicker. *Tell me!*"

Helga twitched as that probe got closer and closer to the dark hiding place. Another second, and Anabel would be inside, sacking the inner sanctum. *Think, you idiot, think.*

She glimpsed that face, reflected in the shiny paneled surface of the medical equipment on the nearby table, and baited the trap, tossing up a thought tail for that vain bitch to catch. *Mirror, mirror . . .*

Anabel took the bait, like a trout after a fly. She looked into the reflection, and for a brief moment, she caught sight of herself and was distracted by the way that the glitter of the teardrop diamonds in her ears set off the perfectly sculpted angle of her jaw . . . *now!*

Helga punched into the other woman's unguarded mind, and Anabel's reflected image transformed. Her skin wrinkled, horrified blue eyes bulging in dark sockets, her lips shriveling from lengthening teeth. Her skin withered, splitting like old leather. Maggots boiled out.

Anabel opened her mouth to scream, but maggots squirmed out of her mouth, too. She went down to the floor, gurgling and thrashing.

Helga watched her fall. Anabel made noise, but she couldn't hear it. So far away. People were rushing into the room, but she was falling backward, arms out, into the waters of the dark lake. One lingering thought linked her to the chaos of pain, strife. One last desperate wish.

Nina, please try.

And the dark water accepted her, closing over her head.

5

Nobody here. Nobody here.

Nina huddled on the subway seat, twisting her hands together until her fingers were colorless. Scared to death, but not of being noticed. On the contrary.

It was like she had no walls around her mind. Other people's thoughts were trampling through her head as if it were their own. *Mind reading.* It was the only concept that would come to her, but as a definition it wasn't quite right. "Reading" implied a deliberate act, a seeking out. This wasn't deliberate. This was more along the lines of being crushed by stampeding wild animals.

Maybe she was crazy. Or else really, really stoned on Aunt Helga's mystery drug. She preferred the second option. As an explanation, it was simpler, more reductive. Comforting, even. Temporary.

So much noise. If she shut her eyes, hid in the gray fuzz, it helped, but the second she opened her eyes and caught sight of someone, their thoughts slammed into her mind, full force. The train squealed on a curve as it braked. Nina peeked to check the station sign—

. . . she'll kill herself if I leave her, but I'll kill her myself if I don't . . .

It was the guy across from her. Her eyes had brushed over him to read the sign. Young, wispy dark goatee, John Lennon glasses, tattered jeans. Eyes red and puffy from smoking too much pot. The frantic buzz of chronic desperation that emanated from him had snagged her mind.

Images flooded in. *Peter.* Bass player. His manic-depressive girlfriend, Jodie, was on a downswing. His belly hurt like a spear was stuck through it. So afraid of coming back from a gig, finding her in the bathroom, dead. Her empty eyes telling him that it was all his fault.

She jerked her gaze away, squeezed her eyes shut. *I'm imagining this. I'm fried on Aunt Helga's drug, my mind creating things that aren't there. His name is probably Brad or James or Tom. Not Peter.*

But sensible self-talk was irrelevant. She couldn't ride the subway with her eyes squeezed shut. If she was tripping on some powerful hallucinogen, well, tough titties. She'd just figure out how to function normally in spite of it. Junkies did it all the time.

So. A plan. She'd compensate for the drug, with her own more-or-less solid map of reality as she remembered it from her old, unaltered days. Solid. That was her. Nina Christie, solid as a rock.

She focused on breathing, to calm the terror that bubbled and fizzed. She opened her eyes, face turned from Peter. Her gaze brushed over a petite black girl with intricately braided and beaded hair, staring down at her red peep-toe sandals. The look on the girl's face sucked her into a slipstream of emotions: shame, fear, dread . . .

. . . keep the baby? How'm I supposed to feed a baby if Tyrone doesn't want it? Ma'll throw me out, she hates my guts already. . . .

Nina refused to flinch. Solid as a rock. Stay calm. Don't

make eye contact. Don't look at faces. Looking at faces triggered it.

At that moment, a heavy man with a suit and a combover sat down next to her. His massive body pressed against hers. The contact made the volume of his thoughts blare in her head.

. . . stuck-up prick. I'll teach him to talk trash about me, that lying son of a bitch. Firing me in front of Pam and Miriam, fucking bastard . . . I'll burn his house with his whole fucking family inside—

Nina jerked to her feet. The guy's eyes were half closed in his heavy face, lost in his revenge fantasy. Reveling in the image of burning his ex-boss in his bed, the man screaming while flames licked—

It hurt her head. She felt lacerated, stabbing lights blinding her. She wanted to vomit. To be alone, in the dark, in the fetal position. She stumbled down the subway car, trying not to touch anyone, look at anyone, shoving through a dense web of thoughts, feelings. Wispy trails clung to her, the strongest ones wrapping around her like cobwebs.

. . . just can't face another round of chemo. . . .

. . . God, I wish he would call me. Why isn't he calling me . . . ?

. . . where will I find money to buy Angie's meds this time . . . ?

. . . rat bastard. Probably boning that man-stealing whore right now, this very moment . . . dirty bitch . . .

Nina flung open the door at the end, gasping for air, and launched herself out onto the jointed metal platform. The noise hurt, but not as much as the contorted emotional worlds inside other people's heads.

And she'd always considered herself an empathetic person. Hah. She had no clue. No clue at all.

The next car was as crowded as the one she'd left. She couldn't face the gauntlet again, so she clung to the door handle outside, teeth clenched, bones rattling while the train spat out of the tunnel and into a station. *Get a grip.* She couldn't just cower between the cars on a blind subway ride to nowhere. *Toughen up, girl.*

Those people at the hospital had been chasing her, specifically. It had to be related to Helga Kasyanov. She did not believe that her pursuers were, in fact, zombie ghouls. Her map of reality did not stretch that far, and never would. But seeing them as a symbol of death was a message from her subconscious mind that they meant her ill. She'd seen their eyes as they chased her. She'd felt their evil. She was convinced. And so? What now?

The F train slowed. Coming up on Second Avenue, which reminded her of . . . she groped, and the lightbulb lit up in her overstressed brain. The driver! Yuri Marchuk lived in Alphabet City! He knew what Helga had said, and she needed a translator for Helga's recording, now that Asshole Aaro had withdrawn his linguistic help. True, some legwork and phone calls would find her someone else who was competent, as Aaro had so helpfully pointed out, but she was on the verge of a breakdown on a random subway ride, and voilà, she had ended up in Yuri's neighborhood. It was fate. Why look farther? Assuming the guy spoke English at all, of course, but hell, she could try.

As if she would meekly wait on Aaro's convenience. Jerk. It pissed her off all over again, thinking about his grudging offer to call her back when it suited his schedule. Giving her attitude after what she'd been through. She was going to have words with Lily, about exposing her to such a butthead. Rude, insensitive, provocative son of a *bitch*.

She wrenched open the door to the subway car as the train shuddered to a stop, waiting until the others filed out. She cringed mentally, held her blanket of gray, fuzzy mental static tight around her.

No cobwebs clung to her this time. She felt them tickle

her consciousness, but they didn't snag. She was grimly amused. Getting her back up about Asshole Aaro's bad manners had steadied her nerves. To the point where she could actually keep a shield up.

It was kind of funny. Almost.

She fished in her pocket for the address that Bruno's friends had procured for her as she slogged her way up the endless flights of stairs. She emerged onto Second Avenue, blinking in the blazing sunshine, and oriented herself to walk east. Three avenue blocks, then left onto B, and up a few short cross streets, and—no. Wait. What on *earth* . . . ?

Her neck prickled. A snarl of cars blocked the street entrance to Yuri's block. The sidewalk and street seethed with people. She edged closer, checked the address. Consulted the map, the street signs. This was the place. Short, narrow, cramped buildings. Flashing lights. Cop cars. Uniforms swarming. Yellow crime scene tape. Ambulance. An air of grim emergency. Goose bumps popped out on her neck.

She looked around for someone to ask. Spotted a young goth woman with lots of facial piercing. She revved up her shield of gray fuzz, and braced herself, just in case the makeshift barrier didn't hold.

"Do you know what happened here?" she asked the girl.

"They killed Yuri Marchuk," the girl replied, her eyes bright and shining with unsavory excitement. "Tortured him and killed him! He was my downstairs neighbor! Holy shit, it totally could've been me!"

Horror blotted out everything for a moment. The girl's words blurred, then comprehension blared back. ". . . cut him to pieces! Marya came home from work, found him all cut up! Marya's coming out now!"

A square, frizzed, bottle-blond woman in her thirties was being escorted from the building, flanked by police officers. Eyes wide, staring at nothing. She stumbled as if she couldn't quite feel her legs.

The police officers escorted her toward a waiting ambulance. Her hands and shirt were stained with blood.

The sun blazed down, but Nina shuddered with cold. Her teeth clacked. She'd lost the thread of the girl's prattle. Couldn't look away from Marya's frozen, staring face. It was dragging her in, pulling . . .

Oh, no. Oh, please, no. Not her. Not this.

Like a magnet sucking her straight into the other woman's experience. Mind, heart, and body. It hit her like a hammer. *Papa.* Shock, disbelief. Blood. His face. His hands. His ears. His eyes. Oh, Papa. Images, superimposed over the mangled red mess on the kitchen floor that could not possibly be Papa. *Holding her in his arms, feeding her* vareniki. *Yelling, laughing, breath heavy with vodka. Playing with her son. A good grandpa. His hands. His ears. His eyes. God, his eyes.*

Images assailed her, gruesome, bright-edged. Colors surreally bright, especially the awful, arterial red. She couldn't separate herself from Marya's trauma. It was too strong, too loud. It blotted her out.

The girl's voice poked like a needle jabbing. Her hand clutched Nina's sleeve, tugging. ". . . you OK? Hey! You on drugs, or something?"

Nina blinked. Her face was wet. The ambulance was pulling away, pushing its way through the crowd. It took Marya with it.

Yellow crime scene tape fluttered and snapped in the gusty breeze. The images retreated as the ambulance did.

She was Nina again, but she didn't feel like herself. She felt like a year had gone by, a lifetime. Tears ran down her face, into her nose. She was sitting on the cracked, dirty sidewalk, on her butt. Second time she'd whacked it that day. It hurt, dully. "I'm OK," she said, struggling to her feet. "Weak stomach. It's so awful. Sorry."

She backed away. *Don't run. Stay calm.* She spun, looking

for . . . what? Shifty-eyed zombie ghouls, staring at her from a parked car?

Tortured. That poor guy. Keep walking. Keep going. Slow and steady. *Nobody here. Nobody here.* She'd honed the vibe. Every item in her wardrobe was chosen to be unnoticeable.

Her phone buzzed. She fished it out of her purse. It was Shira, a colleague at New Dawn. She held the phone to her ear. "Hey."

"Hey, you. Feeling better? Have you found someone to translate that audio file yet? Because I might have, if you haven't."

"No, not yet." She blurted it out. "He's dead, Shira."

"What?" Shira's voice sharpened. "Who's dead?"

"Yuri Marchuk, the cab driver. The one who dumped me and Helga at the hospital. Someone tortured him to death. There are cops everywhere." She stumbled on a pavement crack, barely caught herself.

"My God! Nina! Where are you? Are you out in the street somewhere? You left the hospital? What the hell were you thinking?"

I wasn't thinking. I was running for my life from zombie ghouls. She bit the words back. That would only confuse and terrify Shira, and her own personal terror and confusion was enough to deal with. She spun, in a slow, wobbly three-sixty, scanning the street for who the hell knew what. "Long story," she said. "Tell you later. I'm in Manhattan."

Shira made a disapproving sound. "Well, that makes my call pointless, because I'm at your house right now. I used those spare keys you left for Derek last week. I was going to pick up some things for you. You know, a toothbrush, a book, some panties, whatever. But you're not at the hospital anymore, so to hell with that."

Nina was touched. "Oh, Shira, that was sweet. Thank you."

"Oh, and a guy came looking for you today, right after I got back from visiting you at the hospital this morning," Shira went on.

"A guy?" Nina's spine prickled nastily. "Who? What guy?"

"He said he was Helga Kasyanov's brother," Shira said. "Sergei. Doesn't look a thing like her, though. He said she's a schizophrenic, dumping her meds, and that she thinks her family is trying to poison her. He can't imagine how she'd have access to anything other than her own antipsychotics, which is toxic bad news for you, but not fatal."

"What? You just told him everything?" she burst out. "About me? Everything that happened with Helga? The syringe, and all that?"

"Ah . . . ah . . . well, I, uh . . ." Shira stammered.

"He was lying, Shira!" Her voice shook. "Helga didn't have a brother! She was married, years ago, but she emigrated with her parents when she was fourteen. She had a daughter, but no brother!"

"Oh. I . . . wow. Well, I told this guy about the recording—"

Nina winced. "Oh, God. Don't tell me, let me guess. He offered to translate it, right? I bet he's just a prince of a guy."

"Nina. Back off. I don't like what you're insinuating."

"What did you tell him?" she demanded. "Did you tell him which hospital we were in?"

"Well, ah." Shira sounded confused. "No, not exactly. He just, ah, guessed it. In fact, he guessed a whole lot of stuff. It was weird. Like, I would find myself talking about stuff that I hadn't known I told him."

"What did he look like?" Nina's heart thudded.

"Ah . . . Nina. You're overreacting, and I don't appreci-ate—"

"Just tell me, goddamnit! What did he look like?"

"OK, OK! He was tall, dark, pretty good looking, some

acne scarring, forty, maybe. Nice clothes. Expensive. Flirtatious. Satisfied?"

"Dark, you said? Not bald?"

"No," Shira said. "Lots of hair. Dark. He had a ponytail, a slick little playboy one."

"Was he with a woman? A blond, pretty one?"

"No, he was alone. Stop snarling. I don't know how I ended up telling the guy so much, but I was rattled by what happened to you too! I judged it to be more important to get a clue what might have been in that syringe. I made a judgment call. I screwed up. Sorry, OK?"

"OK." Nina peeked over her shoulder, scanning the stream of cars. "Did you tell him my name?"

"Of course I didn't," Shira snapped. "He already knew your name."

Then how had he found her? Why was any of this about her at all? She tripped over a broken bit of sidewalk, as images came at her, horribly vivid. Sickening realization, along with it.

They tortured him. Cut him to pieces.

Papa. Oh, God. Your hands. Your ears. Your eyes.

Yuri. Yuri was how they had found her. Oh, poor Yuri.

She pressed her hand against her belly, sick and faint. Shira continued to talk, but Nina's arm dropped. The thin, tinny chatter from the phone had lost all meaning. She thumbed it off as her mind spun, feeling for a pattern, a plan. A way through the maze.

If the ghouls had tracked her to the hospital, they could certainly find her house. But why would they bother? Because of something Helga had said to her? And she hadn't even understood it.

Her phone beeped. A message from Shira. The number that the mysterious Sergei had left. Huh. Maybe she should just call the guy. Maybe he'd explain everything. Or make her an offer she couldn't refuse. She could beg him to call off the monsters. She'd do anything they wanted, if they would just make it all go away. Her snort of laughter disintegrated into tears. She could see it now. Nina Christie, bargaining with zombies, torturers, and murderers, with some coin she didn't even know she had. Yeah, that was bound to turn out real well.

She had to go home, risk or no risk. She didn't have anything to tell the police that wouldn't get her locked in the psych ward. She didn't have a close enough friend nearby to ask for help, not with something as scary as this. She needed clothes, a passport, her laptop.

The subway ride was difficult. Survival instinct prodded her to study her surroundings, but every time she looked at a person directly, the weight of that person's life crashed down on her. She tried staring at feet instead. Feet said less than faces. Still, it was better now. If she kept the *nobody here* pulsing out, the gray fuzz up and strong, she blocked most of it. But it took every ounce of her concentration.

The subway stop was a long walk from her house. Her nervous, ragged trot soon turned into a hell-for-leather sprint, skirt flapping, sandals sliding. Phone in one hand, glasses in the other.

She finally reached the narrow brick row house she'd grown up in. It didn't feel like a safe haven, but it had a door that locked.

She longed for a shower, but her crawlies were creeping worse every second that went by. She just wanted to move. She gathered stuff in feverish haste, scrabbling in the drawer for her passport. She hurried up to her bedroom to change, the small room at the back. Years after Stan's death, she had not been able to use the master bedroom. She could not sleep in a room where Stan had slept.

Stupid, she told herself as she yanked off clothes and pried her fuzzy coil of hair out of the scrunchie. She should sell this place, buy something smaller. It didn't look like she was on track to have a family.

And she heard it. *Squeak-pop.*

She went still as death. The warped stair, the fifth one, made that sound when a foot was put on it. Her insides froze. She listened 'til her ears ached. *How the hell . . . ?* The alarm should have gone off!

There. A shush of fabric on fabric. The faint squeak of shoe soles against wood. Someone coming up the stairs. Slowly. Sneakily.

Ghouls, chasing her. Helga, jabbing the needle into her arm, her eyes reddened, desperate. Yuri's mutilated body. She stared around the room, stark staring naked, lungs clenched around a burning bubble of trapped air.

No way out except for the window, but it was swollen shut, as warped as the squeaking stairs. The house was old and creaky, and she didn't love it enough to take proper care of it. She'd never get that window open, not without a baseball bat.

She grabbed her phone, her purse, and dove for the closet.

She'd paid a considerable sum to a carpenter to design her closet when she'd moved in. It was the only change she'd made. She'd been reluctant to remodel the place until she was sure she could stand to live in it, but the closet was a must. The second bathroom that Stan had installed had created a recessed wall in the back bedroom. It made the closet space much deeper than a closet needed to be, so it had been a simple matter of having a false wall inserted there. A click, and a panel slid open, a space just wide enough for a terrified smallish person to slither into. Just a few feet deep. She'd been storing boxes of her mother's old reference books in there, while she gathered the nerve to get rid of them, but there was space behind the stack of boxes. At eye level, to the side, a tiny knothole made a natural peephole.

Nina pulled the outside closet door closed, and slid into the narrow aperture. *Snick,* the panel clicked into place.

She shivered in the inky darkness. The challenge now was to keep her teeth from clacking. She fastened the manual latch from the inside, so that anyone touching the back panel wouldn't accidently engage the opening device. The guy who built the closet had suggested a panic room, but that didn't feel right to her. If the bad guy knew you were there, he could lay seige. You could be starved out, bullied out, burned out. She didn't want to huddle in a bunker while her assailant banged and threatened. She wanted to be invisible.

The door to her bedroom opened, with its shrill, dry creak.

Nobody here. Nobody here. Nothing to see. Nothing to see.

She kept her fear tucked in tight. Stayed very small. Her hand, clutching the phone, was wet. Sweat pooled on her forehead, dripped down her back. She felt faint. *So small. No one here. So quiet.*

The inner directive seemed to come from so far away. Barely perceptible over the roaring of her ears, the thudding of her heart. Footsteps clumped around her room. Closet doors were flung open. A needle of light from the knothole pierced her darkness.

She leaned as close as she dared to the hole. Saw a man's silhouette, then his face when he used the barrel of a big pistol to sweep her hanging clothes aside. Tall, dark, fortyish. Pouches under his eyes, cruel lines carved around his mouth, pockmarks from acne scarring. A ponytail, like Shira had described. He barked out orders, in what sounded like Russian. Heavy footsteps clomped out. She heard someone in the bathroom behind her. *Crash,* the shower box met its end. Muffled thuds sounded from the master bedroom, on the other side. At least three guys.

Ping. A message arrived on the phone in her hand. Oh *fuck!* She muted the thing with a trembling thumb. It glowed in the dark.

From Lily. The pockmarked guy had heard it. His head turned, his eyes slitted as he scanned for the origin of the sound.

You didn't hear anything, she told him silently. *Random beeps and clicks and squeaks. Clocks, phones, appliances. Every house is full of them.* She pulled in even tighter, smaller, and thumbed open Lily's text. The part of her that read it was a tiny speck, miles deep, inside herself.

**Sorry about Aaro. We'll work on him. With thumb-
screws.**

She hit "reply," texted feverishly.

**Thugsinmyhouse. Inclosetnow. 3+guys?
Spk russian? Callcopsnowpls!!**

Send. Twenty hammer-blow heartbeats later, another message appeared, blessedly silent this time.

On the way. Hang in there.

She stuffed the relief down deep, kept herself tucked up. *Tight and small. Tiny gray thing.* She peered through the knothole. He stood in the middle of her room, eyes closed, nostrils wide. Feeling for her.

With his mind. God. That guy was feeling for her with his *mind.*

She clamped down on panic. *Not here. Nothing to see. Small gray thing. Pebble, dry leaf, gum wrapper, bottle cap.*

But the pockmarked man persisted, his mind prodding for her like a rough, lascivious hand between her legs.

6

"Look, I'm just saying," Miles wheedled. "It's not that much to ask. Listen to it while you're driving to the hospice! You won't miss a beat!"

"Get off my back," Aaro growled. "I have enough to deal with, fending off Bruno."

"Oh, come on. Just show them you care. Throw them a bone."

"Like Bruno would be happy with a bone? He won't be happy until I spill a couple buckets of my heart's blood."

"You could have said what's going on with your aunt," Miles scolded. "It's like you want them to think you're an icy-hearted asshole."

Aaro hung up, without comment. He'd never meant for Miles to know about Tonya at all, but he'd been in the room with Aaro when he got the call, and the guy was a goddamn walking antenna. He hadn't stopped nagging until Aaro had spilled it. Out of sheer exhaustion.

That was the price he paid for having a collaborator. Things had been simpler when it was just him, in sweet solitude. And the three-car accident that had hung him up for well over an hour on the Belt Parkway was divine punishment. Chastising him for not helping the sobbing social worker. Not that she'd been sobbing when she talked to him. Spitting, was more like it. Tough chick. Like boot leather.

After the accident finally cleared, he'd been hanging out in the long line of cars bottlenecked for the exit onto Flatbush, contemplating his sins. The cars were finally starting to move. He'd been spending the dead time staring at his phone. The multimedia message from Nina Christie glowed reproachfully on the screen. He was bored stiff. Might as well amuse himself by listening to the recording. Then he could call her back, let her spit at him again. It had been stimulating, in a kinky, masochistic sort of way. She had a pretty voice. Low, husky. Feminine.

Hell, after hours of staring at brake lights, he was actually getting curious about the damn thing. Desperate for something else to think about. Anything else. Even something suck-ass.

He pulled Nina's number up from the call log, on impulse, and hit "call." Was alarmed at his own action. What, was he going to apologize? Yikes. Dangerous. He didn't know the choreography of an apology.

No problem, though. She'd blocked his number. She didn't want no stinkin' apology from him. She'd given him the digital finger. *Ka-pow.*

Aww. He'd made a new little friend. His very special talent.

He was vaguely surprised to find himself grinning. His facial muscles weren't used to that kind of exercise. They were creaky.

The last bit of resistance in him shifted into something like resignation. OK, already. He'd listen to the recording, then he'd call up Bruno, and give him the gist of it. Bruno could call the woman back. Safer that way, with a nice, thick Bruno buffer to protect him from random, pissed-off female weirdness.

But Bruno called him, just as he was about to call. He hit "talk."

"I surrender," he said. "I'll listen to the fucking file, already, OK? Just leave me alone for a few while I do it."

"Never mind the tape!" Bruno yelled. "Go to Nina's house! Now!"

Aaro was confused. "House? Isn't she at the hospital?"

"She left the hospital! She's at her house, and the bad guys are inside with her! Lily called the cops, but you're closer. Take Flatbush right now, and floor it!"

Aaro gaped. "How do you know where I am? You sneaky son of a bitch, did you tag my phone?"

"Take it up with Davy. He gave me the frequency. That's not the point! Move it, Aaro! She's hiding in an upstairs bedroom closet!"

"Oh, fuck me," Aaro moaned, muscling himself into the turn lane amid blaring horns. So the dismissal from Nina Christie was not the conclusion to this episode, but just a foretaste of pain and annoyance to come. To say nothing of the possible bullets.

"You armed?" Bruno asked.

Aaro grunted his assent. Understatement. Going anywhere within five hundred miles of the Arbatov family made him nervous.

"Nina texted that there's three, maybe more. Speaking Russian, she thinks. Go up Flatbush, left onto Avenue U, and then right on Ramsey. If you hit Quentin Road, you've gone too far, so don't. Three blocks up, third house on the right, five fifty-four. Move your ass!"

The car surged forward. Here was his chance to redeem himself for the colossal fuck-up six months ago, if he chose to accept it.

Bedroom *closet*? How did this shit fall to him? Did he have a note pinned on his shirt that he didn't know about? He'd spent a lifetime deliberately not giving a shit about anybody's business but his own, unless he was paid big bucks to do so. Stone cold, out for himself. Taught by the best. And yet, here he was. Speeding down that exit ramp.

He picked up inappropriate speed. Horns blared. Bruno yakked away at him from the phone that lay on the passenger seat. Aaro ignored him. He'd do this his way, whatever that way might be. He didn't have a clue yet, but something would come to him. He hoped.

In fewer than five minutes, he sped past Nina's house. A bland brick row house among other unremarkable row houses. Unbroken line of cars parked in front. He jerked to a stop around the corner, snapped open the case for the folding stock Saiga. He'd considered himself a lunatic, bringing the shotgun along, to say nothing of the special loaded mags he'd prepared; sintered metal breaching round up top for blasting out a lock, then alternating buckshot shells and one-ounce slugs.

He slid in the mag, racked the bolt, and loped toward her house.

No good way to sneak up on a row house. No time to go around the block to slither in from the back, not if a bad scene was already going down inside. Frontal attack, then. Classic suicidal dickhead style.

He ran up the stoop, tried the handle, using his sleeve. No need to leave a trail of fingerprints back to himself. Not that he expected to live through this. It was locked, of course.

Aunt Tonya. He felt a sharp pang of regret. But he'd see her soon enough on the other side, if he bought it here today. Tonya would follow him out. If that was how it worked. Who knew. Whatever. No time.

The street was deserted. No witnesses. He took a deep breath, swung up the shotgun, took aim at the door lock.

Fuck it. Who wanted to live forever?

* * *

"Nina," Pockmarks crooned. "Nina, where are you?"

He knew her name. Oh, God, that creeped her out. She put her hand over her mouth, pressing hard to keep her heart from jumping out. *Small. Gray. Pebble. Brick. Blank wall. Not here. Nothing to see.*

"If you come out, I won't hurt you," he coaxed, in a deep, raspy voice. "Just tell us what Helga Kasyanov told you. That's all we want. Tell us that, and we'll go away. Never bother you again."

So why did you cut Yuri to pieces? Liar.

She stuffed the thought as it formed, or that rough, prodding mind would sense it. *Gray, small, blank, boring, nothing. Dry leaf. Brick wall. Nothing here. No one home.*

"Tell us, and we'll stop bothering you." Pockmarks's voice was an oily ooze of menace. "We won't bother your pretty friend, either—what's her name again? Shayla, Sharon, Sheryl . . . Shira! Yes, that was it! Pretty, blond Shira. Who lives all alone in her studio apartment on Sixth Street." He made an appreciative growling sound. "Pretty legs. Pretty tits. We won't bother her, or any of the other poor bitches in your shelter. We leave them all in peace. Everything like it was before. Just come out. Talk to us. Don't be scared, Nina."

Brick wall. Blank, corrugated metal. No one here. No one home. She cowered, focusing her energy with all of her strength.

"It would be fun, to pay Shira a visit some night," the guy mused softly. "All four of us. We'll bring some Viagra and some cocaine, and some duct tape. It would be fun. We could have fun with you, too, no?" He grinned, spinning around, groping for her. "You pretty, too? I bet you're pretty. But all women are pretty with duct tape on their mouths. I like a quiet woman. I don't like noise, see." He paused, nostrils flaring wider. "You're very quiet, Nina," he whispered. "The most quiet woman I ever met. I go for that. You know what? I think you will be my very special friend, when I drag you out."

It barely registered. She logged his words for future reference on the edge of her consciousness, but she wouldn't let them inside, to the real her. Where they could hurt. Another trick, from the Stan years.

Steel reinforced, armor plated. Titanium plates. Smooth as glass.

"So? Hear anything?" A different voice spoke, this one familiar. Nina leaned toward the knothole. It was one of the ghoul doctors, Granger, but in his live human aspect at the moment, thank God.

"Not yet," Pockmarks said curtly. "Don't distract me."

"I told you she was good." Granger sounded relieved. "We should both have been able to pick her up from this range. It's not just me, man. I'm telling you, it's the simax. The bitch is totally blocking us."

"And if you would shut up, I could get through it," Pockmarks hissed. "Stop making all this noise. I'll find her."

"We don't have time for you to jerk around," the bald guy said. "Got a text from Phil. Someone called in a home invasion here. Cops will be here soon. She went out a window, and called them. We gotta go."

"She didn't have time," the dark guy said. "Shut up."

She caught a glimpse of the bald guy's face through the knothole before he stomped out. Hooked nose. Cruel, pale blue eyes, shifting and darting nervously. His pink forehead shone with sweat.

Pockmarks twirled again. His spin slowed as he faced her closet. He took a step closer. Her heart juddered, but she held the focus. *Nothing here. Nothing at all.* She could smell his hot, sour breath as he swept aside her clothes. Knocked against the back closet wall.

Brick wall brick wall brick wall nothing here nobody home.

Pockmarks backed away, but her tension did not ease, and

in a moment, she knew why. He went into the adjacent bath-room, eyeballing the discrepancy in the recessed wall. He started to laugh. Then, a light *tappety-tap-tap,* a taunting riff that said, *I know you're in there.* A redoubled prodding, the mental hand, groping for her.

It made her squirm. Despair spread, cold and sickening. He would drag her out and cut her to pieces, like Yuri. Slowly and horribly.

Calm down. Don't freak. Stay behind the wall. Her block-ing technique seemed to settle her nerves, so she ramped it up.

Pockmarks swaggered back into her line of vision, grin-ning. "Quiet Nina," he chortled. "Nice hiding place. But I hear you. You know what I hear?" He flung the doors wide, his grin showing his tobacco-stained teeth. "I hear your quiet! I've never heard quiet so loud! It's deafening me! Funny, huh? You looking at me through this hole, Nina? You like what you see? You haven't seen anything yet. How about this?"

Nina jerked behind the boxes of books, as his pistol swung up. He fired three times, at the level of her knees.

Bam, bam, bam, the instant he was going to pull the trig-ger. Three shots from upstairs. *Shit.* Already?

Boom, his breaching round blasted through the lock. He kicked the door open, breaking the chain, and shot straight through the door.

He peered in. A man sprawled in the foyer had taken a face and chestful of buckshot. Bloodied and silent. Aaro kicked the weapon from where it lay near the man's hand, then spun to shoot up the stairs before the sound even regis-tered in his conscious mind.

Bam. The shotgun slug hit the guy dead in the chest. His back hit the staircase wall. He was big and fat, and made a lot of noise as he toppled and slid, stumbling to his knees, then his face. His body snagged, lodged sideways horizontally between banister and wall.

Bam, splinters and plaster flew. Aaro dove for the entryway to the dining room. He peered around the corner, blasted a few more shots up there with the Saiga. *Bam, bam.*

"Fucking shit," someone hissed from above. "Who the hell . . . ?"

A door slammed. Furious voices, from the direction of the gunshots. Up, to the right.

Nina gasped for air. Was she shot? She'd feel pain, right? Heat, stinging? Her blood pressure was as low already as if she were bleeding out. *Don't faint. Don't puke. Hang on. Hang on.* She did. By a thread.

More gunshots, from below. Who? Police, already?

"You asshole!" The snarl of the balding guy. "Your guys downstairs are both dead! Did you tell someone about the simax? Who did you tell? Who the fuck is that guy down there with the shotgun?"

"I don't know who he is! Nobody knew about this!"

"Well, somebody fucking knows now, so let's get gone quick, before the cops show! Out the window!"

"But the girl? She's in the fucking closet! Right here!"

"Out!" the bald guy bellowed. "You first! I'll watch the door! Go!"

"But the girl—"

"Forget the girl!" the bald guy howled. "I'll take care of the girl!"

A screech, as the warped window sash was wrenched up, and the bald guy peered through the knothole, his lip contracted into a sneer. "Bye-bye, sneaky bitch," he said. "Too bad we couldn't party with you."

She dropped sideways as she sensed his intent, wedging herself tight behind the boxes—

Bam. Bam. Bam. Bam Bam. Bam. Bam. Bam. Each shot that hit the boxes was a punch, pummeling her, crushing her against the wall. The ones that had hit above the boxes pierced holes. Dust and smoke swirled lazily in the sharply defined rays of light that sliced through the closet. She stared up at them, too shocked to scream.

The gun blasts jerked Aaro up from the entryway. He darted up the stairs, clambering over the stiff, his heart stuck high in his throat.

Eight shots. Nina Christie was dead for sure. He'd called it wrong, gotten the chick killed by racing in here like a cranked-up asshole, freaking the bad guys into a panic. He should have come up with something sneakier, smarter. Goddamn them all, his so-called friends, for putting him in this position. Like he didn't have enough to feel like shit about every fucking day of his life.

He slapped the bedroom door open. Window gaping, curtains fluttering, stench of gunpowder. He lunged for the window, caught a glimpse of a big bald guy, staring up at him. Pale snake eyes. Another man, tall and dark, was clambering over garbage cans.

Aaro yanked out the .45, squeezed off two shots. Two more at the bald one. Bullets pumped into the garbage bins, whinged off a parked car as the bald guy dove for cover. The dark guy jerked, stumbled, and kept on going, ducking out of sight into the alley.

Grazed. No pursuit possible. He had bigger problems now.

He pulled his head back in, holstered the gun, and faced the closet. It gaped open. Clothes were scattered on the floor. The back panel was splintered with bullet holes. Now came the ugly part. His mess, his failure. Calling EMTs for a woman who was dying because of his poor crisis-decision-making skills. Explaining himself to the cops, too. And then to Bruno and Lily. Well, then again. Maybe he could arrange to get himself hit by a bus, and just skip that part.

"Nina?" He was disgusted by the hitch in his voice. "You there?"

No answer. Hadn't expected one. Not after eight bullets.

He put his hand against the holes in the back panel. His legs shook. "Nina? You in there? I'm not one of those guys who attacked you. I'm Aaro, the guy who pissed you off on the phone, remember? Bruno told me you were in trouble. Are you shot?" He clenched his jaw, hating the goddamn silence. Hating it.

"Aaro?" It was just a squeak, barely audible. "You're Aaro?"

"Nina?" Hope jolted his insides hard, and a hot rush of moisture fogged his eyes, making him blink. "Nina? Are you shot? Are you hurt?"

"I think, ah . . . I think I'm OK."

He rattled the panel, pounded it. "How do you open this thing?"

"Just a minute," she faltered. "I have t-t-to undo the latch, and I'm kind of wedged in here, so . . . um . . . hold on while I . . ."

He heard a scratching and shifting inside. Then a rattle, a click.

The panel slid open. Nina Christie was huddled inside, stark naked. Curly dark hair draped over her face and trailed over her shoulders. She blinked up at him, her aqua-green-and-gold eyes huge and haunted. She had long lashes. The dark waving hair over her face was snarled in them. Her parted lips looked bluish.

"Nina Christie?" he prompted, feeling stupid. Who else could she be? But he could think of nothing to say to the naked chick who had just dodged death. Not like he had a lot of clever conversational gambits floating up to the surface of his mind in the best of circumstances. He just scooped up whatever was floating on top of his mind, like pond scum, and plop, there it was. No filters. What you see is what you get.

He squatted down so that they would be eye to eye, and peered into the dark recesses of the closet. A heap of boxes. Piled one on top of the other. They looked like textbooks. She'd wedged herself behind them. So that was what had saved her life. It was no thanks to him.

Her blinking shook loose the tears that had gathered in her eyes. They flashed down her cheeks, glinting. "A-a-a-aro?"

Uh oh. The way she stared up at him gave him a twinge of dread. All big-eyed and misty, as if he were God, her saviour, her hero. She was in for a rude shock when the truth became clear. Wouldn't take long for that to happen. It never did.

"Yeah, that's me." Discomfort roughened his voice. He tried to look unthreatening, a talent at which he did not excel. "Bruno sent me."

"B-b-bruno?" The girl was scared stupid.

He fought for patience. "Bruno. Your best friend's future husband? The father of her unborn child?" He fought down his natural urge to be a sarcastic asshole, but she didn't react. She just crouched there, staring up at him, with those huge, shocked eyes. Her purplish lips shook. He had to get her dressed, take her someplace safe. What would he do if she collapsed? The Coney Island Hospital? That would involve filling out papers, explanations, accountability. Cops. Bad scene. *Damn.* He made his voice gentle, with some effort. "Come out of the closet, Nina. We have to get out of here. We don't know when they'll be back, how many there are, or anything else. So move."

No reaction. More quivering lips. More blinking. *Shit.* He was going to have to drag her out. He steeled himself for a screaming, scratching, hysterical freak-out. She was entitled.

He reached in, took her hands. They were icy. He chafed

them between his own, and tugged. She came out, offering no resistance.

In fact, she practically flew out, and came to rest right in his arms. There was a weird inevitability to it. A key to a lock. Like they were magnetized. *Snick,* and they were fused, and he was hugging the naked girl. His arms shook, his guts vibrated, his heart tripped over itself. He was squeezing her too hard. Had to loosen his grip. He'd scare her worse than she was already.

He couldn't. His eyes watered, and what the fuck was that about? He hid his face against her hair, used it to blot the tears away.

This was stupid. They had no time to indulge in masturbatory hugging bullshit, with bullet holes smoking and cops on their way. But what was he supposed to do, fling her off? Her face pressed against his shirt. Her eyelash flutters tickled his collarbone. Her breath bloomed, humid against his chest. The sensation rocketed through his nerves.

Whoa. Back off. Don't start with that crazy shit. Don't even start.

Then he caught her scent. And oh. God.

He lived in a forest. Outside his house, the spruce, cedars, firs, and pines towered hundreds of feet over his head, a vaulted expanse of flickering green. When it rained, which was often, the earthy sweetness of pine needles, tree bark, loam, and moss rose to meet the falling rain. The meeting point of earth and water. Perfect balance. The intersection of opposites. It was the exact scent of Nina Christie's hair.

He'd bought that property for the smell alone. It had been raining when the agent showed him the place, and he just couldn't resist it.

So her shampoo has a nice perfume. Get the fuck over it. He knew how to dismantle a foolish notion with a few hard, well-placed blows.

But the damage was done. Now he was hyperaware of

her. His body felt like one big eye that could not close. He caught sight of the mirror on her closet door. There he was, clutching the gorgeous naked chick. Like he was about to push her down onto the floor and fuck her.

Wow. So pale. Curvy. Her dark hair draped in swags over his wrist. His fingers looked very brown against the pale, smooth skin.

His fingers tightened. She was silky. Softer than the girls he usually ogled, but maybe he'd been missing something, favoring the taut, lean ones. Her breasts pressed against his chest, springy and soft. Her bare, tight nipples brushed his chest. Her locks of dark hair tapered off so that the tips barely tickled the swell of her ass. He wanted to pet that peachy, shadowy cleft. His body, jangling with adrenaline, did its fucking stupid animal thing, and sprang to attention. His hands had taken off without permission on an exploratory mission, fingers splaying greedily to feel the dip of her waist, to grip the curve of her hip.

For God's sake, get a grip, you oversexed bonehead. This woman was all fucked up. She wasn't coming on. She didn't need any attention from the beast lunging on the chain, so back *down,* already. Now.

He clenched his jaw hard enough to cause nerve damage, and dragged his mind away from the hot throb in his crotch. Good timing, decency, self-control, gallantry; none of those items were featured on his resume.

He'd just pretend this was normal. Gunfights, pulling zaftig naked girls with bouncing tits out of closets. No biggie. All in a day's work. Nina Christie did not need his engorged prick bobbing hopefully in her direction. She needed a hot cup of tea, a shot of Demerol, a trauma therapist. A police escort.

Bummer for her. All she had was him.

7

Nina couldn't move. Some crucial part of her nervous system was blocked. She shivered like a baby bunny, hiding her face against the man's shirt. Unwilling to let the moment pass. Once he let her go, she'd be alone. Bereft even of this brief fiction of safety.

She knew it was a fantasy. It would flicker out in a moment, and reality would thud heavily down. She knew that, even while she clung to him like a strangling vine. Just a wishful feeling she'd latched onto, in a moment of weakness. So sweet. To feel protected. Just for a moment.

The guy was being a good sport about it, patting her, holding her awkwardly. Probably terrified she was going to freak out on him. She didn't have words to reassure him. She wasn't ready to let go yet. She pressed her face against his shirt. Her shallow, hitching gasps informed her that he was sweating, and that he smoked.

What was she doing trying to catch his scent, anyway? She shouldn't be sniffing the guy who had just saved her from a gruesome and protracted death. She should be thanking him.

Yes. Thanking him would definitely be in order.

She lifted her head. Her voice wouldn't respond. Her teeth chattered. She forgot what she was trying to say, and just stared, transfixed, at the shape of his jaw, the grim lines carved around his mouth. His beard stubble. Sealed lips. Fierce green eyes. Oh. Wow.

"Look, lady," he said. "I'm sorry to push you, but how many of them did you hear? I saw four. Took down two, saw two head out the window. Did you hear more?"

She managed a negative jerk of her head. *I heard four, too, but I only saw two.* She wanted to be calm, controlled. Not the cowering woodland creature, nose twitching and whiskers trembling. Wasn't happening. "J-j-just, ah . . . j-j-just the four," she forced out.

He frowned, a faraway look in his eyes, profoundly still. Listening, head lifted like he was smelling the air. His green eyes had a luminous glint, like a nocturnal animal's, gathering all available light.

"We need to get out of here," he said.

Duh. She knew that. She wasn't stupid. Just mute.

"I don't think there's anyone left in the house, but I'm going to go and check. We need to get out of here," he repeated, more loudly.

Yeah? By all means, check. Tears were leaking down, clogging her nose. Oh, how she hated tears. They made her despise herself.

"You have to let go of me, Nina. So I can go check. Understand?"

His hands folded over hers. Big, warm, long-fingered, with a texture like polished wood. She was so busy enjoying his warmth, it took a few moments for the meaning of his words to sink in.

Let go. Oh, God. He couldn't move, because she was clutching his shirt, in a shaking, white-knuckled death grip. How embarrassing.

"I'm just going to, ah, open up your fingers," he said. "So I can go make sure all's clear. Why don't you throw on some clothes?"

Throw on some—oh, *shit!*

She jerked away, and thudded onto her butt on the floor, legs curled into an awkward, coy mermaid pose. Waves of heat and cold throbbed through her. It was like one of those stupid, banal anxiety dreams. Naked at the grocery store, the bus stop, the subway. Everyone leering, judging. While she shrank in on herself and tried to hide.

Silly. Like being unclothed was such a big deal, considering the circumstances. His fingers were spread out, wide and splayed, like they hadn't been quite ready to let go of her yet.

His eyes had a pull that sucked the air right out of her lungs. His gaze charged the air with heat, shivering awareness. Heavy, almost ominous. And it just kept getting hotter, and heavier. No end to it.

Except for the obvious end. She didn't know how her mind actually ran that far ahead of her, but it did, all on its own, and suddenly, she saw it, in full, glowing detail. Grabbing him, greedily. Pulling him down on top of her, right there, on the floor. Wrapping her legs around him. Clinging to his big, hard body and taking him inside. Way down deep. Never letting him get away. *Mine.*

She was so shocked, she panicked, and snapped right back into default mode. Gray fuzz, the *nobody here, nothing to see, no big deal.*

But the trick didn't work on Aaro. His energy didn't change at all. He just kept looking at her, with those hot, hooded eyes. Not leering, just looking. Long, and steady. His eyes looked . . . hungry.

She wasn't used to it. She'd had men look at her, of course, in spite of how she dressed. Some men would look at anyone, no matter how drab. Equal opportunity oglers. Their gaze left a residue that made her want to bathe. But Aaro's gaze didn't make her feel small, or dirty, or worthless. In his eyes, she felt uniquely visible. Lit up, a strobe light in a disco. She could be seen through walls. Seen from space.

Her eyes darted frantically before being dragged back to his grim stare. Her room stank of gunpowder, someone had just emptied a pistol at her, and she was indulging in sexual fantasies about her rescuer?

Stress response. Put it behind her. Move briskly on. A tangle of clothing lay on the floor, swept to the ground by Pockmarks's gun barrel. She reached, grabbed a high-necked, long-sleeved, plain gray rayon blouse, struggled into it. Groped for a baggy apron-style smock of coarse navy-blue linen, tossed it over her head. It floated down like a parachute. She tugged the loose ensemble into place with difficulty, being so sticky with cold sweat, and ventured a glance at Aaro when she was decent again. His sharp cheek-bones were flushed.

"I'll just, ah, check the place out," he said gruffly. "Get on some shoes." He flung the command over his shoulder as he walked out.

Nina got to her feet, caught herself against the mirror. The room bobbed like a rowboat. Her image looked pallid, foggy, and blurred. Her hair clung to her face, teased and tangled up into a big, scary snarl.

Focus. Shoes. Glasses. They'd been on her dresser. The stuff that had been up there; lamp, stained-glass box, alarm clock, a photo of Mom, a picture of herself and Lily, a dish of rose-petal potpourri; had been shoved off, shattered onto the floor.

She fished her glasses out of dried petals and glass shards, and perched them on her nose with a trembling hand. Sandals, now. The comfy ones that she could walk for miles in, without blisters.

Or else sprint for her freaking life, as the case might be.

She tried forcing a comb through her hair, and promptly

concluded that it was a project for another moment. She pulled the snarled fuzz into a messy braid. She usually twisted it into a knot, but her shaking arms weren't up for coiling a bun, and she didn't want to dig through broken glass for hairpins. Not a day for an updo.

Her purse had been in the closet. She knelt to fish it out, found her phone on the floor, too, tucked it in her pocket—

"You ready?"

She spun around, hand clamped over her face.

"Sorry," he said gruffly from the door.

Her eyes zeroed in on the gun he held in his hand, and froze there like a terrified rabbit. "I'm OK," she whispered, lurching to her feet.

"Good. Let's go." He stepped inside, took her arm. "Just so it's not a surprise. There are bodies. One on the stairs, one at the front door. Just be ready. Lots of blood."

"B-b-b-bodies?" Of course there were bodies. She wasn't one of them, thanks to Aaro. Focus on that. Get a grip.

"I heard shots, when I was coming in," he said. "Sounded like they were killing you sooner rather than later, so I went for it. Wasted them."

Wasted them. His tone sounded so . . . offhand.

She wavered at the top of the stairs and clutched the newel post, staring at the blood-spattered corpses. Aaro tugged, but her fingers would not let go. Her nervous system had been hijacked again.

Those men had tried to kill her. She was glad he'd killed at least some of them. She was no shrinking violet. She'd experienced violence. She saw the consequences of violence every day. So *chill*, woman.

"Nina." The edge in his voice jolted her, releasing her grip. "Move."

She picked her way over the sprawled legs of the corpse on the stairs, trying to avoid the blood trickling down the steps.

A stomach-flopping wave of cold rose inside of her. Her vision went dark, sounds distorting . . .

"You OK?" Aaro's harsh voice dragged her back. She really did not want to fall to pieces in front of that guy again. *Yes.* Her lips formed the lie, but just a feeble puff of air came out. Not enough to voice the word.

His voice came back into focus again some moments later. He was cursing. She could tell from the tone, the punching cadence, though the language was incomprehensible. His fingers bit into her arm, hauling her up. She'd fallen? Yikes. It would seem she had.

The wall thudded against her back, propping her up. She watched as Aaro ran back up the stairs, bending over the corpse and rifling it. He came away with a pistol and a magazine. He shoved the gun into the back of his jeans, the magazine in his pocket, and strode down to crouch over the body in the foyer, where he repeated the performance.

"Don't the, um . . . won't the cops need to see the . . ." She licked her lips. "For ballistics testing, I mean? Shouldn't you leave those?"

"They might be useful. I've got some firepower with me, but more is better, and I don't have time to mess around procuring them. Might as well take these."

"But, ah . . ." Her voice trailed off as he ran his hands over the man's body, and shoved up a pant leg. He unbuckled an ankle holster from a hairy ankle, and held the pistol out. "Want it? It's a Micro Glock. Good size for you. Small, easy to use."

She recoiled. "Oh, God, no."

"Suit yourself." He shoved it into his jacket pocket, and took her hand again, pulling her stumbling through the dining room and the kitchen. He pulled the back door open, peered out, and gestured for her to follow him into the alley. "Let's go."

She gaped, blinking in the flood of afternoon sunlight streaming through the door. "But, ah, shouldn't we wait?"

"For what? For them to come back with reinforcements?"

"Don't be a smart-ass," she snapped. "I mean, for the police. Won't they need, you know, a statement? Don't we need to file a report about what happened, look at mug shots, all that?"

"Not if I can help it," he said.

"But . . . but . . ." She gestured over her shoulder.

"Yeah, there are bodies in your house, and you've got a choice to make. I owe Bruno a favor. If you come with me, I'll protect you as best I can until we connect with the bodyguard Bruno's arranging for you. Or you can wait for the cops. In either case, I'm out of here, with or without you, in the next ten seconds."

"But I . . . but why—"

"Aaro is not my real name. I've been cultivating this identity for twenty years, but in New York, I'm likely to come into contact with people who know my original name. If my new name gets linked to it, my cover is blown. My savings, my livelihood, my property, all of it gone. I'd have to start from zero again with fuck-all, and I'm too old for that. The favor I owe Bruno is big, but not that big. So choose."

"Ah, but I—"

"Quicker." He peered out the door again. "Walk out the door, or stay and take your chances with the authorities. I can't tell you which option is more dangerous, because I don't fucking know."

Nina was aghast. She had to make a life-or-death decision now?

"It just feels wrong, to disappear," she faltered. "Don't they need us to tell them what happened?"

His shrug personified pure masculine arrogance. "They don't always get what they need. A phenomenon commonly known as 'tough shit.' Familiar with it? You should be. It's smeared all over your life."

Anger prickled up her spine. "Don't condescend to me, Aaro."

"Stay, then. Tell them all about it. Hope it works out for you." He vaulted down the stairs without a backward glance. *Bastard*. Her hands fisted with rage, but even so, the decision made itself in a flash.

No way was that guy walking away from her. No. Freaking. Way.

"Don't leave!" she blurted, voice cracking.

He did not turn his head. "Then haul ass."

She scurried after, and he seized her arm, pulling her along in an awkward, scrambling trot. "Could you just give me a ride to New Dawn?" she asked. "It's only fifteen minutes away. I'll call the police when I get there, and tell them what happened, and then I—"

"Shhhh." He spun, scanning the area. "Shit," he muttered.

"What?" She twirled, too, but heard nothing and saw nothing.

"They're watching us," he said. "They'll follow."

She looked around wildly. "But where? I don't see—"

"Me neither," he said. "I feel them. They make my balls itch."

"Oh," she said inanely. "Must be nice to have an early warning system. Are you sure it's not just a fungus?"

He yanked the car door open. "Don't bust my balls while I'm trying to keep you alive. It fucks my concentration. Get down."

He looked thunderously annoyed, but that seemed to be his default expression, whether holding her naked body in his arms or frisking corpses to scavenge their firearms. He grumbled something guttural that sounded viciously profane as he slid into the driver's seat.

"What did you just say?" she demanded.

"That we're totally fucked," he said. "Get down. I'll try to get you there in one piece, but do your part not to get your head blown off."

She studied his scowling profile from her crouched position, head sideways on the seat. "You're not inspiring confidence," she told him.

"It's not my job to inspire confidence."

He drove fast, once she gave him the address. Centrifugal force tossed her from side to side as he surged and braked, took curves on squealing tires. He went the wrong way down one-way streets, too. She heard a lot of blaring horns, the occasional outraged shout. She didn't analyze his route, just stared at the taut mask of concentration that was his face. She couldn't look away. It was like a superstitious thing. The world would disintegrate to chaos without him. His ferocious focus was what held it together.

And that kind of clingy, needy crap would get her into deep doo-doo. No way could she pin that kind of responsibility on him.

There was probably a name for what she was experiencing. Some clinical pathology she'd studied in college. She had to just endure it, not analyze it. Groveling gratitude and anger were a tough mix. Together, they curdled into something caustic and unappetizing.

He jerked the car to a stop. "Stay there," he ordered, shoving the door open. Seconds later, her own door popped open. "Stay next to me. I'll get you in there, but I can't stay, not if there are cops involved."

She nodded, eyeing the very large and intimidating shotgun he held so casually. It would freak her colleagues out, if he carried that thing into the New Dawn admin office. Too bad.

He'd pulled over across from a side entrance to the building, into a parking spot on the narrow street. The sky felt open, strangely threatening. Her eyes darted, searching for their attackers.

"Call the cops as soon as you're inside, and don't leave that building again without a police escort or Bruno's guy," he said.

"Um, OK." She forced down the urge to beg him to stay. If he couldn't, he couldn't. He'd done enough. She'd be OK once she was inside.

"I don't like this." He stared up the street. "This feels wrong."

"Balls itching again?" she asked.

His chin jerked. "They're on fire."

"Mine, too," she told him.

"Oh, yeah?" A grin flickered on his face. "You ready?"

Just then, a black Audi with tinted windows turned the corner, and the full force of their murderous intention blew right through her like a weird ghost wind.

. . . that's her . . . die, bitch . . . cut our losses . . .

"Watch out!" she shrieked, as the window started buzzing down.

Aaro grabbed her, shoved. The pavement heaved up to greet her. *Smack,* she was on the sidewalk. *Bam-bam-bam,* the world exploded.

Glass shattered, pattering down in a glittering hail. Car alarms started squealing everywhere. Aaro leaped up as the bullets whizzed, swung up his shotgun. *Bam-bam-bam.* Glass shattered. A huge crunch and smash. Shouts.

Aaro dropped, crawling around to the front to peer around the tire. A constant stream of foreign profanity was coming out of him again. She no longer needed a translation.

Even she could tell that they were, indeed, totally fucked.

* * *

Take that, dickfaces.

He scooped Nina up as she rasped in air, and heaved her into the front seat again, broken glass and all. Slammed the door shut.

"Stay down," he told her. "Hang on tight to the door handle. Gonna be a wild ride."

He dove in, head ducked, and started the motor. The street ahead had been clear, so he wrenched it into gear and punched the gas, hoping it still was. *Bam, bam,* a bullet caught the side window. Glass flew, stinging his face. Hot blood trickled down.

A second ticked by. He bobbed up over the dash just in time to veer out of the way of a parked car he was about to swipe. Out the rear-view, shrinking into the distance, he saw the dazed thugs spilling out of the wrecked Audi. The bald one, the dark one. The dark one aimed . . .

Aaro punched the gas and swerved. Nothing hit them.

Nina gasped for breath. "How did you . . . what did you—"

"Blew out their windshield with the shotgun," he explained tersely. "Tires, too. They spun out. Crashed into a parked car."

Fuckheads had problems now. They'd gambled on speed, surprise. They'd lost big. *Too bad, pussies. This round goes to me.* He wished he could overhear the talk they'd have with their boss tonight. The debrief and the subsequent reaming would be hugely entertaining.

Wind blew through the empty, blasted windshield, blowing trickles of blood sideways on his face as he sped down the street, hitting all the greens. The option of unloading Nina at her place of work, surrounded by caring friends and colleagues, was no longer feasible.

He mourned it, sharply. It had been so perfect. Leaving her with people used to protecting women in danger, who already had systems in place for it. Bruno's new bodyguard detail could have met up with her there, and the responsibility for keeping her in one piece would have been shuffled off of his shoulders. Whatever. Spilled milk. Let it go.

He turned off the next side street, and screeched to a halt. He fished his duffel and laptop out of the backseat, and yanked the bullet-warped passenger door open. "Come on, let's go." He tugged Nina, but she would not budge. She'd been scared into silence.

Just as well. Less provocation. Upped his chances of success at pretending to be a civilized human being for any length of time.

"Nina." He cleared his throat. "Let go. Please."

A shudder went through her. She scrambled out. He hooked his arm around her shoulders, leaving his gun hand free, and hauled her toward Flatbush.

She scurried to keep up. "Should we be going toward such a big street?" she asked. "Those guys—"

"We need a taxi. Better if you hail it. Cabs don't stop for me."

"Not me," she said. "I never have any luck with—"

"Shut up and hail the fucking cab." He jerked her arm up high.

"You don't understand! They don't stop for me, either!" she yelled.

He gave her a disbelieving stare. "Why not? You're a woman, you're young, good-looking, not slutty or sloppy or punked out, you're not wearing leather, your hair's not green. What's not to stop for?"

"You'll see," she muttered grimly.

She stared into the street, arm up, lips flattened to an angry line, and maybe it was her pissed-off vibe, but a river of empty cabs with their numbers lit flowed by. Aaro studied the drivers, perplexed. They didn't even flick their gaze over to check out a possible fare and then dismiss her, like they did to him. They didn't seem to see her at all.

Fuck it. The cars had slowed for the red, so he chose an

idling cab at random and jerked open the door without a visual invitation from the driver. He bundled Nina inside,
shoved in his duffel, and climbed in.

"Hey! Wait! I am not in service!" The turbaned Sikh driver swiveled, his eyes alarmed. "I was on my break! You cannot get in here!"

"Your light was on," Aaro said calmly.

"But I—"

"Take us to the car rental on Wilburn," Aaro said, cutting
off his protests, and suddenly was conscious of the trickle of
hot blood rolling down his temple. He looked fresh out of
mortal combat.

He gave the guy a smile that spoke of a long, painful
death.

The cabbie whipped his head around and laid on the gas.

Aaro peered out the window, trying to define the thought
that hadn't had a chance to form yet, with all the chaos and
noise.

"I saw your face, right before that Audi pulled up," he
said. "I saw the car turn the corner exactly when you did, but
your face changed before the window rolled down. You
knew that car, Nina?"

He tried to keep from sounding accusatory, without much
success. Nina still looked affronted. "No! I have never seen
that car!"

"Then why the look?" he pressed. "What gave you the
jump on them? Out with it, Nina. If I'm going to help you,
you have to tell me everything. Every last nasty, secret detail. Every sore and every score."

Her throat bobbed. "My personal life is boring and quiet.
I do not have nasty, secret, private details to titillate you
with. No sores, no scores." She spat the words at him. "And
I did try to tell you everything. I tried this morning, when I
sent you that file, remember? We'd both know a hell of a lot
more if you'd condescended to help me earlier!"

"Don't scold me," he ground out. "Just tell me how you knew who was in that car."

Her eyes flicked away. "Um. Well," she murmured. "It's just that, ah, Shira told me about this guy, Sergei. He came to the shelter to ask about Helga Kasyanov, and me. And, um, she saw his black Audi."

She was lying. Like a rug. Her lie buzzed against his nerves. It bugged the living shit out of him. "Who the fuck are Shira and Sergei?"

"No need to snarl," she said. "Shira works with me at the New Dawn administration office. Sergei is the dark guy with the ponytail, the one who was at my house. The one shooting at us, outside the office."

His jaw gaped. "What the fuck? You mean, you *know* this guy?"

"No!" she wailed. "No, of course I don't know him! I only heard about him from Shira! He came looking for me after I got needle stuck, and said he was Helga's brother! I got a call from Shira after I left the hospital, and—"

"Yeah, that was another question," he broke in. "Why did you leave the hospital? What the hell were you thinking?"

Her gaze flicked away again, and she waited a little too long to answer. "The doctor said she couldn't justify admitting me," she said. "I seemed fine. So I left."

Another lie. He stared at her, through slitted eyes, and decided to wait and see where she was going with it. As soon as he found the hole in her story, he'd stick his hand in it and unravel the whole fucking thing. "Fine. They told you to go. Where did you go?"

"I went to Yuri's house in Alphabet City, to see if he—"

"Who's Yuri?"

"If you'd stop interrupting, maybe I could get through a complete sentence! Yuri Marchuk is the guy who was driving Helga this morning. He dumped us both off at the hospital and beat hell out of there, but Connor McCloud got someone to run his license plate number, so I had his name and address. So after you so courteously blew me off this morning, I left the hospital, and took the subway, to the East Village."

He stared at her, waiting for it.

She exhaled sharply, and dug into her purse, rummaging until she came up with a travel pack of wet-wipe napkins. She fished one out, handed it to him. "For your face," she said, gesturing with distaste at the bleeding slice on his temple. "All that blood. It's distracting me."

Distracting her? He stared at the moist towelette, his nose wrinkling at its powdery perfume. He'd stink like a baby's ass.

Hell with it. He wiped the blood off his face with it, as best he could. The chemicals that dampened it made his cuts sting.

What a woman. She'd escaped a violent death twice in twenty minutes, and still had her wet wipes at the ready. He crumpled the bloody rag in his fist. "So? You tracked Yuri down. And then?"

"I went to his address. But when I got there . . ." She sucked in her lip, pressing down so the pillowy pink softness became a pale, sexless line. "It had yellow crime scene tape strung around it. An ambulance. Police everywhere."

His dread intensified. "What happened in there?"

"He'd been murdered." Her voice was small. "Tortured to death. A neighbor girl told me. I—I saw his daughter come out of there. Marya. She was soaked with blood."

He closed his eyes, dismayed. So bad. Worse than he'd imagined.

Nina forged on. "I was coming home, and Shira called me. She said this guy came by who said he was Helga's brother. I know Helga personally, and I know that she never had a brother, but Shira didn't know that. Shira's description of this guy matched the guy who shot up my closet. Tall, dark, ponytail, acne scars. And, um, a black Audi. I didn't put it together until the car window came down."

It exploded out of him. "The fake brother, the murdered cab driver? Jesus, Nina! You didn't think to mention those little details to me before we get mowed down by a hit squad?"

"And when might I have done that? When have we had time for a chat? Between hails of bullets and the high-speed car chases? I am doing my best, Aaro! Don't you dare get in my face!"

He swallowed it back. No point driving her into a frenzy. This was a true McCloud-style clusterfuck. And he was in it up to his neck.

"I didn't put it together until I saw the car and remembered Shira . . . oh God! Shira!" Her eyes went huge. "I am such a self-absorbed idiot!" She dug in her purse, the big pocket of her skirt. "Oh, *shit!*" She turned blazing eyes on him. "I lost my phone! Give me your phone!"

He snapped into defensive mode. "What do you want it for?"

"Shira! That guy who shot up my closet, he knew her name, and where she lives! He taunted me with it! Give me your fucking *phone!*"

He hissed silent obscenities through his teeth. He did not want his number on any register that connected him with this, but Nina was going to totally lose her shit if he didn't oblige her. He gave into the inevitable, and handed her his phone. The account was registered to another name, but those identities were expensive to build.

Nina punched in a number and hunched over it, waiting. "Shira?" she said, voice wobbling. "It's me . . . yes, I know. Shira, you have got to hide somewhere. You're in danger, and I . . . I know. I was the one they were shooting at . . . of course I'm fine! Would I be calling if I weren't? The guys know where you live, Shira. You need to go into hiding . . .

no, not me! I'm fine! This guy saved me. Shira, you have to . . ." A loud burst of words from the phone, and her gaze slid over him, uncertain. "He's . . . well, I just met him, and there was a lot going on. He's a friend of a friend." Another burst, shrill and tinny. Aaro's fingers curled into fists as he waited for Nina's response.

"I'm in a cab," Nina recounted. "We got away, and we . . . no, I don't know where. It's complicated . . . no, I can't tell you his name at the moment. But I'm fine. He saved me, Shira. Really. I'm not being constrained, or anything, believe me. I'm fine."

Oh, for fuck's sake. He grabbed the phone from her. "Shira?"

"Who the hell are you?" The woman's voice was shrill.

"I'm helping Nina go into hiding. You should hide, too. They know your name, where you live. Get out of town. Go someplace random."

"Look here, mister. You tell me who you are this minute," Shira ordered. "I've got your number, and I'm giving it to the cops!"

"If you care about your friend, you won't do that." He broke the connection, turned off the phone. He pried it open, pulled a new SIM card out of his wallet, and changed it out. *Ka-ching.* He started mentally totalling up how much this fiasco had cost him financially. How much worse it was liable to get before he could extricate himself. Ouch.

"What, are you a new person now?" she asked. "Just like that?"

He braced himself for more attitude. "Pretty much."

She harrumphed. "Well. In any case. Thank you. Just so it gets said, before I start screaming at you again."

He was startled. "Huh?"

"I'm just saying it now," she repeated. "You seem to bring out the worst in me, Aaro. But I appreciate being alive. So, uh . . . thanks."

His face was trying to grin again. He put a stop to it. He had no business encouraging her. That just led to misunderstandings. "Don't thank me," he said brusquely. "I'm doing this for Bruno. I owe him—"

"Yes, you told me. This big favor you owe him. I totally get that."

"Don't thank me. It's nothing personal. I'll hook you up with your bodyguard detail, and disappear. And you can forget I ever existed."

She gave him that are-you-for-real stare. "Your rudeness goes above and beyond the call of duty, Aaro. A normal person would have to make a huge, deliberate effort to be as needlessly rude as you are."

"Guess I'm not normal," he said. "I'm not even breaking a sweat."

"You just can't stand it when I try to be nice to you?"

"Don't try," he told her. "It's a waste of energy."

"That's excellent advice," she said, tight-lipped.

"I'm just a font of good advice today," he said. "That one's right up there with my other big winners. Like, 'Get your head down before it gets blown off.' And 'Put your clothes on.'"

Nina blushed. "Asshole," she muttered.

Ah. That was more like it. He relaxed a little. On familiar ground.

She fumed silently for a few minutes before her next swipe at him. "So besides routinely pissing me off, do you have a plan?"

"Not really," he said. "More like a grocery list. New vehicle. Phone call to Bruno, to set up a rendezvous point. Someplace to hear that file. Hotel room." His eyes flicked over her. "And a new look for you."

That put her right back on edge. "What's wrong with my look?"

"They've seen you," he said. "They got a good, long look.

Tent frock, bad glasses, long hair." He lifted his hands when she glared. "Don't get huffy. This is about you not getting dead. Nothing personal."

"Shut up," she snapped. "Or do you think that your bad attitude will create a magic shield that bullets can't penetrate?"

He thought of it wistfully. "Wouldn't that be convenient."

"So people shoot at you a lot, then?"

"More often than I'd like," he admitted.

"Have you considered trying behavioral modification to address that problem?" she asked, a little too sweetly.

He shrugged. "It's more time effective to just shoot back."

8

Nina kept her hot face turned away. He was goading her. Shame on her for getting sucked into it. She didn't recognize the person who currently possessed her body. Scolding, screaming rants; what was up with that? Was she infected with a super-contagious rudeness virus?

She went to insane lengths to avoid confrontations. Violence, physical or verbal, shortened her breath and messed with her digestion. Sometimes she had to turn off the TV or walk out of movies if the screen characters were fighting. It was classic Stan fallout, of course, so she should be able to deal with it, right? But alas, it was never that easy. Just one damn mountain to climb after another. A girl got tired.

Unfortunately, all of life's endeavors that were worth the effort required the basic guts to face down opposition. Especially if one was advocating for victims of violence and abuse. No matter what one did, there would always be someone pissed off at her for doing it, or who thought that it had been done wrong, or whatever. It was a natural law, like thermodynamics. If you did anything beyond eating your breakfast cereal, you were sure to catch some shit for it. It all boiled down to getting a frigging spine. She tried, every day. With limited success, but hey, the effect of constant water on a stone, right?

Look at her now. Mobsters started shooting at her, and she morphed into a screaming virago, haranguing a tough guy twice her size who was carrying four—no, was it five guns, now?

Was it Helga's drug? The thought chilled her.

She thought, suddenly, of that awful subway ride through New York, other peoples' thoughts and feelings tromping through her head. It had been so terrifying at the time, but the concept of terrifying was a lot more relative than she had ever imagined. Getting shot up by mobsters put other scary things into perspective very quickly.

So did hanging out with Aaro. He made her feel, well . . . *electrified* would be the most delicate way of putting it. Her hair was practically on end. She felt bad for lying to him. Or, well, not exactly lying. She'd just withheld a few details. Zombie ghouls, mind reading. She just wasn't ready to watch that smolder of awareness go chilly and distant, then turn to distaste. Counting the minutes 'til he could get rid of the crazy girl. Pass her off to the guys in the white coats. Talk about a turnoff.

Did that mean that she was considering turning him *on?*

That fleeting thought knocked a door open in her head, and the blistering fantasy she'd had outside the closet door came roaring back.

Did he want her, too? It occurred to her that she should know. Why hadn't Aaro's thoughts invaded her brain, like everybody else's?

She tried to drop the gray, fuzzy shield that had already become automatic. It was hard to let it down. She felt naked without it. She waited, for his thoughts to flow in and illuminate her.

Nothing. Absolutely zippo. She tried again. Harder.

"What?" he said, his voice testy. "What's with the look?"

She couldn't think of a lie fast enough, so the truth flopped right out of her. "I was trying to read your mind."

The glance he gave her from under his hooded eyes made her notice how insanely long his eyelashes were. "What did you read?"

"Absolutely nothing," she said.

"You don't need to read my mind to know what I'm thinking. There are other indicators." He paused. "Big ones."

She stared fixedly as the apartment buildings, storefronts, and schools crawled by. Bastard. Messing with her head. Heat and sweat, rising in her body. She must look like a tomato. And now they were mired in a snarl of rush-hour traffic. No end in sight.

"We're going to be here for hours," she muttered.

"Get down." He gripped her leg below the knee, pulling it so that her bottom slid forward over the slippery leather seat. His touch set off tingling sparkles over her skin, through layers of rayon and linen.

"Stop that." She batted his hand away.

Aaro slid down to join her, but the position forced him to fold one leg up against the back of the driver's seat, and angle the other one sideways, in her direction. His knee gently prodded hers. Contact, again. More tingles, more ripples. "I said, stop it," she snapped.

"Can't help it," he murmured. "I'm just. . . . really long."

"Would you cool it with the penis references, Aaro?" she snapped.

"You said it, not me." He looked away, but she could tell from the eye crinkles over his cheekbone that he was grinning.

Heat rose into her face. His slow-spreading grin maddened her. "What?" she almost yelled. "What's the smirk about?"

"Don't freak out," he said. "It's normal. What you're feeling."

"What do you know about my feelings?"

He gave her an offhand shrug. "Happens to me, too," he said. "It's normal. Post-combat stress reaction. Don't sweat it."

Oh, for God's sake, was he suggesting . . . Her eyes flicked down to peek at his muscular thigh, to see if he—

Yes. He was. And she'd fallen right into his trap. He was laughing, under his breath, a deep, quiet rumble. Smug, self-satisfied *bastard*.

"Mind in the gutter? Don't be embarrassed. You're not alone."

She squeezed her eyes shut, but it was impossible to block him out. He was overwhelming in the small space. Feelings pulsed through her, breath-stealing, heavy. The pull, the hot yearning. What the hell?

"You're dreaming," she whispered, swallowing hard.

"Yeah," he agreed. "I still smell your hair. My hands remember everything. The curve of your back. The feel of your skin. Your hair, over my arm. You know those dimples over your tailbone?"

"I do not want to know anything you might say about them."

He ignored that. "I want to lick them," he whispered dreamily. "I want to memorize that creamy, perfect dent shape. With my tongue."

His words awakened sensory receptors in each of the places he had mentioned. Tendrils of heat curled out of them, tightening her nipples, clenching her toes. "I can't believe you just said that to me."

"Neither do I," he admitted. "I don't usually talk this much. Talking gets me into trouble."

"That I can well believe," she said fervently.

His grin carved grooves into his lean cheek. "But not this kind of trouble," he said. "This kind is special."

"Special how?" It popped out before she could squelch it. She had only herself to blame, for egging him on. Stupid woman.

"Specially insane," he said. "Coming on to a woman like you."

Outraged vanity jolted her bolt upright. "A woman like me? What's that supposed to mean?"

His hand clamped on her knee and yanked her back down. "Keep your head low," he said. "You know what I mean. A woman like you, with all the baggage and the expectations."

"I have no idea what you're talking about," she said.

"Then you're playing dumb," he said. "I mean, the kind of woman who'd get all uptight when I cut out in the morning before she wakes up. And then don't call."

She snorted. "Why am I not surprised."

"I like to keep things casual," he said. "I'm not looking for attachments. I'm always up front about that. Always."

It bugged her, that he'd pegged her as clingy, needy. More trouble than she was worth. "What makes you think I'm so hungry for attachment?"

"All women want attachment. Unless they're damaged."

"So do men." She wasn't even sure exactly what they were arguing about, but she couldn't shut herself up. "Unless they're damaged, too."

"Right," he said. "There you have it."

"So you're telling me you're damaged goods?"

"Duh," he said.

A heavy silence followed his blunt assertion. She looked away, angry and restless and bothered. "Wow, Aaro. How very seductive."

His shoulders lifted. "Just telling it how it is."

"OK," she said, shaky and angry. "Message received, loud and clear. I appreciate the warning, but it's unnecessary. I want nothing at all from you. And I'm damaged goods, too, for the record. So drop it right now, before we both say things we'll regret."

"I knew you were. Damaged goods, I mean. I see it from your look. You dress to disappear, and you pull it off, even with a body like yours. I wouldn't have thought it was possible. Just a hell of a thing."

She was alarmed. She'd tried to kill this conversation, and instead, it was spiraling out of control. "That's not what I meant," she said. "And I didn't ask for a critique of my fashion sense."

"We all get stuff we don't ask for. Want to know the weird part, though?" His narrowed eyes were fixed on her, hot with fascination. "My dick is still as hard as cement."

She jerked back against the door. "Don't talk to me like that."

She hated how she sounded. Tight, tense, prissy. One of those silly, not-worth-the-trouble women, full of baggage and expectations.

"I'm not usually this bad," he said. "I mostly keep my trap shut. But I guess, once you've killed two guys, dragged a stark-naked girl out of a bullet-ridden closet and then gone through a drive-by shooting with her, you feel entitled to skip the small talk."

That sneaky bastard. Taking up all the oxygen molecules. It wasn't fair. His long, lean, graceful body was sprawled on the seat in apparent relaxation, but he wasn't relaxed. He buzzed with intensity. Ready for action, like a panther poised to spring. It unnerved her. The heaviness of the air.

"Who would know, to look at you?" he almost whispered.

"Know what?" she squeaked back.

"How soft your skin is," he said.

Her face got hot. Her breath snagged. And stuck.

"The way your hair swirls down into those wisps that brush the top of your ass. The hollow, here." He touched her collarbone, hidden under the buttoned blouse. She jerked back as if his finger were a red hot brand.

"And that thing you do with your lip," he went on. "You suck it in, squeeze out all the pink color and that round, pouty shape. Does it embarrass you, to have lips that make guys think about sex?"

"Stop," she warned. *Please.* Before she fainted.

"And those tits." He shook his head in wonderment. "Women would pay huge money for world-class tits like that. That perfect pear shape, those pointy brown nipples, *mmm.*" He made a caressing, molding gesture with his hands. "But you hide them under a tent. It's a secret. Right? Nobody can know. Or the sky will fall down."

Her nipples, upon being nominated, were making a spectacle of themselves, poking through jumper and blouse without the benefit of her minimizer bra with its fierce underwires and its modesty cups.

She sucked in her lip, felt herself doing it, noticed him notice. So much to feel self-conscious about. Worse than being naked. "I don't—"

"But I know, because I saw it." His voice was a charm, working on her like an actual physical touch. Like a silk scarf trailing over her naked skin, subtle as a whorl of smoke. "Am I the only one who knows what's under there? All that bounty? Jesus, is that even possible?"

Nina sucked in air designated for telling him to stop talking trash, but it got trapped in her lungs when he hooked her skirt, and lifted it, exposing her knee. The fabric tickled her legs. She coughed, to shock her voice back into functioning. "You're messing with my head, Aaro."

"It messes with mine, that you've got no underwear." His voice was pitched just for her ears. "I never said I was fair. Or smart, because coming on to you is stupid. Like, cutting-my-own-throat stupid."

His words were offensive, but she couldn't call him on it,

not with her throat quivering like this. He broke eye contact, to look at the street signs. He checked the time on his cell phone. "In this traffic, I estimate we'll get to the car rental place in fifteen minutes."

Her toes curled up. "Um . . . meaning?"

"Meaning if you slid down a little bit more, all those folds of tent fabric would come in useful. I could slide my hand up your thigh. . . ." He touched her knee, and her leg jerked nervously. "Feel your skin as my hand slides up. Just my fingertips, barely touching you. Taking my time. Until the edge of my hand touches the swirl of your muff, right over your clit. That vortex. Like a cowlick. But I better not even think about licking. Licking's for later."

Stop it. She mouthed the words, but the sound wouldn't follow, and he wasn't looking at her face, he was looking at her thigh, part of which was now bare. His big hand closed over her knee.

And her knee felt so warm. Sparkly and strange.

"When my hand got up to the hot stuff, I'd brush the tip of my finger up and down your slit." His voice was barely audible. "Until you started to make noise, move against me. Then I'd open you up, play with your clit, until you were slick and juicy. I'd slide my finger into your pussy, really slow. Feeling inside you, petting and stroking, listening to how you breath, still playing with your clit, 'til I feel what kind of touch makes you wild. I'll work it . . . slow and soft, deep and hard, whatever you like. Show me as we go. Until you come and come and come. As many times as the trip allows."

"You are outrageous." The words had no air behind them.

"Yeah. Thinking with the little head. Gets you every time. My mouth is watering." He lifted his hand, clenched it, flexed it. "My finger is tingling, just thinking about putting it inside you."

She dragged her tattered dignity together. "I'm impressed with your altruism."

He slanted her an ironic look. "Nobody's ever accused me of altruism before," he said. "How do you calculate?"

"This erotic scenario. Other than your tingling finger, it's all for my benefit. Not a single thought for yourself. How gallant, giving all the orgasms to me. Can't help but make a girl wonder about your agenda."

"You're smart to wonder." She could hear the smile in his voice. "And yeah, there's an agenda. It's all about effective time management."

That took her by surprise. "Excuse me?"

"If we play now, then when I get you to the hotel room, you'll be ready," he said. "What I want requires a locked door, a whole lot of girl lube, and ideally, soundproof walls, though that's probably too much to hope from a mid-range hotel. And after a few hours of what I've got in mind, you won't be accusing me of altruism anymore."

She blinked at him, intimidated. "Um. That sounds alarming."

"It'll be awesome. But it'll be very mutual. I'm a calculating, selfish dickhead, but I do excel in a few things. One is kicking asses. The other I can demonstrate to you right now. Say the word."

His hand on her knee was a silent promise. Waves of energy pulsed from it, straight up her thigh, to pool between her legs, a hot, liquid shimmer of terrified anticipation.

The words just popped out of her, the ultimate buzz kill. "And afterward?" she blurted. "What then?"

Tension gripped the air. For a moment, the silence was absolute.

"Like I told you," he said. "My job is to keep you alive until we hook up with Bruno's guy. After that, you're not likely to see me again. I have my own reasons for staying as far from New York City as possible."

"So what you're suggesting is just a short delay," she said. "In taking me to this rendezvous, I mean."

His grin transformed his face. "It would be a long delay," he said. "A long, juicy, excellent delay. Nothing short about it."

"And just how would you explain that to Bruno and the guy he—"

"Bruno doesn't have this number. He can stew in his own juices. I'll call him when we're done."

When we're done. So flat, so final. She stared down at his fingers, dark against her thigh, trying to think of something to say that was not either prissy or inane or disgustingly clingy.

She needed to be cool, detached, with a guy like this. She gathered her wits, and opened her mouth. "So this is just multitasking for you, then? Killing time while we're stuck in traffic? Getting the tiresome chore of foreplay out of the way in your downtime?"

"Let me do my thing," he suggested. "Tell me afterward if you think it was tiresome. If it felt like a chore. I know how to make a girl come. And I have grasped the concept of delayed gratification, at least when it comes to sex. That's all that can be said for my evolutionary development, though. As for the rest of me, we're talking rudimentary brain stem. The stuff we have in common with crocodiles and sharks. Basic motor function. Making money. Procuring food. Fight and flight."

"You are so full of shit, Aaro," she told him.

That devastating grin made his eyes glow. "You've found me out."

The taxi lurched to a halt. Aaro's gaze fell to her breasts, which jiggled and swayed as they rocked back against the seat.

Her face bloomed hot. "Considering the mortal danger and the mobsters and all that, don't you think we should be more, um, alert?"

"Nah." His voice was offhand. "I'm plenty alert. Trust me. If I were any more alert, I'd have a heart attack."

She choked off the urge to giggle. "So it's all about living life to the fullest? Seizing the day, in the face of doom?"

"I hadn't thought about it in those terms," he said. "I'm not all that deep, to be honest. But what the fuck, right? Let's seize the day. One excuse is as good as another for me."

She shook her head at him. "I cannot believe, after what just happened, that I am having this conversation."

"Me, neither," he said. "But I saw you before you put that bag over your head. The damage is done. Now my dick wants what it wants."

"Bag over my head, my ass," she grumbled.

"Let's not talk about your ass," he said. "At least not until you give me an answer. Then we can go into the subject. In great . . . depth."

She stared up the length of his long, lean body. Presenting himself to be admired. Arrogant jerk. But she couldn't stop looking, at his sharp cheekbones, his hawk nose, his intense, brooding eyes. His face was starkly handsome, even shadowed with stubble. His brown hair had come loose of its tie to hang around his jaw. And she didn't even like long hair on men. She thought it looked affected, effeminate.

Not on Aaro. He was gorgeous. He exuded sexual readiness.

She was actually considering it. Imagining him naked, fulfilling all his heated promises. Imagining herself enjoying every shuddering, succulent minute of it. Heart thudding, thighs clenching.

It was only the most colossally bad idea ever conceived in the history of bad ideas. She was already torn apart. No need to jump up and down on the disassembled pieces. That was what sex with Aaro would do to her. He personified everything she avoided in men. He was rude, aggressive. Too big.

Damaged, by his own admission. He loathed attachment, avoided intimacy. He just wanted to fuck her, plain and simple, before handing her over and walking off into the sunset. He didn't try to put any sort of spin on it, he just said it. He seethed with bad attitude, suppressed violence. He was trained to kill easily, without remorse. Not that she could presume to criticize him for it, considering.

Plus, he smoked.

No, it wouldn't work. Fear and excitement would cancel each other out and leave her stranded at flat zero, miserable and angry at herself for being so stupid. For doing that to herself, despite the alarms, the warnings. All for a stupid little itch that longed to be scratched.

Not in this lifetime. Subject closed, *ka-chunk*, like a bank vault.

She shook her head. "No."

Aaro lifted his hand off her leg without a word, but the silence in the taxi sagged, *whump*. As if the air had turned to lead.

She felt bereft, as if he had taken something from her, something she needed. That sparkling energy of . . . well, she couldn't call it a flirtation. It had been too blunt, too weirdly honest and raw and shocking. Not a flirty vibe at all. But almost, well . . . fun.

And as if she could say no to the man who was keeping her alive. As if she had anything else to offer to convince him to keep on doing it.

She muscled the stab of panic down. She wasn't going to start trading sex. Not for anything. Now or ever. She had enough problems.

Then it occurred to her. After all the terror she'd gone through, she hadn't given her attackers a thought for the past fifteen minutes.

Aaro's indecent proposition had wiped it all right out of her mind.

* * *

Dmitri Arbatov climbed off the motor scooter he'd taken from some terrified teenager, circling the shot-up mess of a Lincoln Navigator that Nina Christie and her protector had escaped in. He'd happened across the car by chance, in their last, desperate attempt to pick up the scent, but he was a short-range telepath, not a tracker like Roy.

Even Roy was in trouble now. They'd gotten out of range while they were grounded with the trashed Audi. No way to pick up the trail of their prey.

His thigh throbbed where the bullet had grazed it. His pants were soaked, one of his shoes filling with blood. Mikhail's and Ivan's corpses had been left in Nina Christie's house for the cops to comb over, and he was defying orders from Oleg at this very moment. He was supposed to be lurking outside Aunt Tonya's hospice, waiting for Sasha to show up.

He was going to catch hell for this.

The thought of the impending conversation with his uncle made him physically sick, but being dry of psi-max for eight weeks was worse. Roy was so fucking stingy with the tabs. When Roy had called, he'd leaped at the bait. Six tabs, ten mg's apiece up front. When they got the girl, another ten. Oh, yeah. He was all over that deal.

Now the girl was gone, and the dose he'd taken for the job was wearing off, leaving him blank, blinded. When he came down from psi-max, he got so thin. Flat, like a piece of paper. He hated that shrinking feeling. Like a hard-on gone south at the worst possible moment.

He craved that rush, when his inner eyes and ears suddenly opened, and he could see the gears crunch and spin in people's heads as if they were made of glass. He knew what moved them, what scared them, what they craved. He owned them. He saw what people thought of him, too, but what the fuck, he was used to being hated.

But he needed a steady supply. Unacceptable, for Roy to own his ass like this. Ever since that night down in SoHo, a year ago. Roy had been calling him for extra guns, false identities, or the services of Oleg's elite computer hackers. Roy had been drunk, expansive. He'd passed Dmitri a little red tab. *Take this. See what happens. Go on. Trust me.*

He didn't, of course, trust Roy. Not at all. But he was curious, so he tried it. And he'd spent the rest of the night in the parking lot, reading every person who walked by. Discovering the man he had been meant to be. The man with the amazing secret weapon, who could not be fucked with, or sneaked up upon. Not when he was using.

Fury seethed and bubbled in his guts when he thought of Nina Christie. Sneaky little cunt. Tiptoeing around him somehow. He didn't understand how she'd blocked him for so long. No one else ever had.

He'd gotten a glimpse of her with his actual eyes before they opened fire. He hadn't been impressed. A mouse of a girl: pale, wispy, shapeless. Big glasses, baggy dress, bad hair. But Dmitri didn't need for them to be raving beauties. Like he'd told her, all women were pretty with duct tape on their mouths. That frantic look in their eyes, the muffled grunts and whimpers, that was what got him off.

He'd seen what went down on the street with her that morning with Kasyanov, through the tattered veil of Yuri's memories. That pathetic fuck had been so easy to read, the torture hadn't even been strictly necessary, but he had to make it look good. The scenario was that Yuri was a dealer and thief, gone into business for himself. There could be no mercy for such a man.

Through Yuri's memories, he knew that Helga had said that there were two doses of this Psi-Max 48 left. Then Kasyanov had shot up Nina Christie with one dose before she spazzed out. This left one dose unaccounted for. They'd searched Christie's house and found nothing. He had to find Nina before Roy killed her. Because that dose was his.

He wasn't satisfied with these pissant ten-mg tabs. He wanted the real deal. The new stuff. Permanent change, that was what Kasyanov had promised them. Rebirth, as his true self. His best self.

Dmitri circled the fucked-up Lincoln. He wrenched the door open. He'd need a tab tonight to deal with Oleg. That evil old goat was so good at mind-fucking, he didn't even need psi-max to help him do it. He knew what he would see in Oleg's head, though. *Sasha.* The long-lost, perfect son who'd had the good sense to disappear twenty years ago.

Oleg said that Sasha would come back now that Tonya was dying, but why? Dmitri couldn't imagine why anyone would want to see that crazy old hag. *Sasha.* Always smarter, stronger, tougher. Dmitri had fantasized since boyhood about slicing open Sasha's abdomen, pulling his guts out loop by loop so he got a good, long look at them. The daydream drifted through his mind as he yanked open the glove box.

If he got that dose, Sasha would be in his power. Sasha's eyes, wide with fear, cowering, pleading. His secrets, naked to Dmitri. *Yes.*

He sifted through the broken glass on the floor, and was rewarded by a battered Samsung smartphone that had slid under the seat. He held it up, and his thumb lit the display, showing a text message.

On the way. Hang in there.

The screen was still unlocked. This gift had come to him even without the psi-max. And Sasha would come to him, too.

9

He should be grateful, Aaro reflected. She'd saved him from his own idiocy. Good thing, too, because he wasn't free to fuck her brains out, anyhow. He was going to Aunt Tonya. A hospice visit was a guaranteed buzz kill. He'd been talking with his dick. It wasn't real big on details like timing.

He should be on his knees in front of her, kissing her feet to thank her for her strength of will. Kissing his gratitude up over her instep, her ankle, her calf, then up her silky thigh, right on up to heaven's gate. He'd end up muff diving in a New York cab.

His cock twitched. So much for situational awareness. Speculating about the flavor of her pussy made his jaw ache. It was going to be a long, painful while before he could schedule a tension-relieving appointment with his own hairy-palmed right hand.

It had been months since his ill-fated tryst with the robot princess, the chick who'd been sent to spy upon him, during Bruno and Lily's adventures six months ago. Naomi had been the name on her fake documents. Not her real name.

Neil King's robot spawn were dead now, so there was no one
left to ask. Probably she hadn't had a name at all.

That somehow-less-than-human thing called Naomi had
self-destructed before his eyes at the Portland cop shop the
morning after he'd fucked her. Brainwashing-induced convulsions. Snapped her neck. So horrible, it had put him off sex,
even a testosterone-loaded horndog like himself. He'd begun
to wonder if he was cured of attacks of inconvenient lust.
Maybe the trauma inflicted on him by the robot princess had
simplified his life. Imagine, not having to feed the slavering
beast ever again. Sweet, unbroken solitude. Ahhh.

But think again. One look at Nina Christie's naked body,
and the beast woke up with a roar, ready to rock and roll. He
was cured.

And she was having none of it.

Whatever. He'd just clench his teeth, keep the girl alive
until he could pass her off to Bruno's guy. Except that Aunt
Tonya couldn't wait for Bruno's guy. He glanced at the car
clock. Visiting hours were long since over. If he drove Nina
to her rendezvous, that was another delay. If he waited for
the bodyguard to drive to him, same problem.

Nah. The zombies and mafiya thugs could all get fucked.
He was going to Tonya now, and Nina would stay nailed to
him, at the cost of dragging her with him to his aunt's
deathbed.

That decision made, he concentrated on driving, not looking at Nina. Strange, that her repressed, buttoned-up vibe
should turn him on so much. Her heat and softness, hidden,
secret. The severity of her disguise jazzed him all the more.
Like it was all just for him.

Dumb fantasy. She wasn't for him. She'd said no, remember? His hard-on was all alone in the world. So. Suck. It. *Up*.

The cab driver pulled up outside the car rental, collected
his fare, and accelerated away with a palpable air of relief,

and for the second time that day Aaro rented a car. The line was shorter this time, and a good thing, too, with Nina clamped under his arm. Even under layers of fabric, he felt her heat, smelled that forest-in-the-rain scent. She was silent, tense. Vibrating at a crazy frequency. A high-pitched, constant buzz, silent to all but him. Like a dog whistle.

And he was the dog. Heh.

They finally took possession of a modest Toyota Yaris, which was all the place had available with no notice. By the time they were on the road again, his hot itch had subsided. The sexual frustration was still there, but now he was just irritated at Nina for provoking it, rather than at himself for feeling it. Which was unfair, but fuck it. A guy clawed his way up the cliff face of his day with whatever handholds stuck out.

The urge to go on the offensive was too much for him. He needed a distraction. Tough shit for her. "So let's hear about it," he said.

"What's 'it'? It's been a full day. Be specific."

"Cut the sarcasm, and tell me what those guys wanted from you."

She looked bewildered. "I already told you everything!"

"No," he said. "That's your cover story. I want the real story."

She looked outraged. "It is the real story!"

"Three things," he said. "One, you have that weird-ass closet, and something is up with that. Two, you recognized the car before the tinted window came down. Three, you lied to me back in the cab."

"What makes you think I lied?"

"I have an ear for it," he said. "And a person does not custom design an expensive secret hiding place in her bedroom unless she's got something to hide. What do you keep in there?"

"Nothing! I keep boxes of books in there! Pharmacological reference books! They belonged to my mother!"

He grunted. "You made a false-backed closet to store your mom's reference books? Come on, Nina, you went to college, you can do better than that. What is it? Drugs? Counterfeit money?"

"No!" she hissed. "I made it for me!"

This was getting stupid, and he was irritated already. "What do you mean, for you? Why, for you?"

"After what happened to me today, you still have the nerve to ask me that? What do you think I was doing in there, Aaro? Playing with myself? I needed a place to hide!"

She was shrieking at him. He'd driven her past the limits of her self-control. Another item from his short list of special talents.

"That won't fly," he told her. "When normal people get paranoid about home invasion, they don't build trick closets. They buy expensive locks, motion sensors, fancy alarm systems, iron bars."

She shrugged angrily. "So I'm not normal. What a surprise."

That put his teeth on edge. "Lady, I am risking my skin to keep you alive. Do not give me any fucking attitude."

She stared ahead. "I'm sorry. I appreciate what you did for me."

It made his ass clench. That super-controlled tone. He preferred it when she yelled at him. "I don't need apologies or thanks," he said. "I just want you to be straight with me. What is up with the closet?"

She twisted her fingers together. "It's, ah . . . it's hard to explain."

He waited a teeth-grinding minute. "Explain it anyway."

Her voice was small. "I guess I have got something to hide."

"Yeah?" He waited for it. "What?"

"Me," she said.

His look demanded that she expand on that.

"I need a hiding place," she admitted finally. "Wherever I sleep."

They stopped at a long light. He took the opportunity to stare at her stark profile. She was looking into her lap, as if she were ashamed.

He had no business poking into this woman's private hang-ups. But he wasn't going to be poking into anything else private of hers.

So fuck it. He wanted to know. "Why?" he insisted.

The weight of the silence compelled her. "It's my stepdad."

Shit. This was going to suck ass. He braced himself for it.

"Yeah?" he prompted, merciless. "What about him?"

"He was an asshole," she said. "Having a place to hide was important. The need stuck with me. I need to have a hiding place, a good one, or else I can't sleep. That's all the closet is for me. A non-pharmaceutical treatment for anxiety and insomnia. Satisfied?"

"Not yet," he said. He glanced over, at the tight braid, the pressed-flat lip, the baggy clothes. Nope, he wasn't satisfied, not yet, and probably not ever, not with all that baggage draped over her. "He messed with you?"

She squinted at him. "Excuse me?"

"Sexually, I mean," he said. "He abused you?"

"No," she said hastily. "Um. Not too much, I mean."

They drove for several minutes in silence while he chewed on that. "That explains it," he said finally.

"Explains what?" Her voice shook with nerves.

"The bag over your head," he said. "Girls usually go one of two ways when that happens to them. Either they go super-slut, start coming on to the whole world, or they shut down the sex thing and just hide." He slanted her a quick, assessing glance. "That would be you."

"I do not need your cheap pop psychology bullshit personal analysis of my personality flaws, thanks very much," she flared.

"No thanks necessary. Going back to your stepdad. What exactly does 'not too much' mean?"

"Fuck off, Aaro!" Her face had gone pink. "I don't want to talk about that to anybody, much less to you, much less today! We've got more important things to talk about!"

"OK," he said, with a meekness that surprised even himself.

He gave her a moment to chill before goosing her along again. "So, about all these more important things we have to talk about."

She sniffed, hard and angrily. "Yes?"

"Talk about them. Start with the lies you told me before."

She stared at him, looking trapped. "Fine," she said tightly. "But you're going to think I'm crazy."

He shrugged. "Crazy's OK, as long as you're honest."

"OK, then. I think Helga's syringe had something really, um, unusual in it."

"And you think this because?"

A nervous, hitching sigh shuddered out of her. "Because since this morning, I'm, um, different. I see things. Hear things."

"Be more specific," he prompted.

"I don't know where to begin," she said helplessly. "There were these doctors, at the hospital. They said they needed to run more tests. I blinked, and suddenly they were, um . . . zombies."

That took him by surprise. "Zombies," he repeated.

She shot him a defensive glance. "Zombies! Familiar with them? Disgusting animated rotting corpses? They mostly populate cheesy horror films? They shamble around, grunt, eat human flesh?"

"Ah." He was at a loss for words. What the fuck was a guy supposed to do with a statement like that? "Uh, OK.

What did these zombies do to you, at the hospital?" he asked cautiously.

"Don't do that," she said, her voice quavering. "Don't you dare!"

"Dare what? Jesus, Nina, I barely spoke!"

"Don't use that super-careful voice, like I'm going to start frothing at the mouth! I know they weren't real zombies, OK? I get that, I know I was hallucinating! But they chased me. That was why I left the hospital in such a hurry. I ran to the subway. I took the F train."

"To the East Village," he supplied. "To Yuri's apartment."

She looked relieved, that he was picking up the thread with no apparent freak-out. But he was good with weird. He'd grown up with Tonya; he hung out with McClouds. Weird was mother's milk to him.

Even so. This girl's story was seriously out there.

"So, the subway is when the strange part happened," she faltered.

"Stranger than zombies?"

She was too intent on her confession to react to his sarcasm. "I hear thoughts," she blurted. "It started on the subway. Then I heard Yuri's daughter, Marya, when she came out of the house. I saw . . . what they had done to him. In her head. So horrible."

"Nina," he began.

"That was how I knew about the car." She hurried on, like she was afraid he wouldn't let her finish. "The guys who shot at us. It wasn't their car that I recognized. It was their thoughts. I heard that they were going to kill us. Like they were shouting it at me."

He looked at her. He tried breaking it into smaller pieces, like fruit in a blender, wood chunks in the chipper. Zombies? Mind reading?

It was too thick and gummy. It clogged up his pipes.

"What?" Her voice was sharp. "What's that blank look about?"

He shook his head. "I'm sorry," he said helplessly. "It's just, ah, extremely weird. Even by my standards."

"There's more." She looked almost desperate, words pouring out. "One of the doctors who chased me? He was at my house."

"I didn't see any zombies at your house, Nina."

"Not in his zombie form," she snapped. "I'm talking about the tall, big guy, with the red burn scar on his neck. He called himself Granger at the hospital. I heard him talking to Sergei. Do you believe me?"

He lifted his hands. "Nina, where do I even start with this?"

She looked away. "I understand," she said, coolly. "I shouldn't have said anything. I guess I just made things worse."

He was cautiously impressed. She'd gone through hell, then been forced to deal with a snarling bonehead like him, and she still came across as regal. "Are you having hallucinations now?" he asked her.

She sniffed. "Not as far as I know. Are you a hallucination, Aaro?"

"Trust me, your mind couldn't spontaneously make up anything as irritating as me. So, visual and aural hallucinations. A lot of stuff could have that effect. Common recreational drugs. LSD, psilocybin."

"But what about Marya? Yuri's daughter? I saw what they did to him, through her eyes! It was horrible, and it was real! I swear to God."

"You could have imagined it," he said. "I'm imagining it right now, and I wish I wasn't. Doesn't take much to fill in the details."

"Then what about the Audi? The guys shooting at us?

How could I have imagined hearing them?" she demanded. "It was real, Aaro!"

He shook his head. "I'm withholding a conclusion for now."

She pressed a trembling hand to her mouth. "You think I'm lying."

He thought about it. "Nope," he said. "Stoned off your gourd on some severe hallucinogen, maybe. But not lying."

She choked on her giggles. "I don't think I should find that statement comforting, Aaro. Yet strangely enough, I do."

He was taken aback. "Treasure the moment," he advised her. "I don't do comfort very often. Blink, and you'll miss it."

That earned him another giggle, one he hadn't known he was fishing for, but he liked it. And he'd better stomp that shit right now, and hard. He could not let himself be entertained by this freakfest. That way lay disaster. An unsettling thought occurred to him, all at once.

"Are you reading my mind right now?" he demanded.

"Um, no." She looked nervous and defensive. "I, um, can't seem to read yours. Maybe it comes or goes. Or it depends on the person."

"Huh," he said slowly. "Is that so. Just me."

Her face tightened. "Please, drop it."

He shook his head. "Go over it again. In sequence. And don't leave out any of the weird stuff this time."

To her credit, stressed out as she was, she gave him a detailed and yet cogent debrief, starting that morning with Helga's attack on the street. He listened without comment, up to the part where he pulled her from the closet. There she stopped, and waited.

"So?" she said. "Any blinding insights, Aaro?"

He ignored the sarcasm, too busy feeling the bars of an invisible cage materializing around him. Dismay, weighing him down like a ton of cold lead. This felt like some heavy shit. These bad guys weren't going to be scared off easily.

"You heard the zombie guy say that the cops were on

their way," he repeated slowly. "That was before I shot out the lock. You were smart not to wait for the police. They got tipped off when Lily called nine one one. This is something big, well organized. Lots of resources, if they have an informant with the cops. What did zombie dude say, exactly? That he should've been able to pick you up from this range?"

"Yes, he said, um . . ." Nina squeezed her eyes shut. "He said it was something like . . . simax. He said, 'the bitch is totally blocking us.'"

"You know what he was talking about?" Aaro prodded. "A blocked radio frequency, maybe? Could someone have planted a trace on you?"

"Not unless it was in that syringe," she said. "No one else has touched me, except for the doctors at the hospital. The real ones."

"Simax," he repeated to himself.

She shook her head. "I don't have any idea what simax could be. Nor do I have a stash of it hidden in my closet."

"I believe you," he said. And surprisingly enough, he did. The asshole stepfather, the closet hiding place story, it rang true.

He screeched to a stop at the red light. There was an entrance to a gas station near at hand. He yanked the car over onto it, and braked. He could not process all this information and drive at the same time.

"Son of a bitch," he murmured.

"Yeah. Tell me about it." Nina was swiping at her eyes with her knuckles. "What am I going to do with this, Aaro?"

He shook his head. "I don't know."

It was the exact wrong thing to say. Her face crumpled. *Shit.* What a dickbrain. "I'll tell you what you do." The words popped out before his brain could put on the brakes. "We find someplace safe. We'll listen to the recording. We call Bruno. That's the plan. You like that plan?"

She sniffed, and nodded. "OK." She gave him a wobbly, brave little smile. "I like that plan."

Her smile was what did it. It was a bad idea, the worst, but she got sucked into the tractor beam of his body, or maybe it was her body that generated the beam, but before he knew it, his ass was poised between the seats, and she was fitting perfectly, right under his arm, like when he'd pulled her out of the closet. Except that she wasn't naked this time.

Naked was better. His body throbbed, remembering how that had been. Her amazing, fragrant softness.

She went tense, and arched away. And what the fuck was he doing, coming on to a woman who had already said no? He retreated to his own seat, embarrassed. Started up the car.

Her mouth was bloodless and flat. "I'm sorry," she said. "Try to understand. I only met you a little over an hour ago."

"During which time I killed two men, and saved your ass twice," he felt compelled to point out, and immediately hated himself for doing so. What, like she owed him sex for that? Was he that desperate?

There was an uncomfortable silence.

"I know," she said softly. "We've definitely cut through the small talk. And speaking of small talk. Where are we going?"

Deft change of subject. The woman was slicker than she appeared. "Brighton Beach," he said.

She stared, astonished. "Excuse me?"

"Did Lily tell you where I came from?" he asked.

"She said something about your family background being, um, checkered," she said delicately.

He laughed. "Nice euphemism."

"Well, not to say anything against your family, but—"

"Feel free. They won't hold back when it's their turn to weigh in."

"Shut up and let me finish," she snapped. "Those guys in my house. Some of them spoke Russian. I heard them."

"So you say. Couldn't vouch for it. I didn't hear them talk."

"Is not all of Brighton Beach and Sheepshead Bay a hotbed of expat Russian immigrants?"

"It is," he affirmed.

"So, aren't our chances of meeting people who might have an interest in ripping my head and limbs off statistically higher in Brighton Beach than it would be in, say, Peekskill, or Bridgeport?"

"They are," he admitted. "Theoretically."

"Then why in holy hell are we going there?" She was yelling again.

He thought of ten different replies to that in the space of a fraction of a second, but what actually came out surprised him.

Just the truth. Dull, flat, miserable. "My aunt's dying," he said.

She was startled into silence, but it couldn't last long. Sure enough, she coughed delicately. "I'm sorry. And your aunt is . . . ?"

"Tonya Arbatov. She's in a hospice. Ovarian cancer. End stage. Dying any time now. She might be dead already."

"Ah," she murmured. "You were close?"

Close? For a second, he thought he'd have to pull over and throw up. Close? She was only a fucking million miles away. Like that star they'd seen on the Jersey Shore, forever out of reach. The memory of those weeks with Tonya and Julie, in the shabby motel. Those card games, movies. Seagulls on the pebbly beach. Close, his ass. He wasn't close to anything on earth. He'd cut all ties. He was out there in fucking orbit. "Haven't seen her in twenty-one years," he said.

"Oh. And yet, you—"

"I'm going to the hospice. Now. I was heading there from the airport when I got your call. That was why I blew you off. She's dying. I didn't want to miss my chance to say good-bye."

"Oh, God, Aaro." She sounded pained. "You could have said something. If I'd known that, I wouldn't have—"

"Told me to fuck off? I didn't take it personally. Why should I tell you? It wasn't your problem."

"Would you stop being such a hard-ass?" she snapped.

"No," he said.

She made a frustrated sound. "So you're heading there now?"

"*We're* heading there," he told her. "You're stuck to me, until I hand you over to Bruno's bodyguard. Afterward, we'll listen to the file, call Bruno, meet up with the bodyguard, whatever you want. But now, now, we go to the hospice. Clear?"

"Crystal." She glanced at the car clock. "Can't imagine it'll still be visiting hours when we get there. It's late."

"They'll let me in," he said. "They have no choice. I'm armed."

She gave him the big-eye. "Aaro? You're making me nervous."

"How about we both just shut up, then?" he suggested.

But she just couldn't resist. "Will I meet the rest of your family?"

"Doubt it," he said.

"No? If she's dying, I imagine that—"

"They ignored and neglected her her whole life, when she wasn't locked in the nuthouse. They didn't give a shit about her before. They'll give even less now. She has no money to leave, no power or status to pass down. She'll be alone. Like she always was."

Nina looked down. "That's so sad," she whispered.

He snorted. Sad? Hah. That didn't come close to describing the sucking black hole that was the Arbatov clan's collective emotional vibe. God grant he could just slide in, say good-bye to Tonya without attracting any attention. Attention from Arbatovs tended to be toxic.

It wasn't a very hopeful thought. Hard as he tried to keep his head down, if there was a shitstorm to be caught in, his natural trajectory would always swing him through the middle of it.

He sped past the hospice, circled the block. Checking for Arbatovs and other unspecified dangers. It looked quiet.

Nina cleared her throat. "So. If you haven't seen her in so long, then why are you so—"

"Don't want to talk about it."

She flinched back, stung. He stopped, maneuvered into a parking space. "I'm not happy about that," he said stiffly. "That I haven't seen her in twenty-one years. And that now she's dying. That bums me out."

She nodded. He took that to mean she accepted his half-assed, oblique apology. Which was the only kind he could manage.

"Come on," he said. "Let's do this."

10

It didn't take a degree in psychology, or even a seminar in people management, to see that Aaro was going to have problems getting in to see his aunt. Nina watched him antagonize the receptionist with his brusque tone, his sharp imperatives. He repeated the performance with the woman's supervisor. A few more minutes of that, and his fate was sealed. They weren't going to let him in. He kept making the situation worse. As it escalated, she was nervously aware of his firearms.

She didn't think for one second that Aaro would hurt those women, but they wouldn't know that, if he lost his temper.

"You don't understand," he repeated. "I *am* immediate family. I have a different surname, but I was like her son, for years! Just tell her Sasha is here. She'll tell you!"

The supervisor's head kept shaking, arms folded tight across her chest. "I'm sorry," she said. "Visiting hours were over hours ago, and her family has requested that access be limited to a preapproved list."

"I just bet they have," Aaro growled. "What about what Tonya wants? She'll want to see me. I guarantee it. Just . . . go . . . *ask her.*"

"She is *resting.* Please, go, sir. Or I will call the police."

"I need to see her now." Aaro's voice was getting louder. "She's dying! She could die tonight! You know that!"

"I'm sorry, but you're not on the list Mr. Arbatov gave us, and I—"

"Listen to me, lady." He leaned over the desk 'til the woman jerked back, eyes wide. "Do not try to tangle with me."

"Aaro!" Nina grabbed his arm.

He shot her a fulminating glance. "What?" he barked.

"Shhh. Calm down," she whispered. "This isn't helping."

"But she . . . is . . . *dying!*" The words punched out of him. "I am not going to let a fucking list keep me from seeing my—"

"Shhhh." She tightened her fingers around his arm, which was very thick and solid and sinewy. She dug her nails in, hard, and pulled.

He finally let her drag him away from the scowling hospice personnel. "Outside," she murmured. "Where we can talk."

She nudged him to go out first, and slid a folded square of paper into the door to block the lock as she exited.

It was chilly. Nina shivered in her thin rayon layers.

"So?" he rapped out. "What are we doing out here, wasting time? Those cast-iron bitches aren't—"

"Shhh," she soothed again. She patted his shoulders, awkwardly. "You're going about this all wrong."

"Wrong how? I want to see her! I explain the situation, I ask permission, and those hags both stonewall me! She could be dead tomorrow! I am going in, whether they like it or—"

"Be quiet!" She dug her fingernails into his arm again. "You do not want those women to call security. Or the police. Do you?"

"Of course not," he muttered. "But I can't—"

"Shut up and listen, you stubborn lout," she whispered. "Stop banging your head against the wall! There are better uses for it!"

He looked away, mouth tight, then pulled his smartphone out of his pocket, and tapped at the touch screen. She peered over to see.

It was a building diagram. She stifled a hoot of laughter. How classically Aaro, to come to his aunt's deathbed armed with a blueprint of the building, as if going on a black-ops mission. He angled it so she could see, and pointed. "Second floor. Room twenty-four twenty-five, unless they've moved her since this morning. End of the second corridor, on the right."

"You've done your homework," she said.

"I'd be an asshole if I didn't." He caught her gaze, narrowed his eyes, defensive. "Go on," he said. "Say it."

"Say what?"

"That I'm an asshole anyway. I saw it in your face."

"If you want the title so badly, just take it," she said coolly. "Don't ask me to participate in your weird little mind games."

He dismissed the interchange with an impatient flick of his hand. "There's an entrance on the other side," he said, pointing. "Another emergency exit, here. This one, I'm less likely to meet anyone coming out. Maybe I can pick the lock. Or I could shoot it out, like yours."

"Shoot . . . ? Good God! Are you nuts?"

"Not at all," he said. "It's not like I need a long-term entry strategy. A breaching round would make a lot of noise. But I could—"

"Don't be ridiculous! You don't have to go to such obscene lengths. I'll open the door for you. From the inside."

His brows knit. There was a baffled silence. "What the fuck?" he said. "How do you propose to get in there? We just tried that."

She shook her head. "No. *You* just tried that."

"If they said no to me, they'll say no to you."

"No, they won't," she said. "Because they won't see me."

He just stared at her. "How do you figure? You'll have to buzz to get in. You think they won't notice?"

She jerked her chin toward the door. "The door is still open," she said. "I stuck a piece of paper in the lock just now."

Aaro started to turn his head to look. She cupped his hot face, jerking him sharply back around. His beard stubble scraped against her palm. "Do not draw their attention to it, idiot! Or you'll wreck it."

His eyes went narrow. "You're weirding me out, Nina."

"You should be used to it by now," she said. "This not-being-seen thing, it's a sort of talent I have. Or you could call it a dysfunction, depending on your point of view, and what you want to accomplish. But if I don't want to be noticed, they won't notice me."

He gazed at her for so long, so intently, she started to fidget.

"You can make yourself invisible?" he said.

His incredulous tone stung her. "Don't be absurd. Of course not. I just slide by, without making an impression. It's handy, sometimes. And sometimes it's a big pain in the ass. Like, when I'm waiting in line at the coffee shop. On a bad day, I practically have to set off flares to get a goddamn latte and a scone. That's the downside. Remember what happened with the taxis? Classic. It's not so great for getting asked out on a date, either. But . . . well, whatever."

"I see," he said. "Came in handy, with the dickhead step-father, too, huh? So this is why he messed with you, but not too much? Because you learned how to be invisible? Even to him?"

She flinched, uncomfortable. "I never claimed to be invisible," she said crabbily. "I said unnoticeable. People see me, for God's sake. They just don't notice me. Or remember me."

"Of course not, with that bag over your head," he said.

She flapped her hand at him. "Never mind, OK?" she said tightly. "Forget I said anything. If you don't want my help—"

"I never said that." His big hands fastened firmly over her elbows. They sent sweet shudders of warm awareness shooting up into her chest, speeding her heart. "I just don't want to let you out of my sight."

She had to force herself to remember. Nothing personal. He'd said so. Repeatedly. He owed Bruno that favor, and he was paying up. *So don't get gooey.* "There's hardly anyone inside," she told him. "Patients, night staff. Nobody who's gunning for me in there. I'll be fine."

Aaro was shaking his head. "Won't work. They saw me with you."

"Wrong," she said. "They saw you, Aaro. Believe me, they will remember only you. You are super-memorable. You used up all their RAM. Just let me try, OK? The worst that can happen is that they stop me, scold me, and send me out with a flea in my ear. Big deal."

"I don't like it," he repeated.

It came to her as she gazed at his face. A flash, as if a curtain had been twitched aside. She saw inside him. Or rather, *felt* inside him.

And an ache of longing twisted her throat, like a screw turning to unbearable tightness. How lost he felt, how sad.

The shadows, the chill. How violently he hated needing or asking for help from anyone.

It made her eyes fog up. She clenched her body, made her voice businesslike. "So? Go to the entrance. Wait for me to open the door."

"If you're not there in five, I'm coming back for you," he warned.

"You have to be patient. I have to wait for my moment."

He scowled. "Either you can do this, or you can't."

"No," she said stubbornly. "You have to wait for the right moment. You have to be patient. Do you understand the concept? At all?"

"No," he said grimly. "I am not patient."

"Tough. Give me more than five. You want to see your aunt?"

He let out a sound, half groan, half growl. "Ten. No more."

She made a shooing gesture. "It's impossible to disappear with you throwing off that frequency. You're, like, Times Square. Go, go."

Aaro turned, and disappeared into the shadows.

Nina let out a breath that felt like it had been sealed in her lungs since the moment she'd first seen him. The darkness pressed on her now that Aaro was gone. *Get it together, girl.* This was her chance to be of use to this guy, and in some small way make up for his much bigger favor of saving her life. She did not want to screw it up.

She maneuvered herself into the shadows of the bushes, into a position that allowed her to observe the receptionist without being seen. She waited, settling her mind and nerves. *Not here. Not here. Just air.*

The receptionist got up, leaned on the door frame, chatting with whoever was inside. *Not here. Not important. Just air. No big deal.* She sauntered to the door, shoved, caught the square of folded paper as it opened. She drifted along while the woman talked, passed the desk, cleared it, and was out of the receptionist's current line of sight.

Elevator, or stairs? She opted for the elevator, pushed the call button. Waited. *Nobody here. Nothing but air. No big deal.*

The elevator opened. There was a janitor inside, with a garbage cart that blocked half the elevator cabin. A black man in his fifties. He had the blank, indifferent look of a person at the end of a long shift. Sore feet, sore back, no energy to be curious. Nina stepped in, and the guy put his hand over the numbered buttons, in automatic politeness.

"Where to?" he asked dully.

"Second floor, please," she murmured. He pushed the button.

They stared side by side into nothing as the cabin hummed up. The door opened. She nodded as she exited, but his eyes were closed.

She walked down the corridor, *nobody here, no big deal,* following the route Aaro had indicated. Around the corner. There were personnel in the medical station, but they didn't see her walk by. At one point, a nurse came out of a room, and headed purposefully down the hall, walking past Nina without turning her head. She'd gotten here at the end of a shift. That was lucky. Everyone tired, thinking about dinner and some mindless TV. She paused outside the room. It felt rude to shove open a door without knocking, but drawing attention to herself by making a sound was crazy. She turned the knob, and pushed.

It was a normal-looking bedroom, with a dim, mellow-golden bedside lamp. Not a sterile white hospital room, except for the bed, which was an automated hospital bed with rails and an IV rack.

A wasted form lay in it, eyes closed. Nina stopped at the door. The woman had high, jutting cheekbones like Aaro's, an oxygen tube taped beneath them. Her skin was yellow, her eyes were closed, sunk deep in shadowy eye sockets. Her head turned, and her eyes opened.

The impact of her gaze made Nina gasp as if she'd been splashed by ice water. She went from feeling invisible to feeling intensely visible.

She tried to speak, but she was immobilized by the dying woman's intense, haunting gaze. Pressure built, as if she were holding her breath. She was about to panic when the tension abruptly eased.

The woman tried to speak, but her hoarse rasp did not carry.

"Excuse me?" Nina said, feeling inane and helpless.

The woman twitched her fingers. It was hardly visible, and yet it was an unmistakable "Come here."

Nina couldn't disobey. Charisma and a compelling personality must be genetic traits that ran strong in Aaro's family.

Close to the bed, Nina saw every detail of Tonya Arbatov's skull pressing against the yellowed parchment of her skin. Her thin fingers twitched imperiously. Nina could come no closer, so she did the only thing she could think of. She took the woman's hand.

Tonya's fingers were cold, but the crackle of awareness was anything but. It thrilled through Nina's nerves, too sparkling to be fear, too nervous and unsettled to be joy. Vividly, intensely aware.

The dying woman began to speak. Nina bent low, putting her ear closer to the woman's mouth. "I'm so sorry," she murmured. "Again?"

Tonya sucked in air, and let it out in a long, slow wheeze, forming words as she did so. "You bring my Sasha?"

Nina stared down at her, that thrill of emotion jangling through her again. The woman's eyes shimmered with happy tears.

"How did you know . . ." The question trailed off. It was stupid and irrelevant, under the circumstances, and Tonya didn't have the strength to answer anyhow. Twenty-one years, no warning, no word, and somehow, she just knew that her beloved nephew was out there.

Tears rushed into Nina's eyes. She had to make this happen, before Aaro panicked outside and spoiled everything. "I'll get him for you," she whispered. "I have to hurry. We're not supposed to be here."

Tonya Arbatov made a wheezy creaking noise that sounded like distress. Then Nina realized that it was laughter.

"Go, go," she mouthed, her voice inaudible. "Get my Sasha."

Nina shoved open the door, bolted to the end of the corridor. She was so rattled, she didn't establish the drone of *nobody here, no big deal* in her mind. God forbid anyone see her now. She was so excited.

She slid the square of folded brochure into the stairwell door and ran down the stairs. Aaro glowered through the small glass window. She ran at it full tilt, shoved it open. Aaro burst inside, grabbing her arm.

"What the fuck took you so long? It's been sixteen minutes!"

No time for scolding, not with his aunt waiting, tears of joy in her eyes. "Shut up!" She towed him toward the stairs. "Come quick!"

"You found her?"

"Yes. She knew you were coming. She's waiting for you. Hurry!"

But he dragged his feet, slowing at the foot of the stairs. "How, ah . . . how is she?"

It stabbed into her again, that sudden glimpse into his armored head. He was so afraid of what he was about to see. And she could not help him with that. Not one little bit.

"She's dying," she said. "She's emaciated, jaundiced, bald. But she's lucid, and she's alone. Now is your chance. Come *on!*"

They hurried up the stairs. The corridor was still deserted. Aaro hesitated again outside the door, but Nina shoved him in. They damn well were not going to all this trouble to get kicked out by a night nurse.

Aaro stared at the woman on the bed. His aunt's eyes streamed with tears. Such a blaze of love shone out of her skeletal face, it could only be described as beautiful.

Nina waited at the door, to give them some privacy. Aaro bent over his aunt, spoke to her for a minute, and turned, beckoning her. "She wants you, too."

Tonya was waggling her fingers as she approached, a clear invitation, so Nina took the woman's cold hand once again.

Tonya's eyes cut from her to Aaro, and back again. The tender gleam in her eyes started to sink in, and with it, a terrible realization.

Oh, God. The woman thought that she and Aaro were a couple.

She was appalled. Of course Tonya would think that. It was a natural assumption. Like a guy would dream of bringing a woman to his aunt's deathbed if she wasn't his fiancée, or at least a serious girlfriend. Any guy at all. Let alone a guy like Aaro.

Oh, this was bad. The dying aunt, all misty-eyed and contented to see her darling boy finally settled before she died. But a deception of this magnitude felt immoral, whether it was intentional or not. She shrank away, but Tonya's fingers tightened around hers.

"This one, she is perfect. Pretty, too, eh? But she doesn't know. She needs you to show her how pretty she is. Perfect for you, Sasha."

Aaro grunted. "Pretty, yes. Hardly perfect. You should hear her scold me."

Tonya's chest jerked, creaking laughter. "Good, good," she wheezed. "You are terrible. From minute you were born. Of course she scolds. She is smart to scold you. You would crush a weak woman beneath your boot." She looked up at Nina, her eyes sparkling. "Yes, scold him, scold him," she urged. "He is bad boy. Needs strong hand."

Nina opened her mouth to explain that she was just a . . . well, hell. Her imagination failed her. A friend? Could she be defined as Aaro's friend? His protectee, rather. Did having a violent adventure in common make people friends? God forbid she made any more friends like that. She wouldn't survive the bonding experience again.

Aaro was speaking again, but she didn't catch his words, just Tonya's response. "Yes, and she has gift, too. Like you, Sasha."

Aaro shook his head. "No, Aunt, you've always been wrong about that. I don't have the gift. Not like you."

"Oh, yes, you have gift. You just never let it out of cage. I understand. You are smart. You didn't want to end up like me."

Aaro looked tormented. "Aunt, I didn't want—"

"Shhhh." She patted his hand. "One day you will open cage. And she . . ." She flapped her fingers at Nina. "She has it, too. Like you, but different. Just different enough to complete you. Very good girl." She patted Nina's hand, smiled up into Aaro's eyes. "I am so happy."

Aaro sank down to his knees next to the bed. He hid his face against the bedclothes. Tonya stroked his tangled hair. The protests, the explanations, the *Oh, no, we're really just friends* that Nina had been trying to phrase dissolved. Tears welled up, spilled over. Aw, hell. She couldn't disappoint Tonya now. She'd been set up, boxed in, and there was nothing she could do to fix it. She and Aaro were going to have words. But not now. Not while just looking at him made her cry.

Tonya's eyes were fluttering. The brief but intense conversation had exhausted her. "You come back tomorrow?" she rasped.

He lifted his head. "If they let me in. They don't like me much."

Her lips twitched. "I will tell them I want my Sasha. Maybe they will listen. But your clever lady will get you in. Her gift is strong. Strong with strong. Makes both of you stronger. Very good. Son of my heart."

"I'm sorry, Aunt." She could barely hear his gruff, choked voice. "That I was gone so long. That I didn't visit you."

"No, no." She shook her head, smiling. "No, Sasha. The one thing that gave me peace was to think that you were free, somewhere. Like we dreamed of, remember, Sasha? That star we saw?"

His head jerked, affirmatively. "I remember."

"I see it now, Sasha. I will be that star now. You go out, look in the sky, say hello to me, ey?" She put her hand on his cheek. "I did not want you to come, risk you getting snarled in Oleg's web. But now . . ." Her gaze flicked to Nina. A smile creased her face. "With her, you are strong enough to face even Oleg." She petted his hair. "I am so happy."

Her eyes fluttered shut. Her hand went limp.

After a few moments of listening to her labored breathing, Nina realized two things. Tonya was fast asleep, and Aaro was not going to move one inch on his own initiative. His shoulders shook.

"Aaro," she said. No reaction. Not even a twitch.

It was up to her. She grabbed his arm, pulled until he was on his feet, stumbling as if half asleep. Nina peered into the hall and hustled him out, her arm around his waist. She got him down the stairs, and onto the street. Aaro showed no signs of resuming his usual executive control of the universe, so she linked her arm through his, and towed him in the direction that she vaguely remembered him parking the car.

"I shouldn't have left her there alone," he said starkly.

"How old were you when you left home?" she asked.

His brow furrowed, as if the question were too difficult to process. "Sixteen," he said finally. "Almost seventeen."

"For God's sake," she muttered. "Sixteen is a child. You should not have been responsible for yourself at that age. Let alone for an adult."

"I should have come back for her," he repeated.

Nina stared around the deserted street. There was a bench on the sidewalk, a bus stop. She steered him there, poised him over it, and shoved until he thudded down. He stared at the passing cars, blankly.

She hated to see him like that. It was like a fist, squeezing her heart. She wanted to pick him up, cuddle him as if he were a small child. As if. But the impulse was too strong to resist, so she did the next best thing. She sat on his lap. Wrapped her arms around his neck.

His arms clamped around her. His arms were very strong, and they held her very tightly. It gave her a dizzy thrill, which she squelched, sternly. This was about comfort. He'd comforted her, in his own rough way. Now it was her turn to comfort him.

He vibrated, as if a tremendous voltage was running through his body. He pressed his hot face to her shoulder, and hung on.

They must have been there for twenty minutes, but time warped and stretched, bloomed into something new and strange. She felt him, so intensely. His body and hers, every point of contact thrumming. The throb of his heart reverberated through her body. The pulse of his breath against her collarbone. Every ticklish swish of the breeze moving her skirt against her legs. Her bottom, perched on those hard, powerful thighs. The warm, earthy smell of his hair filled her nose.

A car drove by, stereo bass thumping loudly. A guy hung out of the window, and howled, "Get a room, asshole!"

Aaro lifted his head, without meeting her eyes. "Good idea," he said gruffly. "You need rest. And we need to listen to that recording."

They stared at each other. He looked nervous. And flushed.

She realized that she was petting him. Stroking his hair. Her hand was actually sliding down to touch the jut of his high cheekbone.

She jerked back, horrified at herself, and scrambled off his lap, smoothing down her skirt. She was sending crazy mixed messages to this guy, and that was totally unfair. And dangerous.

"Uh . . . sorry," he muttered.

"I don't need your goddamned apologies," she snapped.

His mouth twitched. "Uh, yeah. Thanks for getting me into the—"

"I don't want your thanks," she said coolly. "I owed you a favor. Don't take it personally, OK? It's not about you. It's just payback."

He blinked, and a quick, appreciative grin flashed over his face. "Ah. OK. I see. Tough bitch."

"I'm learning," she said. "I'm learning fast."

"My aunt said you were strong," he said.

"I know. I was there. Right next to you. In case you didn't notice."

An odd look flashed over his face. "Huh? Come again?"

"I heard what your aunt said," she snapped. "That you'd squish me like a grape if I weren't strong. And I don't appreciate being called a scold. It's unfair, considering the day we've just had. And what on earth possessed you to let her think that we were a couple?"

His jaw sagged. "But I . . . but we . . . but I didn't say—"

"You said nothing to make her think otherwise." She hadn't intended to lecture him right off the bat, but she hadn't expected to embarrass herself by petting him, either, so what the hell. "It was inappropriate, to deceive her like that. No matter the circumstances."

"Nina," he said slowly. "Explain something to me."

"I'm not the one who should be explaining myself. What was all that stuff about gifts?" Freed from the spell of their timeless embrace, she had to cover her discomfort with brittle chatter.

"Nina, do you speak Ukrainian?"

"Of course not," she snapped. "Would I have been calling you to translate for me if I did? What are you talking about?"

He seized her shoulders, gave them a hard squeeze. "Aunt Tonya was speaking Ukrainian, Nina," he said. "The whole time."

She stared at him. "No, that's not even remotely possible," she said. "I don't speak a word of Ukrainian, or Russian, and I understood every word your aunt said. I get by in Spanish, and I studied some French in college, but Slavic languages are a complete blank to me. She was speaking English, Aaro, and you just didn't notice."

Aaro was shaking his head. "Tonya never learned English very well. She didn't want to come to this country in the first place. She was in love with someone back in the old country. My father forced her to come. Not speaking English was one of the things that kept her so trapped. She wasn't speaking it tonight. I remember what she said, and how she said it. It wasn't English. And I wasn't speaking it, either."

"But I . . . but she . . ." Her voice trailed off. "How could I . . ."

"The mind-reading thing, maybe?" he said.

She shook her head. "It didn't feel like that," she faltered. "I . . . it was the words. I heard them. With my ears. I swear, I did."

They stared at each other. Aaro wrapped his arm around her shoulder, sweeping her into a trot. "Fuck it," he said. "It's one more weird thing, in a long list of weird things, and it's not even the weirdest of the lot. We'll process this later. Forget about it."

That would be a neat trick. But Nina put her arm around his waist and let herself be borne along anyway.

The weight of his arm around her shoulders felt very, very good.

11

Fay Siebring picked up the telephone, and put it down again. *Get it over with.* When Tonya Arbatov had been admitted to the hospice, Oleg Arbatov had requested a meeting with her. Oleg was a tall, thick-bodied man, once powerfully handsome, now riddled with disease. A cancer survivor, she'd heard, but it had not affected the force of his personality one bit. His face was pitted, yellowish, his eyes sunken, but deep in their pits, they burned with an unabated fire. His voice was a rasping growl that made her flesh crawl. His charisma was enormous.

Oleg had explained, in correct but heavily accented English, that Tonya Arbatov was to have absolutely no visitors except for the immediate family, and if anyone else requested to see her, that person was to be denied entrance, and Oleg was to be immediately notified. Not that such a thing was likely, he assured her, but Tonya had suffered from mental illness for most of her life, and was very fragile. He wanted to ensure that her final days were tranquil and secure.

Fay had explained that though his care for his sister was noted, their patient-based care policy dictated that Tonya's personal wishes regarding visitors would be considered above any other—

"That is your son? And your daughter?" he'd interrupted, pointing at the picture on her desk of Cass and Wills. His long, misshapen yellow fingernail looked like a devil's horn. Fay was startled by the impulse to knock the picture face-down to stop him from looking at it. "Ah. Er . . ."

"Cassandra," he murmured. "Pretty. And William. Fine-looking young man. So tall. Basketball, no? I see why."

She froze. Their names. How in God's name had he known . . . ?

"I heard that Cassandra has applied for the Seaver scholarship. Should help paying for Northeastern. Congratulations on her getting in, by the way. Great accomplishment. Good school. Expensive, though, hmm? For a single mother, working in health care administration."

"How do you know . . ." Her voice trailed off.

Oleg smiled. His teeth looked sharp. "I can make sure Cassandra gets the Seaver. A word, with people I know, and the thing is done."

Fay's vertebrae stacked up in a burst of maternal pride. "I appreciate the thought, but Cassandra is by far the best candidate, and I don't think she needs any help at all to—"

"Oh, Ms. Siebring. No. We all need help. You, William, Cassandra. Me, too. It would be a shame, if the scholarship board learned of that unpleasant business . . . the shoplifting incident? That Target store?"

Her mouth sagged. "I don't know what you're talking about."

"Sixty-five dollars worth of stolen makeup." He shook his head. "And your William, too. I hear he likes high stakes poker, and him only twenty-four." He clucked his tongue. "No job yet, I hear. I heard you're refinancing your house to try and cover his debts. That's how our economy got in trouble in the first place, you know."

"But I . . . but he—"

"It would be an honor to help," he said. "So sad, if a promising young man's future was compromised because of a youthful mistake." He smiled, his sunken eyes twinkling. "I will buy his debt. Thirty thousand, wasn't it? It is nothing to me, Ms. Siebring."

Fay could not even speak. Arbatov patted her hand. His hand was heavy. Cold. *Iron hand in a velvet glove.* The phrase popped into her mind, but Oleg wore no glove. It was just a cold, naked, iron hand.

"All I ask is a little help, Ms. Siebring," he said. "A little cooperation. Can I call you Fay? I feel as if I know you."

"Ah . . . of course." Her throat was dry. "Ah, thank you. But that won't be necessary. About Cass, and Wills, I mean. Ah." She could have kicked herself, for revealing their nicknames.

He smiled, pleased. "Wills, and Cass. Charming. Well, Fay. You know who to call." He pulled out a checkbook, and a heavy golden pen.

"Oh, no. I cannot accept that. If you give it to me, I will rip it up."

He glanced up, bushy eyebrows steepled into a wounded frown. "Don't hurt my feelings, Fay."

When she did not reach out to take the check, he laid it on her desk. It was for fifteen thousand dollars. "Cash it," he urged. "A graduation gift. A token of my esteem. Clothes, books, sorority fees. Heaven knows we wouldn't want her forced to shoplift again." He chuckled at his own wit. "She'll be able to use it even if she does get the scholarship. Because, of course . . ." He winked. "She will get it."

Fay clutched the edge of her desk. Oleg laid a card next to the check. "My cell," he said. "If anyone but the people on my list attempts to visit Tonya, contact me. Do we understand each other?"

Fay nodded mutely.

Oleg rose heavily to his feet. "Good, then. Good luck, for your beautiful children. And good health."

The whole episode played through Fay's mind as she stared at the phone. She hadn't heard from Oleg since. No one had come to see Tonya. She'd begun to hope that the situation would pass without incident, that the woman would just die. And if she just didn't cash the check . . . it was like it hadn't happened. A horrific story to tell friends at a dinner party, years from now. But she'd been lingering every day until midnight, in terror of missing a possible visitor. Or worse, of letting anyone else on the staff know how shit scared she was.

Do we understand each other?

Oh, yes, sir, Mr. Arbatov, sir. Don't hurt my babies.

She dialed the number, her belly spasming.

"Yes?" That grating rasp again. She heard it in her dreams.

"Mr. Arbatov. It's, ah, Fay Siebring, from the hospice."

He grunted impatiently. "Well?"

No question about his sister, who was one of the most solitary patients their staff had ever seen. "Your sister, ah . . . she had a visitor."

"Who?" His voice sharpened.

"A man, in his late thirties," she blurted. "Very tall, big, dark-haired. He said he was her nephew. That his name was Sasha."

"I thought I told you to let no one see her!"

"I didn't let him in, of course! I told him there was a short list, and that he was not on it, just as you said! And he left!"

"Go to Tonya's room," Arbatov barked. "Do not let him see you."

"Mr. Arbatov, he's not here! I told him to go, and he—"

"Shut up. If Sasha wanted in, he is in. How long ago?"

"Ah . . . er . . . maybe about a half an hour ago?"

"Half an hour? Why did you wait so long to call? You idiot!"

She floundered. "I, ah . . . I had business to attend to, and I—"

"Take your cell phone. See if he is there! If so, hide in an adjoining room until he leaves. Then follow him. Do not let yourself be seen! Call me when you know where he is. Understand?"

"Ah . . . ah . . ."

"Move, bitch!"

She leaped to her feet, knocking files off her desk, and bolted, racing past Jolene's desk without responding to the receptionist's questioning tone. She sprinted down the hall to the elevator.

Do not let him see you. And how was she to accomplish that? She peered out of the elevator. Hurried, panting, down the hall. Outside Tonya Arbatov's room, she clutched the doorknob with a sweaty hand, turned the knob, and held her ear to the crack. Voices. One was deep, male. Her heart banged against her rib cage. Tonya's voice was too soft to make out, but the man responded, loud enough to hear that he was speaking Russian. She pressed the door shut, and slid into the next room. Fortunately, the occupant was deeply sedated. She punched the "redial."

"Yes?" Oleg barked.

"He's in there now," she whispered.

Oleg gave a noncommittal grunt. "Good. Wait."

So she did. Seconds dragged by. She twitched, fidgeted. Oleg had no problem with the silence. He sat like a spider, waiting for the bug to hit the web. Her eyes fastened on the IV drip of the sleeping patient in the dim room. Her ears strained for the sound of the adjoining door.

At last, the click of the door closing. "He's leaving," she whispered.

"Eh? Well, then! What are you waiting for? Follow him! Fool!"

She peeked out the door. Sasha was accompanied by a woman. From behind, she gave the impression of being from another time, costumed. Amish, maybe, with her dull, full-skirted dress, her long, severe braid. Her arm was around Sasha's waist. She seemed to be steering him down the corridor. Fay did not remember her from the conversation with Sasha. Or did she? Fresh fear jarred her.

Don't let him see you. As if it were so easy for her to lurk and skulk. She was in her fifties, forty pounds overweight, arthritis in both hips, high heels that she cursed herself for wearing.

She waited until the stairwell door slammed shut, and clattered to the end of the corridor to peek through it. Another tense wait while the woman had shepherded Sasha safely out the exit to the street, and she scrambled after them. She ran out, panicking when she saw no one, running into the street, spinning until she—yes, oh, God, thank you. There they were. Halfway down the block.

The woman pushed him onto a bus stop bench, and sat on his lap, hugging him. Fay eased herself into the shadow of a locked newsstand. She was almost certain the woman had not been there when Sasha made his blustering entrance. She whispered into the cell. "They're sitting at a bus stop on Mercer, near the corner of Sprague."

"They? He is not alone?"

"He's with a woman," she whispered. "A young woman."

"Ah. A woman. Hmmph. A bus, you say?" Oleg's voice was heavy with disbelief. "My Sasha is waiting for a *bus?*"

"Ah . . . I think they are just, um, talking," she said inanely. "She's sitting on his lap. What do you want me to do?"

"Wait," he said. "Watch them. My people are on their way. You watch until they arrive."

A cramp clutched her belly. "What are they going to do to them?"

"It is not your business. Shut up, ey? Sasha's ears are sharp. I am hanging up now. Call me if they move."

She did as she was told, dreading what might happen when Oleg's people arrived. She just hoped they wouldn't hurt Sasha and the young woman. Or if they did, that she wouldn't have to watch it.

But before anyone could arrive, the couple got up and took off again. This time, Sasha no longer stumbled. He slid his arm around the woman's waist and swept her along so she had to scurry to keep up. Fay scurried, too. They got into a car. Lights flicked on, illuminating the license plate. She held up her phone, clicking for the camera app, but the car was pulling away, and she wasn't quick enough.

She just stared at the plate, repeating the number to fix it in her mind. She tried to catch the make, the model, but all she could see from this distance was that it was a black Toyota of some sort.

It pulled away, taillights receding. She doubled over, hands pressed to her knees. Her pants had turned into sobs, but she had to make this call before she forgot that plate number, before he decided to punish Cass and Wills because she was such a goddamn, stupid cow.

She pushed "redial." The line clicked open. "And?"

"It was a black Toyota," she blurted, and recited the license plate number to him before he could reply. "It's heading west, on Reading."

"Are you in a car following them?"

As if. She almost laughed, but that could get her children killed. "No," she croaked. "I'm on foot. I can't see them anymore."

"Fucking amateurs," he grumbled. "Twenty years, and my Sasha is driving a fucking Toyota? What a joke. Are you sure it was a Toyota?"

She gabbled for a moment, at a loss. "Ah, um, er, yes, I think . . . I . . . I think it was a black Toyota four-door, I'm almost sure I saw—"

"Never mind. Shut up, Fay. Go home." His voice was benevolent now. "I will let you know when you are needed again."

Her legs wouldn't hold her. She sank down, shaking, like a junkie having d.t.'s. People avoided looking at her, just as she herself avoided looking at people reduced to trembling on the sidewalk. She thought of Tonya Arbatov, hooked to her morphine drip. A turn of the dial would up her dose, until her organs shut down. And it would all go away.

Fay held strong opinions about physician-assisted suicide and euthanasia. She was a crusader for pain control and quality end-of-life care. Now look at her, tempted to abandon her cherished ideals. Tempted to go to Tonya Arbatov's room, and end it. Oleg would have no more reason to remember her existence. Or Cass's, or Wills's.

Except that then, instead of just being a mafia stooge, she'd be a murderer, too. And if Oleg ever found out what she had done . . .

The very thought made her queasy and faint.

"Why did you disobey me, Dmitri?"

Oleg's voice seemed gentle, but every cell of Dmitri's body knew better. It literally *hurt,* to stand in front of Oleg and withstand his disapproval.

"I gave you orders to watch the hospice. Did you not take me seriously? Did you think, ah, foolish old Uncle Oleg, he is just a stupid old man, ey? He will never notice. Did you think that of me?"

No. Dmitri could not make the word loud enough to be heard.

"No, nephew? Then this stupid, tired old man is even

more confused." Oleg's eyes glittered in his sunken eye
sockets. Dmitri could not look him in the eye. He'd topped
up, and he regretted it. When he used, there was no protective barrier of incomprehension between him and Oleg's de-
rision. He felt it all. . . . *junkie scum is stoned . . . a blessing
that my poor brother is dead . . . cannot see what a worthless
turd his son has become.* . . . It made his eyes sting, his nose
run, his nerves twitch.

"You were not at the hospice when he came. I had to use
that cow Fay Siebring to trail him, which she succeeded in
doing for exactly two hundred fucking meters. Where were
you, Dmitri? Drinking, gambling? Shooting up one of your
drugs, fucking one of your whores?"

"No," he said.

"Then what, Dmitri? Tell me."

Oleg was not a telepath, but he had power. Certainly the
power to make Dmitri feel lower than a cockroach.

"Tell me, nephew!" Oleg's command reverberated through
him.

He had no choice but to tell the truth. "I was, uh, on another job."

Oleg's thick eyebrows twitched up. "Ah! You should have
told me, nephew, that you no longer work for me, just as a
professional courtesy. So, then. A new boss? Tell me about
him. He must pay well. This Versace suit, those Ferragamo
shoes; is this new boss a billionaire? This new job is more
important than the task of waiting for your cousin?"

The impulse to babble was overwhelming. "Not a boss,"
he blurted. "A business partnership that I'm, er, exploring.
An incredible opportunity. A man I know is producing a
unique designer drug—"

"A drug," Oleg repeated heavily. "Ah, yes. They are all so
unique."

"He, ah, had an urgent problem today, and needed some
support with personnel, so he, ah, called me."

"Ah, yes. Ivan and Mikhail were your personnel support, no? Both dead, I hear. A detective came to talk to Yevgeni and Stefan. Their bodies were in the house of, what was the woman's name? Nina Christie? He is very interested in talking to you. But of course . . ." Oleg made an expansive gesture. "We have no idea where to find you. You are as elusive as the wind, nephew."

"Thank you, Uncle. I—"

"Fuck your thanks." Oleg's voice crashed down. "You are using this drug, no? You dare come to me stoned, and think I will not see?"

"I—I—"

"Are you addicted?" Oleg thundered. "Tell me the truth!"

"It's not like that! It's a different kind of—"

"I see. You are not working for me, or this other man, either. You are his bitch, Dmitri. You are just a drug whore now."

Dmitri kept shaking his head. "No. If I got a steady supply of this, it would make you more money than you could even imagine."

Oleg snorted. "I can count somewhat higher than you, nephew. Drugs are money, Dmitri, nothing more. But you know what kills the money? Using them. Use them, and you have unfastened your pants and bent over. But I should not talk to a junkie. They cannot hear."

. . . piece of shit . . . cannot be my heir . . .

"This drug is different," Dmitri insisted. "It lets me read minds."

Oleg began to laugh. "Why on earth would you want to do that? People's minds are full of garbage! What is the profit in reading them? I would pay to be spared such a thing!"

"It's not always telepathy!" he protested. "Different abilities manifest for everyone who takes it! Telepathy happened to be mine. It augments whatever natural latent ability that—"

"Shut up. A drug is a drug, and I have never seen any natural ability in you, latent or otherwise." He reached down, finding the spot on his nephew's thigh where the bullet had grazed him beneath the suit pants. His uncle's big fingers clamped.

"Uncle, I'm sorry," he began. "I . . . oh, *fuck* . . ."

Oleg squeezed, until blood soaked through the dressing, his pant leg. The room swayed. A sound came out of him, thin and anguished.

Oleg let go. Dmitri fell to his knees. Oleg examined the stamp of blood on his hand and wiped his hand on the front of Dmitri's dove-gray shirt. "The pursuit of this drug is a dangerous activity?"

"You don't understand." Dmitri couldn't stop the bleating words, though he knew it was futile. "It's like . . . like a superpower, uncle."

idiot . . . fucking cockroach . . . got men killed for his dose . . .

To his horror, his uncle reached out again, plucked open the lapel of his suit jacket, and pulled Nina Christie's cell phone out of it. How the hell had the old man known?

"This phone is not your style, Dmitri. Over two years old."

Dmitri shook his head. "It's mine. I have many phones."

"Then you will not mind if I crush this one, under my foot?" Oleg dropped it on the ground, poised his heel over it.

"No!" Dmitri yelled.

"I see." Oleg picked it up, and tucked it into his coat. "Don't worry. I will keep it safe, and Yevgeni will ferret out all its secrets tonight, ey? Don't try to be a superman, Dmitri. Go out, and look for Sasha, like all the rest of my men. He drives a 2012 black Toyota. Memorize this plate number." His uncle passed him a small slip of paper.

Dmitri pocketed it, watching his death play out in several different ways in his uncle's head. . . . *strangulation, drown-*

ing, faked suicide, from a drug overdose, perhaps . . . believable . . . yes, past time . . .

"Reading minds," Oleg scoffed once again. "Show me how you read minds, nephew. Read mine right now. What am I thinking?"

Fresh blood trickled down his leg, hot and ticklish. "That I am scum," he said. "That you wish me dead. And Sasha here in my place."

"It does not take mind reading to guess that much. Get out of my sight. Be the first to find your cousin."

Or else drive into a lake and save me the trouble.

12

Enigmas made Aaro's teeth grind, which knocked him into standby default mood. Pissed off.

True, weird things had tended to happen around Aunt Tonya, which was why she'd spent so much of her adult life locked inside various institutions. She freaked people out. Made them feel the way he felt right now. Nervous, twitchy, tossed ass over head. Not good.

Like he and Nina hadn't already got a big enough dose of shock and awe that day. He'd only just gotten comfortable with the hypothesis that Nina was whacked out on some garden variety drug trip, that it would pass and be no more than an unnerving memory. But no.

He'd considered himself good with weird, but he couldn't make the ends match on this mess, no matter how he turned and twisted it. So what the fuck. He'd use his usual technique. Put a big, heavy iron lid on the subject, and bolt that fucker down.

"A question, please."

Nina's voice had that prim tone that set his teeth on edge.

He struggled to keep his voice even moderately civil. "Ask it."

"I asked you this before, but we got distracted by the, um, foreign language thing," she said. "I still think you're re-membering wrong, and that she was speaking in English, be-cause it's the only—"

"Drop it, and ask your damn question."

It took a few moments to get her pump primed again. "Why in God's name did you let your aunt think we were a couple?"

He spotted a chain hotel, and changed lanes to turn into it. "What does it matter? You've never seen her before. You'll never see her again. She'll be gone from this earth in days, and I'll be gone from your life. What do you care what she thinks?"

She shook her head. "It doesn't seem right, lying to some-one who's on her way out. If you're not going to be honest to a dying person, who will you be honest to, for God's sake?"

"Honesty's overrated," he muttered.

"You mean, overrated when it's inconvenient for you, right? You demanded honesty from me, remember? Every sore and every score?"

"That was different," he grumbled.

"You mean, honesty isn't important if you're not the one being deceived, right? Be consistent, Aaro!"

"You weren't dying," he pointed out.

"I came pretty damn close today, if you recall!"

"Yeah, I recall just fine." He jerked to a stop in the tem-porary parking in front of the lobby, and killed the engine. "It's been a hell of a day. I'm dead tired. Don't ask me to measure up to your goddamn high standards tonight, Nina. Just shut the fuck up."

She turned eloquently away. Silent reproach, the Nina Christie special. They just sat there, in silence. Laying on the guilt, with a trowel, while he thought of how she'd made it happen for him at the hospice. Getting him in to see Tonya with her magic sneakiness.

Hugging him afterward, during his meltdown. He still hadn't recovered from that. His dick was still tingling. More than half hard.

She'd been nice to him. Nicer than he deserved. His words echoed in his ears. Made him feel like dog shit.

Aw, fuck. He was not cut out for this, wanted no part of it. The impulse almost choked him. The declaration got past the roadblocks by brute force, hurting his throat as it came out. "Sorry," he snarled.

She glanced at him, tight-lipped. "For what?"

He shrugged. "For what I said."

"Hmmph," she grunted. She gave him an assessing look. "God, that must have cost you."

"Already regretting it," he said, through his teeth.

"Stop!" She held up her hand. "Hold it right there. Don't spoil it. Or your heroic efforts will have been in vain."

He didn't recognize the convulsive explosions bursting out of his nose and mouth for a moment. Then he realized it was laughter.

He tried to choke it off. It wouldn't stop. Then Nina started up with it, too, and he was fucked.

They snorted and giggled helplessly for about five minutes before the convulsions died down into a tense, charged silence once again.

But it was different now. The laughter had softened something inside him. He could almost, well . . . breathe. Sort of.

Nina seemed to be still waiting. For explanations, excuses.

He fidgeted, and took a stab at it. "Didn't seem like such a big deal, at the time," he said. "If it made her happy to think I was all set with a woman. And to be honest, since you like honesty so much, I was using a language that you don't speak. So I thought you'd never know."

"Ah." She chewed her lower lip, subdued. "I see."

It occurred to him, though he'd have cut out his tongue rather than admit it, that he'd kind of enjoyed the harmless fiction while it was happening, if enjoyment was a word that made sense in such a grim context. Bringing a girlfriend to meet his aunt. Showing her he'd found a woman who, amazingly, tolerated him. Who, miraculously, wanted to be with him. Letting Aunt Tonya enjoy the fond fiction that he had, well, hell. A future, of some sort. A life, to look forward to.

The discomfort that followed upon that thought was sharp to the point of pain. He flinched away from it.

"I need to go check in," he said brusquely. "It's better if I go alone. The less we're seen together, the better." He pulled the Micro Glock out and handed it to her. "Take this. No safety. Just point and shoot."

She waved it away. "No, thanks. I'm not comfortable with it."

Oh, for fuck's sake. He shoved the gun into his pocket again. "Lock the door," he snapped. "Do your invisible thing. Do it hard."

She nodded.

The check-in process was swift, fortunately, because he would have ground his teeth to nubs if he'd had to wait long in line with Nina alone in the parking lot. But in a few minutes they'd taken possession of a hotel room. He laid his duffel on the bed. Tossed his jacket.

Nina stood in the entry hall as if awaiting permission to take up space. Her face was pale, eyes huge. So tense, she felt compelled to cover those tits with the purse so he wouldn't see them bob and sway.

Too late. He'd seen it. He'd see it in his dreams. Forever.

I could fix that. Relax you like you've never been relaxed before.

Sit on it, horndog. He'd accepted "no." Resigned himself. Then she complicated things by sitting on his lap, pressing her ass against his erection. Petting him until he practically hyperventilated.

But she'd said no. It would be lower than dirt to pressure her now. But oh, man, it was hard. Rock hard. He tore his gaze away, and it landed on a pile of local restaurant menus, which reminded him that there was more to his body than an engorged cock. He hadn't eaten since early West Coast morning, and little enough then. Food might steady them. He rifled through menus, grabbed the phone. "Pizza OK?"

She looked affronted. "How can you think about food now?"

"You intend to fast until things are back to normal?"

She shook her head, resolute. "Nothing for me, thanks."

He called the pizza place, ordered a large cheese pie delivered to the room, in case she changed her mind. He longed for a cold beer to wash it down, but he had no business touching anything that could lower his inhibitions. Damn. He knew he could make her like it. He'd turned her on in the taxi. He'd seen it in her eyes, felt it crackle in the air. She'd been interested, intrigued. Freaked out and confused, sure, but curious as hell. White-hot for him. Trying to keep it hidden.

Whenever he closed his eyes, he saw it. Himself, on top of her luscious spread-out body. Mounted up. Riding hard.

He had to redirect the blood flow in his body, fast. He pulled out his smartphone, pulled up the file Nina had sent. Had to put that unruly mind to work, before it fucked him up.

"*. . . give me that!*" It was Nina's recorded voice, but sharp and tense.

"Oh, my God. You're going to translate that right now?"

Nina's exclamation covered the scuffle that followed, and Aaro paused the recording. "Yeah, so shut up," he said tersely. "I need to concentrate. Go do something else. Quietly. So you won't be tempted to interrupt me."

Nina tossed down her bag and sat on the bed opposite

him, open challenge in her steady gaze. "I'm staying right here."

He sighed. So much for his distraction. "Suit yourself, but keep it zipped. I'm going to listen through, start to finish. Don't ask questions until I'm done. Hell, maybe you'll even understand Ukrainian now."

"I doubt that," Nina said.

He ran it back, hit "play" again. "... *give me that!*"

A squeaking, panting scuffle, and then Nina's sharp yelp, as the needle jabbed her. He'd been braced for it, but it still made him wince.

There was a moment of near silence, just a thudding sound, ragged breathing, and Nina spoke again. *"Helga,"* she said, hoarsely. *"Oh, God. Helga? What was ... wha—why did you do that? Wha—what the fuck was in that needle?"*

"Yes, that is good, you remember me, Nina!" It was Kasyanov now, speaking Ukrainian, her voice shrill and quivering. *"You must do exactly as I say! I will die today, so I cannot advise you again. It is too late for me to get the second dose, but not for you. It has to be you to help me, Nina. You have the talent. I sensed it when you were a child. You have enough control of your psychic abilities to handle this much enhancement, and I must enhance you. Someone must stop Rudd, and help my Lara. Forgive me, Nina. Please, forgive me."*

He clicked on "stop," unnerved. He looked up at Nina.

"You understand anything she's saying?" he asked.

Nina shook her head, and he could see from the expectant look on her face she truly didn't. If she had, it would have scared the shit out of her. He let out a slow, measured breath. Pushed "play."

"I must inject you with a dose of concentrated simax," Kasyanov went on. *"It would kill most others, but not you, my dear. You will experience strange, frightening effects before you settle. I cannot predict what they will be; it is different for*

everyone. But you must get the B dose in time. You have three days, maybe four, before your mind breaks down, like mine has. I tried to stop Rudd, but I failed. Forgive me for forcing you to this task, my dear. I have no choice. You do not deserve this, but Rudd took my Lara, and he will kill her if you do not help. Rudd forced me to produce this drug. It is called simax. He wanted a formula to stabilize the psi, and I created one, finally, but I made it a binary dose. Two parts, understand? I offered Rudd the A dose, but I hid the B doses. I meant to make them let Lara go for their second doses. But they injected me with one of the A doses, instead! I took the last two A doses with me when I escaped, but I hid the B doses before I—

"What have you done to her, you crazy bitch?" It was a man's voice, Ukrainian, with the accent of Odessa. A cigarette-roughened rasp, sharp with outrage. "You didn't say you were going to kill her!"

". . . *for graves!* Helga was shouting over the man's interruption, the word "graves" inexplicably in English. *I sent a letter to Joseph,*" Kasyanov continued her desperate, unbroken gabbling in Ukrainian. "*You should see him there. Wycleff Library. Understand? Inside it! Watch for graves! So dangerous, the most dangerous of all! You have to go to—*"

"Get away from her! I am not going to jail for this!" The man, again.

"*I am not trying to hurt her, you idiot! Listen to me, Nina. I am putting the other A dose into your purse now. It is of no use to me now. I am dying. But you might be able to use it as a bargaining chip.*"

"She can't understand you, you fucking lunatic!" the driver bellowed.

"*Her phone is recording me, you fat fool, and she will find a translator. Shut up. She is fainting. Help me get her into the car.*"

"Oh, fuck, oh, fuck," the guy moaned. His breath got shorter as he presumably heaved Nina's body into his car. *"I'm going to jail for this."*

Kasyanov's monologue was covered by Yuri's scolding and yelling. He strained to identify the words. *"Graves,"* she repeated, in English again. *"Get the B dose, Nina. Wycleff Library. You have three days, maybe four. I'm already on day five, but . . . Nina, do you hear me? Nina, wake up! Please, oh, please . . ."*

A strange choking sound began, and from then on, nothing else useful could be deciphered. The driver started shouting, in what sounded like total panic. After a minute or so of chaos, the recording abruptly ended.

Aaro couldn't look up for a minute. He groped for words. Someplace to begin that wouldn't scare her. But there was no such place. There were no such words.

"It's bad, isn't it?" Nina's voice was carefully even.

He nodded, swallowing hard.

"The drug she gave me. Is it the same thing that killed her?"

"Sounds that way," he said reluctantly. "It also sounds like schizophrenic rambling. I would dismiss it as bullshit, if not for all the strange things happening to you today."

"What is the drug?" She looked like an ice sculpture.

He shook his head. "Not clear, from the recording," he said. "Something she developed herself. I'm guessing it's this simax that the zombie goon was talking about. She says it's a binary formula."

Nina blinked. "Meaning?"

"Meaning you take the A dose, and then you take the B dose that completes the process," he explained. "Kasyanov was injected with the first dose against her will. She was unable to get the second dose in time. She says, uh . . ." He hesitated. "You need it within three days."

"Ah. And what happened to Aunt Helga was the result of

not getting the B dose in time? Convulsions, coma, internal hemorrhaging? That's what I have to look forward to?"

"If you don't get the second dose. If what she says is true."

"It's true," Nina said. "She had nothing to gain by lying."

He nodded. It felt true to him, too. No point denying it. "One more weird thing," he said. "She said that the other A dose is in your purse. That you might be able to use it as a bargaining chip."

"My purse?" Nina's eyes got very big. She lunged for the bag that lay on the bed beside her, ripping stuff out and tossing it onto the coverlet. Her rummaging hand stopped suddenly, and she slowly drew out a cylinder of rolled-up bubble wrap. She peered into the end.

"Here it is," she said, her voice hollow. "But this isn't the dose that I'm supposed to find and take, right?"

He took it from her, and peered at it. Five cc's of innocuous, colorless liquid. Son of a bitch. "No," he said. "It's another A dose. She said she took the A doses with her when she ran. It's not clear where the B doses are. She starts to tell you, but it's garbled, there are interruptions. It's hard to make out."

"Why did she attack me?" Her voice was so rigidly controlled, it sounded robotic. "Did she explain?"

Aaro's jaw twinged, pain stabbing mercilessly up into his ear. Goddamn irritated nerve. "I'll just type it out for you, and you can—"

"Just give me the gist of it, Aaro!"

He closed his eyes. "It's bad," he said. "It sounds like she's sending you off on a fucking quest. She was forced to produce a drug for this guy, Rudd. I assume the stuff they were talking about at your house. Simax. It's a drug that, uh, enhances you. That was how she put it. Though it's not clear what exactly she means by enhancement."

"I think I can venture a guess," Nina said. "After what's happened today."

He shrugged. "Anyhow. Her daughter is being held hostage. She wants you to save her daughter, and stop this guy Rudd, the one who took her daughter. I guess, injecting you is . . . incentive."

"Incentive." She frowned, blinking rapidly. "I see. So now, it's just a small matter of saving Lara, who I haven't seen since I was seventeen, and stopping, what, a criminal mastermind? Before I die of brain meltdown? In three days? Right? That's about all of it?"

"Yeah." He coughed. "That's about all. You know. No biggie."

She clapped her hands over her mouth. "Don't you dare make me laugh, or you know I'll start to sob," she warned, from behind her fingers. "And you will be screwed, Aaro. This is so not funny."

"Course not!" he agreed hastily. "Serious as . . ." He choked it off.

Her face convulsed. "As death?" she said, voice shaking. "Go on. Say it, you big chickenshit."

She struggled with the hysteria, shoulders vibrating. He kept his mouth shut so he wouldn't do any more damage. Finally, she pulled it together. Her face smoothed, like she was ironing it out. She'd crossed her arms over her chest. Her lip was pressed down, but still quivering.

Aaro pulled his laptop out. "I'll type a transcript." He crossed his legs, perched the computer on his knees, and set the file to play again.

Nina sat down on the bed behind him, and hung over his shoulder. Her hair tickled his neck. Distracting, but he wasn't going to give her a hard time about it now. He would just try not to make any sudden moves. Like grabbing her. Holding her. Comfort, right?

She watched the transcript growing on the screen with no comment. He stopped after a few minutes to crack his knuckles.

"My God, you type fast," she observed.

"I spend a lot of time on the computer."

He felt her scrutiny. "You don't look it," she observed.

He shrugged. Wasn't touching that one with a barge pole.

"What do you do for a living, anyway?" Her voice had a chatty tone that put his teeth on edge, but who was he to judge her convoluted coping mechanisms tonight? So he played along.

"I test cyber-security," he said. "I mount attacks on computer security, and analyze the results, make recommendations."

"So essentially, you hack for a living," she commented.

"Nina, you want me to type this thing out, or do you want to make idle chitchat and judgments about how I make my money?"

She looked reproachful. "Don't snap. I'm hanging on by a thread."

"Not fair," he growled. "Don't guilt-trip me."

"Life's not fair. Neither am I. That's a phenomenon commonly known as 'tough shit.' Familiar with it, Aaro?"

In spite of all the drama, he felt his mouth twitch. She was tough. Chill. No tears, no whining. She just kicked him around, to blow off some steam. He hadn't known that steely quality was so sexy. He steered clear of women's problems. Courage, fortitude; those character traits didn't usually emerge during hot trysts in motel rooms.

He'd never been particularly interested in such traits before, truth to tell. He wasn't all that deep. Him, the sharks, and the crocodiles. He stopped at tits and ass. A guy needed to evolve a little further to appreciate those subjective, emotional qualities. Way further. That stuff was a fucking quagmire.

But it sure revved his engine tonight.

13

The text grew on the screen as fast as she could read it, but Nina couldn't follow. It was too strange. A story that happened to someone else. This was not her world. Not her reality. She kept getting distracted by random things. The shape of Aaro's earlobe. The way his hair grew off his forehead. The roar in her ears. The room was tipping, swaying.

Aaro typed like he did everything else—hard. His fingers pounded on the keyboard like a hailstorm. Her eyes burned. She wished, suddenly, that she could just lean against his back. It seemed so warm, so broad. She could just . . . rest there. Maybe even breathe a little.

She stopped herself, kept her spine stiff. No. Flipping. Way.

The pounding stopped, followed by random sporadic tapping. She squinted at the screen. He was in some e-mail program, attaching a file to a long list of addresses with a three-word message: "Talk to Bruno."

"Who are you sending it to?" she asked him.

"Bruno, and Miles, this guy who works for me. Awesome hacker. I'm asking him to do some digging. The McClouds, too, and Nick Ward, Seth Mackey, Val Janos, Tam Steele. You know them?"

"I've heard of them," she said. "Lily told me stories about them that curled my hair. She loves them. She said I'd meet everyone at the wedding."

He grunted. "Maybe you'll meet them sooner." He pulled out his cell phone, punched some keys. "Yo, Miles? Yeah, fine, as you can see. . . . I figured they'd all be having kittens by now. I'm sending you the transcript of that file . . . yeah. Couple things. Dig up anything you can find on Helga Kasyanov, her daughter Lara, and anybody who might be associated with them named Joseph. Also a place called the Wycleff Library. And do some filtering on that audio file. There are places when the woman's voice is covered by a man's. Scrub out the man. Yeah . . . yeah, right. Good. Later, then."

He hung up, rolling his shoulders. "Miles is on it."

The room phone shrilled. It jangled four times before Nina reached out. Aaro batted her hand down, grabbed it. "Who is it?"

He listened for a moment. "Yeah," he said. "Yeah, put him through." He hung up, looking glum. "Bruno followed the trace on my phone," he said, in response to her questioning glance. "Forgot all about the damn thing. He called the hotel, told them to connect him to the big dark-haired guy who checked in at ten forty-eight P.M. Son of a bitch."

Nina was startled. "He put a trace in your phone?"

"Never again," Aaro said darkly. The phone rang. He picked it up.

"Yeah?" He jerked the phone from his ear as shouting burst from it. "We've been busy," he muttered. "Sorry. Things got away from us."

Another explosion made him flinch again. "Nina is fine." Aaro's eyes flicked to her face. "She's. . . . I need to . . .

whatever." He held out the phone. "He's popping an artery. Calm them down. Lily wants you."

Nina clutched the phone to her ear. "Yes?"

"My God." Lily's voice was froggy. "I was so worried. You're OK?"

OK? Was she? With this drug wreaking havoc in her head? Assassins chasing her? Cryptic instructions from a comatose woman her only guide out of doom, and Aaro, driving her nuts? Was that OK?

She made an arbitrary decision. Yes. OK meant "not cut into little chunks." She was fine. Great, even. Living in the goddamn moment.

"More or less," she said. "Lily. Sweetie. If you cry, I'll cry, and I can't break down now, OK? I've got to be tough. Help me with that."

"OK," Lily squeaked. "Sorry. I'll . . . I'll try."

"Lil, Aaro translated that file, and he—"

"Oh, really? Did he finally condescend to do that? I can't believe he said no this morning! I'll rip that jackass limb from limb when I—"

"No," she broke in. "Don't. He had his reasons." *And besides. I need him in one piece.*

Lily floundered. "Uh . . . what? What reasons are those?"

She ignored the question. "Just don't tear him limb from limb." She was careful not to look in Aaro's direction. "He was amazing, actually. He saved my life. Twice. I'd be dead, if not for him."

"Ah. I see." Lily sounded mollified. "Well, good, then. He's racked up some points. But tell me, what in God's name were the two of you doing at the Mercer Street Hospice for forty-two minutes, of all places?"

"Visiting Aaro's aunt," she said.

"Let me get this straight. You take time out from running for your very life from deadly assassins to make a hospital call? Nina? *Hello?*"

"She's dying," Nina said. "It was now or never."

Nina got the uncomfortable sensation that her friend was smiling. "I see," Lily murmured. "Defending him now, are we?"

"I am not, by any means," she snapped. "It's not like that. He doesn't need defending."

"Oh, for fuck's sake." Aaro grabbed the phone back. "Give me Bruno, Lily," he snapped. "We don't have time for this."

He listened for a moment. "OK. Her flight is Delta two forty-eight, one thirty PM tomorrow to Seattle, got it. Yeah, I'll take a picture right now, with my cell. Send me his e-mail. Don't send him over tonight, though. She needs . . . OK, I'll ask her." He held the phone up. "Bruno's asking if you want him to send the bodyguard to pick you up now, or do you just want to crash here and catch up with the guy tomorrow morning? He wants to hear it from you, since I suck, and cannot be trusted." He waited. "Nina," he prodded, after several seconds. "Decide."

It was no decision at all. She didn't want to watch Aaro walk away. He made her feel . . . *safe* was not the word, but whatever it was, she wanted more. A lot more. As much as she could get.

She pitched her voice so Bruno could hear it. "I'll stay," she said, and blushed, as if Lily and her guy could see how crushed out she was.

Aaro put the phone to his ear again. "Don't send the guy too early. The airport is forty minutes from here. Traffic's not bad in the morning from this direction, so don't send him before ten. Have the guy bring her some cash, too. She's broke. Oh, and one more thing. That tracer chip stays in the trash. Don't you ever tag my phone again."

Aaro slammed the phone down. His fingers tapped and fisted in the covers. He was tense, too. Big surprise.

The silence made her sweat. She wondered if he would

see her decision as a declaration of intent. She wondered if it *was* a declaration of intent. It wasn't like she had much experience with those.

What the fuck, let's seize the day. One excuse is as good as another for me. His words echoed in her head. She should definitely be seizing her days. Particularly if she only had three of them.

She pushed that thought away, and opened her mouth to tell him . . . what? *Damn.* She was such a wuss. She just couldn't.

She wanted to burst into tears. "I, um, have to take a shower," she mumbled, fleeing into the bathroom.

The challenge was on, as the shower hissed. Trying not to think about her on the other side of the wall, naked, wet. Those suckable tits gleaming with soapsuds. Rivulets rushing over luscious curves into cleavages, crevices. Dripping off the thick, dark ringlets of her muff.

Sharks and crocodiles, man. He'd surpassed himself this time. Sex hormones pumped out unchecked, after all that they'd just been through. He should be turned off by problems this huge. His balls should have crawled right back up into his body. He should have told the bodyguard to get his ass over here pronto. Good-bye and good luck.

What the *fuck* was wrong with him?

He should at least be working on Nina's problem, if he wasn't going to jettison her tonight. He dropped his face into his hands.

Forget it. He wasn't rational tonight, and couldn't pretend to be. Bruno and his gang were flogging their brains against Nina's problems now, and his own part in this adventure would be over when the bodyguard showed up. He'd hear how the story played out via Miles, who talked to some Mc-Cloud or other every day. His part was done.

That should make him relieved. But it made him feel heavy. Like his limbs were made out of lead.

A knock sounded on the door. He grabbed the .45, jangling unpleasantly with a fresh jolt of adrenaline. "Who is it?"

"Pizza delivery." A bored young voice.

Oh, yeah, that. He cracked the door a slit, gun at the ready. Pimply seventeen-year-old, padded rubber pizza bag, it all looked legit. He peered down the corridor in both directions and concluded the transaction with lightning speed, shoving money at the kid, slamming the door before he could make change. He'd given the pizza boy a two-hundred-percent-plus tip, but what the hell. Kid didn't know what he was risking, hauling a pizza up to the likes of them.

He set it aside, and mounted the portable squealer door alarms he'd gotten from the McClouds' catalog of goodies. He'd made fun of himself when he'd packed them. Check him out, scared shitless to get near the Arbatovs. Pussy. To think he'd given Nina a hard time about her trick closet.

How was he supposed to distract himself when she came out? Hot and soft. Fragrant. Damp. Pantiless. He'd turn the TV on, maybe, though he hated squawking screens. Something loud and obnoxious.

She didn't come out. The water just kept running, and running. He mounted the squealers. Checked and re-checked guns, inventoried the ammo. Minutes ticked on. He thought how she'd sat on his lap on the bus stop bench. Her weight innocently perched on what instantly had become an aching hard-on. Though she hadn't seemed aware of it.

Had she been aware . . . ? Could she be expecting . . . ?

No. No way. Don't even go there. Don't even *start.*

Too late. His brain was out of the starting gate, hurtling full speed into erotic fantasyland. Stripping off his clothes, strutting into the bathroom. Whipping aside the curtain. Let-

ting her take a good, long look at what she was dealing with
before he stepped in. Seized her.

His heart thudded. Sweat popped out at his hairline.

Had she even locked the bathroom door? A discreet turn
of the handle would answer that.

Oh, fuck, no. He sat on the far side of the bed, just bearing
the weight of his massive overload of adrenaline-fueled lust.
It wasn't worth the risk. If he got something that big that
wrong, he'd have to shoot himself in the head just to save
face.

After a nerve-shredding eternity, the bathroom door clicked
open. Perfumed steam stole into the room. He heard Nina's
padding bare feet.

He did not turn. Her bed creaked as she sat down.

He dug for his lighter and smokes with a hand that shook.
Careful not to look at her as he lit up. Waited for the stern
commentary. He could practically do a countdown. Five.
Four. Three. Two.

"Um." She cleared her throat. "I don't think this is a
smoking room."

Right on cue. He found himself smiling as he took a deep
drag and slowly blew it out. "It is now," he said.

"But there's a sign on the desk that says—"

"Too bad."

She did her impatient sniffing sound. "You do this kind
of thing on purpose, don't you? You deliberately rent a non-
smoking hotel room so that you can smoke in it? For the
pure pleasure of breaking the rules? You just have to be bad,
at all costs?"

His smile became a grin. He was careful to keep his face
averted.

"I actually don't remember the smoking or non-smoking
interchange with the desk clerk," he said. "I was too busy
worrying about someone garroting you in the parking lot
while I was gone."

He smoked in sweet silence for a minute, the time it took for her to wind up the scold mechanism again.

"That's bullshit," she informed him. "You've just got to be in everyone's face. It's how you define yourself. You wouldn't know who you were if you weren't being a pain in the ass to someone. Right?"

He considered that possibility from all sides as he basked in the nicotine chill. "We all have our schtick," he offered.

She snorted. "Don't you get sick of it? Doesn't it make you tired?"

"Still not breaking a sweat." At least not for the reasons she meant. He thought of her rosy buttocks, her sweet, lickable dimples. He fought the impulse. Like he'd fought before.

He lost, again. "You're right," he said. "I'm bad. I know it. I don't know how to be any other way, and it's too late for me to change."

"God, Aaro. That's so self-defeating."

"Nah, just honest." He twisted around, fixed her with a narrow gaze while he blew out a long stream of smoke. "You hate smoke?"

She waved the question away. "Of course. I'm a nonsmoker. Cigarette smoke is toxic. And nasty."

He blew out another long stream of it in her direction. "Make it worth my while to stop," he said.

Her eyes went wide. Those long lashes, all around, like coal smudges. He kept his eyes on her, letting his meaning sink in.

"I'm bad," he went on. "But there is that small skill set I told you about earlier. The short list of things at which I am expert. Who knows, they might make up for my more glaring faults." He shrugged. "At least a few of them. You won't know unless you try me."

"There you go again," she said. "Being bad. Trying to shock me."

"No, just proving you right," he said. "Don't you like to be right?"

"I don't like to be played with." Her voice trembled.

He smiled slowly. "You've never felt me do it."

"Aaro." She swallowed, a few times. "This isn't fair."

He shrugged. "Life never is."

"With all that's happening, this is hardly the time . . ."

"This is the time we have," he said simply.

The truth of that statement reverberated like a big gong.

Silence spread afterward, heavy and liquid. The energy between them shimmered like a desert mirage. He felt her response. Awareness. Desire. She wanted it. No matter how scared she was.

Time to lighten up. Stave off her impending panic attack. Pissing her off again should do it. He finished his smoke, stubbed it out.

"You know what your problem is?" he said, lighting up another smoke. "You're not used to a strong come-on. You've never developed a standard set-down strategy for dickheads like me. You never needed to, with that bag over your head."

"Quit it with the bag bullshit," she snapped. "I'm sick of it."

He gestured with the cigarette. "But that trick won't work with me. I've seen you without the braid, the tent, the buttons up to the neck. That thing you do with your lip."

"I do not do anything to my lip!"

"You hide it. Like you hide all the good stuff. Your lower lip is pink, like a satin pillow." He stared, fascinated. "But you suck it in, squish it flat. I understand, if you don't like a guy looking at how hot and soft your lips are. Imagining them closing around his dick."

He saw from the look on her face as she sprang off the bed that he'd pushed too hard. *Shit*. Dick-for-brains. Literally.

He moved without thinking to head her off before she got

to the door, which was wired shut with squealers. He grabbed her before she could yank the knob. She batted at his arms.

He held her fast. "I'm sorry," he said. "That just slipped out."

"I can't stay here with you," she burst out. "I can't deal with you."

"You can't leave now," he said. "You have no place to go. And you don't have cash with you, either, right?"

Her eyes slid away. "I can go to a bank—"

"No. You can't use your bank card, or your credit. You can't go to the cops. The mobsters got tipped off about Lily's nine one one call. You can't go to your friends. You'd put them in danger. Like Shira's in danger now."

"I put you in danger, too!"

"That's OK. I was born to be put in danger. It's all I'm good for."

She stared at him, breathing hard.

"I'm a pain in the ass, and I'm crude and lewd, and I stink of toxic smoke, but I'm all you've got, for now. So use me."

"Yeah?" Her eyes blazed at him. "And just who do you think would really be getting used, Aaro?"

"It wouldn't be like that," he told her. "I wouldn't use you."

"Right," she muttered. "And until you hand me off tomorrow, it's my job to make this bullshit worth your while?"

He was about to snap back at her when the look in her eyes finally came into focus for him. Comprehension slipped in, like a knife between his ribs.

She was scared of him. Of course. Like he should be surprised, knowing what he knew about her. Being what he was.

He stepped back, hands lifted in the air. "I won't lay a hand on you unless you tell me to," he said. "And I would never, ever hurt you."

She still huddled, big-eyed, tight-lipped. Unconvinced.

"I'm sorry," he said, with some effort. "I didn't mean to scare you. It was just the hard-on talking. It talks loud, but it's not the boss."

"I wasn't scared." Her chin went up. "That's, um. Good to know." Her eyes darted around, finding no good place to rest. "So what is this huge favor that you owe Bruno, anyway? I've been wondering."

His first impulse was to slap the question to the ground, hard enough so that it never dared to rise again. That, however, did not jibe with his current attempt to not be a dickhead. The words ground out.

"Not technically a favor. A fuckup. I have to make up for it."

"What fuckup?" she prompted. "What happened?"

He let out a savage sigh. "You know what happened to Lily? When she got abducted by King's goons? The hospital at Rosaline Creek?"

"She told me the story," Nina said.

"Right. Well, that was me. That happened on my watch."

She looked blank, so he tried again. "I was the asshole who was guarding Lily when that happened. Do you understand me now?"

"Ah," she said softly. "Yes. I do."

He was inexplicably pissed that she had no more to say than that. "So," he said. "There it is. That's it. That's the fuckup."

"That's all?"

"What, that's not enough for you? You need more? They took her! I couldn't stop them! She almost died, and so did Bruno! All because of me! So as you can see, my track record sucks. Big time."

"Your track record's pretty good with me," she said.

He waved that away, with an angry swat.

She studied him. "Lily told me how they set up that scam. I would have been fooled. Anyone would have been fooled, Aaro. Anyone."

"Yeah, well, anyone wasn't. I was."

"So you need to redeem yourself? For not being perfect? Is that why you're going to all this effort? To make up for that?"

He stuck his cigarette back in his mouth and sucked on it, to preclude letting anything stupid blurt out.

Nina twitched the cigarette out of his mouth. "Put this out."

He gaped at her, smoke still trickling from his mouth. "Huh?"

She grabbed a cup from the table, and tapped out his smoke in it. Then she turned, and gave him a smile that almost stopped his heart.

"It just became worth your while," she said.

14

Nina couldn't read the look on his face. The few hours that she'd known him, he'd been so armored, so totally 'fuck you,' it took a minute to recognize his expression, and another one to believe it. Fear.

Aaro was scared. Of *her.* Holy shit. No one had ever been scared of her. But this guy, this rawhide-and-gunmetal guy who blazed raw sex appeal—he looked scared of her.

The realization gave her the urge to giggle, which she suppressed. Giggling would kill the moment. She did not want this moment killed. It was astonishing. She wanted to treasure it, follow it. See where it went.

Maybe it was the way he felt about his failure in guarding Lily. He pretended to be indifferent and cynical, but it was bullshit. He cared desperately. It was killing him. Like he cared for his dying aunt. It fogged her up, just thinking about it. He'd revealed so much of himself when he let her witness that. He'd handed her his operating instructions.

She wasn't afraid of him anymore, and fearlessness felt good. The voice of reason still yammered away in the back of her head, and yeah, it was still the worst idea in the history of bad ideas. He was a stranger, a totally inappropriate choice for a lover, badly behaved, and there was no guarantee the sex would work, however excited she might be.

In fact, chances were statistically overwhelming that it would be a disaster. Sex so far had been lots of staring at ceiling tiles, discomfort, embarrassment. Afterward, trying to explain. Reassuring her partners that it wasn't their fault, it was her, not them, blahbity blah blah.

She'd started to wonder if she was, well, different. Some people were straight, some were gay, some were bi. And some were asexual. She'd been getting comfortable with the idea. Thinking that it might be OK, to be "a." What a relief, to just relax. Give up the fight.

And *ka-boom*. Her mind was yanked open, shields down, no gray fuzz, no *nobody here nobody here* churning out. She was oh, so very here right now. So present. Like never before.

It was madness. But it felt like magic.

She laid her hand on his chest, and the contact made her nerves tingle, a zillion little bells ringing. He was hot. The fabric of his T-shirt damp. So hard, that lean economy of muscle beneath it. He smelled of smoke, the tang of male sweat. His heart thumped beneath her palm. Her fingers dug into his sinewy bulk. *Mmmm.*

"All this effort, just to make up for being human," she said.

His eyes narrowed. "If you're trying to make me feel better about fucking up, don't bother. I don't need someone to hold my hand."

"It's not my job to comfort you," she said. "And it wasn't actually your hand I was thinking of holding."

His chest jolted, but he jerked the laughter and his grin promptly back under grim control. "So what are you doing?"

"I'm calling your bluff. You are so busted, Aaro. Was it all just so much calculated bullshit, this amazing skill set of yours? Did I have my mind in the gutter when I assumed that you were offering yourself up as a sex toy when you invited me to use you? Am I that far off base?"

"Uh, no." A muscle pulsed in his jaw. "By no means. My mind lives down in the gutter. It maintains a full-time residence down there."

"Thank goodness. I'd have been mortified, if I'd gotten it wrong."

"I'm just surprised, at the about-face. I thought you were scared of me. Scared of sex. That you thought I was a pain-in-the-ass buffoon."

She smiled, dug her fingernails in. Feeling his nipples tickling her palm through his shirt. "So you figured you were safe, right?"

His face was a taut mask. "Don't push me."

"Why not? You push me. But you know what?" She delicately scraped her nails down over his chest. "I see right through it now."

He flinched back. "What the fuck are you talking about?"

"That bag over my head," she said softly. "You wear one, too. Takes one to know one. That's why I couldn't read your mind, even though I can read everyone else's. Your bag is a shield. Just like mine."

He cleared his throat. "OK. I think you're nuts, but I'll play your game. What do you think you see in there? This one's for free."

She ran her fingertips over the rasp of beard stubble. He was so skittish, so painfully macho. He wasn't going to want to hear about his grief and loneliness. It would just embarrass him, which would piss him off. Not conducive to what she had in mind.

She let out a careful breath. "I don't think you want to know."

He snorted. "Easy answer."

"Easier for you, definitely," she agreed.

The silence thickened, and when she put her finger to his cheek again, he leaned into her touch, like a cat. The shimmer of awareness intensified. "So it's official?" His voice was almost belligerent. "You're letting me fuck you tonight. Awesome. Let's get started."

She stifled a giggle. "There you go again. Get it through your head, Aaro. The rude-and-ugly bag over your head won't work. I've seen through it. The spell's broken. It's silly, now. Give it up. Behave."

"The desire to get laid can make even an asshole behave well for a little while. Then it passes, and it's like it never happened."

She tried not to smile. "Is that a warning?"

He shook his head. "A reminder."

"You're not an asshole," she said. "I don't know why you want to convince everyone that you are, but with me, you might as well stop."

"You're projecting a fantasy onto me," he said grimly. "Don't."

She flapped her hand at him. "You think too much, Aaro," she said. "Stop it before you hurt yourself."

His chest jerked in harsh laughter. "Nobody's ever accused me of that before." He grabbed his duffel. "I need a shower. I'm foul. I was traveling for hours even before the mortal combat. Give me a few."

He vanished into the bathroom. Nina sagged down onto the bed.

The sky had fallen. Pigs flew. Hell was frozen over. It had made dreamlike sense, while he was standing there, zapping her with his wild energy, but once he fled into the bathroom, her insecurities crowded eagerly back. Maybe he'd come on to her out of habit. Some men didn't know any other way to behave with a woman. And now, he was forced to deliver on his big talk, to salvage his macho image.

Then again. That erection had seemed very, very sincere.

The shower was hissing. The pressure was on. She'd never had such an intense reaction to a man. In personal relationships, she avoided intensity. She'd had plenty of that as a kid. She got plenty more working for the women's shelter. She preferred careful, polite, safe guys.

And look how well that was working out for her. It had been over a year since her last attempt at sex. Though she hadn't been aware of any feelings of deprivation. Not until she met Aaro.

Yes, this attack of mad, mindless lust was totally Aaro-specific.

The shower stopped hissing, and she was still wearing the glasses and tent dress he so despised. This was her chance to recline naked, be a seductive siren. But she could hardly breathe, let alone undress.

The bathroom door opened. A cloud of steam swirled around him as he emerged, like stage smoke wreathing a rock star as he stepped into the spotlight. He was naked to the waist, and God, he was fine. Black cotton trousers hung low on his lean hips. She drank him in, breathless. That chest, those shoulders, that belly. Solid, massive, ripped. Some scars, here and there. Perfect. In every last detail.

Their eyes met. The energy level roared up and got hotter with every step she took toward him, like the very air would explode. She inhaled deeply as she moved toward him. *Mmm*. Perfumed. He'd washed his hair. And shaved. His long hair was combed straight back from his forehead. Minty toothpaste, shampoo. Aftershave. Deodorant.

She bit her lip to keep from smiling. "Why, Aaro," she said demurely. "Look at you. You primped."

Those massive, gleaming shoulders twitched. "Least I could do."

"You look awesome. And you smell delicious. I'm touched."

"Not yet, you're not," he replied. "Soon, though."

Her mouth had been open, some smart remark on the tip of her tongue. It vanished, melted away in the heat of his penetrating stare.

"You're still wearing your bag," he said.

Her face went hot. "Um. It . . . it doesn't come off so easily."

"Tell me about it," he murmured. It sounded almost as if he had admitted that she was right, about his own masquerade. His own mask.

"Stop that," he said suddenly.

She jumped. "Huh? Stop what?"

"That thing with your lip. Stop doing that."

She bristled. "I know this lip thing is your pet peeve, Aaro, but you're going to have to get over it, because I have no idea—"

"So make it conscious." He grabbed her shoulders, and swung her around so that they faced the mirror. "Look at your mouth. See how the top is soft and pink, but the bottom is squashed flat. Feel the tension?"

"You're a fine one to talk about tension," she said sourly.

"See?" he said, triumphant. "You can't do it when you talk. Whoops, there it goes again! Back into the cage. It got spooked."

"You're making me self-conscious," she snapped. "That's the kiss of death, you know. Freezes me right up. *So* not in your best interests."

"Just look in the mirror." He reached around, touching her lower lip. She jumped, at the intimate contact. Her lips trembled.

"Try to relax," he urged.

She laughed in his face. "With you? Now? Hah!"

He looked pleased. "Look! See? When you laugh, it comes out to play. See? Pillowy soft. And that sexy crease in the middle."

They both stared at her mouth. It hung slightly open, her

breath coming ragged and fast. Her lip gleamed, moist from having been sucked inside her mouth. He began to stroke it. Barely touching it.

The glancing touch was a match to a fuse. She closed her eyes, shuddering. Sensations jolted deep into the most sensitive, secret parts of her body. He put his mouth to her throat. A delicate drag of his teeth down her tendon, a slow lick of his tongue. She whimpered, and drew his fingertip into her mouth. A suckling swirl of lips and tongue.

He made a choked, shocked sound. "Oh, my God."

Nina reached up, took off her glasses with a trembling hand, laid them on the telephone table. The world blurred, leaving just a small bubble of clarity. It was enough. As long as he was inside the bubble.

Aaro kissed her neck hungrily, and fished up the end of her thick braid. Slowly, as if it were some sacred rite, he teased the elastic off and unraveled it. The curly strands slid and wound around his long fingers.

It was like the hair itself had nerves. As responsive as skin, each stroke of her hair against his hand. Every point of contact reverberated through the vast energy field their two bodies had become. His lips were so soft against her throat. The faint nip, the scrape of teeth. A reminder of the depth of his animal hunger. And his immense self-control.

I won't lay a hand on you unless you tell me to. And I would never, ever hurt you.

She believed him. This guy did not tell lies. He didn't know how. He didn't gloss over anything ugly. There was nothing ugly to gloss over.

She felt like an eye had opened up inside her that could see light shining out of him. It relaxed her like sunshine. Unraveled her, like her braid, making her wanton and luxurious. Loosening taut knots of tension with a warm glow of . . .

Trust? Him? Oh, please. Wake up!

She batted the voice of reason away. She wanted to live

this fantasy. She'd never melted in a man's arms. Her sexual experiences had all been carefully planned. And they had all gone exactly nowhere.

But Aaro, his teeth sliding delicately down her throat, made ticklish thrills lick over her skin, and damp heat rush into her face, between her legs. Her nipples went taut, her knees went weak.

Aaro could take her anywhere . . . and everywhere.

His arm tightened, pulling her back against him. His erection prodded her bottom. Her eyes were squeezed shut. Air would only come into her chest in little jerky starts. She felt dizzy. She opened her eyes, barely recognized herself. So pink. Eyes glowing and dilated.

He loomed, a raptor guarding its prey. His hands slid up, cupping her breasts. Even through two layers of cloth, with pockets and buttons and embroidery and stitching, the soft, stroking contact sent licks of fire curling through her. She leaned back against him, craving more.

And suddenly, his hands dropped.

She almost stumbled, without the support. What the hell? Had he changed his mind? One glance at the loose, revealing pants draped from his hips showed that whatever might be going on in his mind, his body was still hugely enthusiastic. His erection tented out the fabric as far as it would stretch. "Ah . . . are you OK?" she asked.

He shook his head. His hands fisted, opened, fisted again. "I just need to know the rules, that's all."

She was baffled. "Rules? I didn't know there were rules."

"Usually, there aren't. I follow my instinct, and it works fine, so far. I've gotten no complaints. But you . . . you're different."

Different? That quenched some of her glow. "You mean, a woman like me? With all the baggage and expectations and whatnot?"

"No," he said, with a sharp sigh. "That's not it. Not at all."

"I don't have any expectations of you," she said. "Really, I don't. Please, don't flatter yourself, or insult me. I'm not that stupid."

"It's the stepdad thing," he blurted.

That doused her buzz completely. Her belly clenched. "Ah. So, that's, um . . . a turnoff for you?"

"Fuck, no! It's not like that! My head and my dick are both about to explode. Look at me. Do I look turned off to you?"

She looked him over, and her lips twitched. "Um. No, not really."

"That's my problem." His hands began to open and close. "I've never been this wound up. I'm on the edge of a . . . a fucking cliff."

"Oh. I see," she said, though she didn't, really. "Well, don't worry so much. What you were doing was fine. Super-deluxe, in fact. Go ahead, fall off the cliff. I think we'll, um . . . catch each other."

"I'm afraid of scaring you." His voice was raw. "Because of your . . . because you have . . . you know."

"Issues?" she supplied.

He waved his hand impatiently. "I don't want to fuck this up. All that bullshit about my sexual skill set, fuck it, Nina, I didn't know you would have this effect on me! You suck on my finger, and I practically came in my pants. I am this far"—he held up a thumb and forefinger—"from doing that. If you look at me funny, I'll come."

Her heart did a painful little somersault. "It's better that way," she offered. "I prefer it, actually. To not be the only one who feels unsure of herself. I like you that way."

"Yeah? You think you'll like me that way when I'm pounding away on top of you? All two hundred and thirty pounds of me?"

Her thighs squeezed together, and her heart tripped quadruple time. "Um, yes, actually. I think I'll like you just fine," she said, touching his bare chest. "No one's ever wanted me that much."

"You didn't want anyone to," he said. "You didn't allow it."

She acknowledged that with a nod.

"But you want it from me," he went on. "Why?"

Her hand splayed out, feeling the buzz, the heat, the powerful throb of his heart against her palm. "I don't know," she said. "It's a mystery. You showed me yours. So now I'll show you mine."

She shook her hair back as she slipped off the broad linen shoulder straps of the jumper smock. The weight of all the skirt fabric tugged the loose garment down. It caught on her hips, then fell.

Aaro's breathing became an audible rasp. "Ah, Nina."

She looked down, so very glad she'd shaved her legs. It had been a random impulse, an excuse to stay under pounding hot water a little while longer before work. To think she'd been humming, depilating her legs without a care, oblivious of the terrors the day had in store for her.

It was hard to undo the blouse. She'd never tried to undo buttons while her fingers trembled. But one after the other, she tugged them loose, took as deep a breath as her lungs would accept, and shrugged it off her shoulders. Ta da. Her tits. There they were, in all their glory. She shut her eyes, overwhelmed by it. She'd never felt so seen. So known.

"Open your eyes, Nina."

Her eyes opened as he shoved the loose pants down over his protruding erection. It sprang up, bobbing and swaying.

Bigger than her initial estimate. Long, broad, the gleaming head a flushed purple, a tangle of dark veins throbbing on his thick shaft. She wanted to grab, squeeze. Feel his vital energy pulsing in her hand. At her service. Oh, boy. So beautiful. Heavily muscled legs, the lean, perfectly modeled dips and curves of his hips and ass.

She stumbled forward, grabbed him. Pressed her face to his chest. Hot, smooth, and he smelled so good. His skin was supple against her lips, springy chest hair tickling her nose. His nipples were small, tight, and puckered. She loved his taste, when she took the nub into her mouth. The hint of salt. She licked, drawing a strangled sound from him with each flicking caress. His fingers dug into her bottom.

She grabbed his cock, stroked, squeezed. Just as good as she'd thought. That hot, vital throb. Vulnerability and power. His skin was so soft and smooth, sliding over the pulsing, steely hardness.

"Fuck," he rasped. "Nina. Please. Didn't you hear what I said? About self-control? About coming in my pants? Did that sink in?"

"Sure it did. It inspired me. Besides, you're not wearing pants anymore. Come whenever you want."

She sank to her knees, and took him into her mouth.

Half of her was shocked to her toes. The other half cheered like a sports stadium gone mad. Their tangled clothes padded her knees. She gripped his shaft, stroking. His pubic hair was thick and springy. She inhaled soap and hot man musk, licked off precome. Salty, perfect, magic. He stared down at her, his face a mask of tension. A man driven to the edge. And she wanted to be the one who set him soaring.

She sucked him deeper. He made a sound like air escaping from a truck tire, and grabbed her hair, trapping her in place.

Sound seemed amplified; the rattling hum of the air conditioner, the buzz of the bathroom fan. Televisions babbled in the guest rooms on either side of them, voices in the hall swelled in volume and receded. Aaro's panting. The soft, wet sounds of her mouth. His shaking fists, wound full of her hair, next to her ears. Light from the wall sconce hit one side of them and left the other in shadow. Her knees wobbled on the snarl of discarded clothing. Her own heart thudded.

She couldn't boast of much technique, but he seemed to enjoy her efforts. And oh, he was delicious. She loved his taste, his texture, the metallic flavor of his shaft against her tongue. The broad, flushed cockhead, the tracery of swollen veins beneath her hands. Salt, sweet, slippery. She stroked his long, slick shaft two-handed while she licked his glans, tongue swirling, teasing. So excited, she felt faint.

"Oh, God. Oh . . . *fuck*." He flung his head back, and came, with a guttural sound, thrusting even deeper into her mouth.

She clutched his thighs. Powerful jets of come pulsed out of him. A lot to contain. He clamped her in place until the shudders tapered off to delicate flutters. She struggled to breathe, until Aaro unwound his fingers from her hair, pulled his gleaming cock from her mouth.

With her guard down, fear and uncertainty made a surprise attack, whammo. She'd felt so connected, but suddenly he felt like a dangerous stranger again. She couldn't look up, once fear had rushed into that vast space that had so inexplicably opened up inside her. Fear that he would look smug, triumphant. Or worse, contemptuous.

It felt strange, being naked. On her knees. She hadn't felt submissive or ashamed while it was happening. She'd felt like a goddess. Not now. It had all slipped away, and left her nervous and small. She tried to get up, knees wobbling.

She wiped her mouth. Swallowed, with some difficulty. Her face felt hot, buzzing. Her throat, melted and shaking. Defenseless.

And so damned nervous and self-conscious. She heaved upward, on wobbly knees. "Give me a hand up. I need to go rinse my—"

"No." He sank down next to her. "Not yet."

She squeaked in surprise as he jerked her closer, tight against his body. He cupped her face in his hand, and kissed her.

She had about as much experience kissing as she did with

fellatio. Which was to say, not much. But it wouldn't have made any difference if she had been an expert. Aaro was in absolute control, and her body knew it. She responded instinctively to his every silent, implacable demand. Her lips parted when he wanted them to, his tongue thrust, seeking, tasting, exploring her. Pleasing her.

He lifted his head. "I wanted to taste myself on your mouth."

"Oh," was all she managed, before the masterful kiss resumed.

Going down on him had turned her on, but kissing him lit up something even deeper, wider. Lights flicked on in all directions inside her, into the far distance. Color and sparkle and heat, as far as she could feel. She took what he offered, offering herself up in return. Cupping his cheek as if his face were precious, intensely dear to her. There was no end to it. No limit to how good he could make her feel.

Which meant that the opposite of that was also true.

She shoved that bone-chilling thought away, and threw herself back into the kiss. *Seize the day, damn it. Might not be many left.*

He leaned back, after several long, panting, clinging moments, and his expression made her eyes fill. It looked like . . . tenderness.

Tears flashed down over her cheeks. She was a fucking idiot, getting all emotional about this.

He brushed her tears away with his knuckle, and licked them off.

"Wouldn't have taken you for the kissing type," she said.

"You'd have been right," he said. "It's never been my thing before."

"Oh. Well, you're awfully good at it. For a non-kisser, I mean."

"Glad it works for you. Beginner's luck."

The words seemed banal, silly, but she had to keep it

light. She'd promised him. No expectations. She was putting aside the baggage, the issues. She didn't want to scare him away. Not yet. Please, God. Not yet.

She tried to smile. "That was, um . . . intense."

"Yeah. Blew my every last functioning brain cell right to hell."

She licked her lips. "I got the timing wrong," she said shyly. "Making you come before we could, um—"

He grabbed her hand, and pulled it, wrapping her fingers around his extremely stiff cock. "Not a problem."

She squeezed appreciatively. "I thought, recovery time, and all."

"Not tonight." He threaded his fingers through her hair, lifted heavy skeins, letting them slide through his fingers. "You just did us both a big favor by taking the edge off."

She blinked. "You call that an edge?"

"Now I can make up for the fact that you made me come first. You have to come at least ten times now, to compensate for that."

She giggled. "That's overkill. I'm so ready."

"Yeah? Let me see." He reached around to her bottom, stroking the undercurve. She was sopping wet, shivering. When he tickled the tender seam of her vulva, she moaned, squirming. He let the tip of his finger slide inside her, to the first knuckle. Circling, stroking. She reached down to squeeze his cock. Their moans became a sighing duet.

"Oh, fuck. Not again," he growled. "Nina. Damn it. Stop."

"It's too much fun," she protested. "I can't stop."

"So much for taking the edge off," he grumbled. "You've got me right back where I started. On the edge of the cliff again."

"It's your own fault, for being such a great kisser."

His chest vibrated as his mouth covered hers again, his hand delving boldly. Swirling, stroking, in, out. She arched, writhing. "I've never been this ready in my life," she said, when they came up for air.

"Not for me." He laid his open mouth against her throat, nipping, tonguing. "You're so tight. You hug my finger. I want you soft, open, soaking wet down to your knees. Ten orgasms. Then we'll see."

"Don't be ridiculous," she scoffed. "We'll be here all night."

He smiled with all his teeth. "You say that like it's a bad thing."

She giggled helplessly at that, and in the meantime Aaro yanked at bed coverings and pillows, piling them on the floor.

He lifted her so that they faced the full-length mirror, and her giggles choked off. She wasn't quite ready to confront the brazen spectacle of the new, improved Nina the hellcat wanton in her studly lover's arms yet. It was like looking at a too-bright light.

She tried to curl up, to hide the tender bits, but Aaro was having none of that. He perched her on the pillows, and positioned her, limb by limb, legs splayed wide, knees bent, the soles of her feet propped up flat against the wall on either side of the mirror. A wildly erotic pose.

Her face burned. "What's this?"

"It's a visual thing," he said. "I want you to see what happens when I touch your pussy. Anatomically, that's hard, without a mirror. Just go with it. Look. You're so hot."

Um. Easier said than done. She wasn't used to staring at her intimate parts at all, let alone having a gorgeous naked man watch her do it. Her face was hot pink, her mouth even pinker. Shiny, flushed.

Aaro ran his hand up her thigh. "So fucking soft," he whispered.

Too soft, part of her wanted to scoff, but she was not going to ruin the fantasy by focusing on how she wanted firmer thighs, and besides, he wasn't complaining. *Just go with it.* The muscles in her legs and her butt clenched and released as he slid his hands toward her groin. His palms felt tough, smooth, hot. He nuzzled her neck, parting her muff, opening tight-furled folds, stroking. They gleamed, glowing pink. He splayed his fingers in a vee on either side of her mound, lifting until her clit popped out of its hood, shiny and taut and eager. Everything shone with lube, a foggy soft-focus glow of arousal that made it hard to breathe. There was a heavy, liquid ache in her lower body. She felt like the lightest touch could make her scream with pleasure and unravel.

His teeth grazed her, nipping and dragging just as he opened her and slid his finger inside, pushing with a low, triumphant growl into the snug channel. She gasped, and lifted against his hand. Offering herself.

He thrust again, easing two fingers in and out, in and out, then took his own sweet, tortuous time about licking his fingers. "You taste so sweet. I want to lick up your juice. Look. Open your eyes."

She opened her eyes, to see his two fingers disappearing inside her, caressing some excellent spot in there and simultaneously doing something amazing with his thumb to her clit. She lifted her hips, clenching around his hand. Wiggling so much, he lifted her, clamping her against his chest while his other hand plunged and delved and thrust. She made strange, high-pitched sounds as the ache swelled . . .

And broke. Pleasure shuddered through her in rhythmic waves.

She became aware of the slow, sensual rasp of his tongue against her throat, her ear. Licking away sweat. Her eyes fluttered open, lazily.

One of his arms was clamped across her pale belly, her breasts propped on top of it. The other tenderly cupped her mound, petting the wet ringlets as if she were a fuzzy kitten he was coaxing to purr. Every delicate stroke sparked a rippling shudder, a delicious sparkle.

Time stopped, as she stared into his hooded eyes. She was caught and held like a vise by what she saw in there. So many things that he desperately wanted to say, but couldn't. He was trapped behind inches of soundproof, bulletproof glass. She actually felt the pressure bottled up inside him. How strangled he felt. She felt it in every glance, every stroke of his sensitive hands. The desperation of his ravishing kisses.

She dragged in a deep breath. "I want it now," she announced.

He looked disapproving. "I wanted to go down on you first."

"Do that later, if you want," she said. "But do this now. Right now. I want you inside me. And I want you to kiss me while you do it."

His eyelid twitched, wary as always. "Kiss?"

"Remember? The lip contact thing? Mouth-to-mouth, intermittent tongue action? Afraid of multitasking, Aaro? Too much challenge?"

His grin was gone before she could be sure she'd seen it.

"I'm afraid of everything right now," he admitted.

"I'm surprised you admit that, knowing you."

"Yeah?" His eyes narrowed, glittered. "You think you know me?"

She stared straight at him. "Yeah, Aaro," she said. "I think I do."

She wondered, in the stark silence that followed, if she'd gone too far, presumed too much. Then she saw another very fleeting smile.

"Maybe you're right," he said, and leaned to snag his bag. He dug through it, pulling out a flapping tail of condoms. Ripped one off, deftly rolled it into place. Then he stretched out against the heap of pillows, lounging in a deceptively lazy pose, stroking his flushed cock, which lay stiff against his belly. He braced it, so that it stood conveniently vertical.

"Help yourself," he said. "At your service."

She was dismayed. She'd been hoping to abandon herself to his amazing skill and experience. "What happened to the two-hundred-and thirty-pound wild boar who couldn't control himself?" she complained.

"I want to be sure that I don't muscle you into anything. Only way to be sure of that is to have you drive. At least the first time."

She licked her lips. "How many times did you have in mind?"

"For as long as you're having fun."

Wow. She took him in, the whole length of his lean, solid body, his simmering vibe of controlled power. She sensed that it was difficult for him to be passive. His natural instinct was to take control and run the show, start to finish. He cared a lot about not screwing up. That moved her. He gazed at her, his sharp cheekbones flushed, his mouth grim. He seemed to be relaxed, but it was all for show.

"I give you permission to drive," she said, just for the hell of it.

"So? I never asked permission in the first place. Touch me."

She edged closer, perched on her knees, and grabbed his cock. His fist clamped around hers, guiding her on the tight, swirling pull all the way up the lubricated latex that covered him. Beneath it, he was so taut. Stone hard. She petted and squeezed until his breath hitched.

"Show me you want me." His low, rasping tone made her body clench. Yearning sharpened into something approaching pain, but there would be no relief until she took it herself. In both hands. So to speak.

So she did, struggling not to laugh. It felt awkward and

strange. Mounting up on the oversized phallus of a gorgeous sex god commando warrior. Not on her usual daily to-do list.

She swung her thigh over his. He gripped her hips, positioning her, helping to find just the right spot, the right angle. Then he petted her bottom, stroking her butt cheeks, cupping and spreading them so that her slick folds parted for him, just as he nudged inside her.

He prodded her with the bulbous tip of his cock, moistening himself. Petting, twisting, and rocking, pressing against the resistence inside. A soft, pleading caress. Not pushing. Just waiting.

Their eyes were locked. He was so big and blunt, lodged . . . just so. Oh . . . *God*. She wiggled, as her own weight forced her down over him. Thick and unyielding, but she was so excited, even the tight, stinging stretch around him was an afterthought to the excitement.

He stroked her hips as she got used to his girth. Feeling his heartbeat pulse deep against her womb. "You're so tight," he whispered. "But you take all of me. You're perfect."

She had no idea what next, immobilized as she was by his big cock throbbing inside her, so she defaulted to mindless babbling.

"I have no idea what I'm doing, but I'm glad it works for you," she said. "But what about the kissing? Weren't kisses part of the deal?"

"Be my guest. Kiss me, fuck me, ride me. Do as you will with me."

"It's not the same," she informed him. "I want kisses like before."

"Picky, picky." He jackknifed up so fast, it rocked her backward, but he caught her before she fell. He sat beneath her cross-legged and set her astride his lap facing him, legs around his waist. "Fucking complicated woman," he complained, and kissed her again.

If anything, it was more devouring than before. Or maybe

that was the effect of having him stuffed three miles up inside her body. She wrapped her arms around his neck, and devoured him right back. So hot and strong. He smelled good, tasted good. Toothpaste, aftershave, tickling her nose. The tang of salt. She was weightless, suspended in a molten liquid, clinging to him. His big body was her anchor, her lifeline.

The sinuous dance began, with such inevitability, there was no telling who initiated it. It was timeless, the deepening strokes of his cock, of his tongue, the rise and fall and pulse of her hips. His arms trembled, his fingers dug into her hips. She twined, flowering, fruiting, heavy with juice, flowing abundance. Her chest was going to supernova. She felt godlike, blessed, yielding to every thrust, each plunge of ravishing pleasure. Every stroke a new revelation. Surging, falling.

It could have been hours. She came more times than she could count, pleasure cresting through her until she was liquid and boneless, again, and again. She was a shimmering cloud, contained by his fierce embrace. Defined by the strong body clutching hers.

He held his own release back, even when she urged him on, but finally flipped her, pinning her against blankets and pillows. He lifted his mouth to stare into her eyes. "You sure? This is OK? Me on top?"

She nodded, gasping vainly for air.

"You want me to fuck you harder?"

"Yes." The words came out a tight, breathless squeak.

Air rushed out of him. He folded her legs high, rearing up onto his knees, and set a jarring rhythm. She gasped with each hard, slapping thud, staring into his face. His eyes burned with intensity.

It was squeezing her heart into a new shape. She came hard, racked with pleasure. He let go, too, pumping deep.

Some time after, she felt him move, and when she opened

her eyes, he had withdrawn, in every sense. He sat, back to her. Slumped, his head hanging between his shoulders.

And cold reality hit, like a gust of icy wind. She'd gotten a mad, crazy crush on this guy. He'd compounded the problem by fucking her brains out, intensifying the phenomenon.

In the silence, she finally felt just how deep the chasm beneath her feet actually was.

15

Aaro got to his feet, staggered toward the bathroom to get rid of the latex.

This part of the sex act was always his least favorite. The lead-up was fun, imbued with anticipation and sexual urgency. The long, juicy, bouncing ride was great. The fireworks at the end were awesome.

Then came the aftermath. The chilly, awkward moment when he never knew what to say, because anything that came out of his mouth would be offensive. Unless he told lies. Which he abhorrred.

He never learned. He made the same mistake, over and over again, sucked in by his dick, against his better judgment, every time.

But his judgment had never been this bad.

Women always wanted to be held after sex, but that felt like a lie, too. Forced. That was why he chose his sexual partners so sparingly. Once his dick was appeased, he just wanted to get gone.

But this was different. Worse. Gut-churning fear. Clinging to her, like he'd die if he let go, what was up with that?

And his guts right now, aching and squishy. Sick with anxiety. And *kissing?* What the fuck? Kissing was not part of his repertoire, ever. He went down with gusto, but he was careful to avoid protracted staring into a woman's eyes. His favorite sexual scenario was a long, juicy lick-down, to cover the girl's quota of orgasms, concluded by an energetic, pounding fuck from behind. Minimal eye contact was key. He did not kiss. Not ever.

With Nina, he hadn't been able to stop.

He did not want this. He had enough problems. Nina was chipping down walls he needed to survive. He'd known her for a few hours, and he was already completely fucked up.

Oh, yes. You have gift. You just never let it out of cage. I understand. You didn't want to end up like me.

His aunt's words made his guts squeeze with guilt. It was true, though. He didn't want to end up like Tonya. It was a bad scene, when boundaries between people's heads blurred. People got scared, angry. They took steps to protect themselves. People got hurt.

Maybe it was just the sex, but he'd had lots of sex. In all of it, he'd never felt like he'd cracked his insides open and mixed himself with somebody. He'd never wanted to claim a woman for his own. Other men did, but he'd pegged it as hormone-fueled bullshit, an evolutionary maneuver to trick men, against their own best interests, into taking off the latex, perpetuating the species. Like the world couldn't use a purge of the problematic human race. He'd seen the dangerous phenomenon in action in the McCloud Crowd, as they paired up.

But she could almost have tricked him into it tonight. Those big eyes with that amazing iridescent mix of colors gazing up at him like she really saw him, really knew him. That curvy body, her hair tickling his shoulders as she writhed, sighed, stroking his cock inside her hot little cunt. So fucking beautiful, he was afraid to look at her again.

Every detail of her was incised on his memory. Her bountiful tits, bouncing with every stroke of his cock. Her eyes, gazing into the deepest part of his head. The place where he'd always been alone.

He had sought aloneness all his life. It was safer, simpler. But she'd crept inside him. And the weirdest, most fuckedup part of it was that he kind of, almost . . . liked it. Almost as much as he hated it.

The hungry beast had tricked him into this. He'd been infiltrated. She could fuck him up from the inside. No one had wielded this kind of power over him since he was a kid. And he had not liked being a kid.

He splashed water on his face for a while, gathering the guts to walk out there again. When he stepped out, he saw that Nina had remade the bed. She was curled up in the sheets, hair rippling down. She glowed, in the dim light. Waiting, as mysterious as a sphinx.

What the fuck is the matter with you? What is your problem?

The perfectly reasonable question screamed through the ether at him. He deflected it, instinctively. "You, uh, OK?"

She nodded, letting him hang there. Twisting slowly in the wind.

So he tried again. "Did you, ah . . . did I—"

"It was amazing, if you were wondering," she said. "I can't believe that I actually have to say that."

Air rushed into his lungs, so fast, he felt dizzy. "Thank God."

"You were worried?" She sounded amused.

"I didn't want to fuck it up for you. And I didn't want you to think about Stan."

Her eyes went wide. "How did you know his name?"

He shrugged. "You told me about him. Remember? In the car?"

"I never told you his name," she said quietly.

"So you let it slip and you don't remember."

"No, I did not do that," she said stubbornly. "I make a point of not speaking his name. It's, like, a superstitious thing with me. I did not say his name, Aaro, so how did you know it? Did Lily talk about me?"

He shook his head.

They stared through the cavernous space that suddenly opened up between them. He didn't like it. He wanted back, through the maze of crazy, the unanswered questions, the hidden perils. He wanted to find his way back inside her. He fucking ached for it.

"It's too weird, Aaro," she whispered.

"We could put it all aside and just have sex again," he suggested. "Take our mind off the weirdness."

She dissolved into silent, shaking giggles. "Actually, not to offend you, but the sex is part of the weirdness."

He went as tight as piano wire. "I'm too weird for you in bed?"

"I already said it was amazing. Don't fish for compliments."

"Then what the fuck do you mean?" His voice came hard, and her smile faded. He'd killed the giggle fest, like an asshole.

Her lashes swept down. "Never mind," she said. "It's nothing."

"Like hell." He stood there like an idiot. So, what the fuck? Should he leave her alone? Sleep in the other bed? With the guns?

Fuck it. He'd gone this far down the road to destruction. Why not cruise a little farther? So he'd lie in bed with her. Big fucking deal. Other men did it, on a regular basis. It would either kill him, or it wouldn't. He jerked the coverlet and sheets aside. "Scoot over."

She did so, slowly, eyes big and nervous.

He had every intention of just holding her, maybe even

trying to talk. Damned if he knew about what. All they had to talk about was the stuff of nightmares. Subjects best avoided. But when he seized her, it happened again, like that afternoon, when she'd fallen naked into his arms out of her trick closet. Except that this time, he was naked, too.

Snick. A key to a lock, a hand slipping into the perfect glove. Her curves just . . . *fit.* So sweet. Lust, of course, followed right after, huge and mindless. He fought the beast. Wait a goddamn minute. This was a postcoital cuddle, enjoying the glow, relaxed and sated. Right?

Not. He didn't remember how he got there, but he found himself on top of her, elbows propped on either side of her chest, mouth at conveniently close range to her lush tits.

She looked breathless and somewhat dazed. He lowered his head, suckled one of her tits, and it was just like when he'd kissed her before, like he was parched in the desert, and she was sweet relief. He cupped her tit in his hand and laved on it while he petted her slick folds with the tip of his cock. Caressing her until she was shivering and squirming, making those awesome, breathless, whimpering sounds.

Time to shrink-wrap himself, before he did something unforgivably stupid, but his hips kept driving forward, nudging his cockhead deeper into the plushy, suckling kiss of her tight pink pussy. The slick balm of her lube on bare skin was irresistible. She squeezed him, clutched him. Pulling him into herself.

"Um," she quavered. "Aaro?"

"I know," he muttered. "I have to get a condom. I'm sorry."

"Um, actually . . . you said you didn't have any diseases, right?"

He stopped moving, transfixed by the implications of her question. "Yeah? Haven't had sex in months, and I've had bloodwork since then. I'm clean."

"Me, too," she offered. "I'm not fertile right now. Just

finished my period, so it's an OK time to . . . well, anyhow. If you wanted, ah—"

"You'd let me come inside you," he said, dumbfounded.

She blinked, dazed and misty. "If you want," she whispered.

"Want?" He laughed at that. "Don't trust me. I could be lying. Guys will lie through their teeth for anything that feels this good. Even a good one will lie. Like a dog on a rug. And I'm not a good one."

She licked those luscious lips, and twined her arms up under his arms and over his back, petting him. "I know you love to make people think you're bad," she said. "But you're not. And you don't lie, either."

"How do you know that?" He was yelling now. No clue why. The woman was offering him something he wanted more than his next lungful of air, and he was scolding her for it, for fuck's sake.

"I just know," she said. "Maybe the same way I understood Ukrainian? The way you knew Stan's name? What do you figure?"

Poised above her like a stone statue, it occurred to him that if that didn't scare his dick south, nothing would.

It didn't. By no means. But he still reached over to the bedside table, grabbed the condoms, and ripped one off, fumbling under the sheets almost angrily until he got the damn thing onto his cock.

"Are you mad at me, for offering?" Her voice was small.

"No." He rolled onto her, fitting his cockhead against her pussy again and petting her to lube it up. "But I won't allow you to be that stupid. It sets a bad precedent. Don't trust me like that. Just don't."

She stared into his eyes, put her hand against his cheek. She was ignoring his warning. He could see it in her face. Goddamnit.

But it was too late to stop. One deep, slick lunge, and he lost himself inside her once again. And they were off and at it.

Fucking busywork. Once away from the direct effects of Oleg's intimidation, Dmitri's anger bubbled up, almost boiling him alive. It was humiliating, driving around to look for Sasha's stupid car. His uncle just wanted an excuse to put his execution plan into action.

It had been two hours since Fay Siebring had seen Sasha drive away. He could be on the Jersey Turnpike, in upstate New York, Pennsylvania, Connecticut. Flip a coin, pick a direction. Flip a thousand coins. Never more than now had he wished for long-range talent. And he'd peaked, too. Already starting the long, sad tail. Turning back into a paper man.

Fuck this. Dmitri jerked the car around in an abrupt U-turn. His thigh throbbed as the tires bumped over the median. He headed back the way he came, fumbling for his pills. He might have a short-range talent, but no one knew Sasha's vibe better than Dmitri. It had grated on him for his entire fucking childhood.

If anyone could sniff out that arrogant bastard it was Dmitri.

By the time he got back to the hospice, the dose had kicked in. He was himself again. His true self, three-dimensional, rounded out. Hot, hungry, and brilliant. He parked next to the bus stop where Fay Siebring claimed to have seen his cousin with that woman on his lap, and stared at it, thinking about Sasha. Getting into his cousin's head.

The way his cousin hated his family, he'd have settled as far from them as he could. And he wouldn't plan to linger. He'd want to be here and gone. Chances were, he'd been traveling all day, from someplace far. He had the woman, too. If she'd been traveling with him, she'd be tired, whining for some place to rest. She'd sat on his lap. Women sat on men's laps to make their dicks hard. It worked for Dmitri, so he expected it would for Sasha, too. The girls had always liked Sasha.

So. A woman sits on Sasha's lap. Next logical step, find a bed to fuck her in. Conclusion: Forget the turnpike, upstate New York, and Pennsylvania. Sasha was nearby, in a hotel, in a bed.

Dmitri cruised the parking lots of eight hotels on the strip before he found Sasha's black Toyota Yaris in a hotel lot in Canarsie.

He parked opposite it, and just sat there for a good ten minutes, astonished that Sasha hadn't second-guessed him. His cousin had done the dumb, predictable thing. He was no paragon of brains and cunning. He was just another asshole. Easy to herd.

Dmitri could take him now. It was all different now.

His first impulse was to call Oleg, bleat the happy news. But when he pulled Oleg's number up, his finger hovered over "call."

His success wouldn't matter to Oleg, not set against years of failures. The old man would still despise him. And now Sasha would be there, in Dmitri's face. Inviting comparison.

He needed to find a way to turn this to his favor. He strode through the lobby, took the elevator to the top floor, and started strolling the corridors, burning hot with psi-max. He was so excited, it extended his range by a good two yards. He was usually good up to about twelve to fifteen feet, but tonight he was having no problem reaching across the bathrooms to the beds beyond. Touching sleepers' minds with a feeler. Most slept, at that hour. Some watched television.

He could tell none were Sasha without breaking stride. His feeler was a long, extended tongue. He dipped it in, tasted them. Sipping the meaningless drivel of people's dreams, spitting them out, moving on.

He hit gold on the second floor, the door next to the stairwell. That time, he flicked out his tongue, touched a dreaming mind . . .

And saw Aunt Tonya.

She was smiling. Not the sad-eyed, shuffling skeleton she'd been when last he'd ignored her at some gathering or other at Oleg's house. She was younger, dark hair barely streaked with gray. Taller, with dark, mysterious eyes. She pointed at a star. Dmitri had never seen colors like that sky. Cobalt blue, so bright it made something ache inside him.

"That will be our star." Tonya's voice was tender. "See it?"

He'd seen stars. He didn't understand why this one should make his pulse race like his heart was trying to break out of a cage.

Then, suddenly, Aunt Tonya's face changed. Her eyes refocused, grew cold and hard. She made a sharp warding gesture. "You don't belong here! You were not invited! Be off with you! Scat!"

He was flung out of the dream, so hard he stumbled back, making a muffled thud against the opposite wall, like a cat kicked out the door.

Sasha had thrown him out. Tonya had warned him, from the inside. Bitch. He'd never liked that woman.

Having found his cousin, it was just prurient curiosity, but he tasted the woman, too, just to see what type of female turned his cousin on. And if she did the same for him. He touched her with the dream-tongue, and flinched back. Her dream was darker, nastier. She was curled into a box, as small as she could make herself. A man raged in the room outside the box. Glass broke, thuds, things falling. A woman screamed. There was the sound of blows, cries of pain.

The sides of the box pressed her inward, like the machines that squeeze cars into a cube. *Nobody here. Nobody here. Nothing but air. Nothing but air.* Silence, immense quiet, like a smothering blanket—

Ke-rack, the top of the box was ripped off, and he stared up, blinking, into a reddened, empurpled face. "Quiet girl," the goblin said. "All women are pretty, with duct tape on their mouths."

Dmitri recoiled, and just gasped against the wall, for a full five minutes before the true meaning sank in.

That had been him. Himself, but uglier. Those were his words.

It was *her,* in there! The quiet girl! Naked and lying next to Sasha!

His mind reeled. His cousin was fucking Nina Christie! Sasha must know about psi-max. He was probably on it. He wanted more. He wanted the new formula. It was Sasha who had saved her today, Sasha who had killed Mikhail and Ivan, Sasha who had shot at him, wrecked his car. So typical. As soon as Dmitri found something that would put him ahead of the pack, Sasha came along to try to take it from him.

But not this time. The psi-max itself wanted to be his.

He walked down the stairs and out, euphoric. Didn't see a thing until the gun barrel was jammed into the nape of his neck.

"In you go, big boy," a female voice taunted. "We need to talk."

A door on a big SUV slid open, and he was shoved inside.

Anabel used the gun barrel to prod Dmitri Arbatov into the back of the SUV. "Hands out where I can see them."

"What the fuck is this? I did what you asked me to do! And more!"

"I just bet you did." She followed him in, jabbing with the gun. "A lot more."

The tab of psi-max that Anabel had taken on the way over had finally kicked in, and that was good, because her head was so not in the game tonight. Kasyanov's rotting corpse trick had thrown her off her stride. She couldn't stop shivering, reaching to touch her own live skin, shuddering at the memories of maggots, stench, rot.

With Kasyanov dead now, there was no one left to punish. Faithful old Roy was always good for a few kicks to the head, but his reactions were on par with a cinderblock's. After a few years hanging out with Harold Rudd, Roy was just too damned accustomed to pain.

But this Arbatov guy, hmm. Big, strong, not bad looking. He might be different. She liked to surprise them. Make them squeal.

She shrugged her leather jacket open, to show off her tits. Arbatov's eyes were drawn down instantly. She wagged her gun at him.

"You boys were bad today," she said. "Bad enough that you went to Yuri's house without me. But going to Nina Christie's, too?"

"We didn't need you," Roy repeated, sick to death of the scolding she'd been flogging him with for over an hour. "One fucking telepath is enough to deal with at one time."

"Ah, ah, ah!" She waved the gun again. "You know how I hate being sidelined. Thank God you two didn't manage to kill her, considering that Kasyanov bit the big one today. She's our last link."

"You were busy humping the senator. We couldn't wait around for your legs to close." Roy gestured at Arbatov. "And since he was the one who probed Yuri, it made sense for him to be the one to come."

"Yes," Anabel said sweetly. "And just look how that turned out. I'm surprised the boss hasn't asked me to put you down."

Roy's face was beet-colored. "He needs me," he insisted.

She rolled her eyes. "You just keep telling yourself that, honey."

"Humping what senator?" Dmitri asked.

Anabel leveled her gun at him. "Did I tell you to speak, pig?"

His leer faded as she probed at his mind . . . and found it blocked. A good block, too. Seamless and tough, like a walnut. Roy said the guy had first-dosed just over a year ago. Most new ones learned blocking techniques by that time. Nothing she couldn't get through, of course. No one could keep her out for long. And to think Roy preferred to team up with this mafiya swine rather than her. She ran over his block, as if she were palpating a guy's bicep. "Got something to hide from me, Arbatov?"

He eyed the gun, then her tits, in the low-cut, black, stretch-velvet minidress she had elected to wear. "No."

"Then why this big wall?" she murmured. "You're, like, stainless steel, Dmitri. You're so . . . *hard* . . . in there."

Arbatov licked his lips. "Standard operating procedure. Like keeping your pants zipped up."

Oh, dear. Sometimes men made it so easy, she was almost sorry for them."Well, Dmitri. There are times to zip, and times to unzip. What kind of time do you think this is?"

His mouth worked as she maneuvered herself up onto her knees, and swung her leg over his. Showing off gartered black lace hose . . . and no panties. She started to sparkle. She couldn't resist. The looks on mens' faces were her reward, that fog of mindless hunger. Dog-like worship. The sweat, beading on their brows. The bulge down below.

Roy groaned. "Anabel, for fuck's sake—"

"Sssst!" She braced herself with her gun hand, and shimmied until the stretchy velvet skirt rucked up, and Arbatov could see her neatly trimmed, silky, dark blond muff, swaying over his groin.

"At least point the fucking gun away from me," Roy growled.

Fair enough. She rested her gun hand on Arbatov's shoulder, so that the barrel pointed toward his head instead, but he didn't notice. He was in thrall, gasping for breath, fumbling desperately at his crotch. She cooed her appreciation when he finally managed to whip out his tool, gripping it at the base with his hand, offering it to her.

She squeezed it, leaning the gun against his shoulder. He glanced down at it, his face shiny. "Uh, are you going to put that gun down?"

She smiled brilliantly. "No."

He whimpered, but offered no protest. To his credit, his cock stayed hard. He was beyond speech, but it wasn't words she wanted. Sounds magnified in the dark interior. Shifting seat cushions, the creak of leather, Arbatov's rapid panting. She swayed over him, kissing his tip with her labia. Teasing brushstrokes of lube, like she was dabbing at the canvas of a painting. Roy tapped at the steering wheel with the butt of his gun, bored and uncomfortable. Poor Roy.

Arbatov made the mistake of thrusting his hips up, and found the gun jammed beneath his jaw. "Ah, ah," she whispered. "Be good."

"Oh, God," he whispered.

No, Goddess, she almost said, but it was redundant. Her divinity was reflected in his eyes. She saw herself as they saw her when she sparkled. Imbued with perfection. Shining, perilous, glorious. She undulated, coordinating the brushstrokes of her snatch with mental brushstrokes against that tough shield. Brushing, flicking. Weaving over him, back flexed, hair tossing, until veins popped on his forehead.

She gripped his shaft to guide him, as she sucked his cock inside, and felt his shield falter, crack . . .

She sank in her claws. He cried out, startled. Too late. Once she was in, she was in. No one had ever been able to dislodge her.

Except for Nina Christie, that morning. And Kasyanov.

She shoved the thought away and rifled through the contents of Arbatov's mind, made her discoveries, drew her conclusions, in a few breathless, panting seconds. She processed information very quickly. She also discovered that the contents of his mind repulsed her.

Once she had what she wanted, she was instantly annoyed with the stiff rod poking her from below. The man's grunting and heaving disgusted her now. She slid off and shoved the gun under his chin.

"You've been holding out on us." She flung a triumphant glance at Roy. "He found her cell phone, and did not tell us! Can you imagine?"

Dmitri reached, trying to pull her back down. "Please," he begged.

"No!" She swatted him away. "Jerk it off yourself!"

"Not in the car, he won't." Roy pinned the guy with a cold gaze.

"And they're here," Anabel said. "Right here, in this hotel. Isn't that just sweet, Roy? That they're curled up naked in bed together? When do you suppose Dmitri would have told us?"

"You fucking sewer rat," Roy snarled.

"Oh, but it gets better," Anabel bubbled on. "His plan was to get Kasyanov's last dose of the super psi-max . . . and take it himself, and fuck all the rest of us!" She waved her pistol. "But that's not the kicker. That guy who mowed you assholes down like grass? He's Arbatov's *cousin!* What do you make of that, Roy? Do you smell a conspiracy?"

Roy lunged between the seats, and pinned Dmitri against the backrest, the gun digging into his throat. "Cousin, huh? The whole thing was a setup, right? You son of a bitch. You told him about the drug, right? You had a thing going behind my back?"

"I didn't! I haven't seen that asshole for twenty years! He's been in hiding! He came now because of . . ." He choked, against the pressure of the gun barrel. "Aunt Tonya," he coughed. "In the hospice. Dying."

Roy glanced at Anabel, and she gave him a nod. "True,"

she said. "I felt the surprise. This is fresh. He just found out, right before we got here. The aunt, that's true too. Cancer. Poignant, isn't it?"

Anabel leaned closer to Dmitri. "Sasha, hmm?" she taunted. "The cousin you love to hate. So tall. So handsome. So smart. Oleg's favorite. I'm wasting my time riding you. I should go upstairs, and mount up onto that big, hot cousin. Is his dick bigger than yours, Dmitri?"

Dmitri stared at her, stark loathing in his eyes. "Shut up, whore."

Roy dug the gun in. "How shall we kill this douche bag?"

She shrugged. "Quickly. I want to meet Sasha. He's the one who's got the goods. Give me the phone, Dmitri." She waited a moment, and pressed the gun barrel up beneath his ear. "The phone. Now."

"My uncle took it," he muttered, sullen.

Anabel exchanged disgusted glances with Roy. "Oh, for God's sake. Where do you keep your psi-max? I don't want to have to grub on your corpse for it, and it's too precious to waste. Roy, take it from him."

She held the gun under his chin while Roy groped roughly on the guy's chest. He found his pillbox, ripped Dmitri's shirt, yanking it out.

"Good," she purred. She rummaged in her purse, took out a syringe with untraceable poison she'd prepared, and plunged the clear liquid to the top. They all watched a drop swell and quiver on the needle tip, lit up like a gem by the light that came from the stairwell door.

"Night night, Dmitri," she said softly. "It's been real."

"No! Wait!" he shouted. "You don't know Sasha! You'll need help to take him! You saw what he did at Nina's house, remember?" He turned to Roy. "I can help you when he comes!"

"I don't think we need your help, Dmitri," she told him.

"I can make it so you don't have to deal with him at all! Those two walk out in the morning, I take Sasha off your hands, and there's your girl, swinging in the wind, all alone. You won't even have to deal with a body, because I'll take him away with me! No muss, no fuss!"

Anabel exchanged dubious glances with Roy.

"Plus, I listened to the recording Kasyanov left, and it's all in Ukrainian. You need me to tell you what was in it! She talks about Joseph. I had my hackers check. It's Kirk, her ex-husband! He must know about the drug, because she mentions him twice, so she must have sent—"

"We'll take care of Kirk," Anabel said. "Don't trouble yourself."

"I have men, in Portland! It's an hour's drive to Kirk's from Portland! I could have men there in an hour! We could have answers *tonight!*"

Roy shrugged. It was true that they didn't have enough personnel to man a complicated job like this. And no one wanted to tell Rudd that.

"What do you want in exchange?" Anabel asked.

Dmitri gulped. "A hundred tabs."

Anabel and Roy burst out laughing. "How about your life?" she said. "And if all goes well, we give you back these." She rattled the pillbox she had taken from him.

"But I need more. . . ." His words trailed off, swallowed. "I'll need one for tomorrow. When they come out."

"I don't think it's necessary. Too many telepaths only fuck things up. But here. If you must." She shook out one, and tossed it on the floor of the car. He dove, pants still undone, to scrabble for it.

"Where is his room?" she asked. "And his vehicle?"

"Room twenty sixty," he said. "It looks out over this parking lot. This is the car, right next to you. Remember. Sasha belongs to me."

Anabel shook his pills. "Don't get grabby. It'll have to be slick, quiet. We don't want noise, police, nothing. No messes."

"We can plan it now," Dmitri said eagerly. "Right now."

Anabel looked at his unzipped pants, his unquenched erection. "Go wait in your own car. We'll plan this, Dmitri. You follow orders. Get out of here. Now. You smell like blood. It makes me queasy."

Dmitri got out, muttering. They watched him limp back to his car. Anabel noticed Roy staring at her. "What?" she snapped.

He gestured toward her crotch. "Pull the skirt down."

Anabel laughed as she wiggled the tight skirt down over her bare ass. "What, Roy? Jealous?" she crooned. "Want a piece of candy?"

"Anytime, anywhere," he replied, hoarsely. "But you're such a bitch. You'd never give it up to me, would you?"

"Hmm," she murmured, tugging up her stocking. "No, I don't think so. You're a hound dog, Roy. And bestiality just isn't my thing."

"Come on," he said. "You'd do dogs. You'd do anyone."

She thought of that helpless, dazzled look of adoration her lovers gave her when she sparkled, and blew him a kiss.

"No, Roy," she said. "Dogs don't have anything I want."

16

It was the dark cavern again. The chill air clung to his clammy skin, heavy and unwholesome. The cavern extended into the dark, with many dark nooks in which anything could be lurking.

In the middle of the chamber lay a girl, dressed in a wet, dirty nightgown. Julie. She lay on her side on the jagged rocky floor, as if her body had been dumped there.

He knelt. She was dead, of course. Her face was gray, tinged with green. Her long dark hair was tangled with seaweed. Her blind, open eyes were full of silent accusation. Eternally asking the same question.

Why didn't you save me?

He woke with a jolt, and found his limbs tangled with Nina's. Her hair draped his chest, tickling his jaw. Her weight pinned down his gun arm.

Two things happened. His cock hardened, and his stomach dropped. Like a rock lobbed over a freeway overpass, about to crash into a windshield and cause a twenty-car pileup. This scenario was exactly that bad, that stupid. What the *fuck* had he been thinking?

Alarm pulsated like a strobe light, jangling his brain. He tried moving slowly, but he was tangled up in all that curly hair, terrified of waking her. *Danger.* It was all around. He felt it, smelled it, tasted it. He'd always had an instinct for it, but danger had always threatened from the outside. Guns, knives, grenades, bombs. Not his own gut-twisting issues with sex and intimacy. He couldn't tell them apart. Fear was fear. Who knew what this red alert was about? No one could have found them. No one could have connected this hotel to them. Except from the hospice. But he would have noticed if they'd been followed.

Or would he? He thought of the shell-shocked state he'd been in when they left. Nina had practically been carrying him.

She felt his tension and stirred in his arms. He angled himself so that she slid off his plank-stiff body and thudded onto the sheets.

She rubbed sleep from her eyes and hoisted herself up onto her elbow, lush breasts dangling. Her puzzled, misty gaze took on focus, and started looking worried.

Yeah. As well she might. They stared at each other. His stomach kept plummeting while pressure built inside him, like steam.

"Wow," she murmured. "Eight thirty. I can't believe it's so late."

"You slept like a rock," he said. As if he hadn't, too. He should have stayed awake. But no, he'd forgotten about the mortal danger and conked out into a postcoital haze after the three-hour fuck fest.

Dickheaded self-indulgence. Selfish, brain-dead asshole. He deserved to get bombed into a thirty-meter crater for being so sloppy. He wished there were two of him so he could kick his own ass.

"Looks that way," she said cautiously, wary of his steel-cable tension. "Um. Aaro. Are you, uh, OK?"

"You told me you couldn't sleep." The words blasted out like an accusation. "You said you could only sleep if you had a hiding place."

This hung in the air. She finally spoke. "I guess you were my hiding place last night."

Her tone was gentle, but he still recoiled. "Don't lay that on me," he said. "I can't carry it. I can't be that for you."

He felt her hurt vibing against his back in the appalled silence.

"I'm not laying anything on you," she said. "I was just saying."

He shook his head, and declined to reply, or to look at her.

"So," she said, after moment. "It's like that, is it?"

Yeah, it was exactly like that, and too fucking bad. Welcome to cold, hard reality. He'd warned her. She'd practially signed a waiver. He had never misrepresented what he had to offer on a personal level.

Which was exactly nothing.

He got busy with the coffeemaker, just to do something with his hands. Hoping she'd just chalk one up for experience, and they could get through the morning without any more misunderstandings.

She went into the bathroom. The shower started to hiss, but not for long. He could tell by the look on her face when she came out, wrapped in a towel, that she'd been working up a rant. She groped for her clothing. "This sounds like my cue to grab my clothes and split."

"If you want to die young, sure."

She tried to cover herself, but the towel wasn't up to the task. It took a better class of hotel to get towels big enough to wrap all the way around ta-tas that luscious. Her glance fell to his crotch, skittered nervously away. He glanced down at his massive hard-on. Let out a harsh laugh. "Take a look at the circus sideshow act. Sad, isn't it?"

Her chin went up a notch. "It didn't have to be."

"No?" He grabbed his cock, massaged it with a rough hand. "So you'd service me again? Great. Get over here, lose the towel, bend over."

"Why are you doing this?" Her voice shook. "Do you suffer from some rare mental illness? Why do you have to be so ugly?"

"It's my nature," he replied. "I'm hardwired that way. I warned you last night about that, Nina. Repeatedly."

"Oh, shut up!" she snapped. "I am so sick of your bullshit."

There was a tune he'd heard before. "Of course you are," he said. "It happened even faster than I thought it would."

"What?" she yelled. "What's happened? Other than you freaking out on me, and acting like a spoiled child?"

He gestured at the space between them. "You, hating my guts. You were halfway there yesterday, more than once. The only thing that kept you from going all the way is because you wanted me to fuck you."

She was so angry, her tits slipped out of the towel and she didn't even notice. "You arrogant son of a bitch," she breathed out.

"Yeah, yeah. And now you're all confused, because I'm not following the pretty script in your head."

Her mouth flapped in outrage. "What? I don't have any script!"

"Sure you do. You can't help it any more than I can help being an asshole. But I'm not going to play nice. Get it through your head."

She drew herself up, fiercely dignified. "It's through my head. You can stop hammering it in now."

He was breathing hard. "Good," he said. "That's good."

They stared at each other for a moment, but the horned berserker that had taken over his body wasn't done hacking and rending yet.

"So," he said. "Do you still want it?"

Her eyes narrowed. "Want what?"

He gestured at his cock, still cluelessly begging for action. "This."

She stared at him, mouth hanging open. "You just can't stop pushing, can you?" she asked, in a wondering tone. "You have to push us all the way off the cliff, no matter what. You just can't stop."

"I could make you come again before we hit the rocks," he offered.

"News flash, Aaro. We've hit the rocks already," she informed him. "We're splattered all over the place down there."

"Oh, no," he assured her. "You have no idea. There is so, so much farther yet that we can fall."

She clapped her hands over her mouth, and for a second, he was afraid she was going to burst into tears.

It was with huge chagrin that he realized she wasn't crying. She was laughing. At him. He stared at her, unsure if this was a worse state of affairs, or better. "Yeah," he said, through his teeth. "Yeah, go for it. I know I'm just a big laugh riot."

"You're ridiculous, Aaro," she told him. "And I am still not fooled."

"You're superimposing dumb girl fantasies over everything I say. I'm trying to be straight with you. That's all I've got to offer."

She gave him a cautious nod, her lip trapped between her teeth.

"I will be straight with you," he went on. "And I'll try to keep you alive. And I will fuck you properly. If you want me to. That's it."

"Hold on." Her eyebrow twitched up. "That's three things."

His brain wouldn't process that, being starved of the oxygen-bearing red blood cells which had all defected to his crotch. "Huh?"

"First you say it's only one thing you have to offer. All of a sudden, it's three. Watch out, Aaro. Before you know it, you're going to start opening doors for me. Flowers, chocolates, champagne . . ."

"You're doing it again," he growled. "Stop that shit, Nina."

"And you're panicking. Chill, Aaro."

Her lips were still twitching. So he was an object of amusement to her now. He was that desperate, that pathetic. That transparent.

He should say something vicious, to drive the nails deeper into the coffin. But he couldn't. Nothing was coming to him. Not while she looked at him with that hot glow in her eyes. His cock throbbed with each heartbeat. They stared at each other, tension tightening. That high-pitched hum of sex about to happen. Amazing, juicy, improbable sex.

If he didn't kill it, right now. He could. But God, he did not want to. He opened his mouth. A croak came out. He coughed. "No promises."

She wrinkled her nose. "Not even common courtesy?"

"Right," he said, and the part of him that just could not shut the fuck up kept on blathering. "Here's a tip, to put you on the right track."

"This is sure to be fascinating," she said. "Enlighten me."

His eyes dropped to her muff. Fuzzy ringlets that hid juicy, pink, folded secrets. "Shut me up," he told her. "The sooner my mouth has a job to do, the sooner I'll stop shooting it off."

"Ah," she murmured. "You mean, um . . . ?"

"Stop playing coy." It burst out of him, steam blasting out of a valve. "Get over here and sit on my face."

"Stop it." Nina's voice rang out imperiously. "Don't say another ugly, vulgar, hurtful word, Aaro. Just shut . . . *up*."

His chest heaved, painfully. "Make me."

Make me.

The words rang, flung down, like a gauntlet. His tone was pure taunting provocation, but after yesterday, her reality had split. There was the old reality, which had become transparent, and the new one, the real one, shining underneath. She heard things, saw things, knew things she'd never known before. With her new ears, she heard very clearly that his words were not a taunt.

They were a plea.

She'd felt it last night, too, but today the sensation was stronger. He was trapped behind a booby-trapped, land-mined fence, strung with razor wire, desperate and alone. If she had half a brain, she'd leave him there, write him off as more trouble than he was worth. He didn't expect her to do otherwise. No sane, self-respecting woman would put up with the shit he dished out. That was the point. He did it on purpose. It was his automatic security system, functioning exactly as programmed.

And she saw right through it.

The feeling was seductive. She felt flooded with energy, bright and hot. She tingled and glowed. Fearless. Inspired. She followed the inner prompting, let the towel drop to the floor, let her spine stretch up to maximum height and then a little more. Shoulders expanded. Hair, tossed luxuriously back. Boobs, tilted provocatively up.

He opened his mouth. "Don't start to—"

"Shut up." The punch of power behind her words startled him.

His chest jerked, with ironic laughter, but he did not

speak. He just swallowed hard, staring hungrily as she came closer.

Every step she took, the glow of power got hotter, stronger. When she was inches from his body, the buzz of his aura electrified her. Her nipples hardened, her hairs rose up, her lungs hitched.

She didn't touch him, just let the charge build as she looked him over. Reached out, boldly stroking the angles and dips and bulges. Not a pinch of fat on the guy. All lean, taut, sinewy. No soft spots, inside or out. She dragged her fingernails in his chest hair. His nipples were as hard as little rocks. The arrangement of the muscles and tendons in his throat was a marvel of human physiology. She wanted to sink her teeth into his deltoids. And his ass, oh. She'd never been the ribald, ass-ogling type, but there was always a first time. And as for his manly member, ah. She wanted to make him gasp, sigh. To knock that frozen look off his face. To make him relax. Trust her.

Talk about the impossible dream.

But now, he needed something else, something so hard to grasp, she had to feel her way toward it . . . or she'd blunder right past it.

"You know what I think?" she said, her voice throaty and low. "I think you're sorry Bruno's bodyguard is on his way. I think you're going to miss me." She gripped his cock. "I'm sure this fellow will."

"Nina," he began, in a tight, warning tone. "I can't—"

"Shut up." She put her finger on his lips. "Didn't you hear me the first two times?"

His lips twitched under her finger. His lips were so soft, so warm. She had to stay on top of this. She channeled all the most regal queens and empresses of history. "I did not give you permission to speak."

She felt his teeth beneath her finger as his grin flashed. "You're getting off on this," he said softly. "Check you out."

"Shut up," she snapped. "You're breaking the rules."

"There's rules now? Since when?"

Since you begged me for them, lout. "Shhhh." She swatted his chest, and put her hands on his big shoulders—and pushed down.

His eyes widened, startled, but he sank to his knees, fascinated.

She grabbed his hair, pulled his face back, and perched a leg up on the bed, waving her muff inches in front of his delighted face. "This is the part where you make up for every rude, nasty, unnecessary thing that you just said to me. Make me forgive you."

His eyes lit up. Seized her hips in his big hands, and put his mouth to her without an instant's hesitation.

It took her about three seconds to realize that she was in big, *big* trouble. It was so good. Amazingly good. She clutched his head, fingers tangled in his hair, shaking and wobbling on one unsteady leg, the other cocked high on the bed, with that luscious candy-swirl of pleasure undoing her from her core. He licked and delved and probed, and thrust two fingers up to his knuckle, curving them and petting her inside.

She teetered, stuck on the caressing prong of his fingers, legs shaking so hard she was sure she'd topple. Sore from the night's marvelous excesses, but still going off in delicious little explosions. She was about to fall, but to stop him, to ask for quarter in any way would wreck her upper hand, and he needed her to be strong for him.

She didn't pretend to understand it. She was improvising, but he was melting her down, and the ache swelled bigger, brighter—

It bloomed, and spread out toward infinity in great, pulsing, black and red and rainbow-spangled waves, and she lost herself with it.

She may have toppled, or flopped on top of him, or fainted dead away. But when she came back to herself, they were kneeling, facing each other, and Aaro held her. Or she'd have been a heap on the carpet.

Her eyes fluttered open. He was smoothing strands of sweaty hair off her face. His eyes swam into focus. His grin carved deep grooves into his lean cheeks, made his eye crinkles fan out. He was so gorgeous, her breath stuck halfway inside and just sat there, like a rock.

"Can I use my mouth again?" he asked.

After an embarrassingly long interval, she found the power of speech again. "Only to kiss me."

His kiss broke her heart. His demanding hunger, her frantic surrender. No controlling him now, not a chance. He tossed her onto the bed, opened a condom, and rolled it on one handed. Mounted her, never ceding for a moment in his devouring kiss. He slid his cockhead against her slick folds and stared into her eyes. Every slow increment of his penetration, she felt a deeper claiming. After all his trash talk, how desperately he tried to distance himself from her.

He couldn't. Not against this. Neither of them could.

She felt devoured. She loved surrendering to his worshipful skill. She whimpered and gave in to the luscious slide and thud of his big body, forcing her into another wrenching climax. She arched, sobbed. He stifled a shout. They clutched each other.

Aaro finally rolled onto his back, but kept her clamped against him. She ended up on top, thighs twined around his. His half-hard cock still clasped inside her. He wound his fingers into her damp hair, and gently lifted her head. "I didn't ask, this time," he said, frowning.

She gave him a lazy, sated smile. "You sure didn't. You trashed my dominatrix fantasy, throwing your weight around like that."

He did not relax. "Is it OK?" he persisted. "You're OK?"

She folded her arms over his chest and propped her chin

on them. "Let's put aside your annoying habit of fishing for compliments, and address the more burning question."

He looked spooked. "And that is?"

She toyed with his chest hair. "Did you get your ya-ya's out?" she asked. "Have you calmed down? Can we talk rationally?"

His mouth tightened. "You fucked me just to calm me down?"

She jerked up onto her elbows. "Don't start, Aaro. I'm warning you. Do not even start. Behave. Or else."

"Or what?" A wary smile twitched the corners of his mouth. "Or you'll sit on my face again?"

"Whatever I have to do." She tried to sound stern.

"As a deterrent, it's not real effective," he said. "My mouth waters just thinking about it. You'd have to kick me away and handcuff me to the radiator to make me stop." His cock swelled inside her with those words. She clenched around him, the small muscles inside fluttering.

"Would you kick me away, Nina?" he murmured. "Cruel goddess."

She moved over him, gasping. Ready again, so soon? They were so wet and slick from her lube, the slide of his cock inside her was a long, tender, liquid kiss inside of her, pulsing tenderly.

"Do you always wake up in such a bad mood?" she asked.

"Mostly," he said. "It's better now. I don't usually inflict my shitty morning mood on another person. I make a point of being alone."

"You never have girlfriends stay the night?"

He shook his head.

She pushed herself upright, which only served to emphasize the fact that he was still wedged inside of her. And that, in spite of their charged conversation, he was fully erect. His heartbeat throbbed inside her. Their eyes locked. He grabbed her waist, lifting her up to give himself room for a longer stroke. Slid his shaft halfway out. Let her sink slowly, deliciously back down. Pulsing, wiggling.

"Do you ever get tired?" she demanded, breathless.

"Not of you."

She harrumphed. "If you're trying to distract me, it's not going to work," she informed him.

"But that's what you just did to me," he pointed out. "It worked, too. And it's an infinitely repeatable solution. Yum. Cool."

"It's not the same thing," she said sternly. "I was distracting you from your catastrophically bad attitude. I think we should talk."

"About my bad attitude? Fuck, no. Let's not and say we did." He circled her clit with his thumb. "This is way better."

She laughed. "You actually think we can avoid all awkward conversations indefinitely by distracting ourselves with sex?"

"Worth a try, isn't it? Who knows how long we could spin it out?"

A lifetime? She tried to erase the thought, it being inappropriate and impossible. She pushed his chest. "I'm a little sore," she whispered.

He drew away instantly, pulling out of her. "Sorry. I overdid it."

"It's OK," she murmured, curling her legs beneath her on the bed. "You look scared," she blurted.

His gaze slid away. "Shitless," he admitted, after a moment.

"Why? What's so scary about me? I'm so goddamn harmless!"

"Harmless?" His voice was heavy with irony. "My ass." He still avoided her gaze. "I don't want to hurt you," he muttered finally.

"Then don't," she said.

He rolled over, hiding his face. She tried to coax him back, but he wouldn't budge. After a few moments of that, she realized he was right.

It wasn't that simple. It should be, but it wasn't. She was torturing the guy needlessly, asking for things he just didn't have to give.

Oh, the hell with it. She draped herself over him, covering him with her body, her hair. Trying to memorize the shape of his big body.

She slid off when he started to fidget. "What now?" she asked.

He rolled onto his side. "What we've been doing," he said. "I try to keep you alive. You try to tolerate me."

"There's only so much I can tolerate," she said.

His face was sullen and guarded. "I know."

"You know you can't throw fits like that, right?" she pressed. "We got through it this time, but it's not something I can tolerate again."

He nodded.

"So you'll be good?" she persisted.

"No promises."

For God's sake. Defending his right to be a jerk. She sighed. For some reason, it seemed important to convince him of this one, small thing. "I'm not asking for promises," she said, an edge in her voice. "I just want you to try to behave. I won't be here much longer, so it's not even that big of a deal. Will you just *try* to be good?"

It sounded like he was coughing up rocks. "I'll try."

That was it. The best she was going to pry out of him. A reluctant promise to try not to be horrible. She was such an idiot. She headed into the bathroom. Barely recognizing the woman in the mirror. Cherry red, puffy lips, eyes dilated, hair big and crazy mussed.

Of course, the guy was gorgeous, and a god in bed. He'd saved her life, and then screwed her brains out all night long.

There would have to be something wrong with her if she hadn't gotten a huge crush on him.

There were plenty of things wrong with her already, of course, but she'd never thought that wanting impossible things from inappropriate men was high on her list of personality flaws.

Tears pricked her eyes. Absurd, to get all emotional over him, the way he held himself back from her. She set about washing off the latest evidence of her poor judgment, lecturing herself in the toughest possible terms. Whoop-de-fucking-do, Aaro promised to try not to be mean and horrible to her for the next hour. What a prince of a guy.

Give him a freaking medal, why didn't she.

17

*B*e good. Tough directive. Hard to define. All the different things it could mean. He avoided ambiguity whenever possible. He kept things simple. Binary-code-type simple. Black or white. Dots or dashes. True or false. One or zero.

Never two.

When Nina came out of the bathroom, he grabbed his cell, desperate for something to distract him from the promise he'd just made. He didn't know if he could follow through on it. Had no evidence to suggest that he could, and a lot that would indicate that he couldn't. It made him frantic. It was so fucked up. So stupid.

"Who are you calling?" Nina asked.

"Miles," he said.

Her eyebrows went up. "It's barely six in the morning there."

"I pay him enough to call at three A.M." It began to ring. "And he's not asleep. Miles never sleeps when he goes into computer world."

Miles picked up. "Hey," he said. "Found out stuff. Weird stuff."

"Why am I not surprised," Aaro said.

"I did my best to filter out the guy's voice on the file. I'm sending the scrubbed file to your phone right now."

"Good," Aaro said. "And the rest?"

"Could you put that on speakerphone?" Nina's voice had that whip-snapping bite to it. He kind of liked it. He clicked on the speaker.

"First off, Kasyanov is supposed to be dead," Miles announced, on the speakerphone. "She died three years ago. A fire at the Morgensen Memorial Research Center, outside Spokane. A guy named Joseph Kirk was married to her in the eighties. He met her in some think tank. They had a daughter, in 1986. It says here, 'survived by a daughter, Lara Kirk.' She attended the San Francisco School of Fine Arts. Up-and-coming sculptor. Galleries were taking notice, collectors snapping up early works. Until she disappeared."

"Let me guess. Four months ago? Right?"

"Uh, yeah. She's a missing person now. I have the number of the detective handling her case. Haven't called him yet. Too early."

"Forward it to me," Aaro directed. "Where's Joseph Kirk located?"

"He's the head of the science department of a small liberal arts school, Wentworth College. About an hour from Portland."

"You haven't talked to him yet?"

"It is six A.M. Some people actually do sleep, you know."

"Call me when you find out more." He hung up, and noticed Nina gazing at him, her face perplexed. "What?" he demanded.

"Why did you ask him to call you?" she asked. "The bodyguard will be here soon. He should call Bruno with new info. Or me."

Who knew why? Why the fuck did anyone do anything?

It was a valid question, but it made him feel pushed away, and pissed off.

"You don't have to pretend it's your problem anymore," she said gently. "You're excused. You've done your part. You did it wonderfully."

Excused, his ass. "I'm not pretending anything," he muttered.

Nina stared down at her clasped hands. "So she died, in a fire three years ago? That fits with what Helga said. That the guy had imprisoned her, forced her to produce this drug for him. Poor Helga."

"You feel sorry for her, after what she did to you?"

Nina shook her head, picked up the room phone.

"Who the hell are you calling?" he demanded.

"The hospital," she replied. "Maybe Helga woke up. Even if she still can't speak English, she could talk directly to you."

He sat and watched as she went through the process of getting through the hospital switchboard. She kept her voice pleasant, despite being put on hold, over and over. "Yes, I was calling to check the status of a patient, Helga Kasyanov," she said. "She's my aunt. Is she . . ."

Her face went pale and hard. "I see," she said tonelessly. "Thank you very much." She set the phone delicately back into the cradle. "She died." Her voice cracked. "Yesterday."

Oh. Well, fuck. He let out air. Not that he'd really had much hope for help from that quarter anyway. Not after listening to that file.

"So." Nina rubbed her face. "She said she was injected five days ago? It's Friday. She told me I had three days. But she lasted for five."

"If what she said was true," Aaro said.

Nina shook her head. "It was the truth. She was dying, and she knew it. She had no reason to lie."

It burned him, being handed a problem that he could not

solve. He wanted to give her something, resolve something. But he came up blank. Blowing steam out his ears. She located her clothing under the coverlet on the floor. "Don't bother putting those on," he said.

She shot him an are-you-kidding look. "Aaro, seriously—"

"I wasn't proposing more sex," he assured her. "It's just that you can't wear those again. It's too dangerous."

A knock sounded on the door. He leaped for the gun, gesturing for Nina to retreat into the bathroom. She scurried in, alarmed.

He sidled toward the door. "Who is it?"

"It's Roxanne." A bored, cigarette-roughened female voice with a strong Brooklyn accent. "From the front desk. Last night, remember? I picked up that stuff you wanted at Fausta's."

The steel bands locked around his lungs released a small notch. After the goatfuck at the hospital last year, he was wary of everything. Little old ladies, poodles, cream puffs, anything and everything that looked innocent could hide dumdum bullets in the fluff, just waiting for you to lower your guard so they could fuck you up.

"Just a minute." He yanked his jeans on, fished for his wallet, peeled two C-notes out of it, as arranged last night when he'd checked in. An expensive fee for services rendered, and he was probably being paranoid, but he did not want Nina Christie walking out of this hotel looking like the woman who had walked into it the night before.

He shoved the pistol into his jeans, and eased the door open. It was Roxanne. Chubby, bleached hair, bad perm. Not the best candidate for this errand, but if she ever got questioned, it would be long after the fact. He opened the door wider. "What have you got?"

She hoisted up a bunch of shopping bags. "What you asked for," she said. "I spent until the money was gone, like you said. You said go sexy. I did my best." She held up a smaller bag, pink and green stripes. "This is the underwear. Thirty-four D, you said." She ran an assessing eye over him. "You said size eight, right? I hope they're not for you, buddy, 'cause if they are, they're gonna be way too small."

A startled laugh snorted out before he could stop it. He took the shopping bags she held out. "Not for me," he assured her.

Roxanne scoped his bare torso for a moment, and peered into the room. He shifted to block her view. "Want me to wait while she tries 'em on?" she asked hopefully. "I could take 'em back, if they don't fit."

He just bet she would, for another two hundred dollars. "Don't worry about it," he said. "Did you get makeup and scissors?"

She passed him a bag. "Receipt's in the bag. Your change, too."

He peered inside. It looked in order. He eyeballed the clothing. The underwear one was packed with lacy, silky stuff, in bright colors. The clothing likewise. On first glance, he saw spangly denim and a froth of pink gilded ruffles. Loud, he'd told the girl. Sparkles, sequins, color. He wanted Nina to look the opposite of how she usually looked. Bright and tight, red lipstick, cat eyeliner. Tarry mascara. Big hair. Tops of her tits poking out. All dusted up with glitter powder. He could hardly wait.

He passed the money to Roxanne. "Thanks for your help."

She fingered the bills, ogled his pecs. "Anytime," she assured him. "Call me for anything. Happy to help."

He closed the door. Now came the fun part.

Nina waited until the hotel door closed. No shoot-outs. Not even any harsh words. She came out to investigate. Pink shopping bags?

"What is that stuff?" she demanded.

"Your new look." Aaro sounded pleased with himself.

He dumped clothes out onto the bed. Fluffy, glittery, shiny, clingy costume pieces. She stared at them, aghast.

"Ah, Aaro?" She gestured toward the garish tangle on the bed. "I can't wear that stuff." She lifted the skinny jeans, artistically ripped at the knees and spangled with sequins. "These are a size eight! I can't wear eight! I won't be able to breathe!"

"Sure you will. They're super low-rise. They won't be anywhere near your lungs," he informed her. "Can't wait to see them on you."

"But . . . but . . ." She stammered for a moment, and finally wailed the words. "They're not my style!"

"That's the idea." He dumped the drugstore bag, popped the haircutting scissors out of their molded plastic, and struck terror into her heart with his next words. "We'll start with the hair."

She backed up. "Get away from me."

He came on. "Into the bathroom," he said. "Less mess."

"No!" she yelled. "What part of no is so hard to understand?"

Aaro gave her the look he usually reserved for facing down armed assassins. "The part about the people trying to kill you? Those people got a long look at you! You can't walk out in that baggy frock with your hair down to your ass!"

"They won't remember me! Nobody ever remembers me! You saw that! At the hospice, remember? The taxis, on the street?"

"Yeah, and we're changing that, one hundred and eighty degrees. Because the guys trying to kill you? They saw you, Nina. Your image is firmly fixed in their long-term memory, trick or no trick. I guarantee it."

Nina's head just kept on shaking. "You are not a hair stylist! No matter what other talents you may have. You'll butcher it!"

"I didn't want to have to say this, Nina, but you leave me no choice. Am I going to have to perform cunnilingus on you again?"

She exploded in helpless giggles. Aaro wound his hand through her heavy, wet hair and lifted it, hefting its weight. "Usually, in a situation like this, I would make a woman plainer, less noticeable," he said, his voice more gentle. "This is the exception. They're already looking for someone unnoticeable. It's safer to go the other way, at least for today. I won't butcher your hair. I want you to look good."

"So I really look that bad?" she retorted crabbily.

"We're not having that conversation." He cupped her ass. "You know what I think of your looks. You can barely walk this morning. Feel this." He pressed her against the omnipresent bulge of his erection. "Do you need me to show you the depths of my appreciation again?" he whispered. "I stand ready to serve."

"No," she murmured, abashed. "Not now."

"Into the bathroom, then."

He situated her in front of the mirror. She stared at herself, her mouth flat and colorless. This was awful. She liked keeping the hair a no-brainer. A braid, a bun, a ponytail. A bad haircut could irritate her for years. Sameness and severity suited her.

But this wasn't about her looks. This was about survival. The thought was depressing. The end of her fantasy idyll was at hand, and all she had to look forward to when it was over was the ugly reality.

The danger she was in. The mystery drug in her body, Helga's unsolvable riddle. The fear, the dread, the helplessness.

Aaro used the comb he found in the bathroom toiletries

basket, and worked through her tangles with more patience than she had herself. "You've done this before?" she asked.

"I had a little sister, once," he said. "I used to help her."

A sister? She was curious, but his tone of voice didn't invite any more questions. She closed her eyes, let him have his way, and by the time he was done, it was drying, springing up into corkscrewing ringlets. He smoothed it over her shoulders, his warm fingers sending tingling sparkles over her skin before he started to cut.

She squeezed her eyes shut, wincing with each muted *snick*. He took it slow, careful and deliberate. Finally, he fluffed her hair up with his fingers. "Open your eyes."

She did so, and blinked, startled. It looked good. On top, it was shorter, different lengths that all sprang up into a playful halo. In the back it was longer, bouncing, tickling her. The longest curls brushed her shoulder blades. She switched her locks from side to side, watching them swirl and flop. Wow. It looked cute. Jaunty. And memorable.

Aaro's face was impassive, but smugness emanated from him.

"You missed your calling, Aaro," she said. "You should have been a ladies' hairdresser. Complete with the earring and the lisp."

"So if I run through all my other identities, I have another career option," was his reply. "Get dressed."

The clothes were a whole new challenge to her sensibilities. The outfit Aaro chose was a tiny microfiber pink tank, the sparkly jeans she'd objected to, and a terrifyingly brief, sheer blouse that fastened in one point over her bosom, showing loads of cleavage and an inverted vee of pale belly, framed by fluttering swags of gilded pink-and-gold ruffles. The print on the blouse was a loud swirl of butterflies, and it floated in a long, frilly tail over her ass. The skin-tight jeans actually fit—sort of. They clung to her hips, showing a terrifying expanse of hip as pale as milk, having never seen the light of day.

And the underwear, oh, God. A lacy fuchsia push-up bra, a matching thong. And the makeup. His directive was to put on ten times as much as she was comfortable with. The threat being, if he wasn't satisfied, he'd make up the difference himself. She had to go back three times to trowel on some more before he was satisfied.

He took care of the glitter spray himself, spritzing her until she coughed and choked and waved the toxic cloud away. He dusted her hair, her face, her shoulders, her boobs, and after a brief pause, her belly, too. Like she had any damn business drawing attention to it.

Aaro dragged her to the mirror and loomed over her shoulder, clutching her waist, his fingers dark against her belly. *"Mmmm."*

Nina stared at her crimson lips, her mascara-gummed lashes. "I look grotesque," she said tartly. "I look like a drag queen."

He shook his head and brought his hands up to cup her breasts, petting them in their scratchy push-up lace until her nipples tightened.

"No," he said. "Drag queens don't have this effect on me."

"You'll get glitter on your lips. And don't use your perpetual hard-on as an indicator of how good I look, you oversexed freak."

"Freak?" He peeked up from his nuzzling, aggrieved. "Me?"

"Yes, you." She gazed at herself in the mirror. Unhappily. She hated the way the clothes made her feel. For any other woman, this would be fun. Dressing up, being someone else. What was the harm?

It made her so tense, she could hardly breathe.

"I can't stand the way men will look at me," she blurted.

Aaro looked up from the nuzzling. "I know," he said. "I get that. But you're forgetting something."

"What is that?" she demanded.

"Me," he said.

She was still blank. "What do you have to do with anything?"

"It goes like this. The guys catch sight of you. They start to sweat. They look again." His predatory smile sent her hormones zinging. "Then they look at me." He nipped her shoulder, and soothed the fleeting sting with a swipe of his tongue. "And then they look away."

The focused sensuality of his mouth moving at her neck overwhelmed her, a sweet, rippling rush, oh dear God, how did he do that? Heating her up, from the inside, like a shot of magical liquor.

Fantasy bullshit. She locked her knees. "You won't be there when guys are ogling me," she said.

His hands dropped, and he stepped back. "Whatever. Put the bag back over your head when I'm gone. No one will stop you."

She made a final, desperate attempt to act like a grown-up. "Look, I'm grateful to you," she said. "You've done so much for me already. It's time for you to go concentrate on your aunt. So thanks. Really."

"I told you already," he cut in. "I don't want thanks."

"Shut up. I know you hate being thanked, and I know about the thing with Bruno, and I don't care! I'm thanking you anyway! You, yourself, Aaro! Not a middleman, got that? It's just Nina and Aaro, in the room! Me, thanking you for keeping me alive! Can you handle that?"

"What the fuck?" he asked, plaintive. "Are you mad at me again?"

She sighed and looked up, praying for patience.

*   *   *

Aaro's first impulse was to blurt out something dangerous and stupid. Once that impulse was squashed, nothing
else bobbed up into its place. Leaving him stupid and sputtering.

He played it safe and bland. "You're welcome," he said.

She waited for a moment. "That's all?"

"What do you want from me? You want me to thank you
back?"

She winced. "God, no. For what? I don't need to be thanked
for having sex with you. I did that for me, and I'm glad I did.
I'll never forget it, as long as I live." She hesitated. "Even if
that's just for three days."

"Don't say that," he said sharply. "Don't even think that."

They stared at each other. He breathed hard, heart kicking up.

She groped on the table for her glasses, and his hand
flashed out, blocking her. "Uh uh. No way," he said. "Those
stay off."

She looked horrified. "Aaro, I'm blind without them!"

"Blind, maybe, but different. More likely to stay alive."

She muttered a protest, but complied, tucking them into
her big black purse. "Should we, um, go on down?"

"Wait 'til the guy calls," he said abruptly. "It's safer in
here."

"OK," she whispered. "I'd rather say good-bye in private
anyway."

He nodded. He didn't want to say good-bye at all. His
throat was tight. The silence felt taut with a strange pleading
pressure, as if the words themselves were longing to be said,
held brutally back. She bit her lip, but released it when she
tasted the lipstick.

He cleared his throat. "One last thing."

"And what's that?" Her chin went up.

One long step brought him to her. He ran his hands over
her shoulders. The sheer fabric of the filmy blouse snagged

and caught on the rough spots on his fingers. So soft. He
fluffed a handful of her hair, let the springy curls bounce.
That was her true nature, he thought. Now that he'd sheared
off the weight of that massive, heavy braid, it sprang up, *ka-
boing*. Defiant, sassy, and wild.

"Aaro," she said warily. "I hope you, ah, aren't thinking—"

"Shhhh." He sank to his knees. "I haven't kissed this part
yet."

Nina jerked away, but too late, he'd grabbed her ass and
yanked her close. She batted at his head. "What do you think
you're doing?"

"Just this." He pressed his face against her belly, rubbing
his cheek against that strip of pale, fragrant, soft skin.

She dug her shaking fingers into his hair while he wor-
shipped the soft swell of rounded belly. It made his palms
sweat. It ripped the lid right off all the things they'd been trying not to say or feel, and now it was all clawing to get free.
Now he wanted to tear off those jeans, whip the pink, lacy
fuck-me thong down, and bend her over and squeeze himself
into that tight, hot hole again, 'til his cock was bathed with
her slick juice, gleaming as he pumped and plunged. He
wanted her to make those sounds for him, the whimpering,
the moaning. Those sweet, frantic kisses, clinging, yielding.
He could not get enough of it.

Nina felt the point of no return bearing down on them
like an eighteen-wheeler, and pushed at him. "Aaro. Stop.
You have to stop."

"I know." He staggered to his feet, wiping his mouth.

Nina's face was stern, but her crimson lips twitched when
she looked at him. "Um, your face is covered with glitter now."

"Kiss it off," he invited her rashly.

Her eyes went big. "Well . . . then there's this lipstick,
and I—"

"I do not fucking care." He grabbed her.

The kiss jerked him around to where it wanted him, a

force of nature that had to have its own desperate, twining way. They ended up horizontal on the messed-up bed, he had no idea how, fingers wound into each other's hair. He pressed the bulge of his cock against her groin, pulsing it, tenderly. The ache was killing him.

His cell phone buzzed.

They froze. The phone rang again. Aaro lifted off. Flopped heavily onto his back, staring at the ceiling. Ah, fuck. Too heavy to move.

Nina slid off the bed. She knelt on the floor, digging into the pockets of his leather jacket. The cell buzzed, buzzed, buzzed.

She retrieved it, and handed it to him. It rang twice more before he could even lift his arm to answer. "Yeah?" he asked dully.

"It's Wilder, the bodyguard," the guy said. "Bruno Ranieri sent me. I'm in front of the lobby. Six two, brown crew cut, blue jacket, gray Chevy Tahoe. You want to take her out the front or the side?"

Aaro shook the fog of sex from his head, and rapidly decided he liked the clearer visual of the lobby's traffic circle better than the parked cars on the deserted side lot. He didn't like the shrubs, but the cars were worse. "Front," he said. "Be right down."

He hung up, and got grimly to it. He took down the squealers, strapped on the various guns, stuck an extra in the back of his jeans. He'd come back up, and get the rest of his gear after Nina was gone.

"Aaro?"

He rounded on her. "What?"

"Wash your face."

He stomped into the bathroom to clean off glitter and crimson-lipstick clown smears. She followed him in, grabbed her own washcloth.

They scrubbed, side by side. He didn't even dare to look

at her. That jittery feeling kept growing. His fuck-up alert. Like a car with sensors that beeped when you were about to back into something. He was trying so hard to do the right thing, but the sensor kept shrilling.

Nina hoisted the plain black bag over her shoulder. She'd stuffed the other clothes he'd gotten for her into a shopping bag. "Shall we?"

"Put on more lipstick," he told her.

Nina sighed, and leaned in to the mirror, reapplying the bright crimson. He peered into the corridor, and they were off.

He matched his steps to hers, his mind buzzing. He'd go see Aunt Tonya, then fly back to Portland tonight, to aid in the community effort to keep Nina alive. Bruno could use his help putting the pieces together. Another brain and gun wouldn't hurt. He'd be able to check on her.

Tonya would approve. Applaud, even. Protecting his lady friend.

Don't even start with that shit. Shut up, asshole. Snip snip with the bolt cutters. Follow through. Move the fuck on.

He'd never realized how unpleasant that voice in his head was.

Down the elevator, through the lobby. The fuck-up sensor blared louder, shriller. His balls itched. But not a thing was out of place.

Outside the sliding door, next to the gray Chevy Tahoe, was a tall guy with a big jaw and a salt-and-pepper crew cut. He saw them, and nodded. He was just as Bruno had described him, and just as he had described himself. Everything was exactly as it was supposed to be.

Apparently. He slowed, pulling Nina closer.

She sensed his tension, peeking nervously up at him. "Aaro?" she murmured. "Isn't that the guy?"

"He looks like it. *Shhh.*"

"Aaro," she whispered. "Something is weird in here. You feel it?"

"No shit." The automatic door slid open. He jerked to a halt.

"When did you meet Davy McCloud?" he called out.

Wilder's face was expressionless. "Ninety-three," he said. "Iraq."

It was the right answer. Still, he hesitated. *Don't want to let her go, lover boy?* That fucking cold voice, again.

They stepped through the door. At that moment, another SUV pulled up, right behind Wilder. Aaro flicked his gaze over it. Gray Ford Expedition, woman driver, bobbed dark hair, sunglasses.

The woman got out, as Nina took a timid step out the door. She was thick-waisted and awkward, wearing a baggy, nondescript blouse. She jerked open the back door, grabbed her suitcase, and pulled it toward the hotel entrance, passing on Aaro's other side.

Nina sucked in a sharp breath as the feeling of danger opened up beneath her, like a dark mouth gaping hungrily. "Aaro! Watch out!"

He spun, instinctively, to block the baton whipping at the back of his head, caught it on his forearm, a white-hot crack of pain.

His body took over.

Nina flew through the air toward Wilder's car. Wilder yanked the back door open and was reaching for her when another body hurtled against her. The bald guy with the scar, a snarl on his savagely reddened face. He jerked Nina back against himself, his meaty arm across her neck. She wiggled, squirmed, and chomped on his arm. He bellowed, and Wilder's boot flashed out. A pistol flew into the air, clattered to the ground, and Wilder charged him.

It was really confusing after that, with two big guys grappling around her body, but when the bald guy was too busy fighting Wilder to hold her, she wormed away and scrambled back against Wilder's Chevy. Wilder jerked the bald guy's arm back, and smashed his bald pate into the car window, crunching it inward and leaving a bloody stamp around the rounded hole. She craned to see Aaro. He had flung the attacking woman to the ground, was running to the car. She was rolling to her feet, wig and glasses askew. It was the blond doctor, wearing a foam-padded vest beneath her oversized blouse. Aaro whipped out his gun.

Pockmarks stepped out of the hotel. "Hello, Sasha."

Aaro froze, for a split second. Pockmarks's gun whipped up. *Bam.*

Wilder crushed her against the car, knocking out her wind. His weight bore her to the ground. A bullet had taken him in the head. The exit wound had taken out his temple, his eye. It was a red crater. The car was spattered with the contents of his skull. The one eye he had left stared at her, blank and empty.

She barely felt it when Aaro jerked her up, tossing her into the car. She barely heard the gunshots. Felt the percussion with her body, like faraway thunderclaps. A door slammed shut, the engine surged.

Aaro was driving, shouting as he took the curve, flung her back against the seat. He braked, flinging her forward. She slid onto the floor.

The car roared as he turned onto the street. Aaro was too shocked to keep up his shield. She felt how terrified he was, how guilty. It blazed out, raw and jagged, blood tinged with battle fury . . . *got Wilder killed . . . almost got Nina killed . . . brain-dead asshole . . . Dmitri? What the fuck?*

She curled up into a ball and willed herself into nonexistence.

18

Miles parked the Wrangler outside the overgrown lawn of the old Victorian house that belonged to Joseph Kirk. He'd been trying to call the guy since seven A.M. It was early, it was rude, but fuck it, this was Aaro's girlfriend. Aaro needed a girlfriend. If the guy cared enough to stick his neck out this far for her, then this chick was definitely the one.

He stared up at the house. He'd checked out the photo portrait of the guy in the Wentworth College website. Self-important professor emeritus. Handsome older guy, pointy Freud beard. He had that annoying pose; holding chin with the thumb and crooked forefinger, the "Bow down, o clueless ones, before my wisdom" pose. Miles had spent years in academia. He could smell their affectations from miles away.

In any case, he was glad for something that took him out of the temple of trees Aaro called home. Working for Aaro was OK, once he got used to the guy's rudeness. The guy was ambitious, and ferociously smart. Miles liked working with smart people.

The McCloud Crowd and Seth still had their panties all in

a wad since Miles had bailed on them, but he couldn't be within a two-hundred-mile radius of Cindy Riggs. Cindy, who had gone off a few months ago on an up-and-coming alternative rocker's big concert tour, and come back the rocker's concubine, mouthing unbearable platitudes. *I'm, like, so sorry, Miles! I love you, too, but my love for Aengus blew me away.*

His own fault, to have tried for so long to believe that she had hidden depths. Cindy was fluff. It was sad, even. Not worth being angry over. And yet, he was. Oh, man, he was.

She didn't deserve this much airtime. He had his doubts as to how long Cindy's fling would last, but he'd be damned if he'd wait around to pick up the pieces. Move on, man. Fuck that.

So he'd come down to work for Aaro, like joining the French Foreign Legion to forget his tragic past. Sweet deal moneywise, since Aaro paid him well to do something he'd probably be doing at all hours for free. The problem with living up in Aaro's extension, north of Sandy, Oregon, was that the situation had a lot in common with all the worst aspects of living in his parents' garage. Just tattoo a big L for loser on his forehead. No one to talk to but trees and chipmunks. And himself.

He had to get his ass out there, get a fucking social life. He and Aaro were sexless robot hermits in their cyber-lair. He only crawled out of his computer to sleep, usually during the day. Or work out in Aaro's gym. Or sprint through the forest until he collapsed.

The McCloud-style adventures were over. He'd just revert to being a bug-eyed, number-crunching, code-cracking geek freak in a basement. Making a pile of money that he had no heart to spend. Who the fuck cared.

Yet here he was. He even had a gun. He had no license to carry concealed in Oregon, but Aaro's tales of psycho killers and mafiya drive-by shootings had made him nervous enough to bring the Glock Sean had given him last year for his birthday. The insane lengths those McCloud guys had gone to, to man him up, Jesus. He was proficient with it, but he felt like a fraud when he carried a gun.

He walked up to the porch, which was covered with a drift of pine needles. He peered through the window, saw a dim foyer. Curtains over the front windows were drawn. No reason for his neck to prickle. Nothing weird about an empty house. He took a flagstoned path that curved around the house. Time to go back to Sandy and crawl into the computer, where his talents were put to their best use.

He rounded the corner and looked up onto the back porch.

The back door had a missing pane. Someone had broken in.

Shards of glass littered the porch floor. He reached into the hole, turning the knob. He wore thin leather gloves, since the crime lab in Clackamas already had his DNA and fingerprints in their databank, after that mess that came down with Kev. He was highly motivated to never have trouble with the law again, ever.

Just wearing the gloves made him feel in the wrong. He wished Sean were there, or Davy, or Aaro. To help him make the right decision.

Grow up, man. They can't hold your hand forever.

He padded through the mudroom. Stopped to listen. Creaks and pops, wind whistling. Trees swaying. He stepped into the kitchen.

It was trashed. Only the table was intact. It held a plate with the remains of fried eggs, crusts of toast, a half cup of coffee. He touched the cup. Cool. The coffeemaker by the sink had a half a pot still steaming. Every cupboard and drawer was open, contents flung out on the floor. Same with the fridge.

He picked his way through broken glass, pickles, relish, smashed eggs, cherry tomatoes. In the dining room, the papers and academic journals had been flung to the floor. Living room, same deal. Couches and easy chairs slashed and gutted. Pictures torn down, the backs ripped off. Books swept off the shelves.

A photograph caught his eye. He leaned to pick it up. A black and white taken at the coast, of a girl sitting on a rock looking out over the churning surf, dark hair flying like a banner. Big, mysterious eyes that looked like they could see for a million miles. She was . . . wow.

He turned the photo over. *Lincoln City, OR*, and a date, ten years ago, scrawled on the back. This must be Lara. In her twenties now. Slender, gauzy peasant blouse that blew flat against her high, beautiful tits, which were evidently feeling the chilly coastal breeze. If he was a dad, he wouldn't hang his daughter's nipple hard-on up on the wall for every passing random schmuck to slaver over. But maybe these cultured, academic, artistic types were different about stuff like that.

His cyber-digging had revealed that she was an artist. She looked the part. Those big dreamy eyes.

Miles shook off the spell, and squelched the impulse to slip the picture into his jacket. That would be stealing. Not to mention vaguely kinky and stalker-ish. He put it down where he'd found it. Mooning over dream babes on the job. *Lack of vigilance will get you killed.* A McCloud creed that he seemed to have internalized.

It occurred to him, as he picked his way over the smashed coffee table, that Lara Kirk was the first woman he'd scoped that he hadn't automatically compared to Cindy. Of course, he'd just invalidated that miraculous event by noticing it, and congratulating himself for it.

There were more pictures of Lara. In one, she was about eight, in a dark-haired woman's lap. She had a somber, thoughtful look.

He climbed the stairs. As he made his way down the corridor, a noise began to register. The shower. The bathroom door hung open. The walls of the corridor sweated from the steam that floated out.

All the horror flicks he'd ever seen ran through his head. He braced himself, and peered in. Empty, thank God. He turned off the water. Condensation slid down the mirror. He stared grimly at himself. His jagged hair stuck straight up. He'd chopped it off himself with kitchen shears while freshly in mourning for the Cindy of his dreams who had never existed. His hooked schnoz, his clamped mouth, his sweaty forehead. The medicine cabinet hung open, the sink full of stuff they'd scooped out. Shaving stuff, nail scissors, dental floss.

The bedroom had been torn apart. Bed coverings ripped away, mattresses slashed. There was a suitcase, though someone had emptied its contents onto the floor. A briefcase, gutted. Kirk had meant to go somewhere, but he hadn't taken his suitcase or briefcase with him.

Miles picked through the papers scattered across the floor. One proved to be an e-boarding pass. A flight for Denver, leaving at eleven fifty-five A.M. this morning. He memorized the trip code and put the paper down where he had found it.

That was it for the upstairs. He crept back down. The professor had gotten up, put coffee on, made breakfast. He'd gone upstairs, prepared his suitcase, gotten into the shower . . .

And something very bad had happened. Miles went steadily toward the one door he had not yet tried.

Oh, man. Don't. Not the basement. That never turns out well. Going down into the basement was for blond actresses with bobbing tits, doomed to die screaming. He turned the knob, flipped on the hanging chain light. Dust and mold, bare wood steps, basement floor of oil and damp, stained, rough poured concrete.

He smelled it halfway down the stairs. He didn't want to believe it, but his nose did not lie. His heart was stuck in his neck, choking the air out of him. The smell got stronger as he descended. He'd smelled it before. Wished that he hadn't. Voided bowels. The fresh, meaty smell of blood. Like an anvil, careening through space toward his head. He tried to prepare himself, but he still wasn't ready when the sight hit his eyes.

The professor was naked, seated against a support column, his arms jerked back at an agonizing angle, hands cuffed behind it with plastic ratchet cuffs. Blood was everywhere. He was still, eyes staring. His fingers and his toes were gone. Something red and fleshy was stuffed in his open mouth, and his crotch . . . oh, sweet holy Jesus.

A whimper jerked out of his throat. He struggled not to retch. Oh, God. How fucking horrible. The guy was surely dead, but Miles felt a ceremonial necessity to check his pulse. He owed a fellow human being that much, no matter what. He crept closer, trying not to look at those red stumps. Blood still oozed. The people who did this must have left moments before he arrived. He pulled off a glove. Couldn't feel for a pulse with leather on his hands.

He touched the guy's carotid. Nothing. His fingers came back red.

He got up the stairs, tears streaming down his face. Rinsed blood off into the kitchen sink, hand shaking. Put the glove back on. He dialed nine one one. "I'm calling to report a murder," he told the dispatcher, in a voice that was unrecognizable as his own. He gave them the address, let the phone dangle as the woman exhorted him to stay at the scene.

Not. He stumbled out the door and broke into a run. To get as far away from the house as possible before he lost his breakfast.

* * *

"Ah . . . Mr. Arbatov, would you sign the guest book before—"

"Shut up." Oleg kept on down the hospice corridor, fingering the flash drive that contained the footage of Sasha and his woman friend.

He stared at his pitted, jowly face in the reflective metal surface of the elevator panel as he went up to the second floor. He looked old. Felt old, upon seeing Sasha in that video. So many lost years. It had an odd effect on him, to see his grown-up son. Like seeing himself thirty years ago, though Sasha was unquestionably better looking, having gotten his mother's dramatic bone structure to mitigate the bull-like Arbatov genes. Oksana, his first wife, had been very beautiful. His throat still caught when he saw her in photos. A rare occurrence. His wife Rita made sure that pictures with Oksana were kept well out of sight.

But his son's green eyes and severe mouth, that was pure Arbatov. Sasha looked good. He had not gone to fat, nor did he have the broken veins or pitted skin of an alcoholic and a junkie, as his cousin did. The two were profoundly different, in every way. Although when the boys had been children, many had taken them for twins.

Sasha looked strong, restless. Angry. Those were good things to be. Oleg loathed complacency, or anything that smacked of softness.

Sasha's woman had not impressed him, at first glance. A mousy nonentity. Then he'd seen her smooth penetration of the hospice, her perfect timing. He'd barely seen her enter, though he had the video to study. Just a gray flutter, and *poof,* she was gone. Of course, he would have wished Sasha a woman endowed with jaw-dropping beauty, not invisibility. But perhaps this girl had other gifts to bring to the table.

He pushed open the door to Tonya's room. She appeared to be asleep, but he knew his sister's tricks. Sneaky to her last breath.

He bore down on her with all the force of his will. "Open your eyes, Tonya. I wish to speak with you."

Tonya's eyes fluttered, though she stared defiantly at the ceiling. No one but Sasha had ever resisted his will as much as Tonya had. Both had suffered for it. But he could not allow insubordination. Not then, certainly not now, not if he wished to maintain his power and status as Vor. Much as it pained him to be severe with his own family.

With all his freakish intelligence, Sasha had never seemed to understand how much he stood to gain by giving up on his compulsive resistance. He'd never cared about the power he would inherit if he would just listen and obey. He'd fought Oleg with every breath. He had resisted in his fucking sleep. It had made Oleg angry enough to kill, and even so, he'd been perversely proud of the boy for being so indomitable. Only that kind of steel could possibly hope to run the vast and complex underground business empire that Oleg had created.

It was a riddle that had no answer, and then Sasha had fled anyway, making the answer irrelevant. His only surviving child, gone. The self-absorbed Rita had given him her perfect body, but it had born no fruit, and Oleg suspected that Rita was quite satisfied with that state of affairs. She did not want to distort her figure with pregnancy, nor did she want to make any effort on anyone's behalf but her own. Being Rita Arbatov was a full-time job, in and of itself.

"Look at me, Tonya." He let steel show through his voice.

She turned her head. Her dark eyes in her emaciated face were more intense and haunting than ever. And full of relentless hatred.

"Sasha came to you, Tonya. I have video footage, of him, and his woman. You do not protect them with your silence. You only anger me."

She licked her lips. "The closer to death I get, the less

power you have over me. You will not catch them, Oleg. Together they are strong."

"Are they lovers? Married? Where? Are there children?"

Her lips stretched in a deathly smile, showing flakes of
peeling skin, discolored fever blisters. "You will not put your
hands upon their children," she said. "I have seen it.
Dreamed it."

Oleg waved that impatiently away. "What name is he
using?" he demanded. "Who is the woman?"

"Her name was not important. She is strong enough for
Sasha. That was what is important."

"I do not wish to hurt Sasha," Oleg snapped.

Tonya made a wheezing sound, lips drawn back. "No?
You never meant to hurt Julie, either, ey?"

Rage surged inside him. "I never hurt Julie," he said
harshly.

"You did not protect her," Tonya forced out, breathless.

"From what?" he said harshly. "Herself?"

"You never asked yourself why she was so sad? Why she
got so thin, why she ate her fingernails and cut her arms
with a knife? You never noticed the light in her eyes going
out? No, it was enough for you that she obey you. That was
all you ever wanted from any of us."

"Be silent," he snarled. "I did not come here to be scolded."

She laughed again, harshly. "Then you should have
stayed home."

He leaned over her, letting his will batter her. Her lips
drew back from her teeth as she withstood the gale. When a
thread of blood began leaking from her nose, he leaned back
in the chair, and waited.

Tonya could not speak for ten minutes. She dragged air
stubbornly into her lungs. Gasp after gasp, rattling, whooping. So painful, so useless. Life, maintaining itself when all
pretexts for living were gone. Were it he in that bed, he

would have put a bullet in his head long before. When it came to that, he'd made arrangements. His body had declined as far as his dignity would allow. One more sacrifice, one more compromise, and he would be running to meet the reaper, arms outstretched. But first, he wanted his son. Just that.

"You know where Sasha is," he said. "You've always known."

Tonya shook her head. "I never saw much with those drugs pumped into me," she said. "And you gave the orders for that, brother."

"If you had helped, instead of spitting in my face." His voice shook with anger. "If you had done as I asked, and used your gift to help me find him, I would not have been forced to punish you! Stubborn cow!"

"Why not leave him in peace?" Tonya shook her head. "You and Dmitri, both of you. Obsessed with him. After twenty years."

Oleg frowned. "Dmitri doesn't give a shit about finding Sasha. He's out chasing some new drug. I hope it kills him. Worthless turd."

Tonya shook her head. "Dmitri is hunting them. They have something he wants more than life. I've dreamed it. He will kill for it."

Tonya's predictions, when her eyes had that unfocused glow, were to be heeded. Tonya had dreamed Oksana's breast cancer long before the doctors had diagnosed it. "What did you see?" he asked.

"I saw Dmitri creeping into Sasha's dream," she rasped.

Tonya's sepulchral whisper had begun to annoy him. "Don't play oracle with me. I'm not in any mood to interpret fucking metaphors."

"Last night, he sneaked into Sasha's dream," Tonya insisted. "And he will attack again. Sasha is my heart's treasure. You expect me to give him to you? When you have never done anything but punish him?"

Oleg coughed. "I do not wish to hurt him."

"Then stop Dmitri," she said. "That is all you can do."

Oleg took out the cell phone he had taken from Dmitri the night before. He held it up where Tonya could see it. "Dmitri is hunting the woman who owns this phone. Her name is Nina Christie. Have you ever heard of her? Have you seen her in your dreams?"

Tonya shook her head. "I do not know the name."

"There is a great deal of senseless babbling on this phone that I wish to have explained," he said. "Some of it in Ukrainian, of all things. But this speaker, I believe, is the woman herself." He punched the audio file, set it to play on the speaker.

". . . Helga. Oh, God. Helga?" The female voice was low, quavering with shock. "What was . . . wha—why did you do that? Wha—what the fuck was in that needle?"

Startlement flashed in Tonya's eyes. Oleg clicked the file off. "Who is she?" he demanded. "Do you know anything about this needle attack? Who did it, when it took place?"

Tonya shook her head.

His teeth ground in rage. "You will tell me. *Now*."

"Or what?" That silent, wheezy laugh again. "Or you will kill me? Do it, Oleg. You've kept me locked in a cage for long enough."

"Is this what you want?" He lifted his hand to the knob that regulated the morphine drip. A little turn to up the dose would depress her respiration, and she would be dead in hours.

Her eyes fixed on his hand, her mouth a martyr's clenched grimace. "I would not sell my darling to you, even for that." Her mouth worked. Spat at him, with surprising energy.

He wiped the spray of spittle that had stained his snowy

shirt cuffs, and reached up to the knob. He turned it, but not to increase the drip. The other way. The drip slowed, stalled, and stopped. Oleg grasped the call button that dangled from the head of the bed, and looped it over the IV rack. Out of her reach, unless she stood, and Tonya could not stand. The tumors had metastasized to her spine, fracturing it. She did not have the strength to scream. She could barely croak.

Tonya's eyes filled with dread. "That will kill me, too."

"Of course." He gave her a wide smile. "But the death will not be gentle. But why should death be gentle, when life never is?"

"Fuck you, Oleg," she whispered.

He leaned over her, staring into her eyes. "That woman. How do you know her?" He let his will bear down, and this time, she cracked.

"Came . . . came in, with Sasha," she gasped out.

He was jolted by the unexpected implications. "This is Sasha's woman? This is she?" He shook the phone. "Dmitri is hunting her?"

"Both . . . both." Tears streamed down her cheeks. "Both of them."

The door burst open. Fay Siebring bustled in, a bright, nervous smile on her face, prattling about a call from the scholarship board, but Oleg's attention was elsewhere. His sister tried in vain to get Fay Siebring's attention, plucking the woman's jacket, begging in her broken English for help, but Fay ignored her, and focused only on him.

Oleg held up his hand to forestall the spew of words. Leaned to kiss Tonya on her clammy forehead. "Good-bye, little sister," he whispered. He took Siebring by the arm, and led her toward the door. "Excuse me, but I must be on my way," he said. "Will you see me out?"

The door swung closed on Tonya's breathless sobs.

He escorted Siebring down the hall, pretending to listen to the nonsense the woman was spouting. It occurred to him that Tonya might well die, if he did not say something to a staff member before he left. He did not know how dependent upon morphine she was.

But the equation was so simple, he could not understand why Tonya never seemed to learn it. No opposition meant no pain, no punishment. Plus everything her heart desired, or at least everything that money or fear could buy. Which was quite a bit, in the end.

So simple. So fair. It was not his fault if the woman was too stupid to make the connection. To protect her own best interests.

He left Fay Siebring in mid-sentence, and walked away, saying nothing about Tonya at all.

19

With all Rudd had to worry about, he had to clean up for his cleaning crew, too. That idiot Roy, the only one who could have followed the two fugitives, had gotten his head smashed, and the resulting trauma had put him out of commission for hours, at which point the runaways were hundreds of miles out of range. Anabel had barely had the presence of mind to get her colleague loaded up and away before the cops showed. A bloody corpse. Hysterical witnesses. God, what a mess.

Back to doing things the old-fashioned way. Using his naked and unassisted intelligence. Fortunately, he still remembered how, unlike his assistants. He gazed up from his car at Nina Christie's house, still festooned with crime scene tape. A cop stood sentinal, looking bored and hot. He dragged a pack of cigarettes out, tried to shake one out. It was empty. The guy tossed the pack to the porch floor in disgust.

Rudd estimated the distance between himself and the cop. Right on the edge of his range, but he could do it. He'd waited until just before peak dose to try. One had to time these things just so.

He reached, harder, farther, stretching . . . contact. He was only a rudimentary telepath. At peak dose, he could catch random glimpses, or follow thoughts if they were strongly projected with intention, if they were emotionally charged, or if he knew the context well. Otherwise, not so much. But this guy was easy, even for him. Simple, predictable. He was hot, he was bored, his ass itched, he was frustrated at pulling this kind of duty and being passed over for better assignments. Irritated at his wife over some long-standing fight. His thoughts flowed through Roy's mind, fuzzy and staticky, but clear enough.

. . . fucking hot . . . kill for a cold beer . . . need more smokes . . . wonder how long I'll have to wait to get laid again this time . . . go find me a friend with benefits, that'll teach the snotty bitch to give it up. . . .

And so on. Rudd hung on to the contact, and began to funnel his coercive energy against the guy's mind, like he did to punish Roy, but harder. And suddenly, full force.

The policeman doubled over, clutching his head. His thought processes disintegrated into shock, terror. *Pain.* He groped for the walkie-talkie at his belt. Rudd ramped it up before the man could say anything into it. It felt good, to unleash the full range of his abilities. Like a full-body stretch after sitting in a cramped plane seat for hours.

Rudd got out of the car. Time to get on with it. The man dropped the walkie-talkie. It tumbled down the steps. The man thudded to his knees, tipped. Rudd heard a *crack* as his head hit something.

Rudd nudged open the gate, kicked the walkie-talkie with his toe to where it was not visible from the sidewalk. He ran a practiced eye over the cop. The knock to the head plus the previous trauma Rudd had inflicted should keep him quiet.

He nudged the man's legs, bending them at the knees so that they were hidden behind the low wall that bounded the porch, and could not be seen by a casual passerby, and ducked under the yellow tape. He'd waited for the evidence techs to finish up with some follow-up work, and was reasonably sure now that the house was empty, but who knew for how long. He'd keep this quick.

The place was a mess. Trashed by Roy and his mafiya thugs in their search for Psi-Max 48, then worked over by the forensics types. He was under no illusion that he would find Psi-Max 48 here. The drug was with Nina Christie and her brawny protector. But he would walk through, look, think about her. People let down their guard when they were home. Weaknesses were revealed. He had an excellent instinct for weaknesses. There was a zen to it. He'd been pretty good at exploiting weaknesses even before that happy day he'd discovered psi-max.

He started with the upper floor. Several rooms were empty, including the master bedroom. Odd. The bathroom was a heap of glass from the broken shower stall. Meatheads, breaking things for the sake of breaking them. The medicine cabinet's contents were scattered in the sink. Face cream, body lotion, Advil, aspirin, antibiotic ointment. Dental care items. No cosmetics, no contraceptive pills or devices. No antidepressants, antianxiety drugs, opiates, or medication of any kind.

But a woman in Nina Christie's line of work was often compensating for something. Do-gooder crusaders always were.

He was all the more convinced of this when he looked over her bedroom. It was a much smaller back bedroom, looking over an alley. A narrow, antique bed, plain white sheets, a somber quilt. A hard, matted-down futon mattress. A veritable nun's cell. And that closet. She'd hidden in a false-backed closet, Roy said. He stepped over voluminous, dull-looking clothing to take a look at it. Fine work, custom made. The back panel was torn up with bullet holes. No casual hiding place, but carefully planned. This project had cost her money.

The clothing was all in flat, neutral colors that disappeared when you looked at them. Grays, beiges, taupes, the occasional daring navy blue or olive drab or charcoal. She even avoided true black and true white. Evidently they had too much pop.

He nudged at the crumpled rose petals, broken ceramic. A seventies-era picture of a smiling, pretty woman, probably Christie's mother. No jewelry box. What young woman's bedroom was devoid of jewelry? So very austere. His foot crunched over a picture frame. He picked it up. A photo of two young women. A striking strawberry blonde, her arm draped around a smaller woman, whose dark, curly hair was dragged straight back from her forehead. The dark woman wore harsh, unflattering glasses and a drab brown button-down shirt.

That plainer one was clearly Nina Christie. No jewelry, no makeup, no contraceptives. Ergo, no lovers. A custom-made closet to hide in. Hmmm. A deep fault line, just waiting for him to exploit.

His eyes fixed on the other woman. A friend with pride of place on a woman's bedroom dresser, right next to dear old Mom, was another fault line. Love was the best one. It had worked on Helga, after all.

But time pressed. He laid the picture down and swiftly toured the rest of the house. Not much to glean. She hung few pictures, had simple, utilitarian furniture. A china cabinet in the dining room was flung down, its porcelain contents smashed to dust. A mirror over the table had been smashed, cracks radiating out from the splintered hole.

The kitchen was his last stop. He made his way to the refrigerator, and gazed at what was clipped with magnets to the door.

Yet another photo of the smiling strawberry blonde, but this time she was seated with a tall, grinning dark-haired man who had his arm around her shoulder. Each held a squirming toddler on their laps.

A card was stuck up with a magnet. It was made of handmade paper, liberally scattered with pressed wildflowers. On closer inspection, the flowers proved to be yellow mountain lilies, small and delicate, their dried petals wispy yellow threads, like saffron. Inside was printed:

> *You are cordially invited to the wedding of*
> *Lily Evelyn Parr and Bruno Ranieri,*
> *to be held in the Portland Rose Garden*
> *on September 8, at 2:00 PM.*
> *Reception to follow, at the Braxton Inn.*
> *Please RSVP.*

His cell phone vibrated in his pocket. The display indicated that it was Anabel. He hit "talk." "Yes?" He kept his voice cold. He was displeased with Anabel. She'd been coming up blank in every task he set to her.

"I heard from Dmitri," she said. "About Joseph Kirk. In Portland. His men paid Kirk a visit this morning. Questioned him."

"And?"

"Kirk didn't know anything. He really thought Helga was dead, in the fire. No clue. Dmitri's boys questioned him very thoroughly."

"We need to have you read him, too," Rudd said briskly. "Make arrangements to go to Portland immediately. We have to move fast—"

"He's dead," Anabel broke in.

Rudd's manicured fingernails dug into his palm. "He is *what*?"

"Um, they didn't actually mean to kill him," she explained. "They did some cutting, see. And he went into shock. His heart stopped."

"So we'll never know," he said grimly.

"Boss, you remember what Kirk was like," Anabel coaxed. "I think it's true. I think he really didn't know. Kirk wasn't the heroic type. He wouldn't hold back. Not if they were cutting him."

"And now we'll never know for sure," he repeated coldly.

He could not be bothered with Anabel any longer. He hung up, looked back at the announcement. A note was scribbled on it.

> *You're maid of honor, you know, so wrap*
> *your mind around it and don't even try to*
> *fight. I promise, the dress won't gag you.*
> *I ask only one wedding present of you.*
> *Get contacts before you come, and let me*
> *do your makeup. XXOO love you, girl.*
> *Lily.*

Aw. Lily. Hence, the lily-speckled notecards. Sweet little detail, that. Rudd appreciated those subtle feminine touches.

Fault lines. Rudd took the invitation and tucked it into his pocket. He walked out, ducking back under the yellow tape over the door. Glanced at the man sprawled on the porch.

Rudd made contact, though there was very little to make contact with. The man's mind was barely there, fading fast. He hung on by the thinnest of threads. Rudd inhaled, concentrated . . . *pushed*.

The thread snapped, like a cobweb. The man drifted away.

Rudd sauntered back to his car, his good mood restored.

* * *

The goddamned bus went so slow. Aaro needed an accelerator to press, but he was stuck in the back of a lumbering bus, going fifty an hour, with only the .45, the snubby, and the Micro Glock still on his body, plus his knives. The rest of the hardware, plus his laptop, had been left behind in the fracas. He missed it all. Sharply.

If he were behind the wheel, it would be impossible to keep from speeding, though. And the last thing he needed was to get pulled over. Depending on how the shitstorm back in Brooklyn was interpreted by the cops, who knew? He was probaby a wanted man at this point.

It made him want to laugh. After investing all this energy in being unwanted. Now three entirely different entities were out for his ass: his own family, Nina's psycho freak team, and the law. Wow. Like there was even enough room around his throat for all those squeezing hands.

How the hell had that douche-bag Dmitri gotten mixed up in this mess? His long-lost, un-missed cousin. He'd almost shot the guy, until their eyes met . . . and Aaro's flash of hesitation had killed Wilder.

Wilder's death was on him.

"Would you stop that?" Nina murmured, from beside him.

He glared at her. "Stop what?"

"Flogging yourself like that. You didn't kill Wilder. So don't take the blame onto yourself. You have a very bad habit of doing that."

"Get the fuck out of my head, Nina," he warned.

She turned innocent eyes up in his direction. "I wasn't snooping," she said. "I was just trying to concentrate on all the details of Helga's transcript. But your mental histrionics were making it really hard."

"Histrionics? Look, if you're going to start policing the random shit that runs through my head—"

"I won't. Don't flatter yourself. I've got my own thoughts to think, and my own guilt. That guy saved my life. But I just don't feel like witnessing the self-flagellation right now. It's distracting, and it's too damn loud. We're getting our asses kicked hard enough. No need to kick your own ass, too."

"Let's make a rule," he said grimly. "Don't scold me for my thoughts. It's bad enough getting scolded for the things I actually say."

"Let's not set rules. I'm doing the best I can, so deal with it."

Nina still had the harsh black glasses on, having managed to hang on to the purse slung across her shoulder, even through the attack. But with the bouncy hair, the glasses looked different. Funky and daring, rather than harsh and dowdy. Her lips were still stained hot pink from lipstick that had worn off long ago, and her mascara had run into smudgy pools of shadow. She still glimmered with the glitter spray. So pretty, he just wanted to drag her onto his lap and feel her up.

And he was a dirty dog for even thinking about it right now.

She gazed at him, expressionless. Probably seeing every erotic image in his head, in detail. Damn, it was hard to get used to, this telepathy thing. It changed the rules of the game completely.

"You're awfully calm," he said, disgruntled.

Her lips twitched. "You say that like it's a bad thing."

"Just jealous," he said. No point in being anything else but honest with a chick who could read his mind. "Because I'm so not."

"I see that," she said. "I don't know how deep this calm goes. Probably just shock. I'm too hammered to react appropriately."

"Why is it you can read my mind now when you couldn't before?"

"You dropped your shield," she said simply.

"I *what?*" That didn't sound like something he'd do. Ever.

"It's true. Yesterday you were like the door of a bank vault," she said. "And today, it's open."

"I don't feel like I'm doing anything different," he said.

She shrugged. "Maybe you trust me more."

Well, hell. Since she had given him the mental construct, he used it. Pictured those big vault doors swinging shut, with a huge clang.

Nina winced. "Ouch. That was so not necessary, Aaro!"

"Just experimenting. Got to get the hang of it, right?"

"I've figured out how to shield, too," she said. "It's sort of like my invisibility trick, but reversed. Shiny side out. Like a trick with mirrors."

He shook his head. "The technical subtleties of your psychic abilities are too much for me to process right now."

"Then I won't burden you with them," she said crisply.

To his relief, the phone buzzed. Miles. Good. He clicked it. "Hey."

"Where are you?" Miles asked.

He peered out at the freeway signs. "Almost to Cooper's Landing."

"Good. Stay on the bus all the way to Lannis Lake. When you get there, a taxi will be waiting. He'll take you to a house on the lake. It's eighty-five Lakeside Road. About three miles from the town. Right on the water."

"Is anyone there?"

"No, empty. The house key is in a cinderblock near the woodpile."

"Is the owner going to come in on us unexpectedly?"

"They're friends of my dad," Miles said. "It's their vacation home. They retired and went to do a couple of years in the Peace Corps. They're in Central America somewhere, vaccinating orphans. They're never going to know, and if they do, I'll take the responsibility."

"OK. Does this guy have firearms? A hunting rifle, or something?"

"Don't push your luck. He's a retired math teacher. Likes organic gardening. His wife does cross-stitch. They go to Quaker meeting."

"OK, whatever," he muttered.

"You'll be safe," Miles went on. "It's almost a mile from the main road, and there's no way the place can be connected to you."

"Anything new about the transcript?"

"Nothing yet. I tried to find something on the Wycleff Library, but came up blank. I was hoping Kirk could help, but so much for that. He had a packed suitcase, and an e-ticket for Denver. That's all I know."

"OK. Thanks, man."

After he hung up, he set to listening to Kasyanov's monologue again, to keep his mind busy, since when he let his thoughts run wild, they trampled right through Nina's head. But the only thing he gleaned from the scrubbed version was that Kasyanov said something that sounded like "party for" before she said "graves." Party for graves?

Huh. Sounded like fun. The Wycleff Library reference seemed promising, but he'd had no luck digging on his smartphone, either.

After the sixth time through, he switched it off and turned to her. "The simax those guys were talking about in your apartment," he said. "It's got to be p-s-i. Psi-max, as in, maximizing your psi."

Nina's brows snapped together. "Makes sense," she said. "I wish I knew what the hell she was talking about when she says 'graves.'"

"She says it in English," he said. "Just that one word. In the scrubbed version, it sounds like 'a party for graves.' Which makes even less sense. Something hidden in a grave?"

"Brrr," she murmured. "I sure hope not."

"Bruno had to dig up a grave to find something," he told her.

She gave him a suspicious look. "Get out of here," she said. "You mean, moldering corpse and all?"

"Three moldering corpses were involved, as I recall."

"Well, Helga said she'd been imprisoned for three years, and this drug formula is new. So it's not languishing in a grave. Thank God."

They were quiet, each carefully sealed inside themselves as they got closer to Lannis Lake. When they got out of the bus, a cab driver came toward them. "Aaro and Nina?" he asked.

"That's us," he said.

The guy had been paid and briefed on address and directions, to Aaro's relief. Nothing was required of him but sitting in the backseat, slack-jawed with exhaustion, his arm clamped around Nina.

Lakeside Road was narrow and twisty. The driver slowed, and turned into an entrance so overgrown it was barely visible. They got out in front of a cabin by a lake that shimmered in the fading twilight, through trees and undergrowth. The cab bumped away over the rocky driveway. Aaro set out to find the key in the cinderblock. There were several of them, all inhabited by spiders. When he finally found it, Nina was gone. He looked around cursing, his heart in his throat, until he saw her on the walkway leading to the floating dock.

Her back was to him, gazing at the water. "We aren't safe here."

He pondered that hard truth as he admired her ass from behind. "I don't know," he said. "I don't know how they found us before, so I can't guarantee they won't find us again."

"I know how they did." She turned around, and looked at him, her voice barely audible. "They're on that drug. Like me."

He fought the idea. "But Helga said she didn't give it to them. They injected it into her, instead. To test it, probably."

"Maybe not this formula," Nina said. "But she's been cooking it for them for three years. They're all enhanced. In one way or another."

Feeling powerless always made him feel inexplicably furious. "And so?" he snarled. "Fuck it. So we run until they get us. So we fight until we die. End of story."

"Fight with what? We have to use every weapon we have."

"What do you think I've been doing, Nina? Sitting around with my thumb up my ass? I'm being as pro-active as I know how to be!"

"No. I mean . . ." Her voice trailed off, like she was afraid to say it.

"What?" he demanded. "Spit it out!"

"Your aunt said you have talent, too," she stated. "She said, you never let it out of its cage."

"Yeah? My aunt said a lot of things. She also spent most of her adult life in a psych ward, stoned out of her mind on antipsychotics."

She hugged herself, gazing at the glassy lake. "I can see how somebody with this ability could wind up in a psych ward. I also think that she knew exactly what she was talking about. About you."

"I don't believe in fairy tales," he said, through gritted teeth.

She spun on him. "You call what's happening a fairy tale?"

"No, I call it a cautionary tale! Get the fuck indoors. My skin is crawling."

The place smelled of dust, mildew. A combined living room and kitchen. Bedrooms and a bath on the far side. The furniture was shrouded in sheets. Picture windows, covered with dark drapes, led out to a big deck that overlooked the lake.

Nina flipped on a light, and Aaro practically jumped out of his skin. "Turn that off! We'll look like a Christmas tree out here!"

She flipped the light off, enveloping them in shadowy gloom. "I was just going to look for something to eat. Hard to cook in the dark."

Aaro's stomach twitched. He opened the freezer, which was amazingly functional. Some grubbing around yielded a handful of Lean Cuisines. He pulled out five, threw them in the microwave to nuke. "There," he said. "See? I cooked."

"Wow," Nina murmured. "The confidence, the skill, the flair. That was sexy, Aaro. I love to see a guy strut his stuff in the kitchen."

It didn't take much to make his body zing into alertness. "Yeah? You think that was good?" he asked. "You ain't seen nothing yet."

She was silent for a long moment. "Would that be a good idea?"

God, yes. The best idea. The only idea. "What was it you said yesterday, about seizing the day?"

"Was that only yesterday? Seems like years," she murmured. "So, you want to seize the day, Aaro?"

He took a step toward her. "I want to seize everything."

Startled laughter choked in her throat, making her cough. "What?" he asked. "What's so goddamn funny?"

"Nothing," she said. "I'm just not used to being treated like a sexual object. It still startles me."

"Get used to it," he advised.

They stared at each other, and he realized that he was actually enjoying the taut silence, the energy buzzing between them like a wire drawn tight. His body hummed with awareness, hunger.

On impulse, he let out a slow breath, releasing the tension in his head, the locked jaw, the grinding teeth . . . and pictured the vault door, easing open. Heat and light rushed into

cramped, tight places. His chest felt suddenly hot, like a fur-
nace blasted out of his chest. It almost hurt.

She took a startled step back. "My God, Aaro," she whispered.

"It's what I thought you wanted," he said. "Lose the
clothes, Nina."

"Wow. My feminist sensibilities are outraged," she murmured.

"Yeah? I'll outrage them like they've never been outraged
before."

She glowed at him, luminous. Like a torch in the darkness, not to his eyes, but to all his other, secret senses.

She licked her lips. "And I thought that beneath your
mask was the heart of a gallant cavalier."

"No way. This is taking too long, Nina. Are you fucking
with me?"

Her smile made his balls tighten. "I'm working up to it,"
she said.

"Work faster," he suggested.

20

Miles stared morosely out the window of Lily's hospital room. Wondering if sending them to the cabin was the right thing to do. Hey, what could possibly go wrong? He suppressed a bark of laughter.

He glanced down at the smartphone dangling from his fingers. Thinking of fingers was a mistake. The image of Kirk's mangled hands and feet made his belly seize up. He'd been wishing for something to drive the image of Cindy banging the rocker out of his mind. But at this point, Cindy and her rocker would be a relief.

Lily wandered over to look out the window with him. "I'm so sorry you had to see that this morning."

"I'm all right. You're not supposed to be on your feet, are you?"

"That's right," Bruno said, from the door. "Get back in bed, Lil." A few strides brought him over to her. He swept her up into his arms.

She swatted at him. "Stop that! I'm huge! You'll hurt yourself!"

"I can carry you both," he said, hauling her to the bed. "I

think you just get up because you get off on it when I sweep you off your feet."

"I'm just sick of lying down," she complained.

Bruno leaned down and kissed her, so thoroughly that Miles had to curl his lip and avert his eyes. Public displays of passion stuck in his craw these days. At great length, the kissy-face sounds eased off.

"Do you think they'll really be safe there?" Lily asked fretfully.

Miles shrugged. "Not particularly."

Bruno gave him the hairy eyeball, and Miles glared back at him, defiant. "What do you want from me? You want me to lie to her?"

"Yeah," Bruno said truculently. "What the fuck is the matter with you, man? Why upset the pregnant lady?"

Lily patted her guy's shoulder. "Nothing would upset me as much as being lied to."

Miles shook his head. "I just feel like I'm missing something."

"That's because you are," Bruno said. "I'm sorry about that guy this morning, but you're not the only one feeling bad. Remember that."

Fuck you, man. He walked out. Bruno called out after him, but he strode on without turning. He was in too foul a mood to make nice.

He headed out to his truck. There might still be someone in the faculty office to talk to. He had to keep moving, keep active, or those images of Kirk would pile up on him and suffocate him.

He tooled around on his smartphone for coordinates. Back to Wentworth. Same road he'd taken this morning, but that was a different Miles. A callow guy, obsessed with the cheating ex-girlfriend. Now all he saw in his mind's eye was the professor, without his fingers and toes. And various other important bits of business.

He parked outside the science faculty building, and hesitated before getting out, thinking of one of Sean McCloud's many lectures about maximizing his assets. *You got the looks, but you've gotta work it! The biceps alone would get you noticed! Back straight, hair slicked back. You're a six-five beefcake! Chest out! You've got good teeth! Use them!"*

"And the nose?" he'd asked drily, fingering his schnoz.

"Be grateful for the nose. The nose pulls it all together and makes it special. Otherwise you're just another pretty face."

That last bit was just spin, but whatever. He shrugged off his jacket to better display the results of all those hours in the gym. Gazed at his face in the mirror. Pallid, haunted. Not very pretty. Fuck it. His looks weren't important enough to command his attention right now.

The faculty office had a subdued atmosphere of shock and grief. People in the office were bunched up in tight groups, nervously muttering. Some wept. One hefty old dame with an iron-gray cap of hair and a body like a brick approached him. "Can I help you, sir?"

He tried flashing the teeth at her. She looked grimly unmoved.

"Ah, yes. My name is Miles Davenport," he offered. "I was wondering if I could speak to Dr. Joseph Kirk's personal assistant."

"We all helped Professor Kirk," she said. "You can talk to me."

Okay, fine. He regrouped, and dug out a card. "I'm with a private investigative agency. Professor Kirk's family has hired me to look into—"

"Are you a journalist?" she demanded.

He blinked. "Uh, no, as I said, I'm with a private—"

"The police have already been here."

"I'm collaborating with the police," he said, though it wasn't quite true. Only a matter of time, though. He would indeed collaborate with the police, at the earliest opportunity, and to the very best of his abilities. "The professor's family—"

"Professor Kirk had no family," she said triumphantly. "His ex-wife died years ago. His daughter disappeared last year."

"I'm looking into that, too. I was hired by Lara's cousin." Leetle bitty stretch, that one. "I'm trying to figure out if what happened to Professor Kirk is connected to his daughter's disappearance. I know that he was planning on traveling today, to Denver. Do you know why?"

The woman folded her arms over her large chest and stuck out her chin, studying him. He gazed back. No bullshit with the pearly whites or the biceps was going to work with this Amazon. He went for the earnest, sincere, grim and yet studly vibe. A Davy McCloud approach. Easier to execute than sparkling charm.

She scrutinized him, gave him a nod. "Come on back, then."

He followed as she stumped through cubicles. He drew curious glances as he went, but kept his eyes trained on the Amazon. This was her domain. If anyone had the goods to give up, it was going to be her.

She led him into a small, crowded office. "I probably shouldn't be talking to you, but Joseph was sick with worry after Lara disappeared, so thank the good Lord if someone is trying to find her. The poor girl doesn't have anyone left to nag the police. You'll keep looking for her?"

He opened his mouth to explain that he actually hadn't made any progress on Lara Kirk's disappearance, since he had just learned of her existence yesterday. He met her anxious, reddened eyes, and stopped.

"Yes," he said. "I will."

She looked satisfied. "Good. Now, I already told all this to the police, but I'm not sure how well they were listening."

"Did you ever meet her?" he asked.

"Joseph brought her by last spring. Beautiful girl. Talented, too. Joseph showed me a catalog of her sculptures once. I'm not one for visual art, but even I could see she had something special. Joseph was so proud. When she disappeared, he . . ." Her mouth began to shake.

Miles discreetly turned his head, and caught sight of another Lara picture on the professor's desk. Lara, in a bathing suit, hoisting herself up onto a wooden dock. Her slim, curvy body was beaded with drops of water. Innocent, fresh, drop-dead, blow-your-mind gorgeous.

"That's her?" he asked, pointing.

"A trip they took to Lake Tahoe, a couple of years ago," she said, digging a crumpled tissue out of her pocket.

"They were close?"

"Oh, yes. He doted on her. He just wasn't the same since she disappeared. This whole semester, he was like a man in a dream. And then, he got that letter." Her tone changed, gaze shifting side to side, like she was going to tell him a secret.

Miles leaned closer. "A letter?"

She nodded. "I opened it. I opened his mail, even though it's not my job. He was supposed to handle his own mail, but things were getting out of hand, so I started sorting it for him. You know, throwing out the junk, spoonfeeding him the rest. I felt so bad for him, you see."

"Yeah, I see," he said. "So? This letter?"

"So one day, I open this letter, no return address. Just a single sheet of paper, right in the middle of the page, bolded, all caps. It said, "If you want to know what happened to Lara, go to the Greaves Institute Fund-Raiser.""

Miles was perplexed. "That was all?"

"That was all. I tried to convince him to give it to the police. I thought it might have fingerprints, right? Like on TV. But he begged me not to tell anyone. He said, if she was alive, telling the police will get her killed." She pressed her hand to her shaking mouth. "So I didn't say anything. Now he's dead. If I'd told someone . . ." Her face crumpled.

Oh, sweet Jesus. His throat was tight. Her rounded shoulders, the gray cowlick at her nape, her shaking dowager's hump. It burned his ass, that a nice old lady should feel this way. Like it was her fault that these sons of bitches were out torturing and killing.

"It's not your goddamn fault," he said, with some force. "It was those evil bastards, not you. All you did was try to help your friend, as best you could." He reached out, and pulled her into a fierce hug.

He stepped back hastily, horrified at himself for taking such a liberty with a complete stranger. But she didn't seem offended.

She just blinked at him, her reddened eyes glistening, and dabbed her face with a tissue. "Ah. Well," she murmured. "Thanks for saying that, young man. It's good to hear. Whether it's true or not."

"It's true," he insisted. "Don't take it on. The blame is not yours."

She blew her nose. "Be that as it may. The police have the letter now. And the invite from the Greaves Foundation is long gone, so I—"

"There was an invite?"

"Yes, about the fund-raiser. He'd gotten it weeks ago. I asked him then if he was interested in going, but he seemed to barely hear me, so I just recycled it. But you can read about the event online if you want."

"When is it?" he asked.

She pursed her lips, and frowned. "Tomorrow. Saturday night. After he got the letter, he asked me to get him a ticket to Denver."

He grabbed her hand. "Thanks so much, ma'am."

She twitched her hand away. "Don't you ma'am me. My

name is Matilda Bennet. But if you think you're just going to walk into this party, think again, young man."

"Yeah? Why? What's special about this party?"

"Fifteen thousand dollars a head, that's what's special about it."

Miles sucked in a pained breath. The lady nodded glumly.

"Yes, I thought about going, too," she said. "But I don't know where to start. I'd be throwing away fifteen grand I can't afford to eat a tough old chicken fillet, like as not. But who knows what a sharp, resourceful young man all full of fresh ideas might come up with, eh?"

He nodded again. Yeah. Who knew. God help him.

She cleared her throat. "Well, then," she said briskly. "Off with you. Get to it. Do your best for that poor girl."

Miles headed for the door, but she called again. "Mr. Davenport?"

"Call me Miles," he said.

"OK, Miles. You'll tell me how it all comes out, won't you?"

Her face looked so anxious, with those reddened eyes and nose, it just made his heart hurt. "Yes, ma'am," he said. "I will."

Staring down Aaro in this mood was like standing in a strong headwind. She had to brace herself, to shift her emotional center of gravity to face that much raw male sexual energy coming her way.

She couldn't say no, so it was a damn good thing that she didn't want to. He'd burned her before. Now he wanted to do it again. Great. Bring it on. She'd burn him right back. They'd burn together.

She shrugged off the sheer blouse, and peeled off the tank. Undid the clasp of her bra, laid the clothes on a chair.

The house was cool, but she felt like she was on fire. She shimmied out of jeans, panties.

He walked toward her, slow, graceful, catlike. He pulled the gun out of the back of his jeans, and laid it on the nearby tabletop. He made no further move to touch her. Yet she felt stroked. Seen, in every detail.

"Turn around," he said.

She did so, squeaking in surprise when she felt him sink down to a crouch and laid his hot mouth right at the small of her back.

She gasped at the startling sensation. Light, heat, streaming up her spine, down her legs. Tightening her nipples, making her thighs squeeze together. He was kissing the dimples over her tailbone. Petting her, his big hand sliding up between her thighs, finding her damp and soft. Caressing, nuzzling. Making her feel adored, from the inside out.

She didn't want it to end, but when he eased his finger inside her and teased her clit with his thumb, she came as if she'd been primed for it for hours, a huge crashing and rushing. It left her feeling clean and soft.

She got pulled back into the space-time continuum by the sound of his belt unbuckling behind her. She turned, but he jerked her back into position, facing away from him and bent her over the back of the couch, kicking her legs wider apart. "I don't have condoms here," he said. "We left those behind at the hotel. But I won't come inside you."

"Ah . . . OK," she murmured, although he didn't sound like he'd been asking for permission, and was, in fact, already opening her body and positioning himself. "Aren't you going to take off your clothes?"

"No. I want to be ready for anything, and armed. Always."

"But . . . but . . ." She looked down at her naked self, and tried not to laugh. "That's not fair!"

"No, it sure isn't," he agreed, and before she could protest, he thrust inside her. She cried out, the sensation was so intense. Not just his body's invasion, although that was considerable, sore as she was from the excesses of the night before. It was all of him, the thundering wave of hot energy that masqueraded as Alex Aaro, crashing through her. His restless anger and fierce hunger made her fierce and hungry, too.

He held her down against the couch as he slid heavily into her body, seeking out the angle that would stroke his cock against the hot spots. Finding them, teasing them, tormenting them. He knew just how to drive her mad. He reached around and slid two fingers down to tease at her clit, pinning her with his weight. She couldn't move at all, just twitch and strain and whimper at the slow, juicy slide and stroke and push, slide and stroke and push . . . again, again, again, oh *please*.

Her face was shoved against the dusty sheet that covered the couch, mewling and jerking desperately, but he had his agenda, and he adhered to it ruthlessly. Every time she was about to crest, he stopped, held her still until the energy subsided. Then he surged in again, and drove her farther than she ever knew there was to go.

By the end, she was screaming into a tear-soaked sheet. They shot out together into that timeless otherwhere, merging. Fused.

When she floated back, his scorching warmth curved protectively over hers, she found that she had brought something with her. Like a souvenir from the whirlwind trip inside Aaro's well-armored mind.

It floated to the top as he withdrew himself from her. A haunting image of a girl, lying on a rocky floor in some dark place. Beautiful, dark haired. Big, dark, empty dead eyes, full of silent reproach.

She straightened, feeling the hot trickle of his come on her back, her bottom. "Who's Julie?" she asked.

21

Aaro jerked back. "Where the *fuck* did that come from?" She edged back at his harsh tone, bumping against the back of the couch. "Ah, I . . . I don't know. I just . . . I saw . . ."

"What? What did you see?" He hadn't intended to yell at her, but she flinched, arms flying up to protect her face from a blow.

That made his face burn, with a weird toxic mix of shame and anger. "I will not hit you," he said. "So don't flinch. It's not necessary."

"I know that," she said. "It's just conditioned muscle memory."

That pissed him off more. "That's real tragic and all, but don't guilt-trip me with your kinky Stan conditioning. I don't deserve it."

Her eyes burned, even in the dim light. "Guilt trip? You think I did that on purpose, just to make you feel bad? You arrogant butthead! You think it's all about you!"

"Just don't blame me for shit I didn't do!" he yelled.

"Then try not to be such a fucking diva!" she shot back.

"I don't like you turning over rocks inside my head! If

there's a rock on something, it's there for a good reason! Just leave the toxic waste dumps in my head alone! Is that so much to ask?"

She scooped her clothes up and clutched them. "Then you'd better stop fucking me, Aaro. I did not go looking for that. You pulled me in, and gave it to me. Keep your distance, if you don't like it. I did not ask for any of this. And now, if you'll excuse me, I need to wash."

She marched into the bathroom, her back elegantly straight.

Aaro sagged down over the table, spitting the most vile obscenities in any language that he knew. None of it helped. The fucking microwave was beeping, grating on his nerves. Probably had been for a while. When his cock was inside that woman, nothing else existed.

He slapped the microwave door open and shut to silence it, and kicked a kitchen chair across the room. It hit the fireplace and splintered. *Shit.* He was ashamed of himself. Miles had begged him to be careful, and here he was, throwing a tantrum. Trashing the place.

Fuck it. He couldn't fight this. He wouldn't be able to move or breathe or think straight until he fixed things with Nina.

The bathroom opened off the bedroom. He stopped there, stripped off his clothes and holsters and harnesses, leaving them and the guns on the bed. He went into the bathroom, which she had foolishly neglected to lock, naked as the day he was born, and as defenseless.

He'd laid down his defenses. Sacrificed them on the altar of brainless idiocy. It was the only way he knew how to tell her he was sorry for being an asshole. All the other channels were bricked up.

He climbed into the shower with her, over her voluble protests. Didn't even register the meaning of the stream of sharp words. He deserved all of them, so why bother to respond? Yeah, he was a pig-dog from hell. What did she want him to do about it?

He shampooed her hair, staring at how drops of water slid along the perfectly engineered grain of her eyebrow hairs and then tangled into her wet eyelashes like trapped diamonds. Soaping her up with shower gel, rinsing her, again and again. Rinsing was excellent. The truncated nature of his previous sexual adventures had never involved morning-after showers, so it was a happy discovery, all those tender, slippery inside bits that required protracted petting and delving and stroking to get them soap-free. Lather, rinse, repeat . . . repeat . . . repeat. Fingers deep in her pussy, seeking out that hot clenching pulse.

God, he loved to make her come. Any way was fine, fingers, tongue, cock, it was all good. He dropped to his knees to nuzzle Nina's belly, parting rivulets of water with his nose, licking, kissing right down into that sodden puff of hair that he'd been lathering up. He buried his face in it. Sweet relief, oh, God, yes. Oh, God, yum.

What with the curly ringlets and juicy pink pussy folds and the constant rush of water over his face, he wasn't getting much oxygen. Fuck oxygen. He'd gasp and choke and snort along without it, as long as he was drawing out that slick, slippery, sweet pussy nectar.

He had no clue how long he was actually at it. Tonguing her pussy put him in a trance that was light-years out of time, out of everything. Finally, there it was. She gave it up, sobbing. He held her hips to keep her steady, thrust his tongue deeper to savor the sweet, bright bursts of energy against his face. He drank it in, famished.

He stumbled to his feet, rinsing off his face. His cock bobbed hopefully between her thighs, wanting its turn to bathe in that sweet nectar, prod its way into that tight, hot hole, and thrust and heave its way to heaven on earth. *No way. Chill out, mad dog.* She had to be sore, after that last bout, bent over the couch. He had not been gentle.

Nina pushed waterlogged springy curls off her face, and reached down, clasping his cock in both hands. She gave him a questioning look. He almost laughed. Like he would refuse? Not in this lifetime.

He was sore, too, he realized. He'd lost his calluses, after six months of celibacy, but what was a little rug burn compared to a volcano threatening to lay waste to miles of countryside? Discomfort was all a matter of degree. He'd be walking funny for the rest of his life if he didn't come again, and soon.

She reached for the bar of soap. "Should I use—"

"No." He put the soap back, shut off the water. The silence was startling. A foggy, hazy, humid quiet. Hollow plops and drips.

"No?" She blinked water out of her eyes.

He slid his hand between her legs, slicking it up in the slippery well of delicious girl juice that his tongue had brought forth, and rubbed it liberally over his cock. "Balm of the gods," he said. "Way better than soap. I shut the water off so it won't rinse off the lube."

It made him almost faint with lust watching her touch herself to anoint her hands, and then she got down to business, slender hands wrapped around his shaft. He clamped his own hands over hers as she worked his cock, in the steamy, echoey quiet, her face intent, absorbed in the task. Long tight squeezes and strokes that made him gasp, stopping from time to time to moisten her hands in the sacred well. Slip and slide, twist and swirl, pull and squeeze, and oh, God . . . oh, *fuck* . . .

He exploded with a shout. Jets of hot, pearly come spurted out, fountaining over her hands, breasts, belly. He sagged against the wet tiles, staring at his come spattered over her fair skin.

A deep, animal impulse swelled up, taking him over. Before he could rethink it, he was painting her with his come. The tips of her breasts. Her taut, puckered nipples, the heavy undercurves, her dark aureoles. The swell of her belly. That spot right over her heart. The hollow of her collarbone. Slowly, like a ceremony.

Like he was putting his stamp on her.

She didn't object, just leaned against him, shivering. Her face was glowing red, soft mouth faintly open. Her breath came fast. He could feel her heartbeat, tripping, frantic. She grabbed his hand, lifted it to her lips. Sucked come right off his finger. The wet heat of her mouth made something flare, flames doused with accelerant.

He grabbed her, kissed her like he'd die if he didn't get his dose.

She wrestled away after a while. "Aaro," she pleaded. "I can't—"

"Shhh," he cut her off. "Please don't talk. Not yet." He put his finger over her lips. Could not handle anything she might say right now.

She gulped back whatever it was, and let him hug her. They were glued together with his come. Teetering on his own private cliff.

He felt her start to shiver. Turned the hot water back on, sluiced them off. They dried off with somewhat mildewy towels Nina had found, and pulled their clothes back on, such as they were. He ached for his bag of tricks, the extra firepower, the computer, the various other toys and tools. The clothes, too. The ones he had were rank with fear sweat, stained with blood from the luckless Wilder. Nina's were, too, but she just pulled them back on without complaint, sat down with a comb, and got to work on her hair. Aaro climbed onto the bed behind her, laying the gun beside him on the mattress, and tried to take the comb.

She hung onto it. "I can do it myself."

"Please." His voice still shook. "Please. It calms me down."

She gave him a long, silent look, but let go, and did not protest as he started combing.

It was just what he needed. Something long, slow, and careful, so he could concentrate on letting his stress hormones level off. Julie's black hair had been wavy, not curly like Nina's, but it still had gotten tangled into long, terrible fuzzy snarls, and the hell-bitch Rita would scream and threaten her with the shears. Until Aaro intervened. He'd made it his business to keep the hair situation under control. He'd gotten good at it. Even kind of liked it. It was his and Julie's little private thing.

By the time he'd combed out all of Nina's hair, he'd finally gotten himself to the place where he could say the words. Her hair was almost dry. Ringlets twined around his hands as he finger-combed them.

"Julie was my sister," he said. "Three years younger. Committed suicide when she was thirteen. Swam out into the sound one summer night, when we were at our father's beach house. Never swam back."

Nina listened quietly. "I know how that feels."

He grunted, doubting it. "Do you."

"Yes, I do." Her voice was tranquil. "For me, it was my mother."

She turned sideways on the bed to look at him, but he didn't want to be looked at. His throat ached. He didn't want to have this talk, he didn't even want to know, but he'd launched this fucking thing, and it had its own implacable momentum. No way out now but through.

"So?" He couldn't keep his voice from sounding angry.

"How did she do it? Carbon monoxide, alcohol, heroin, razor blades? An oven?"

The words were like blows, but Nina did not flinch.

"She used pills. I knew she was depressed. She hated herself for not being strong enough to leave him. For not stopping what he'd done to me. I wish she'd been stronger, too. But we are what we are."

"That's the truth." The words tasted bitter in his mouth.

"I still wish I could have saved her," she went on. "I felt guilty for years. I dreamed about it, obsessed about it. But it's up to us all to save ourselves, I think. There's only so much you can do for another person. The rest, they have to do for themselves."

Julie's face swam in his mind, as she'd been when they found her. The gray lips, the wide, staring eyes. Her long hair twined with seaweed.

The words burst out of him. "I want to save you."

She gave him that sweet, mysterious smile. "I know you do," she said softly. "Good luck with that."

He wanted to say something sarcastic, to flick that away, maintain security distance. But his sarcasm machine was disengaged.

"I want to save you, too," Nina said. "Though you wouldn't need any saving if you weren't unlucky enough to be hanging out with me."

"Oh, I need it," he blurted out. "I need it bad."

Her eyes widened. Her smile was luminous and tender as she reached out to stroke his bristly cheek. "Promise me you won't misbehave when you get all pissed off at yourself for saying that, OK?"

It was nice of her to try to bullshit him into a lighter mood, but it was a lost cause right now. "I don't know if I can," he said, his voice rough. "Save you, I mean."

Her fingers trailed down his jaw. "Maybe not," she said.

"But one thing's for sure. If we don't make it, it won't be for lack of trying. That's one thing no one in the world could accuse you of."

"Trying isn't enough." He rubbed his face, swallowing to calm down his shaking voice. "Fuck, Nina. I don't have a plan. I don't have shit. I'm nowhere with this. I don't know what to do next. I'm flying totally blind, and it's driving me . . . fucking . . . *crazy.*"

She slid her arms around his waist. He seized her in a hug so swift and hard, she let out a little startled *oof.* "Shhh," she soothed. "I can't think of anyone I'd rather be flying blind with than you."

"Oh, yeah?"

"Oh, yeah," she said. "The perks are amazing. The sex alone—"

"Don't make me laugh," he warned. "It wouldn't be a pretty sight."

"OK," she murmured. "We'll think of something, Aaro. We'll take it minute by minute. And I've got a good idea for the next few minutes."

"Oh, yeah?" he demanded. "What's that?"

"Food. You cooked. That was how you seduced me, remember?"

That seemed like a really excellent idea. The light from outside was all but gone, and Nina rummaged through kitchen drawers and found a flashlight with just enough juice to make a wan, brownish light for them to eat by. Nina unearthed a can of some strange tropical fruit juice, which he pried open with his all-purpose belt knife. The Lean Cuisines had cooled in the microwave, but they were ravenous and didn't bother reheating them, just ripped off the plastic and fell to. Nina went for teriyaki chicken and the Cordon Bleu. He inhaled lasagna, turkey and mashed potatoes, Mongolian beef. They guzzled bizarre papaya cocktail.

Afterward, he persuaded Nina to lie down on the bed,

whether she managed to close her eyes or not. There was no point in him doing it. Whenever his body came to rest, it jolted instantly into compulsive movement again. Besides, he knew what would happen if he got into a bed next to Nina Christie again. Enough. She was tired.

He paced for hours, peering obsessively out the windows. The moon was up, blazing on the lake water, which was glassy and still. No wind at all. The night was holding its breath.

He went to peek in on Nina. She'd fallen asleep after all. She'd borrowed a plaid flannel shirt from their hosts' closet, which swamped her, reaching halfway down her thighs. He'd tucked a wool blanket around her sleeping form. Something about her slight shape, bundled under the bulky blanket, made his chest ache.

That was the moment he felt them. His balls started to itch. The hairs on his neck prickled up. At first he thought it was paranoia. All this psychic shit, stress, and adrenaline, two nights of sleep deprivation, all getting the better of his good judgment and his objective perceptions. No way could they have been tracked to that place.

But he positioned himself at the window with a view of the main road, and waited, gun in hand. Five minutes. Ten. Twenty.

Headlights, finally. Flickering through the trees. Cruising along the winding road, until they reached the approximate position of the driveway. The lights switched off. There was his answer. *Shit*.

He went instantly cold, detached. Their hunters would use the moonlight to navigate the driveway, if they drove in at all. Perhaps they would approach on foot. Running away would be useless in the dark, with the thick trees and the snarls of bracken, jagged rocks, and steep rocky cliffs looming behind. The place had morphed from haven to trap.

"They're coming, aren't they?"

He spun around. Nina stood in the doorway, her voice eerily calm.

"You felt them?" he asked.

"I don't know if I felt them or you, but I felt something go zing."

"Go outside," he told her. "Now. Go out back, and hide in the woods. Move away, as far away as you can, and do your invisible thing."

"No," she said. "I won't leave you."

He could tell from her calm voice that there would be no moving her. It made him frantic. "Goddamnit, Nina, we don't have time—"

"There's no point. I won't make it one step without you," she said. "So we'll face them together when they come." *Die together, too, if it comes to that.* He heard the thought as it formed in her head, and then her gray-fuzz, staticky mind shield surged, and blocked everything.

He pulled the Micro Glock from the small of his back. "Take this," he said. "Six shots. Like I said. Point and shoot. It's easy."

She took it, gazed down at it. "Do we, um . . . have a plan?"

"Sure," he said. "We kill them."

Lily ran her hands through Bruno's hair. She loved the crisp texture of his wild black curls. "You should go on home," she urged. "You're tired, and Lena and Tonio are trying to stay awake for you."

"I know." He rested his head on her shoulder. "They miss you, too. We all do. It's just not as much fun without you."

"Ditto," she replied. "But it'll be over soon. Go on, go to them."

Bruno shook his head against her shoulder. "I don't want

to leave you all alone with this," he said, his voice muffled. "I fucking hate it."

"You're doing all you could," she soothed. "There's no one she could be safer with than Aaro. Plus, I think she, ah . . . likes him."

Bruno lifted his head. "Really? You mean, like, *likes* him?"

"Yeah, I do mean," she said. "He saved her life. Girls notice a thing like that. And he is extremely good looking. Girls notice that, too. That is to say, he is when he's not scowling."

"And when is that?" Bruno asked drily. "God help her, then."

Lily leaned in to him, to get a deeper sniff of his aftershave. "I'm worried about Miles," she said. "He's so thin, now. Hadn't seen him since he ran off to Aaro's lair. He must have lost thirty pounds. And then he had to witness . . . that." She shuddered. "Poor guy."

"Don't think about it," Bruno commanded. "It's bad for the baby."

Lily snorted. "You try that yourself. See how far you get."

"Just try. You have to try."

"Whatever. Now Miles is compensating by playing hero."

"There are worse ways to compensate," Bruno pointed out.

He made no move to go, and Lily didn't have the heart to push him again. They leaned against each other. Bruno reached around her belly, feeling the flop and roll of the baby inside. Nuzzling her neck.

Tension suddenly gripped him, and she turned around to see him frowning intently at the bouquets against the wall.

"Who the fuck is sending red roses to my wife?" he asked.

Lily looked, startled. A dozen big, perfect, red roses, floating in baby's breath, with a few spotted orange tiger lilies as well, making a weird, unconventional bouquet. She'd just assumed . . .

"You mean, those weren't from you?" she said.

Bruno's mouth went hard. "No," he said. "They should have been, but I haven't had time to go to a florist. When did they show up?"

"This morning sometime," she told him. "I found them here."

Bruno unwound his body from hers, slid off the bed, and crouched, examining the bouquet from closer range. "No card." He grabbed the stems, and lifted them out of the heavy vase of smoky, opaque glass, dripping copiously. He peered at the stems, then inside the vase. He reached in. Pried out a plastic disk with a stick-on side.

Lily drew in a sharp breath and opened her mouth, but Bruno shushed her. She clapped her hand over her mouth. He dropped the thing into a pitcher of water, and carried it out of the room.

He came back in, dead pale. "Were those flowers here when Miles was giving Aaro the directions to that house?"

Lily struggled to remember. "Yes," she said slowly. "I noticed them after the fetal monitoring, right before Miles came in. I remember thinking, oh, how sweet, Bruno must have left them for me. Then Miles told us what happened to Kirk, and I forgot all about it."

Bruno pulled out his phone, dialed. He waited, and waited.

He put his hand over his face. "Oh, shit."

22

Aaro crouched just inside the bedroom door, and Nina inside the bathroom, clutching her Micro Glock. He'd decided that the unfamiliar terrain outside was too dangerous. The house at least had cover, right angles. His eyes were adjusted to the dark. He had shut down all extraneous mental activity. The goal was to cap as many as possible, as fast as possible. He wished he had night-vision goggles. But he had what he had. Suck it up.

"Close the vault." Nina's whisper floated from her hiding place.

"Shhh." He visualized vault doors slamming shut—but before he could stabilize the image, something gripped his mind, glomming on like a clutching hand, squeezing, probing, squishing . . . His eyes watered, his head pounded, he sucked in air—what the *fuck* . . . ?

"Aaro? Aaro, are you OK?" Nina's whisper, louder.

He couldn't reply. Couldn't move. Terror and rage built. He braced himself, inwardly, shoving back against the brute pressure, the roaring in his ears. Gaining just enough purchase to breathe, but not enough to move or speak. Footsteps crunched on the gravel outside. Those fucking bastards weren't even trying to be quiet. They didn't have to try.

The goons filed into the house, one, two, three . . . four. Three men, a woman bringing up the rear. Relaxed, sauntering, sure of their success. The closer they got, the stronger the gripping sensation became. His ribs closed in around his lungs. His guts, compressed like a trash compactor. Pain tightened into a terrifying agony.

One of the figures walked straight into a beam of moonlight that came through the picture window. It lit up the smile on his face. He lifted his hand, like a magician performing a spell, and as he did, Aaro's gun hand lifted clear of the doorway and stretched out, where the guy could see it. Aaro's body followed, lurching forward, crawling helplessly. His hand was numb. He could no longer feel it, let alone control it. The gun slid from his nerveless fingers.

"Get him in a chair," the man said. The two men moved to obey, gripping him under the armpits, dragging him into the kitchen.

Bam. Bam. The guy who had given the order let out a cry, and stumbled, clutching his arm. *Nina.* The pressure suddenly let up. Aaro could finally turn his head. Nina leaned out from the doorway, sighting with the Micro Glock—

She shrieked, arched back. The gun fell from her fingers.

The guy walked over to her, pressing his wounded arm, staring down as she writhed and gasped. So the guy could only inflict his trick on one of them at a time.

They flicked on the light, and he was blinded for the time it took them to bind him to one of the spindly chairs, cuffing his hands to the seat, his ankles to the chair legs. They relieved him of the .357 snubbie at his ankle, the Kershaw and Gerber knives in his pockets. He craned his neck desperately for a glimpse of her, straining his ears to hear her voice. *Nina.*

Slowly, his eyes adjusted. The boss man backed into his

range of vision, his hands hooked in Nina's armpits. The woman, a hot blonde in skin-tight ninja black, carried Nina's feet. They heaved her onto a chair and fastened her to it. The boss guy grimaced at the bloody patch on the sleeve of his upper arm, poking at it gingerly. She'd winged the bastard. Pretty good, for a rookie. Too bad she hadn't gotten him through the heart. When the blonde was done with the cuffs, she back-handed Nina's face, hard. The chair rocked up, teetering precariously up onto two legs before it thudded back down.

"That's for shooting him, bitch," she said. "Just for starters."

Nina raised her head. There was a red, angry splotch on her face. The blonde looked less hot with that sadistic grimace on her face.

The bald guy who had attacked them in New York was there, a bandage around his head. Dmitri was there, too. His hot eyes were fixed on his cousin, tongue flicking out to lick his lips.

And that other guy. The one with the psychic taser in his head. Tall, late forties, unremarkable brown hair in a conservative haircut, high-quality casual sportswear. The bland, pleasant good looks of a Sears underwear model. His smile was terrifying, because it was so normal. Straight white teeth, grin lines, eye wrinkles, even a lopsided dimple. It came across as grotesque, aimed at him now, cuffed in a chair, watching somebody hit his girlfriend in the face.

Aaro dragged his gaze away. He was not ready to deal with Mr. Apparently Normal yet, though he was their real problem by far, more than all the others combined. Aaro addressed his cousin. "Hey, Dmitri."

"Sasha," his cousin said. "How long has it been? Twenty years?"

"Not long enough," Aaro said. "You're a long way from the city out here, aren't you? I thought you didn't like nature. Remember how I used to put spiders in your shoes? Snakes in your bed? You were such a pussy about that. I'm surprised to find you in a place like this."

Dmitri's lips curled. "Yeah, I remember. Nature's not my thing. I have you to thank for that, probably. But hate is a strong motivator."

Mr. Normal clapped his hands. "Cousinly love. Warms the heart. Now shut up. Your tender family reminiscences aren't on my schedule."

Aaro stared up into his face. "Who are you, asshole?"

Oh, *fuck* . . . pain slammed into him. Him and his smart mouth. He barely heard the guy above the roar in his ears, the rasp of his lungs. He concentrated—and pushed it far enough back not to pass out.

"I suggest you be more polite when you speak to me," Mr. Normal said. "I'm not used to this much resistance. You must have been enhanced. Are you? Did that lying hag Kasyanov soup you up, too?"

"What . . . are you . . . doing?" he gasped out.

"Look at him. Most people can't even talk when I blast them with this voltage," the guy mused. "Only Roy. God knows, he's had practice."

"But what the fuck *is* it?" The words burst out of him.

Mr. Normal's eyes twinkled jovially. "You are experiencing the effects of my very strong talent for compulsion, Mr. Arbatov. It's my particular specialty. Extremely useful. Perfect for my personality."

Compulsion? "To do what?" he coughed out.

"Nothing, at the moment," the man said. "I'm not focusing right now. I'm just blasting it at you wholesale. But when I do focus, I can push an unsuspecting mind into making any decision I want. Like when your hand decided to reach out beyond the door frame and drop the gun." He clicked his tongue. "Bad decision, but you can hardly be blamed." He preened. "Don't beat yourself up about it."

Aaro strained for traction. It seemed effortless, for the

guy. He stood there, perfectly calm, his face normal, no twitch, no strain, while projecting a battering force that felt like a hurricane wind.

His phone, left next to the remains of their meal, began to buzz.

Mr. Normal scooped it up. "Bruno," he said. "Your friend, who signed your death warrant. We got your destination from him and your lovely friend Lily tonight. And Miles, whoever he is. These people just talk and talk and never stop." He shook his head. "It was almost too easy."

Aaro struggled to bring up the salient details. "You're . . . Rudd?"

The guy looked gratified. "You know about me? Yes, my name is Rudd. Helga told you, I expect. She's been a naughty girl."

Aaro propelled the words out. "Until you killed her."

"No, she did that all by herself." Rudd moved closer, and the energy clawing at Aaro's mind grew stronger. He leaned close to Aaro's sweat-slicked face. "She got what she deserved, for trying to trick me. She was caught in her own trap, that's all. Devious old cunt."

The sick nauseous dark was rising up to swamp him. He struggled to keep afloat. Not that he could help Nina in his current state, but Christ, he didn't want to conk out and leave her all alone.

Too bad. It was getting dark, he was sinking lower, drifting farther . . . and farther, into the dark. . . .

"Uh, boss?" The voice came from miles away. He could not tell whose voice it was.

"Don't interrupt me!"

"You'll blow his mind, boss. Let me just read him first, please!"

The pressure let up. Aaro's head dangled as his vision cleared, dragging in lungfuls of oxygen. "What are you?" he rasped.

Rudd chuckled. "Interesting question," he mused. "And coincidentally, it's my favorite. But are you asking what I was? What I am, which is constantly evolving? Or what I aspire to become?"

Aaro coughed. "You can stop jerking off any time."

Pain ripped through him. He jerked, strained. The chair rocked.

"Be respectful," Rudd warned. "Be very respectful. At all times."

"Don't hurt him, please," Nina begged. "Please, he never—"

"Shut up, bitch!" Spittle flew from the guy's lips as he whirled on her. "No one asked you to talk yet! I'll deal with you later!"

Nina shrieked, cringing as the guy had at her with his mental flail. Aaro struggled against his bonds. "Stop! Please, don't hurt her!"

"No?" Rudd turned back to him, his lips wet. His eyes flicked from Nina to Aaro. "You'll be good?"

Aaro swallowed that down. "I'll be good," he said hoarsely.

"That's better." Rudd sounded satisfied. "As I was saying. What I was, that was the question? I'll tell you who and what I was when I met Helga Kasyanov." He waited, bright eyed, for Aaro to respond.

Great. Kissing the ass of a madman who was in love with himself. Just the thing to brighten his mood. "How?" he growled sourly.

"I sold life insurance to her!" Rudd waited for Aaro's exclamation. He giggled to fill the gap when there was none. "Isn't it perfect? One of life's little ironies. Of course, her daughter had already collected the money, three years ago, when we faked her death. But even so."

Aaro was genuinely baffled. "Life insurance?"

"Yes, it was eleven or twelve years ago." Rudd had a hint

of nostalgia in his voice. "I was back in the Tri-Cities, then. She made an appointment with me. Wanted her daughter's education covered, in case anything happened to her. Lara was fourteen at the time—"

"Where is Lara?" Nina burst in. "What did you do to Lara?"

The man shot her an annoyed glance. Nina twitched and yelped in the chair as if she'd been lashed with a whip. "You be quiet," he snapped. "I wasn't talking to you. Anyway, I sold Helga a policy, quite expensive, but very good, and the next day, she came back to see me again." His eyes drifted up, dreamily, as he remembered. "She told me I had a strong talent of persuasion. That she was involved in a think tank that was exploring all the possibilities of enhancing these innate talents. She invited me to take part. Said my abilities were wasted selling insurance. She was right. I was reborn on that day."

"Kasyanov gave you this drug?" he asked. "This psi-max shit?"

"Not at first," Rudd explained. "It took her years to develop the formula. I was there for all of it. Anabel joined us about seven years ago, and Roy right after her. Helga had no idea what she had wrought." He giggled. "It was all so very secret. It made it easy, in the end, to take the operation over and run it myself."

"And your power to persuade turned into the power to compel, with this drug?"

"More or less," he said. "Everone who is enhanced has their own special twist. Anabel, for example, does invasive telepathy. If memories are stimulated with the appropriate questions, she can pull them out of your head like beads on a string. Roy, here, he's my faithful hound. He can follow your mental frequency from over two miles away sometimes, on a good day. Both very handy abilities to have on my staff."

"Ah," he said. "So what are you now?"

"Ah . . ." Rudd considered the question. "Well, compulsion can be applied in so many ways. Business, for starters. I have made a great deal of money. But I'm bored with that. Always the same. Big yawn."

He paused, waited, eyes twinkling. Aaro gritted his teeth, and did what was expected of him. "So? What's next for you?"

"That depends on many things. One of which is you two," was his response. "We were on a cusp of a new era, before Helga betrayed us. She was developing the formula that would end our dependence on psi-max forever. But she double-crossed me, and you two are going to fix that." His smile widened. "At least, I hope so, for your sakes."

"What is it that you'll become?" Aaro hastened to drag the guy's thoughts from anger and betrayal and back to his own glorious self.

"I was making the shift into politics, you see," Rudd explained. "I need a larger scope. A bigger canvas, for my abilities, my gifts. But I need that new formula first. I want the enhancement to be permanent. No ebb and flow, no needing a fresh dose, no constant strain from the side effects." He looked at Nina. "Helga injected one of the A doses into you, my dear. And you have another dose with you, is that correct?"

Nina hesitated, her eyes darting to Aaro. Anabel hauled off and whacked her again. The sound of contact made Aaro gasp and cringe as if the pain were his own. "Yes, she does," he blurted. "One dose."

Rudd walked over to Nina, and tilted up her chin, squeezing it hard enough to make her squeak. "And how do you feel?"

Nina coughed. "I've been better."

Rudd slapped her again, rocking her head back. "Don't be snotty."

"She won't be," Aaro said hastily. "Tell them, Nina. *Now.*"

Nina held her head up, blinking, but her face was composed. "Yesterday I had some nasty hallucinations," she said. "Also some waves of what I assume was telepathy that I could not control. Today, not so much. I can hear thoughts, but I can block them out at will. Helga told me I had three days, four at the most, without the B dose."

"Or what?" Anabel demanded.

Nina looked up at her, quiet for a moment. "Or I die."

Silence. The four attackers all exchanged grim glances.

"Without the B dose," Rudd repeated. "Well, there it is, then. This is the part where the two of you tell us where that B dose is."

Rudd crossed his arms. The silence grew once again, and took on actual weight as it charged with danger. Impending pain and terror.

Aaro's guts sank. "We don't know where it is," he said.

Rudd glanced at Roy, and made a gesture. Roy punched Aaro in the jaw. The blow snapped his head back, cut his lip against his teeth.

Aaro licked blood off his lip. "It's still true," he said flatly.

"Is it?" Rudd was breathing hard. "Is it? See if it's true, Anabel!"

The blonde approached him now. He winced as the mental hand began poking. It hurt, almost as much as Rudd's mental beating, but in a more intimate way. He resisted, kept those vault doors locked. Like he used to do with Oleg. She battered on them, but the doors held.

"He's blocking me." Anabel's voice was sharp. "The son of a bitch is blocking me!"

The air around her changed. She glowed, eyes sparkling, a nimbus of light gathering around her. "I could get through it." She flicked a coy glance at Rudd. "It would be fun, to do it in front of her."

Rudd grunted. "I don't have the stomach for it at this

hour," he said. "There's a more sanitary way, one that doesn't involve bodily fluids." He gestured at Nina. "Hit her again."

Anabel pouted, but she turned to Nina, hauled off—

"No!" Aaro shouted. "No, don't. I'll, uh . . . I'll lower the shield." He said the words without even knowing if that mechanism was within his voluntary control. He would make it be. *Please.*

Dmitri chuckled. Anabel lowered her clenched fist. She gripped his face in her hands. Her dangling blond hair tickled his neck. So beautiful to look at, and she smelled sweet, too, but something stunted and unclean squirmed behind her eyes. He recoiled, every muscle rigid.

"Open wide, big boy," she cooed.

For a moment or two, he didn't think it was going to happen. He strained to visualize the vault doors. Thank God he had something concrete to imagine. He had Nina to thank for that. For that, and a million other unnameable things. He pushed that thought away. No tender thoughts of Nina with that mind-raping hag hanging over him.

Even so, he seemed to feel Nina, reaching out. A gentle touch, holding him up. He clung to that hand in the darkness, and pictured those vault doors. The image formed, clear and sharp. He shoved them open, slowly, from the inside. They creaked . . . first a crack, wider . . .

Anabel drove inside, violent and eager. He jerked, fighting nausea, panic. His heart thudded as she flailed around inside his naked inner self, hacking and slashing. "I've got him!" Her voice trembled with excitement. "Ask the questions now! Quick! I don't know how long I can hold him. He's very strong! Hurry!"

Rudd cleared his throat. "Did Helga Kasyanov enhance you with psi-max?" he demanded.

Aaro yelled, as Anabel plowed through his mind, prodding and pinching. He could not speak, so it was a damn good thing she answered for him. "He never heard of psi-max or of Kasyanov before yesterday. His friends in Portland asked him to help Nina Christie."

"All right then. What are the effects of the new formula?"

Another assault. He tried not to cry out. He felt torn apart.

"He doesn't know much." Anabel sounded disappointed. "Just what Kasyanov said. He heard a recording, of Helga babbling. She said then that the formula will stabilize the psi, but only if you get the B dose in time, within three days. Four, max. Helga croaked at day five. When I saw her in the ICU, she looked like shit. Like she was melting down from the inside."

"One more question, before we toss you in the trash." Rudd's voice vibrated with anger. This time, he let his coercive power thunder through the words, driving them into Aaro's head like a hammer driving a pick. "Where are the B doses?"

The double invasion was agony. He almost lost consciousness at the noise, the blinding lights, the pain. He was screaming, but he could not hear his own voice. He writhed, flopped. Air rushed past his face.

Thwack, a sideways whole body blow. The world had turned ninety degrees. He was on the floor. Gasping for breath.

"No idea." Anabel's voice was sullen. "No fucking clue. Whatever Helga told them, it wasn't enough. I got something about a library. Something about a grave. Wycleff. Skeletons. A grave. A party. That's it. It's nonsense. Garbage. He doesn't think they'll find the dose, that's for sure. He's afraid she'll die. He's scared shitless."

"How sweet, that he cares," Rudd muttered. "I'm moved."

"Yeah, maybe we could speed things up for him," Anabel said. "Put him out of his misery." She aimed a vicious kick to his thigh. "He's in love with her. They're fucking like bunnies, every chance they get. Love in the face of certain death. Like, *La Bohème,* or something."

"I'm not interested in his sex life," Rudd snapped. "Focus."

"Wycleff?" It was Roy speaking, now, though he could not turn to see. "Why Wycleff? That old goat's been dead for years. Maybe that's what the grave part's about. Or maybe Helga was just delirious."

"Shut up, Roy," Rudd said. "I didn't ask for your input."

They left Aaro forgotten on the floor, coughing as blood ran from his nose down his throat, and turned to Nina.

"You do know that if you block Anabel, we will punish him," Rudd told her. "Understood?"

"Yes." Nina's voice was amazingly even. "I get that."

They asked her the same questions, and got the same conclusions, but Nina didn't shout or choke nearly as much as he had. She just went rigid, trembling and silent, enduring it when they did their mind-rape-and-battery thing. Tough as boot leather. Amazing.

Aaro couldn't see her, no matter how he lurched or struggled or craned his neck. All he could do was watch her feet twitch and her toes curl in the fancy sandals Roxanne had brought, to go with the sexy new outfit. He tried to reach out to her, but he didn't know how. That was Nina's magic thing, not his. He couldn't help her the way she had helped him. He couldn't do anything. He was a useless fucking lump of dead meat. He wanted to hit himself.

Hate them, not yourself, silly. It sounded like Nina's scolding voice echoing through his mind, but she was busy gasping and jerking as they dug around inside her head.

He faded in and out of consciousness. Swam back to the surface to find Roy and Dmitri hoisting him upright. He stared up into his cousin's gloating face. Spat blood into it.

Dmitri wiped the red spatter off. "You'll wish you hadn't done that while you watch me and Roy taking turns with your fuck buddy," he said. "At least this detour is good for something. Always a pleasure getting laid, and getting laid by your woman, ah, now, that's worth something to me. Plus, I'll be able to read your mind while I do it."

"Read my . . ." He stared at Dmitri, sickened. "You?"

"Oh, yeah. Me." Dmitri's smile was broad. "I'm a telepath, too. It's in the family, after all, right? Maybe I got the latent ability from wherever Tonya got it. I love it. Doing . . . *this*."

He dug into Aaro's head, not as deep or hard as Anabel, but it hurt, having that squirming presence inside. Dmitri groped and probed . . . and laughed. "You're as much of a sanctimonious prick as you ever were," Dmitri said. "Always moping, agonizing about hurting people. Fucking wuss. You'd do anything for her, wouldn't you? Never fear, cousin. Whatever you can do to her, I can do better. I'll show you tonight, when the boss is gone. Over and over. In every hole she's got."

"That butthead psycho Rudd is your boss?" Aaro asked. "Oleg was better. Never grew up to be boss yourself, huh? Don't feel bad. Some are born to lead and some to follow, you know?"

Whap. Dmitri's roundhouse to the ribs made him suck wind.

His cousin rubbed his knuckles and circled the chair.

"Stop," Rudd ordered. "I didn't give you permission to beat him."

"You said he was mine after you questioned him," Dmitri said.

"I'm not through yet," Rudd snapped. "Where's the last A dose, Anabel?"

"Found it in her purse." Anabel approached, unwinding the bubble wrap that was wound around the syringe.

Aaro glanced at Nina. She was snowy pale, but eerily calm. Her face had that carved-out-of-marble look, in spite of the blood trickling from her nose and lip. Wild hair, springing in all directions. Undaunted.

Anabel held up the syringe. "What are you going to do with it?"

Rudd gestured toward Aaro. "Inject it into him."

"But . . . but it's the only dose we have!" she protested.

"It's garbage," Rudd said. "A fairy tale. That's all. Kasyanov's dead. Without the B dose, what's in this syringe is a slow poison. If these two can't tell us where the B dose is, there's no one left alive who can."

"No!" Nina's unnatural calm had shattered. "No, please, there's no reason to inject it into him! There's no point! You don't have to—"

"Did I ask for your opinion? Go ahead, Anabel."

Anabel looked as if she were going to cry. "But there's no other—"

"There never will be!" Rudd shouted. "Accept it! We'll find someone who can duplicate the current psi-max we've been using, and content ourselves with that. I've been wasting precious man-hours on a worthless treasure hunt. Score one for Kasyanov. She fucked us. We fucked her back. She's dead. We're flat even. Game over."

Anabel turned and looked them over. "And them?"

"Take them to Karstow," he said. "Lock them up together in the subbasement. Set up video surveillance. Should be entertaining, to watch them break down. We can contemplate our own narrow escape." He wagged an admonishing finger. "It'll be an object lesson."

"But he'll be on psi-max," Roy said. "What if he manifests?"

"If it's a dangerous talent, just kill him. But don't damage his brain. I want a full autopsy. On both of them."

Anabel shoved up Aaro's sleeve. His muscles bunched up as he strained at the plastic cuffs. She punched the needle in, savagely.

Nina screamed for him, though she hadn't screamed for herself.

Nina's mouth was still moving, but his blood pressure was going south, and he could not hear her. Just his heart thudding, very fast, very loud. Falling, falling. Gone.

23

Nina fought back the fear. *Don't faint.* She stared at Aaro, willing him not to be dead. He didn't seem to breathe, and his mind didn't respond when she reached out with hers. *Don't faint.* It was just her, now. All up to her. She had to come up with a plan for them both. Something brilliant, amazing. Hah.

Pay attention, goddamnit. She focused in on the conversation.

". . . us to take them to Karstow now?" Anabel was saying.

Rudd frowned. "Not you. Dmitri and Roy can take them to the Karstow facility. You're coming with me."

Anabel looked put upon. "But Roy—"

"Roy can make do with Dmitri. They'll manage without you. I know you were looking forward to playing with your new toy, but I need you with me at that fund-raiser for the Greaves Institute, remember?"

"Fund-raiser? I have to leave those two fuckups all alone with the captives to go and be arm candy at a cocktail party? Are you serious?"

"I will decide what's relevant, Anabel, not you. This is

Greaves, remember! I have to present my gift! Maybe if you're lucky, your toy will still be alive in a couple of days. You can amuse yourself then. We have flights booked from New York, but at this point, we'll save time driving there directly. Besides, someone has to transport the model, now that Roy will be babysitting these two." He grabbed a handful of Aaro's hair, making his head loll. "Roy, come out with us. I want you to move the boxes of the model from your car into mine, and you might as well carry the man out while you're at it. I have no intention of leaving this place until he's safely locked in the trunk of your vehicle."

Roy sliced through Aaro's cuffs and caught his limp body with a grunt of effort as it sagged. He hoisted Aaro over his shoulder in a fireman's carry, cursing as he staggered out the door.

Rudd gave Dmitri a narrow glance. "Roy will be back in a few minutes, to load her up, too," he warned. "Do not damage her."

"Can we, uh, you know . . . ?" Dmitri waggled his eyebrows suggestively. "Might as well have our fun before she falls apart."

Rudd's nostrils flared in distaste. "Oh, I suppose," he said faintly. "If you must. But I repeat. Do not damage her. I want to observe what the drug does to her at Karstow. Is that understood?"

"Crystal clear," Dmitri said.

Rudd left. Anabel shot Dmitri a warning glance, and followed.

Nina's fear kicked up, tenfold, until it choked her, but Rudd's words kept echoing. *Greaves Institute. Greaves. Greaves?*

The thought evaporated as Dmitri yanked her hair, and leered into her face. His hot breath was sour. She struggled not to gag.

Be clear, be quiet. The less he read, the better her chances of taking him by surprise.

"This would have been more fun with Sasha watching," he said. "But fuck it, I'll manage. I see he's tarting you up. You're showing your tits now. Very pretty." He squeezed one, hard enough to make her gasp, her mind shield roaring up to protect—

Whack, he slapped her. "Drop the shield, bitch. Or I'll break your nose."

She blinked, eyes watering at the umpteenth blow to the face. It was excruciatingly difficult to lower it. But she'd done it when Anabel read her. To protect Aaro. So she knew she could. *Still. Lake water in the moonlight. Not thinking. Mind open, empty, so very still. Opening . . .*

He jabbed into her mind as soon as he felt the yielding. She read what he had planned for her, freezing it somewhere in her head, not allowing herself to react.

Empty. Calm. Still water. Moonlight. "What you have in mind requires taking these cuffs off," she said to him.

"Shut up, bitch. I'm on to your tricks."

"No tricks." She smiled at him. *Still mind. Clear water. Moonlight on a lake.* "I could never pull one over on you. So I won't try. I'm not stupid. But I'm a telepath, too, you know." She peeked up through her lashes. "Don't you think that could be . . . interesting?"

Dmitri's eyes narrowed. His face was like a ruined, night-marish version of Aaro's. Like, and yet horribly unlike.

"What would be interesting?" he asked slowly.

"You and me," she said, trying to sound coy. "Minds open. Joined. Have you ever done that? Joining mentally during sex?" She gestured with her chin toward the door. "Sasha can't do that. He can't read me, and won't let me read him, so that door is closed. But with you, it could be, like, total union. It's just so intriguing, you know?"

She parlayed a shudder of revulsion into what she hoped looked like desire, and formed an image of herself, naked, inviting him.

Lust kindled his bloodshot gaze. "You're a bad girl."

She tried to shrug, but her shoulders were in a state of burning agony. "I know when to switch sides. I like winners. Sasha lost. Time to move on." She gazed at the bulge in his pants, and formed a clear image of herself, kneeling, caressing him with both hands while she serviced him with her mouth. "Untie me," she urged. "I mean, what could I do to you? You're twice my size, and armed to the teeth. And a telepath. So strong. It's just, like . . . wow." She licked her lips. "I go for that."

Dmitri pulled out a knife. The blade snicked out, and he waved it in her face. "Take a good look," he warned, and circled behind her chair.

She bit her lip and stifled a moan as the blade put pressure on the tight plastic cuffs, and then cut through them. She tried not to cry out as her arms fell free. Blood rushed into her numb, cold hands, hurting like fire. Her wrists had a raw, bleeding line.

"Get to it," Dmitri said.

She forced a smile, and got up. Backing away as she tugged off the sleeve of the flannel shirt. It came loose, dropped to the floor.

His brows knitted. "Where the fuck are you going?"

She arched her back. "The couch, of course." It was a balancing act, hiding real thoughts, projecting the false ones. *Calm mind. Still water.* He came closer, until his fetid breath filled her nose. She kept the smile on, projecting a stream of submissive sexual images until he was inches from her face, groping her breasts, with rough hands.

He jerked his belt loose. "Get to it, bitch."

She let her smile freeze, and her gaze drop to his shoulder. She shrieked, backing up a step. "Oh, God, don't move," she said, voice quivering. "A spider . . . oh, my God, it's a black widow!"

"Wha . . .?" Dmitri jerked his head around.

She punched the image into his head. Black spiders, bulbous, gleaming abdomens, crawling on his shoulder, in his hair, legs scuttling on his cheek, his neck—

He shrieked, batting at the illusory spiders. Nina lunged for the heavy old landline telephone on the table by the couch. She swung—

Crack, it connected with Dmitri's head. He screamed, spun. Blood flew. His fists flailed. One caught her a glancing blow on her temple. She lost her grip on the base of the phone, but whacked him again with the heavy receiver on the back of the head, knocking him forward against the couch. She lunged, looped the phone cord around his neck, dragged him off his feet. He fell backward, on top of her.

She hit her head on something as she went down, but hung onto consciousness. She was screaming something, but she didn't know what, obscenities, insults. He was Stan and every other vicious bastard who had beaten or raped or shot or stabbed his girlfriend or wife or kid or anyone weaker than himself, and she was going to destroy that monster once and for all, annihilate him, crush him. The universe narrowed down to that cord. Keeping it taut. He was big, strong. It took everything she had. His blood smeared her hands. She kept screaming, kept pulling. His fingers scrabbled, trying to get a grip on the cord.

His efforts got feebler. He twitched, flopped. Went limp.

She lay beneath his dead weight, panting. Frozen with terrified disbelief. Wary of a trick. She could not believe it.

Move, idiot. Roy would soon be back. She scrambled out from under Dmitri. The cord wound around his neck was bloody. Was he dead? She didn't know. Couldn't bear to check. She scrambled away, snorting for air through snot, blood. Aaro. Aaro. Had to hurry. She saw Aaro's all-purpose belt knife lying on the table, next to the juice can. *Knife.* For the duct tape. That would be good. She scooped it up. Aaro's smartphone still lay on the table, so she grabbed that, too. She looked around for Aaro's other knives, and the pistols he had carried, but Roy had evidently carried them away. The Micro Glock was gone, too.

Roy could be here any minute, but she'd gotten away from him at the hospital by using her invisible trick, so she pulled herself in tight, generating *nobody here, nobody here.* She could do it even while her knees were weak with fear. She had lots of practice.

She scuttled into the brush, but that meant making more noise, thwacking branches, tripping, snapping twigs. The car they'd packed Aaro into had to have been parked on or near a road, either the driveway or the main road. If she left the driveway, she risked getting lost in the dark. The moon was about to set. No more light 'til dawn. But if she stayed on the road, she was sure to meet up with Roy.

nobody here, just the breeze, just a rock, just a tree

Trees. She'd stay a couple yards off the road, creeping, in the shadows of the trees.

nobody here, nobody cares, just the dark

She heard him coming from a good ways off, and scrambled farther into the shadows. Brambles. Blackberries. They clutched at her naked upper arms, raking and scratching. She barely felt them.

She curled up into a tight ball, *gray rock, still water, leaves rustling.* Calm, neutral images filled her mind like a cup, flooding out everything else. She herself shrank smaller and smaller, light retreating into the distance. A pinpoint. Vanishingly small.

Roy's footsteps were heavy, crunching on gravel. As they grew louder, she herself got smaller. Nanoworld small.

He walked past, not ten feet from her, and went on.

It took a few blank, stupid moments to remember who she was, what she was trying to do. Hard to keep the shield up while sprinting, not slide into screaming panic. She tripped over rocks, skinned knees, hands, her breath sawing in her chest. *nobody there, nobody there*

She almost ran into the SUV. She tugged at the doors, which were locked, and so was the trunk. And with all the rocks she'd smashed her bare toes against, it was absurd that it took a frantic eternity to find one massive enough to do the job. Heaving that sucker through the car window, hearing it smash, felt good. Couldn't savor it. Feelings were dangerous. They turned her into a beacon for that hound to home in on.

Cold, stay cold. Lump of ice, gray rock, tiny pebble, nothing at all

She groped around in the dark in the vehicle for the trunk release, finally found it, and popped it open. Her time window was closing. Any second, she would hear running footsteps. Gunshots.

Aaro was terribly still, duct-taped within an inch of his life, if he still had one. She sawed at his bonds, begging him in a sobbing whisper to wake up, wake up, please. She could not carry him. Knees, wrists, head, ankles, upper arms. So much damned gummy tape, and her hands shook, and his knife was sharp, and if she made a false move in the dark she'd open one of his veins and kill him herself by accident.

He moved, stirred. Tears of relief streamed down her face. "Huh?" he muttered. "Wha . . . ? Nina? God . . . my head . . ."

"Get up," she said sharply. "I'm sorry about your head. But if you don't get up, we'll both die! Come on. Hurry. *Up.*"

She tried to lift him, but she could barely roll him onto his side. She pulled one of his legs out, heaving and tugging at his torso. He tumbled out, grabbing the car to keep from falling to the ground.

"Now," she hissed. "Up! We have to go! On your feet!"

He staggered up, clinging to her. She directed him into the featureless dark of bushes and trees. He could barely stay on his feet.

"Be quiet," she whispered fiercely. "Inside your mind and out. Roy's out there. I'm going to try something, Aaro. Are you ready?"

He stumbled to his knees over something, struggled back onto his feet with a grunt of pain. "Ready for what?"

"I'm going to project something into your mind," she whispered. "It's my invisible trick. If you can feel how I do it, maybe you can do it, too. At least you can try. Open the vault, Aaro. Please."

"Be gentle," he begged her. "My head is splitting open."

She dragged him deeper into the trees. "I'll try."

The night was a hell of pain and staggering. Even the light of the moon was too much for his eyes. He could only focus on Nina's crazy invisibility trick if he kept his eyes squeezed shut. So damn hard. Counter to his nature. He liked things to be clear, sharp, chopped off. He hated blurring, fuzz, static. If felt like he was hiding from himself.

Duh, Einstein. That's the whole point.

He kept grimly on with it. Nina was the one with the eyes, and the functioning brain. The one who had outwitted the pack of scum-sucking killers, alone and unassisted, and rescued his sorry ass.

How . . . ? Later for that. It was all he could do to just stay on his feet. Clutching her, for reference, for direction, for everything.

The moon finally set, and Nina let him stop. They huddled up next to the corrugated aluminum siding of some farm outbuilding. Dawn was lightening. His vision was coming back, slowly. He could see the distant lights of the freeway junction, and closer, the back of some prefab strip mall store, recently carved out of the surrounding farmland.

Nina cuddled next to him, fiddling with duct tape that clung to his head. Her lips were soft against his forehead. The contact eased the pain. "Keep it up," she whispered. "He's out there, looking. I feel him."

She projected another wave of her static fuzz frequency. He gratefully caught it, matched it, and they rode it together, lost inside their bubble of *nobody there nobody there nothing but air*. The two of them, fused into a single tiny nucleus. When he gave into it, it was actually kind of restful. He was too tired to resist the sweetness.

Dawn lightened the sky. They were damp, cramped, chilled, and stiff. His headache had subsided to a dull throb with the occasional lightning strike of apocalyptic agony. More or less dealable.

They couldn't stay huddled here forever. He felt in his pockets, tried to speak, but had to cough for a while to get his swollen vocal folds to produce sound, and coughing hurt like a sonofabitch. "Phone gone."

"No, it's not. I have it." Nina dug into the purse that she, amazingly, still had, and pulled out his phone—and his belt knife. "This, too, if you want it back."

He took it, and stared at it, mouth agape. "How the hell . . . ?"

"Later," she said gently. "We have to go."

He nodded, regretting it instantly. "Where?" he croaked.

She smoothed tangled wads of hair back from his eyes. "Well, about that. I heard something Rudd said, after Roy carried you out to the car. He had to go to a fund-raiser party, for the Greaves Institute."

There was something significant there, but he wasn't grasping it.

"Greaves," she repeated. "Graves. Do you think that Helga was saying Greaves, instead of graves? You think it's possible?"

He felt a cold flutter over his skin. "Greaves Institute? Helga said Greaves party. Who is Greaves? Where is the party? He didn't say?"

She shook her head. "All I know is, he and Anabel are driving there now. And it's tonight. We'll find out. Call Bruno now."

"No, wait," he said. "First, we look around for a moving vehicle. If we're on foot, they'll get us. If we call a cab, they'll get us."

They crept through pastures and outbuildings until he saw the one he wanted, parked next to a barn. A rusting '84 Ford F150 pickup. Perfect. God grant it have a few drops of gasoline in it.

Its front driver's side window was smashed in, plastic taped over it, so the door was easy to open. Nina climbed in and watched him peer under the dash, struggling to focus on the wiring harness. The tiny pinpoint flashlight on his belt knife saved his ass, lighting up the dusty power wires, connecting to fuel pump and lights. And starter wires.

He peeled the plastic off the tips of all three, spliced the two that connected power to the components. Touched the starter wire to the splice point.

The truck coughed, and started up. He was so relieved, he almost burst into tears. He bent the starter wire way back, to isolate it as best he could, and guided the car without headlights past the ranch-style house, praying that the inhabitants were sound sleepers.

"Stay invisible," she murmured. "It's too soon to be triumphant."

But no one stopped them as they pulled onto the main road. Less than an eighth of a tank of gas, but that was still outrageous luck.

Nina handed him the cell. He reached Bruno on the first ring. The guy was uncharacteristically quiet when he picked up the line.

"Who is this?" Bruno asked warily.

"It's me," Aaro said.

"Oh, God." Bruno's voice was thick with relief. "I guess you know about those assholes planting a bug in Lily's hospital room?"

"Yeah. It got pretty wild, there, for a while, last night."

"And Nina?"

"She's OK. Roughed up, but OK."

Bruno let out a sharp sigh. "How'd you do it, man? I thought . . . I thought you guys were dead meat. I thought we'd killed you."

"I didn't," Aaro said.

"Huh?"

"They kicked my ass," Aaro said. "I got rolled in duct tape and shoved into the trunk of a car. Nina did it. She got me out of there."

"But she . . . but how . . . ?"

"I don't know. All I know is, she is the wild warrior goddess with the flaming sword of righteousness. Do not mess with her, man, or she will fuck you up."

Nina leaned toward him, impatient. "Later for bullshit, please," she said. "That guy is still looking for us."

"Of course," said Bruno hastily. "So where are you two?"

Aaro hesitated. "You sure there's no more bugs on you?"

"I'm in the middle of the parking lot," Bruno told him.

"OK. We're on Route twenty-nine, at the southernmost freeway entrance out of Lannis Lake. Driving a stolen car. We need to ditch it real soon."

"Hold on, I've got my tablet, I'll Google map it. So what's the plan?"

"I don't have any ID. Lost my wallet. Can't fly, can't rent. Nina still has the ID Wilder brought for her, and the cash. It was in an envelope in the backseat of his car. But neither of us is really fit to drive right now. A bus is our best bet, I guess. But we can't take one from Cooper's Landing or Lannis Lake. They'll be watching. We need to catch one from farther away."

"OK, I'm picking this town at random, OK? Go to Glenville. Southwest of there. Forty miles away, population fifteen hundred."

Aaro looked at Nina's blood-stiffened hair, the marks on her face, the lacerations on her goose-bumped shoulders. Muddy, bloodstained jeans. Bloodied toes. Swaying tits with a nipple hard-on under the frayed tank top. "Is there a strip mall? With a Target, or something?"

"You want to do retail therapy?" Bruno sounded amused.

"We're covered with mud and blood," Aaro said bluntly.

"Ah, yeah. OK. Right. There is, in fact, a strip mall in Glenville, first exit. I'm sending coordinates. And I'll order you the tickets. Where to? Want to bus it to the nearest big city? Or all the way here?"

Aaro hesitated. "Is Miles there with you? I wanted to ask him to check out some data for me before I answer that."

"Nope, sorry. Miles is getting ready to head to the airport right about now," Bruno said. "He's on his way to Denver."

"What's in Denver?"

"Fucked if I know. He's got this wild idea. Talked to a secretary at Kirk's faculty office. The prof got a mysterious letter some time ago, telling him to go to this fund-raiser party if he wanted to find out what happened to his missing daughter. Got sliced into chunks before he could go check it out. So Miles is going. Nobody could talk him out of it. He's got this bug up his ass about it."

Aaro's neck prickled. "Fund-raiser? For what?"

"Something called, lemme see, the Greaves Institute," Bruno said.

The air whooshed out of Aaro's lungs. "Greaves," he repeated, in a whisper. His heart thudded. "No shit."

"Anyhow, I could meet you in Salt Lake City by late tonight, if I stepped on it," Bruno offered.

"No," Aaro said. "Get us tickets for Denver, too."

"Denver?" Bruno paused for a long moment. "Why?"

Aaro started grinning. Having a place to go, any place on earth at all, made him so happy he wanted to break into song.

"We've got a party to go to," he said.

24

The damp dawn air blew through the broken window as Roy speeded around the snaking corridors of green on the lakeside road. Broken glass crunched beneath his ass on the seat. He tasted bile.

Too many disappointments for Rudd lately. This would put Roy's quota squarely over the top, and Anabel wasn't even there to distribute the blame. Though Anabel didn't lose points when she fucked up alongside him, just because she was a pretty girl with a juicy, hot snatch that she offered up to Rudd whenever he needed it for his various projects. Roy's own talent was just as valuable, but damn, it didn't seem that way, without the nympho-bouncing-tits-and-gaping-pussy card to play.

And Dmitri was worthless, as far as distributing blame went. He must have been insane to involve that dickhead.

He'd left the worthless scum lying in his own blood, phone cord noose around his neck, pants around his knees. Nina Christie had taken him. The bitch was tough. Nice tits, too. He'd been looking forward to a piece of that before the long drive to Karstow. A tension reliever, so rare and sweet in these strange days. But no. He never caught a fucking break. Never.

He jerked the car around into the driveway, bumping over ruts and holes. Goddamn shitty ungraded roads, making his jaw clack and his teeth rattle. He could not get a fix on them. Just fleeting traces of the man, never for long enough to pin down their location. They winked in and out, moving, shifting around. Taunting him. Thumbing their noses.

He'd tried blundering after them offroad, in the forest, but that quickly proved to be stupid and useless, without a clear scent to home in on. Then he'd tried in the car, within the range they could possibly be. If they were on foot. But what if they weren't on foot anymore?

He stared out the broken window at the lake. Fucking *fuck*. Chances were, Rudd would make him shoot himself. Tragic suicide, so shocking, we had no idea he was so depressed, blah, blah. He could actually feel the place under his jaw where the bullet would go in.

He should just keep on driving. To Mexico, maybe. But that meant driving away from psi-max. His whole being rejected the idea. Without psi-max, he was nothing. He might as well eat the bullet.

He jumped out of the car and stomped inside, not sure if he was going to revive that asshole or kick him to death here and now. He was tending toward the second option, just to blow off some steam.

But when he walked in, Dmitri was no longer on the floor. The room was empty, tables and chairs overturned, bloody telephone and tangle of cord spread on the floor. Blood drops dotted the linoleum.

He heard water running from the bathroom. "Dmitri! Get your ass out here!" he bellowed.

The water switched off. Dmitri appeared in the doorway, dabbing at his forehead with a towel. He gazed at Roy, cool and expressionless.

"You asshole!" Roy shrieked. "How did you let her go? You have fucked us so far up the ass, we will never stand up straight again!"

"She has another talent." Dmitri's voice was hoarse, no doubt due to being strangled. There was a bloody line across his throat. "She can project images. Same mechanism as telepathy, but active rather than passive. Took me by surprise. Rammed it to me. Sneaky bitch."

"Like Kasyanov." Roy shuddered at the memory. "So, she zapped you with an illusion? What did she hit you with?"

"None of your fucking business."

The guy's eyes were cold. He felt a cold flutter of unease. Before, he'd always had Dmitri by the balls. Roy had the psi-max. Roy made the rules. This did not feel like before. Dmitri was different. And that buzzy glow in Dmitri's eyes, that was different, too. It looked like he'd topped up, but how could he have? He was dry. Roy was doling out psi-max tabs on an as-needed basis. Dmitri had peaked almost an hour ago, and was coming down the other side.

"Get your ass in gear," Roy ordered. "We have to correct this fuck-up of yours or we are both dead meat, you understand?"

"I don't think so," Dmitri said.

Roy stared at him. "Who the fuck asked you to think, butthead? Do you have any idea what Rudd can do to us? He can make you swallow your own tongue, or drink a bottle of Drano, or slice open your own bowels! And he likes it, you hear me? He's a fucking psycho!"

"Where are your car keys, Roy?"

"I'm not giving them to you, so what the fuck do you care?"

Roy cried out at the sudden, painful intrusion in his head.

"Ah. In your pocket," Dmitri said softly. "Just as I thought."

"Stay out of my head, or I will fuck you up! Yeah, they're in my pocket. Right here." Roy held the keys up, rattling them. "So is this." He held up his Beretta with the other. "So don't get any ideas, asshole."

"Speaking of ideas. You never did hear the recording Kasyanov made, did you?"

"No, we did not, thanks to you. Fortunately, we don't need to. Anabel read them left, right, and center. She knows everything they knew. Why are you wasting my time with this?"

"Kasyanov said, 'Graves party,'" Dmitri said. "I didn't catch it before. I thought it was 'graves,' just like Sasha and his whore did. Anabel said something about graves and skeletons. But it's not graves. It's Greaves. The fund-raiser for the Greaves Institute. That's where that bitch Anabel and Rudd are headed, right?"

"What do we care where they're headed?" Roy yelled. "We don't give a flying fuck anymore, remember? We don't have the goddamn A dose, so the B dose is irrelevant! Focus, Dmitri!"

"They care," Dmitri pointed out. "Sasha and his whore care very much."

"They didn't know anything!" Roy yelled.

"Of course they didn't. They had no point of reference. I didn't understand either, until I heard Rudd talk about the Greaves party. But they heard the recording that I heard, and Nina Christie was listening when Rudd ordered Anabel to go to the Greaves party. She's not stupid. If I put it together, she will, too. She and Sasha will go to the fund-raiser. That's where I'll catch up with them. Which brings me to my next question."

"We don't have time for questions! Let's get moving!"

"Answer me first," Dmitri went on, with that same eerie calm. "The first time you gave me psi-max, at the club. Remember?"

"Of course. Why?" Roy shrieked, startled. The invasion was violent this time, like someone was stripping away his siding, ripping open his walls with a chainsaw. Slashing, cutting, tearing.

"Why did you give it to me?" Dmitri asked softly.

Roy did not have to answer. The question itself brought the information up, as if Dmitri had typed key words into a search engine. Dmitri ransacked his thoughts, his memories, his fears, all connected like sprawling webs, each memory tugging a deeper one loose. His life ran past like a sped-up movie. Roy had no idea that Dmitri was such a powerful telepath. Anabel's gift was nothing in comparison.

Dmitri began to laugh. "You meant to kill me," he said, in a tone of amused discovery. "But I lived. I surprised you. That's gratifying. I like surprising people. I plan to do a great deal more of it in the future. But for now, let's just wrap this up. Give me the car keys, Roy."

Fuck you, Roy started to say, before he saw the cobra wrapped around his wrist. He screamed, shaking to fling it off. Heard the *ka-chunk* of jingling keys hitting the floor, the thud as the gun followed.

The cobra sank its fangs into the fleshy part of his thumb. He shrieked. The pain was agonizing. *Trick! It's just a fucking illusion trick!*

He knew it. Knew it for a fact. But still, his heart raced and the snake hissed, venom dripping from its milk-white, gaping jaws.

It bit again. He screamed louder.

"I learned the trick from her. Great, isn't it?" Dmitri's voice came from miles away, over the deafening pound of his heart. "Tell me, Roy. Where is the Greaves Institute party taking place?"

It's just a trick, an illusion, you asshole! He tried to look away from the fake snake, from the burning, freezing agony in his thumb.

It stopped abruptly. Dmitri picked up his keys, and his gun.

"Spruce Ridge, Colorado," he said. "Thank you. Roy. But

the snake is not the real monster in your closet. We should go for the big guns. Like Kasyanov did, yesterday morning. Do you smell it, Roy?"

He did smell it, then . . . and he forgot all about the snake.

That smell. He hated it. It made him want to vomit, made his head pound, his scar itch. It made him feel small, helpless, lower than dirt.

"No." His voice broke. He backed up. It was kerosene. Everywhere. The fumes. They made him queasy. He was dripping with the stuff.

Dmitri smiled. But it wasn't Dmitri anymore. It was Bobby, Roy's big brother. Braces flashed as Bobby grinned his evil grin, a rash of pimples hot and inflamed on his freckled, thirteen-year-old face. Blue eyes glittering with joy as he walked toward Roy with a lit match.

Roy watched Bobby, pleading, babbling. He was only six, and just a little dumb shit, a piece of whining crap, like Bobby always said, and he should just die already and nobody would care. The match flickered in the dim garage, lighting up Bobby's face grotesquely with shadows from below. Roy was huddled, trapped in the corner, the driving lawnmower blocking him on one side, the ping-pong table on the other.

Bobby came closer. The trembling flame came closer. The flame seized onto the fumes, and embraced his arm, flickering and spreading, licking and swirling, as the flames consumed fabric, then skin.

He broke past Bobby and ran for the garage door, but when he burst outside, it wasn't the lawn and pool of the suburban ranch house where he grew up, but darkness, rustling trees, moonlit water.

Water. Yes. Please.

He ran for the water as his skin blistered, charred. Flames licked his chin, agonizing, unbearable. The dock swayed and gurgled beneath his feet. The water was illuminated by the flames. He was a screaming human torch, stinking of kerosene, wreathed by greasy smoke.

He leaped into the air, legs pumping. Hit water, went under. Came up, gasping for air, but the fire seared his lungs afresh.

When he opened his eyes, he saw Bobby at the edge of the dock, holding Roy's car keys and Roy's Beretta, laughing. His face was lit up by the fire flickering on the water. Fire that came from Roy.

The leap into the lake had not put the fire out. He screamed, and kept on burning, burning, burning.

"Fucking ouch!" Aaro jerked away as she made the umpteenth attempt to tease the strip of duct tape out of his hair.

Nina glanced around, and caught the disapproving glare of the blue-haired lady ahead of them. "Shhh," she hissed at him. "You're being a baby. And you're making a scene."

Still, he jerked away again when she reached for his head.

"Aaro," she coaxed. "Get real. You can't go around with that thing stuck to your hair. It's like wearing a sign that says, 'I just escaped from the trunk of a car.' Come on! We don't want to advertise it!"

"You're ripping out all my hair! It hurts!"

"So I'll cut it. Give me your belt knife." She made an impatient sound as he continued to hesitate. "Don't be such a wuss," she complained. "You chopped all my hair off, remember?"

"That was different," he muttered, producing the knife and passing it to her with obvious reluctance. "I had scissors."

"Of course, I can't promise a perfect salon cut, but even so." She sawed at his hair, trying to be careful, but the tape

was horribly gummy, and had latched onto a wide swatch of
the hair on the back of his head. There was no graceful way
to do it, stuck so close to his scalp.

Aaro stared at the clump of hair and tape when it finally
came loose, and gingerly felt the jagged, shorn place at the
back of his head.

"Oh, fuck me," he muttered. "Looks like shit, right?"

Her mouth twitched. "You will need a remedial haircut,
yes. But look on the bright side. You're not still in the trunk
of a car, right?"

"Yeah," he said. "About that. My cousin. Did he hurt
you?"

She met his eyes. "He didn't rape me," she told him.

She felt his mind edging cautiously up to hers, searching
for the truth. "How?" he asked softly. "How in the hell did
you pull that off?"

She lowered her own shield, so he could feel the truth for
himself. "You told me how, actually," she said.

"I did?" He looked baffled.

"Spiders," she said. "You said he hated them. I projected
the image of black widows, crawling on his shoulders. While
he was freaking out about the spiders, I whacked him with
that phone. And then I, ah, choked him with the phone cord.
Until he passed out. I ran off, hid from Roy in the trees while
he was coming back from taking you to the car. No big hero-
ics. Just, you know. Tricks."

His eyes gleamed. "Hell of a trick."

"That's a hell of a cousin," she retorted, with feeling. "If
that's an example of your family, I can see why you wanted
to disappear."

"Yeah, Arbatovs are special that way," he said. "But Dmitri
was never that much of a problem for me before tonight. Just
a pain in the ass. Jealous, sneaky."

"The problem was your father, right?"

He gave her a slit-eyed look. "Are you peeking again?"

"No. Just remembering what Aunt Tonya said, at the hospice," she said. "It sounded like he was . . . problematic."

He choked off his laughter. "You've got this amazing gift for understatement. Funny, though. Last night, when Rudd was kicking my ass, I had a sense that I'd felt that sensation before. With my father."

She was startled. "You think your father used psi-max?"

Aaro shook his head. "No way. He would never use drugs. He's willing to make a fortune manufacturing or selling them, sure, but he despises people who use them. I mean, naturally. Like Tonya is naturally telepathic and clairvoyant, Oleg has a natural talent for coercion."

Nina was sobered by the thought. "Wow. If that's true, then I can certainly see why your shield was so strong."

"Me, too, now that I think about it."

"Speaking of talent," she asked delicately. "Are you feeling anything strange? You know, since they injected you?"

He looked startled by the question. "I forgot all about it," he said. "Too much going on to even think about it. But no, I guess."

"No weird phenomena?"

He grinned. "Nothing yet. No zombies for me. I can read your mind, sort of, but only when you want me to, so I probably just catch what you're projecting to me on purpose."

She looked him over, long body sprawled over the backmost seat of the bus, long legs propped out in the aisle. They had bought plain jeans and cotton knit shirts, but a sponge wash in the Target customer restroom could not erase the marks last night's adventures had left upon them. Aaro had bruises on his face, marks around his mouth where the duct tape had adhered. His wrists had bracelets of dark scabbing, and his hair, well. It had to be said. His hair needed help.

She herself had a black eye, a swollen lip, bruises on both cheeks, lacerations on her shoulders, scab bracelets, and a collection of contusions, scabs, and scrapes, plus a wild

mass of snarled, blood-stiffened hair. They were a mess. The
Target personnel had tried to call an ambulance for them.
Aaro had nixed that idea on the spot, and scared the bejesus
out of the assistant manager in the process.

Yet, battered and exhausted as Aaro looked, he seemed
more relaxed than she'd ever seen him. Smiling, sprawled
out as if he were lying on a beach. Probably just too tired to
be tense.

She wished she could say the same for herself. It was the
morning of the third day since Helga had injected her. She
didn't want her life to be almost over. Not with Aaro smiling
at her like that, making her heart thud and skip. She'd never
wanted so badly to keep living before.

Wrong thought to think. It triggered a greasy stomach
flop . . . and suddenly Aaro's face hovered over hers, smile
gone, his face tight with fear. His voice sounded far away.
"Nina? What's the matter? What's wrong?"

It took time for the power of speech to come back, and
she still couldn't manage to sit up when it did. "Woozy," she
whispered. "Sorry."

"I'm going to tell the driver to stop somewhere," he said,
propping her up on the seat. "I'll be right back. Don't move."

As if she could. *Don't, I'll be fine,* she tried to say, but the
words didn't have enough energy to punch their way out of
her mouth.

25

"We can't stop now." The fat, grizzled driver scowled. "We're behind schedule. You should've gotten her a snack at the rest stop."

"She needs a meal, not a snack." Aaro hung onto his temper, long unused to having to ask permission to get out of a moving vehicle.

"Yeah, and the thirty other passengers on this bus need to get where they paid to go. You're not the only ones on the bus, buddy, so unless she's having a heart attack, forget it. We'll stop at Mormont at the diner, and take a half an hour then."

"How far's Mormont?"

"Hundred and ten." The guy's voice was unsympathetic.

Damn. Two hours, at this speed. Aaro hung between the seats. Hammering the driver to the ground was not an option. So? What?

A thought flashed through his mind, sparked by the recent conversation with Nina. What would Oleg do? Of course, Oleg would never be in a similar situation, being wealthy beyond a normal man's capacity to even comprehend. But if he were . . .

"Go back to your seat," the driver ordered. "You're bugging me, hanging over my shoulder. We'll stop when we stop."

Aaro scooted backward, thinking about Rudd's attack. The way it reminded him of conflicts with his father. He tried to imagine how it would feel to be on the giving end of that, not the receiving end.

And as he imagined, something inside him twitched, stirred . . . and *stretched*. Something strong, restless. Eager to come out and play.

He breathed through the dread, and followed the impulse. Gently . . . *gently*. The guy was driving a large vehicle full of people on a busy highway at fifty-eight miles per hour. *Gently*. He was touching the guy's mind. It felt different from touching Nina's. Prickly, staticky, incoherent bursts of energy. Sometimes he caught an articulated thought, mostly just a blur of anger. . . . *prick . . . looks like a criminal . . . thinks the goddamn world revolves around him and his fluff of a girlfriend. . . .*

Fluff, his ass. The fluff who fought her way free of psychically enhanced killers, rescued his ass from the trunk of a car, and looked smoking hot all the while. He dragged his mind back to the driver's mind. The guy was hungry. Could use a piss. Had prostate issues. The munchies, too. He ate when he was angry. And he was always angry.

Aaro burrowed deeper, leaned on those two points. *A long, loud piss rattling into the john, ah, the relief. After, a hot, juicy bacon cheeseburger with a slab of sliced onion and fuck the heartburn. . . .*

He leaned . . . leaned . . . then *pushed*. . . .

The bus hummed on. Countryside flashed by. Nina was still fainting. The only difference was, his headache was back, a new, improved version. He headed back toward Nina.

So much for his enhanced psychic powers. They were a great big pile of steaming fail, and now his head was going to—

Buzzzz. "Stopping in fifteen, in Caldwell," the driver announced on the intercom. "We'll take a half hour at the truck stop."

Aaro hurried back to Nina, but his Mr. Psychic Hot Shit euphoria evaporated when he found her slumped against the seat, lips blue.

Was it that drug? He shoved the gut-melting fear away. All his energy had to be dedicated to getting them to this Greaves Convention Center, at which point, he'd pick the place up, turn it upside down, and shake it until Kasyanov's B dose fell out. Something had to come to him. He could not stand this fear. Could not banish it, either.

Nina came to while he was carrying her through the parking lot toward the truck-stop diner. She tried to insist on walking. He laughed in her face. She got some color once she was seated in a grubby booth, sipping heavily sweetened coffee, but that was as far toward lunch as they got. The overworked waitress with the mousy ponytail and the swollen ankles ignored them, and continued to ignore them. Five minutes ticked by. Ten. The driver was digging into his burger and fries.

Bugger this shit. Aaro reached out for the woman's mind as she hustled by, getting a weird, disorienting rush of aching feet, exhaustion, and beneath it a sucking-down vortex of money worries, kid worries. She wasn't getting to the day care on time to pick her kids up because Terri hadn't shown up for work, and that lazy bitch really needed to lay off the sauce. Her resentment and frustration seethed, tired as she was.

He called out the next time she swung by. "Excuse me, ma'am, but our bus is leaving. Could you take our order and put a rush on it?"

He slid inside . . . and *pushed.*

The woman turned to say she'd get to them when she could . . . and her face went blank, like she'd just lost her train of thought. "Ah, yeah. What can I get for you?"

They ordered. The waitress scurried to put it in, bawling to the cook that it was a rush. Whoa. That had come to him so easily, it was scary. Or would be, if he didn't have so much other shit to be scared about. As things were, this didn't even make the cut.

His hamburger and her grilled cheese and tomato soup cup came out in record time. Food helped. The shadows under Nina's eyes seemed less pronounced, at least on the side where she didn't have the black eye. The swelling in her lip was almost to normal proportions.

She finished off a triangle of sandwich, licked her fingers. "How on earth are we supposed to dress for this party, anyhow?"

He'd been waiting for that, poised. "What do you mean, we? Miles is coming with me. He's bringing tuxes. You're lying low in the hotel with your mind shielded, clutching a loaded gun. You think I'm letting you anywhere near that psychopathic motherfucker again? You saw what he can do. And that hell bitch blonde of his, too. They're lethal!"

She seemed to grow three inches. "You think Rudd's going to attack us at a big, fancy fund-raising cocktail party, Aaro? A psychic duel, out in front of the ice sculptures? That he'll coerce us into drowning ourselves in the reflecting pool? Hell of a floor show, but I guess for fifteen grand, you're entitled to something spectacular."

"He can be more subtle than that if he wants to be. He was hurting us last night just for the fun of it. He's deadly, Nina."

"You think I don't know that?" Nina's voice was gentle. She reached out, touching his hand. "Dangerous is a relative term, Aaro, when you're dying."

He jerked, like he'd been pinched. "Don't say that!"

"I'm coming," Nina said quietly. "It's day three. This is it for me. I'm a telepath. You and Miles aren't. The party is the only place on earth where this ability might help us. It's our only hope for a clue for those B doses. And even if it's too late for me, maybe I can at least help you."

He kept shaking his head. She was right, but it didn't matter. He couldn't bring her back under the same roof as that sadist. He couldn't protect her from that guy. He'd demonstrated that fact very thoroughly the night before. He could not go through it again. Just couldn't.

He leaned in close, touching the wide, shimmery tingle that was Nina's beautiful mind. Groping around for her thought process. Sensed her determination, her heroic resolve. He looked for weaknesses, but it was hard to find one. Just fear, and he hated to lean on that; she had enough problems, for fuck's sake. But there was no other fault line presenting itself, so he leaned . . . *pushed* . . .

Nina put her hand to her temple, and flapped her hand at him, looking irritated. "Would you stop that, please?" she snapped.

"Stop what?" he asked, all innocence.

"Whatever you're doing with your mind." She took a bite of her sandwich and frowned as she chewed. "It tickles."

He subsided, gloomily resigned. He might have known it wouldn't work on her. That would be too easy. Nothing ever was.

Nina took one of his french fries, and nibbled it. "So, back to my original question. The party. I need a dress, shoes, makeup. Underwear, for God's sake. How can I go shopping if we're trapped on a bus?"

"Miles has your dress," he admitted. "He's bringing it with him."

Her eyes went big. "What? But . . . but how—"

"Lily had him pick up the outfit you're suppposed to wear to the wedding," Aaro admitted. "She had it all ready for you. Guess she didn't trust you to dress yourself for that blessed event. Go figure."

Nina dabbed her lips with the napkin. "Wow," she murmured.

"It's red," Aaro informed her. "With sparkles. Miles peeked."

Nina winced. "Oh, God, I can't wear red. I'll look like a stoplight!"

"So stay at the hotel," he suggested.

"Don't even start," she snapped.

He dumped ketchup on what remained of his fries, and held his tongue, with a huge, muscular effort of will.

"I keep waiting for the other shoe to drop," she fretted. "The psi-max that they gave you. I wish . . . I hope it has no effect on you at all."

"Oh," he said. "Um. About that." He took a moment to wipe grease off his fingers. "Maybe there is something."

"Oh, yeah?" Her gaze jerked up, her face taut. "Tell me!"

He wished he hadn't said anything. Where did this uncontrollable impulse to share come from, anyhow? Info like this might scare her, or skeeve her out. "I think I'm, uh, like Rudd. And Oleg," he admitted.

Nina's brows twitched together. "Coercion? Really? Wow. What makes you think so?"

The fact that we got off the damn bus. The fact that we're eating lunch. "Oh, I don't know," he said vaguely. "Just a feeling."

"A feeling," she repeated, looking at him very hard, but he offered no further explanations. "Actually, it makes sense," she said, after a few minutes. "In fact, it's appropriate. For once, nature knows best."

"How's that?" he asked, suspicious.

"Only a principled person can be trusted with a gift like that."

He coughed, sputtering his coffee. "You figure?"

"Hell, yes! A talent that easily abused? It could be used for every trivial thing a person might want, out of sheer convenience! That power is only safe in the hands of a person who can be trusted absolutely!"

The glow of conviction in her eyes made his stomach sink. "You think I'm principled? And trustworthy? Really?"

"I know you are." She had that ring in her voice. People were turning to look. "I know you. I can read you. You would only use a power like that in self-defense, and under the direst of circumstances."

He didn't understand this irresistible impulse to confess, but he leaned over the table. "I coerced the waitress into serving us lunch."

Nina's jaw dropped. Shock vibrated against his mind like the jangle of an alarm bell. Then came the imperious knock against his vault doors, summoning him to open up, show that it was true.

He did so, docile as a lamb.

She gasped. "Aaro," she whispered fiercely. "That is *despicable!*"

"Yes," he agreed meekly. "Horrible. Heinous. I know."

"Never do that again!" she hissed. "To anyone! You hear me?"

"It was just an experiment," he protested. "I had to see if my hunch was for real, so I—"

"Experiment, my ass! It makes you a monster! Like Rudd!"

"Uh, OK, fine. Never again. Except, uh, in self-defense. And in the direst of circumstances."

"Don't you dare throw my words back into my face, you bastard!" she hissed. "You owe that woman! You *wronged* her!"

He squinted. "Huh? Owe her what?"

"An apology, at the very least! But since that's inadvisable right now, we'll settle for a big tip. A *massive* tip! You manipulative *bastard!*"

He shrugged. "I don't have a wallet," he reminded her. "I'm flat busted, Nina. You're the one with the cash."

She dug into her purse, pulling out the manila envelope from Wilder's car that contained their dwindling cash stash. She pulled out two C-notes, and slapped them on the table. "This is a loan. You will pay me back, Aaro. Every last cent."

He stared down at the money on the table. "Nina. The bill is nine dollars and seventy-nine cents," he said. "That's a hundred-ninety-dollar-and-twenty-one-cent tip."

"I'm so glad you pointed that out!" She dug into the purse again, rummaged, and slapped down another ten. "You should make it an even two hundred. She can use it. Her kids need shoes."

They stared at each other. Her eyes sparkled. There were pink spots in her cheeks. He'd pissed her off so much, it had kicked up her blood pressure. Awesome. That flushed look of righteousness.

The bus driver drained his coffee cup, and stood. "Five minutes, and all aboard!" he bellowed to the restaurant at large, before stumping heavily off to the bathroom again.

"Next time, it will be four hundred," she warned. "Then eight, and so on. You do the math. Never, ever again! Understand?"

"Whatever," he muttered. "Let's get on the bus."

He followed her out the door. Anger smartened her step. At this point, he judged it impolitic to confess what he'd done to the bus driver. It would fry his synapses to give four hundred dollars to that prick, as well as wiping them out of cash. Lucky she hadn't caught it herself while peeking. Nina strode on ahead, still seething. He admired the angry ass twitches as she flounced up the steps of the bus.

She flopped down in the back, staring stonily out the window, clutching the big black purse to her tits like a shield. Blocking him out.

He sat next to her, staring at the back of her mop of wild, flopping, snarled elf-locks. "Nina," he said.

No response. It was starting to piss him off. They did not have time for this self-indulgent shit. He'd confessed, he'd apologized, he'd paid a fucking fine. What did she want from him, blood?

"Turn around, Nina," he said. "Look at me."

She did not. He grabbed her, hoisted her up onto his lap. Wrapped his arms around her, effectively immobilizing her.

He stared directly into her blazing, furious, bright eyes.

"Be pissed, if you want," he said softly. "But don't push me away. Normal couples can have stupid fights. We don't have that luxury."

Raw emotion flashed in her eyes, and for a moment, he was terrified that she was going to cry. But she pulled herself together, brushing at her eyes with the back of clenched fists. "Did you do it to me?" she demanded. "Did you coerce me into anything?"

He didn't bother playing dumb. His silence was his answer.

Her eyes widened."You son of a bitch! What did you make me do?"

"Nothing," he muttered, as the bus lurched into movement.

"Bullshit, nothing! Tell me!"

Aaro caught several pairs of eyes on them. "Tried to coerce you into not coming tonight. But it doesn't work on you. You're safe."

Her eyes slitted. "Let me see."

He closed his eyes, and let those vault doors creak open. At least the experience wasn't painful, like when Anabel and Dmitri did it. Nina's mental touch was delicate, like being brushed by butterfly wings. In fact, it made him hard. Nina felt it, and abruptly withdrew.

"That felt nice," he said wistfully. "Do it again."

She sniffed. "I wasn't trying to titillate you."

"You saw that it's true, right? I can't push you. I tried, I failed. You're safe. OK? You still mad?"

"Yes," she said. "I'm mad because you tried. You *dog*."

He rolled his eyes. "So do I owe you four hundred bucks now?"

"You owe me a hell of a lot more than that!"

He sat there, wondering what to say. "Fine. I'll pay," he said rashly. "Stick around, Nina. I'll just keep on paying. Forever."

The feel of her body changed. Her mind quested, butterfly wings brushing, trying to figure out what he meant. "Aaro?"

It came together, like a landslide crashing down. The decision had been grinding along, making itself for a long time, almost since he'd met her. Certainly since he'd fucked her. Now the decision was made.

He opened up. He liked having her in there, petting, stroking. He let her see what he wanted, what he longed for, what he was afraid of. He was too tired, too blasted apart, to even bother being ashamed of what a fucking mess he was in there. It felt good to be known.

"Don't make the mistake of thinking that I'm principled and trustworthy," he said. "I was raised by a mafiya vor. I was taught to steal and kill and do whatever's expedient. And fuck, yeah, I'll goose a waitress in a diner to get you a sandwich, after you faint on me. I'd do it again, and pay the four hundred bucks. Cheerfully. Or eight, or sixteen. I'm not hurting for money. The fee's not an issue for me. You get me?"

"Ah . . . yeah, but—"

"No buts." He had to get this out, all in one piece. "You see what I am, right? When you look inside? No secrets, right?"

"Yes, but what I meant was—"

"You see that I'm a rude, bad-tempered, suspicious, over-sexed butthead? With zero moral values, and a pathologically bad attitude?"

"Ah . . . yeah, but I also see that you're—"

"I'm all fucked up," he forged on. "I'm going to piss you off on an hourly basis, if not more. But I love you." There, he'd said it.

He just sat there, dumbfounded at himself, staring into her big, startled eyes. "I love you," he said again, more loudly. He liked the way the words made him feel. "I love you. And I want you."

Tears welled into her eyes. They flashed down over her cheeks.

"Oh, my God," she whispered.

The silence that followed was like being boiled alive. As the seconds ticked by, he had to fight not to twitch. "Well?" he ground out.

"That's not fair," she said.

"That's another thing that's good to know up front. I'm not fair, and I never will be. If I can trick or manipulate you into my evil clutches, I will. Count on it."

That earned him a wobbly smile. "So I'm in your evil clutches?"

His grip tightened. "Fuck, yeah. You're not going any-where, anymore. Not without me."

He waited, but it was just silence again. "So? Out with it."

She sucked her trembling lower lip between her teeth, and rested her forehead against his. "I don't quite know what to say—"

"I could give you some suggestions."

"Shut up, Aaro," she scolded. "This is hard to say."

"Fine," he growled. "I'm all ears."

"I guess . . . I'm just enjoying this. All of it. The fighting, the talking. Scolding you. Having you tell me that you love me. It's all part of the fun fiction that we could actually have a future together."

That cut into him, deep and cold. "It's not a fun fiction."

"Aaro, it's day three," she said. "Deal with it. Face it with me, please. Don't leave me all alone with it."

"No," he replied. "I will not allow this to happen. And you're not alone. I'll never leave you alone. Never. No matter what."

He couldn't say it, but there was no hiding from a telepath. She read it in his mind. That if the worst happened, he'd be with her to the last, clutching her hand. Glad to follow along behind, right on her heels. But they weren't going to give up without one hell of a fight.

But he couldn't say those words. Literally. Could. Not.

Emotions flashed across her face, but she just pried her hand loose and pressed it to his cheek. A light, butterfly touch, like her mind.

"OK," she said simply.

"We will get through this," he said thickly. "I want this. Us, I mean. I never have before, but I want it now." His voice broke. He hid his face against her neck. "I want years of it. Decades. I want to be together 'til we're old and creaky and shriveled, with no teeth."

"OK," she whispered again.

"What the hell does OK mean? You never had any problems expressing yourself before! Can you imagine being with me? Forever?"

She wiggled her arms loose, and wrapped them around his neck.

"You bet I can," she said softly. "Let's get old and creaky and shriveled together. I am so on board with that."

The joy that leaped up inside him scared the living crap out of him with its intensity. He had to breathe it down some before he could even speak. "Really?" Bleating for reassurance like a nervous little kid.

She kissed him, his mouth, his cheek, his nose. Little soft, hot points of contact that glowed and sparkled against his skin like stars.

"Really." She leaned back, and gave him the hairy eyeball. "But if you ever try to coerce me again, I'll rip out both your lungs."

"No, never," he assured her hastily, and they melted into one of those hugs again, as breathlessly close as they could possibly get with their clothes on. Tears kept slipping out of her eyes, and he would kiss them away, licking the salty drop off his lips. "Don't cry," he begged.

"I'm just so sorry," she said, her voice choked. "That you got caught in this trap along with me, with Helga's drug. The last thing I wanted was for you to be hurt. I'm so sorry."

"I'm not," he said baldly. "I'm glad."

She blinked at him, looking nonplussed. "Glad?"

"I'm not hurt," he announced. "That is to say, I was hurting before I met you. I've been hurting my whole life, but I'm not hurting now. I'm scared shitless. Greedy for more of the good stuff. But I'm better right now, at this moment, with you, than I've ever been. Ever. In my life."

She smiled through her tears. "Oh, Aaro. That's so sweet."

That bugged him, that his raw confession could be construed as romantic babbling. "It's not sweet," he insisted. "Just the facts. If you're heading for a wall, I want to be with you. We'll hit the wall together."

She wiped her eyes, sniffling. He offered her the hem of his shirt, which made her laugh, and soon they were twined in that breathless hug again, and laughter and tears became indistinguishable.

"Me, too," she admitted. "Better than I've ever been. Mortal doom and psycho monsters be damned."

"Yeah, fuck 'em," he said, with fierce satisfaction.

They swayed together, in a state of perfect grace, for at least twenty minutes. Nina lifted her head. "How long to Denver?"

He glanced at his phone. "Three hours. Miles called us a car service to get us up to Spruce Ridge. Another hour by car."

"Do you think we should study the transcript again?"

"No. I think we should spend the time madly tongue-kissing."

She sucked in her lip to suppress the smile, but the smile won. He had at that sweet, smiling mouth again until she was breathless.

She dragged in air, at one point. "Is this a clever brain-storming technique to help you think outside the box?"

"Sure," he agreed. "Brilliant technique. One thing, though. I want you to do that thing you were doing in my head while I kiss you. Touching me, inside. I liked it. Turned me on."

Her eyes darted toward the other passengers. "We can't get hot and heavy in a crowded bus in broad daylight, Aaro," she said sternly.

"Can we get hot and heavy in the privacy of our own minds?"

"Oh, whatever, OK." She cuddled up, and he didn't even have to make those vault doors creak open for her now. They were flung wide. Hers, too. It occurred to him that when she was like this, wide open and trusting, he could probably pull off the coercion trick.

He banished the thought. He was not going to fuck up his good thing so soon. Besides. She wanted so badly for him to be this heroic righteous dude who kept his promises. He would try to be that, for her sake. Whatever, man. Whatever, if that was what got her off.

The bus lumbered on, dragging them through space and

time toward that wall, but he wasn't thinking about it, or letting her think about it, either. They floated in their magic bubble of ideal perfection, and he wasn't going to let anybody take this away from him.

Not even himself.

26

Stimulating, Oleg reflected, to do for himself a task that he would ordinarily have delegated. He gazed around the bustling waiting room of the OHSU OB/GYN unit. It was physically taxing, yes. Flying to Portland on short notice with health issues like his was not easy. But there were certain things that had to be done by himself, alone.

He sensed urgency, in this hunt. He had no proof that there was a ticking clock, yet he heard the ticking, and he paid attention to it. That was what set him apart from other men. It had made him Vor, made him filthy rich, and kept him alive. So far. He pressed his hand against his liver, ravaged by cancer, surgery, and cirrhosis, peeking with a pang of longing at the Starbucks cup of the woman across from him. Hot, black, strong coffee, just as he liked it. But coffee was forbidden now.

He saw his targets the instant they emerged from the corridor. It would have been impossible to miss them. A tall young man with dark curly hair and dimples holding his curly-headed, shrieking son under his arm. The jowly, rectangular woman in hot pink who dragged a wiggling girl alongside her, the girl a female version of the boy. The old woman was haranguing the man in a dialect that sounded Italian.

The man rolled his eyes. "Get it through your head, Zia. She doesn't like boiled fish and baked apples, so there's no point in you dragging them in here for her. She wants a chicken sandwich with pesto and a fresh fruit salad from the cafeteria, OK? The pregnant lady gets what she wants, *capisce?* So stop throwing your weight around!"

"I'm thinkin' about the baby!" The woman looked hurt. "Looks like I'm the only one, eh? Chicken and pesto, pah!"

"Chicken and pesto will nourish the baby just fine, Zia."

The woman hefted a heavily loaded plastic bag, and dropped it into the trash receptacle next to Oleg. She met Oleg's eyes. *"Puo fare che cazzo vuole,"* she said belligerently. *"Me ne frego un cazzo di niente."*

Oleg dragged the remnants of his Italian up out of his head. *"Giovani di oggi,"* he offered sympathetically. *"Non capiscono niente."* Young people these days. Haven't got a clue.

She gave him a grateful look and took off after the little girl who had disappeared around a corner and into one of the medical suites. "Lena!" the lady shrieked, thudding heavily along. *"Torna qua!* Lena!"

Meanwhile, the man was doing the same thing, running after the scampering boy. Shrill laughter and bellows retreated into the distance.

Oleg got up, folded a magazine, and strolled in the direction from which they'd come. As a distraction, he could ask for nothing better than the Ranieri family. Noise, bombast, color. Constantly moving parts. Perfect. He scanned room numbers. He knew Lily Parr's room, the details of her health, the health of her unborn child. He knew everything in the hospital database, and everything in various other databases. Colorful past. Couldn't wait to meet her.

He turned the knob, and went in.

Lily Parr was curled up on her side, hugging her very pregnant belly with one arm, and tapping a message into her cell phone with the other. She glanced up at him, jerking up onto her elbow. She was very pretty, even eight months pregnant, disheveled and clad in a baggy nightgown. She pushed a hank of wavy red-blond hair from her eyes.

"Hello?" she said cautiously. "And you are?"

Oleg smiled. Her face paled. "A friend," he said gently.

"Friend to who?"

"You, I hope. If all goes well. Don't touch that button, Ms. Parr."

Lily Parr's hand froze as she groped for the call button. Her eyes went wide, and her throat worked as she tried to speak, but he clamped down and simply held her still. "Give me your telephone, Ms. Parr."

She resisted, but she was too inexperienced to be effective at it. Soon her hand began to extend, shaking with terror and tension. Her breath sawed in and out of her mouth. No doubt her heart was racing triple time. Her forehead shone. Her powerlessness terrified her.

He was sorry to upset a lovely pregnant girl. Women were to be cherished, coddled, enjoyed. Particularly beautiful ones, like this one. A juicy, succulent piece of strawberry tart. He'd always liked it when they were ripe with child. He found it stirring. But there was no alternative.

He plucked the phone from her hand, and toggled the display back into the outbox, to read the message that she had just sent.

Yo, Miles. Aaro needs u 2 stop at a drugstore when u get 2 spruce ridge. Get electric hair clippers, razors and shaving gear, black hairpins for Nina, some sparkly jewelry, rhinestones, maybe, 4

hanging out with fat cats. + following makeup, just
give the list 2 the salesgirl.
Lipstick-Lucia Magarelli, long lasting glow, #3245
Autumn Wine. Foundation, also LM, ivory and
alabaster, #149 . . .

The list was long and extensive. Eyeliner, four different
colors of foundation, concealer stick of three different types,
brow enhancers, highlighters, moisturizers, under-eye creams,
and things he'd never heard of. Women's tricks. Bless them.

"Miles," he murmured. "Joining Aaro and Nina in a place
called Spruce Ridge. Where exactly is Spruce Ridge, Lily? I
can call you Lily, no? I feel as if I know you, after reading
that long, thick file. Fascinating life you have led. And your
man, too. That incredible business last year, my goodness.
Shocking stuff. Congratulations on surviving. And on your impending nuptials. All the best. But we digress. Spruce Ridge?"

A small, defiant head shake was her answer, but he leaned
closer, smiling. Clamping down, squeezing. Hard.

She let out a tiny, creaking sound. Tears leaked from her
eyes.

He put his hand on her swollen belly, and her muscles
twitched. That was all the movement permitted to her. "You
need to tell me the location of Spruce Ridge," he said. "If
you care about your little son."

Her eyes widened still more, horrified.

He clucked his tongue. "Oh, dear, have I made a gaffe?
Yes, I saw the ultrasound reports. Had you requested not to
be told the child's sex? Spilled the beans, did I? I'm devas-
tated. Spoiled the surprise for you. Oh!" He gasped, chuck-
ling. "He kicked me! Already defending his mamma. Such a
brave, good boy."

She struggled to speak, and to her credit, got enough traction against his mental pressure to do so. "Fuck . . . off," she
ground out, tonelessly. "Don't . . . touch . . . my . . . baby."

"I don't want to hurt your son." He plugged the key words *Spruce Ridge* into his phone, and surveyed the results. "Hmm. California, Nevada, Wyoming, Montana, Colorado. Help me narrow it down, my dear. This is too much territory for one tired old man to cover."

She shook her head again.

"Denying me is not an option," he said. "I'm afraid I must insist."

Her soft lips pursed. She was wondering if she could stall him until her family got back with her chicken pesto sandwich. Which they well might, if he did not speed things up. He pulled the video stills from his coat, taken from the hospice. One of Sasha, one of his lady friend.

Lily Parr had neither talent nor training in hiding her feelings. She recognized both pictures, and her reaction was strong, and visible.

"You know these two?" He petted her belly, freezing her impulse to slap his hand away before her muscles could do more than jerk.

"You see, I understand how you feel about your son," he told her. "Because this, see . . ." He held up Sasha's picture. "This is my son."

Her eyes fixed on the photo, then on his face. To catalog his features: eyes, mouth, jaw, ear, hairline. It was quite a job of forensic excavation, to find the resemblance the young, handsome Sasha bore to him, in his current age and disease-ravaged state, but it was there.

He studied her SMS. "Aaro," he murmured. "My first wife's great-great-uncle from Minsk bore that name. Does he use it as a surname?"

The stress of resisting hurt her, and might very well hurt her baby. Stupid girl didn't know what was good for her. He clicked through her other messages. "Ah, look at this," he murmured. "From a Davy McCloud, two hours ago. 'Sean arr. Denver eight ten rent car, will be there ASAP, attached aerial view of Greaves Convention Center. Working on floor plan.' My, my! Let me see what happens when I plug Spruce Ridge and Greaves Convention Center into the same search, hmm?"

Tears of helpless rage flashed down Lily Parr's cheeks.

He hit gold instantly. A gala event, to raise funds for the future Greaves Institute, Spruce Ridge, Colorado. He glanced at the map.

"Colorado," he said, staring at Lily. Her eyelids twitched, and his heart exulted. Twenty-one years he'd waited. "Everyone is converging upon Spruce Ridge. Miles, Aaro, Nina, Sean? Glittering earrings to dazzle the fat cats? Makeup, hair trimmer? To clean up for the party?"

She gasped for breath. He put his hand on her belly again. "You did not tell me the name my son is using, Lily," he said softly. "Give me my son . . . and I will give you yours."

Her eyes blazed. He didn't genuinely need to push her any farther, but her defiance reminded him of Sasha's. He pulled her onto her feet. Grabbed her upper arms, and clamped down. Harder . . .

She shuddered, doubled over, and a rush of blood-tinged water flooded down her legs, over her feet, spreading around his shoes.

He stepped back, dismayed. Oh, for God's sake. She'd broken her water and probably gone into premature labor, the stupid bitch. Just didn't know when to give in. An epidemic of poor judgment going around.

Lily slid to the ground, sagged onto her side. Fainted. Maybe the child had shifted down in her womb, with the rush of water. *Damn.*

It didn't happen often, but Oleg knew defeat when he saw it. He took a moment to pop her SIM card out, wipe her phone down and toss it back on her bed, and walked briskly out, leaving the door ajar.

He hobbled down the hall, considering his next dilemma.

It was not unlike the one he had faced in the hospice. But he was not as angry at Lily Parr as he had been at Tonya. And he did not want to deprive the world of a luscious strawberry tart, or her little son.

At reception, he put on a concerned expression. "Excuse me, nurse?" he said, to a snub-nosed brunette in flower-spattered scrubs. "I think the lady in the room second from the end of the hall needs help. I saw her through the door, and it looked as if she'd fainted."

"Thanks for saying something, sir! I'll have someone check it out!"

Oleg smiled his thanks, and forgot Lily as he hurried to the elevator, his mind buzzing with plans. Obtain a tuxedo, donate money to the Greaves Institute, and organize the flight plan to land his private jet as close to Spruce Ridge, Colorado, as possible.

Thaddeus Greaves leaned and looked at the detail of the architectural model of the proposed Greaves Institute that Rudd had brought. Rudd forced himself not to swallow nervously as he watched the man do so. If he did say so himself, the model was stunning. Twelve feet square and three feet high, from the massive, knee-height display table. Every detail picked out. God knows the thing had cost enough.

Rudd watched Greaves pluck a tiny fir tree out of a grove that straddled a greensward, the one that led up Library Hill. He peered at it, heavy dark brows beetling. Greaves was in his early fifties, but looked younger. A fine figure of a man, tall, trim, powerfully built, with olive skin and a shock of gleaming hair that shone a snowy white.

Anabel's moist, mooning gaze annoyed Rudd. That innocent, milkmaid glow made him twitch. Rudd didn't like to imagine what was going on in her fertile, self-serving brain. She was under orders to keep her mouth shut unless directly addressed. So far, she had obeyed. But Anabel was always Anabel.

Greaves peered through his reading glasses at the small tree, and put the pushpin base back, in exactly the tiny hole from which he had taken it. "Pretty. A lovely thought, Harold. Amazing detail. We'll display it in the Great Hall, under the chandelier. It'll look great as a foreground while I make the fawning speeches tonight."

"Yes, the detail really struck me," Rudd said. "This artist specializes in incredibly detailed models. I'm a firm believer in the magic of visualization, and what could be a more potent way to manifest such a magnificent new reality than a facsimile of the new Institute . . . ah . . . Mr. Greaves? Those buildings are glued down. They don't come loose."

"No? Don't they?" *Pop,* Greaves cracked loose and lifted an exquisitely perfect model of what would eventually be the Swayne Chapel. White, simple colonial style. A sharp and perfect steeple.

"Ah, yes, that will need to be glued down again," Rudd said nervously. "They're quite delicate, and if you . . . uh . . ."

His voice trailed off, as the chapel crumpled in Greaves's fisted hand, collapsing into a handful of sharp, painted splinters. The small bell tower snapped off, and fell to the Aubusson carpet.

Greaves placed his heel upon the tiny steeple, bore down. *Crunch.*

"Yes," he said. "Quite delicate, Harold. Just as you said."

Rudd stared at the fragments on the carpet. "Ah . . . if you don't like the model, I can take it back."

"Not at all, Harold! I like it very much!" Greaves assured him. "Even without the chapel, it's a lovely thing. It's a perfect visual focus for this event. Brilliant idea, really. I just wanted to make a point, you see. A large enterprise can function even if a key element is removed. The model is still beautiful. I will still display it, and only the donors who . . . now who is it who donated the money for the chapel?"

"Milton Swayne," Rudd said woodenly.

"Oh, yes. Of course. Milton and his shriveled bitch of a wife, Dorothy. Only they will notice the omission. I'll have to smooth their ruffled feathers. How tedious. Perhaps you'd be good enough to do that job for me? Come up with an excuse? Missing plans, an error on the part of the artist, a box left behind? Something clever like that."

"Of course," Rudd said, his voice strangled.

"Excellent. I'll have it taken to the Great Hall immediately. But first, explain again, because it hasn't sunk in yet. How it never occurred to you that I might like to observe Christie's and Arbatov's reaction to Psi-Max 48 for myself. Did you think that I would not be interested?"

"I . . . I considered it a dead end," Rudd said nervously. "I wrote the new formula off. The B dose is lost, and there's no one left alive to ask where it is, so the A dose is useless. It was distracting my people, taking up time and resources. Those two were probed so thoroughly, I'm surprised they didn't have cerebral aneurisms on the spot, and according to Helga's timetable, the woman was doomed within hours anyway. It seemed like poetic justice, to inject the man. So I . . ."

"Wrote Helga's last formula off. The culmination of her life's work. Injected the last existing A dose into Arbatov's arm, for what? For poetic justice? Spite, pique? To stroke your inflamed ego? It was a childish impulse. Childish impulses are dangerous."

That calm phrase made his bowels turn to ice. "I am sorry if I—"

"Karstow, you said? That's where your man is taking them?"

"Yes, but I will have Roy bring them here, if you would prefer—"

"Yes, Harold." Greaves's voice was thick with irony. "I do prefer."

Rudd pulled out his cell, and inwardly crossed his fingers as he pulled up Roy's number. But sure enough, like the last six times, he got a recorded voice. "Out of area," he said, trying to sound casual. "I'm sure I'll reach him soon. Anabel, try Dmitri's number again."

Anabel pulled out her phone, tried, and shook her head. "Him, too."

Greaves appeared to notice her for the first time. "Keep trying."

"Certainly," Rudd assured him. "Constantly."

Greaves's gaze flicked back to Anabel. "What have we here?"

Rudd turned, knowing what he would see. Anabel had begun to sparkle, against his very specific orders, the treacherous bitch. Watching Greaves give him a bare-ass spanking had turned her on.

"Switch it off, Anabel," he hissed. "You're pissing me off."

"Well, well." Greaves tilted up Anabel's chin, studying her glowing smile. "Look at that. Psi-enhanced beauty and sexual attraction. A talent I have never encountered. And you said she was a telepath."

"I am," Anabel said coyly. "A strong telepath. This is a bonus talent."

Greaves chuckled. "Bonus talent. Excellent, my dear, excellent. Can you do this under any circumstances?"

"Yes," she murmured. "Although it is much quicker and easier when I am, ah . . . genuinely stirred by someone." Her lashes fluttered.

Greaves glanced at Rudd. "What else can this delicious creature do?"

Anabel licked her gleaming lips. "For you, sir, anything,"

she said, in a breathless voice. "Anything you want. Right here, if you liked."

One of Greaves's heavy, dark eyebrows lifted. Anabel drifted closer, imperceptibly, reaching boldly. She ran her fingertip along the bulge of his erection that tented out the cut of his elegant wool trousers.

"Very well," Greaves said coolly. "Let's see what you can do."

Rudd groaned inwardly. Intemperate slut. What was he, the body servant, holding the hot steamed lemon-scented towels for after-sex cleanup? While his own personal, psychically enhanced assistant, in whom he'd invested millions in research and training, prostituted herself? True, her nymphomaniacal eagerness was handy in a pinch, but this situation did not qualify as a pinch. This was just Anabel's pathological boundary issues, and he was sick to death of them.

Anabel was on her knees. She'd undone Greaves's trousers and taken out his rather large penis, and was already slurping away at it with unseemly gusto. Greaves glanced up and caught his eye. "Turn around, Rudd," he said austerely. "I don't care for spectators."

Well, at least he didn't have to watch, but he did have to listen to the wet suckling sounds, and Anabel's throaty moans made him want to slap her. He counted the seconds, hoping Greaves didn't take too long.

Greaves hissed in a breath. Anabel shrieked. Rudd spun around.

Anabel was flying through midair. She slammed against the wall and hung there, legs dangling three feet above the floor, eyes wild with terror. She clutched her throat. Greaves was pressing it telekinetically.

She clawed, making awful sounds, her face growing purple.

"Your whore tried to probe me," Greaves said, in a mild, conversational tone. "Did you put her up to that, Harold?"

"No!" he said, horrified. "Of course not! Perhaps she did it by accident! Sometimes, when she is excited, she . . . ah . . . ah . . ."

Ghostly fingers clamped down onto his throat, too. Greaves had no problem at all directing his talent in two places at once.

Rudd could not speak, or breathe. His larynx burned, as if it were imploding. His eyes popped. His vision started going dark . . . the pressure relented, and he stumbled heavily onto his knees, coughing.

"Do not vomit on my carpet, Harold," Greaves said.

Rudd managed, barely, to obey that command. When the impulse had subsided, he lifted his head. Anabel lay on the floor, whimpering.

"Get up," Greaves said. "I thought that you understood your place in my grand scheme, Harold. And to think that you aspire to the highest office in the land. Really. The mind boggles."

"But I . . . but this is just a—"

"I did not give you leave to speak," Greaves said. Rudd choked off, as the ghostly fingers tightened again. "I am angry. Losing Kasyanov was catastrophic. The publicity, the mistakes, your decisions as to how to dispose of Arbatov and Christie, it is a tremendous disappointment to me. I wish to know the instant you get in touch with that worthless cretin, what was his name?"

"Roy Lester," Rudd supplied, coughing painfully.

"Yes. Roy Lester. I do not want him to stop to eat, sleep, or piss. Just drive. I wish to see what Kasyanov's final masterpiece can do, even if it is incomplete. Information is priceless. And when he delivers them, I want him eliminated. He is not intelligent enough to be attached to this project."

"I already made arrangements," Rudd agreed fervently. "Trust me."

"That's difficult, Harold," Greaves said. "You've made it so hard to trust you."

Rudd glanced at Anabel, wondering if she'd sustained serious injuries in her wall-smack and subsequent fall. He hoped not. For all her faults, Anabel was immensely useful. "I'm sorry," he forced out.

"Good." Greaves walked to Anabel. Nudged her with his toe.

"I'll get her out of your way," Rudd said. "Anabel, get up."

"I will discipline her myself," Greaves said. "Wait outside, in the hall. I told you, I don't like spectators. They cramp my style."

Dismay clutched him. "I . . . I need her, sir. To work the party."

Anabel's limp body rose up, suspended in the air, clawing at her throat again. Her bulging eyes pleading silently for help. As if he could. She had brought this on herself. Trying to use her psi on *Greaves?* Dear God, what a fucking idiot.

"I won't leave obvious marks on her," Greaves said. "Give me credit for some practicality. Out with you, into the hall. This won't take long. But you may be sure, Harold. She will never attempt to use her gifts on me again. And neither will you."

"Yes, sir. I never, ever did, sir," he babbled, and suddenly the ghost hand pushed him on the chest, shoving him backward toward the door. He had to scramble not to fall. He was herded into the hall. The door slammed shut in his face.

The screaming began shortly after. Rudd fidgeted, waiting. Members of Greaves's domestic staff approached from time to time, but when they heard the shrieks, they slipped back the way they had come.

It went on and on. At this rate, Anabel would need reconstructive surgery on her vocal folds. Not that he needed her to talk tonight. But still. At great length, the door flew open, and Anabel was tossed out, by invisible hands. She thudded to the floor and lay, naked, on the hallway carpet runner, her face wet, nose running. Mouth distorted by weeping. She sported a raccoon mask of smeared mascara.

Greaves sauntered to the door, fastening his trousers and buckling his belt. He leaned on the doorjamb, and gazed down at Anabel's shuddering body. "See?" he said cheerfully. "Not a mark on her."

Anabel's clothes and shoes floated through the door, coalesced into a clot above her, and dropped onto her body. She flinched when they hit, sobbing harder.

"Get her cleaned up," Greaves said. "I don't want her leaking bodily fluids on my carpet runner."

Rudd grabbed her arm, but it was like pulling a corpse. He kicked her in the buttock. For God's sake, did the dumb cow have a death wish? He shoved at her with his mind, but it was like pushing his psi against a mountain of broken rock.

He hauled her dead weight bodily to her feet, scooping up her clothes, shoving them against her chest, and dragged her down the corridor naked. No way to wrestle her into the complicated and complex underwear, or her pencil skirt and her silk blouse. Not in her current state. He'd drag her out to the car naked, and dress her there.

Anabel stared back at Greaves, stupefied, mouth agape. He smiled from the door of his library. Waggled his fingers, in a playful farewell. She yelped, and dropped one of her shoes.

The shoe floated up and followed them. Rudd grabbed it. "Thank you," he muttered.

"See you tonight. Be early for the meet and greet. See that she pulls herself together. I want her at her best. She'll be working the room for me. With all of her talents."

Rudd looked at Anabel's mascara mask, the snot running from her nose, her unfocused eyes. So this was to be his punishment. Making bricks without straw. "She'll be great," he promised.

And indeed, she would. If it killed her.

27

When Nina and Aaro finally checked into the hotel Miles had chosen in Spruce Ridge, the blaze of euphoria had faded. Nina missed it, sharply. It had made her feel like there was no stopping them.

Now, she was feeling extremely stoppable. Fluttery, squirmy in her middle. Fear of Rudd, fear of Aaro getting hurt trying to defend her. Fear of that hospital bed, blinking lights, beeping machines. Clinging to Aaro's hand as a drug destroyed her brain. Knowing that he'd soon face the same fate—except that he would face it alone.

They'd spent most of the drive from Denver to Spruce Ridge holding hands, staring at the foothills of the Rockies rising up around them. Shields back up, in default mode. Aaro's face was grim, but she sensed furious activity behind his shield, like he was coming to some momentous conclusion. God forbid he give her hell about going to the party. She didn't want to have that argument again.

They checked into the room Miles had reserved. She had nothing to lay down but her purse. Aaro had nothing but his phone and his knife. Down to bare essentials. No gear, hardly any weapons, just their own naked, nervous selves to pit against Rudd and his goons.

And finally alone. The air ignited as they stared at each other. But not quite yet. "I need a shower," she said. "I still have blood in my hair."

"Make it quick," he told her. "Miles will be here soon."

And this might be it for us. Make it very quick.

Nina stood under the powerful jet of hot water, trying to jar loose the accumulated strain of the last two days, along with mud, dirt, aches and pains. She rubbed globs of conditioner into her hair, rinsed, finger combed it, and stared at her dripping self in the mirror.

She looked pale, and thinner. Splotched and scraped. She'd seen herself with bruises, in the bad old Stan days. But she'd never seen that look in her eyes then. She did not look defeated. She looked scrappy, ready for another round. The wild woman warrior. She liked the way she looked. Aaro liked it, too. Aaro loved it. Loved *her*. Wow.

She dried off, wrapped herself in the towel, and walked out. Aaro sat where she'd left him, at the foot of the bed. He'd stripped off his shirt and his shoes. She stood before him, putting her hands on his shoulders, caressing the mottled marks, bruise upon bruise, purpling up at different stages and colors. Three days' worth. Her champion. She petted them, wishing the needle full of psi-max had given her healing abilities. Now that was a talent that would be worth the trouble.

Aaro seized her towel and pulled it off. She didn't cringe. It felt good to be bare. She could feel exactly how much he liked what he saw.

He stared up into her face, with an odd look in his eyes. Hard, glittering. Challenging.

"Marry me," he said, in a tone of flat command.

She was taken aback. "Ah. . . . well, yeah. I thought . . .

aren't we sort of, um, engaged? After what you said on the bus, I thought—"

"There's no 'sort of' about it. I'm not talking about engaged. I'm talking married. Right now. The whole deal. Better or worse, sick or poor, however it goes. 'Til death do us part." He stopped, swallowed.

Nina was at a loss for words.

He frowned. "What?" he asked. "What's the problem?"

"Ah . . . I'm just surprised, that's all. I don't have any personal experience in being proposed to, but it usually takes a guy a long time to work around to the concept of being even engaged. And even longer to, well, you know. The M word."

"You're that afraid to say it?"

"You're not?"

He shook his head. "No. Not if it's you."

The words burst out. "I'm afraid, Aaro. Of losing you, of facing Rudd. Of death. And I'm afraid of being as happy as you make me feel." She paused. "I'm afraid this isn't real. That it's just a dream."

He ran his hands over her arms. "If it were a dream, you wouldn't be so beat up. And I'm no dream man. You know me."

"Yes." Her soul shook, for joy. "Yes, I do know you."

"I put up a good fight, but once I make up my mind, it's made," he told her. "I want you to belong to me."

The giggles melted into tears. "You've known me for two days."

"Two unusual days," Aaro pointed out. "A day like one of these counts for at least a year."

She clamped her hand over her mouth, and fought for control of her voice. "Are you sure? With all the stuff we're dealing with right now, you think it's the right time to pile this on?"

"Yes," he said. "If I'm going to take you with me to that party, into mortal danger, I'll take you as my wife. Or not at all."

"Ah. So, it's a condition? I marry you, or you won't let me come?"

He crossed his arms over his chest. "That's right."

She nibbled on her lip. "What makes you think you can stop me?"

"Let's not go there," Aaro said. "Just marry me. It'll be easier."

She braced herself against the blast of charismatic male power, and a thought occurred to her. "Are you coercing me, Aaro?"

"No," he said. "My shield's down. Look inside, if you don't believe me. This is just normal, garden-variety bullying and manipulation."

That provoked another storm of giggles. "Well, gee. If you put it that way, how can I resist?"

His eyes blazed with triumph. "So, no resistance? That's a yes?"

"That is a yes," she said. "I accept your proposal."

He pulled her closer, nuzzling her breasts as he stared up into her face, his eyes alight. "Yes," he whispered fiercely. "Yes."

She licked her lips, and waited. "And?" she asked. "Now what?"

"The vows," he said. "Come here."

She looked at his head, between her breasts. "Um . . . I am here."

"No. Like this." He grabbed her waist and lifted her up onto his lap, so that she sat facing him, astride his legs.

"This hardly seems a decorous sort of position in which to exchange sacred vows," she said, embracing him.

"But I love you like this." He slid his hand down between her legs and cupped her mound, tracing the seam of her tender folds with his fingers. "Legs wide open," he murmured. "Wet and soft. Trusting me."

"I do, I do trust you, but . . . oh God." Her voice choked off as he slid his finger inside her. "Stop that. That's not fair."

"Don't you like it?" He thrust in two fingers, stretching her. Her opening clenched greedily around him, quivering.

"I will not exchange vows with you while you're petting my private parts, you dog," she said. "That's an unfair advantage."

"So grab my cock," he suggested. "We'll be even."

"No. Absolutely not. That's for later." She grabbed his hands, and placed them squarely at her waist. "Be good."

He sighed, and lifted his fingers to his face, licking each one. "Later," he said. "Shields down."

"But then you'll see how scared I am," she whispered.

"I'm scared, too," he said. "That's why I want this now."

Her arms tightened around him. "OK, Aaro. So? Now what?"

"You start."

"Me?" she squeaked, outraged. "But this was your idea!"

"Yeah, but you're a girl. You know wedding schtick better than me. When I go to weddings, I hide out and smoke during the vows."

She rolled her eyes. "That is so lame!"

He gave her a pleading look. She harrumphed. "OK, then," she grumbled. "I don't have the presence of mind to come up with anything original, so I'll try to remember more or less what I've heard. And don't you dare laugh or criticize how it comes out. Or. Else."

"Never," Aaro said solemnly.

She took a deep breath, digging into her memory. "OK. Ah . . . do you, Alex Aaro, take me, Nina Louisa Christie, to be your wife? For better or for worse, for richer or for poorer, in sickness and in health, to love and to cherish, as long as we both shall live?"

He gave her that grin that reached all the way to his eyes.

"Fuck yeah," he rumbled, and pulled her in for a tight, hot kiss.

She pushed free a moment later. "No!" she scolded. "Do it properly if you're going to do it! Say 'I do!' And save the kisses for the end!"

"I do, I do. I was just being emphatic."

"Be good, not emphatic! This is serious stuff!"

"Serious. Very." A hot excitement burned in his eyes.

"OK, your turn," she told him briskly.

He looked blank. "My turn for what?"

She sighed. "The spiel," she prompted. "What, am I the only one who has to make the deathless vows? Fair's fair."

He looked clouded. "OK. Do you, Nina . . . what was your middle name again? Lavinia, Lucinda, Lauretta?"

"Louisa," she supplied patiently.

"Do you, Nina Louisa Christie, take me, Alex Aaro, to be your husband? And all the rest, yada yada?"

Seconds ticked by. "No yada yada," she said sternly. "Like hell will I accept a shortcut like that, you lazy dog. Say it. All of it."

He made an impatient sound. "OK, for richer or for poorer, in sickness and in health, to love and to worship, as long as we live?"

"It was cherish, not worship. Even though worship is kind of nice, now that I think about it. And you forgot for better or worse."

"Can't get much worse than this. So what's the word, Nina Louisa Christie? Do you take me, or are you just going to dick me around?"

She couldn't stop giggling. "Oh, yes. I take you. I claim you. You are mine, Alex Aaro. I own your ass."

Aaro's teeth flashed. "Whoa. That was stern. I never heard that line in a marriage ceremony before."

"I thought I'd do some variations of my own. I guess,

um . . . that we can pronounce each other husband and wife." She stroked his cheek, with a reverent, wondering hand. "So? You're my husband."

"You're my wife." His voice shook. "My God, it's such a turn-on."

"Glad it works for you." They stared at each other.

"This is the part when you kiss the bride," she reminded him.

"I'm going to do a hell of a lot more than that to the bride." He pulled her into a devouring kiss, then lifted her off his lap and set her on the bed. He got to work on his belt. "If you want to get married again normally, for the bureaucratic stuff, fine. And the party. If you want to have your friends, the white dress and the champagne and the shrimp puffs, fine. But as far as I'm concerned, it's a done deal."

"Yes." It was all she could say, with her throat quivering like that.

He jerked his jeans down and stepped out of them. His cock sprang up, flushed and stiff. "I want to come inside you," he said.

That was a conversation they didn't have time for, but whatever. Her body answered for her. "You can," she said simply. "I want that."

He stroked his jutting cock, smearing precome. "Miles should be here soon," he said. "I'd rather not start our married life with a quickie, but we're going to have to be real focused."

"I've auditioned you pretty thoroughly at this point," she assured him. "I already know what you're capable of."

"You think?" His grin flashed. "Then I'll just have to surprise you."

He sank down to his knees and pushed her legs apart.

She gasped, grabbing his head as he laved her slit with a long, tender swipe of his tongue. "I thought you said a quickie!"

"I did," he said, teasing her open with his finger. "It can be quick, sure. But it damn well has to be good. For that, you need to be wet."

"I am wet!" she protested. "Saying our vows turned me on!"

"I want you wetter," he said, and put his mouth to her.

She clutched his hair, shivering. Husband. Wow. It had all happened so fast. Her life had exploded from within, become something brand new. And in spite of the danger, something so unexpectedly beautiful.

Nothing could be more different from the drab, uptight woman she had been than this wanton, whimpering, naked girl with the pink face, clutching her husband's head between her legs while he teased her with his tongue. He suckled, coaxed, plunging and lapping, driving her until she exploded. It pulsed through her, a sweet, sobbing eternity.

"Yeah." He rose, wiping his face. "Now we're talking. Scoot back."

She did so clumsily, canting her hips to take him deeper, and crying out in raw delight as he sank his stiff, thick cock deep inside. A long, tight slide and then a tender pulse. So hot. Naked inside her, heartbeat throbbing with hers as he slid and stroked. She clenched him, with arms, legs, her pussy. Clung as he began to move. Slow, heavy thrusts, but it wasn't slow for long. She drove him on, digging her fingernails into his ass. Yelling, demanding, lifting herself. She craved his intensity, his energy. It fired up her courage and faith, her very life force, with each eager, plunging stroke. They drove each other to the brink, diving off together, in perfect trust and abandon.

Later, Aaro slid off, onto his side. Air rushed into the vacuum of her lungs, but she missed the sheer mass of him.

He ran his hand over her breast, teasing her nipple to hardness. He was so gorgeous. Those slanted, smoldering green eyes. The shadow of his beard stubble. His look of utter concentration when he made love to her. "My God, you're beautiful," she said.

He gave her that lazy grin. "That's my line."

"I stole it," she announced. "It's mine now."

"We'll share," he told her. "We're married now. We share everything, right? Isn't that how it works?"

She stared at him, big-eyed and boggled. "Wow," she whispered.

His eyes sharpened. "Regrets?"

"No. It's just hard, you know? To believe it's real."

"Oh, it's fucking real, all right," he said. "I'm holding you to it. Don't think for one second that you can back out now."

She was startled at his intensity. "I'm not!"

"Good," he said. "Because you can't." He sat up. "Roll over."

She was too slow for his tastes, so he flipped her himself, jerking her hips back. She twisted, looking back. "Hey, what are you doing?"

"Admiring my wife. Legs open, awesome cheeks on display for me to pet. Your pussy, red and puffy and shining." He caressed her thighs. "Wet to your knees with your lube and my come. You said you owned my ass, right?" He gripped her ass, positioning himself behind her.

"Yes," she whispered. "Yes, I did say that."

"So I own yours right back. That's fair. Right?" He fitted his cockhead against her labia, stroking and teasing until it was lodged in her tight opening, and surged forward. She moaned, at that deep, luscious slide of perfection. A slow lick; a wet, tender inside kiss.

"I thought we were short on time," she said. "What is this, Aaro?"

"Just sealing the deal." He swiveled. She trembled at the pulsing ache. "I love how you make my cock slippery and hot." He gripped her hips for a forceful thrust. "I love watching it go into you."

She struggled not to collapse onto the bed at the heavy jolt of his hips against hers. "Didn't we just seal the deal?"

"That was just the beginning. I'll keep at it until I feel like the job's done. Could take a half a century or more. Who knows?"

She laughed, and he growled his appreciation. "I love it when you laugh with my cock in you," he said, and drove in again, a jarring thud of contact. He stopped moving, holding her tightly. "Does that hurt?"

She felt his mind questing for contact. Opened every part of herself, in perfect trust. "Do what you want. I like you that way."

Those were the last coherent words either of them was capable of for a long time. After that, it was just gasps, the thud of flesh on flesh, the rattle and squeak of the bed. His anger and fear, his lust and longing, mixed with hers until they were one and the same, and the long string of explosions jolted them even deeper inside each other.

After, he lay there for a long time, his face hidden in her hair. When he finally rolled over, Nina stroked his hair.

"Did you seal the deal?" she asked.

It took a long time to answer. "It'll do, for a little while," he said curtly. "Get in the shower. I don't want Miles to see you in a towel."

"Ooh, possessive," she murmured.

He gave her a sharp look. "You just now figured that out?"

She got to it briskly, then he took his turn. The phone rang as Aaro came out of the bathroom, a towel around his hips. He snatched it up. "Yeah? Good. Come up."

28

Miles didn't know what he was expecting when the door to the hotel room opened, but what he saw was not it.

Nina Christie was so small. Curvy, pretty, a floppy mane of dark ringlets. Big eyes, long lashes. Sweet smile. Nasty bruises. But in spite of being on the run for her life, she seemed to, well . . . glow.

And Aaro? Miles barely recognized the guy. He could have walked past him on the street. And the change had nothing to do with the bruises or his weird hair. It was the underlying muscles in his face. Like, they'd been frozen before, and now they'd thawed and decided to throw a party. Miles had never seen Aaro smile, except for smirks which never got near his eyes, but he grinned while he introduced Nina, eye crinkles creased up à la the Marlboro Man. "Nina, this is Miles Davenport, my colleague," Aaro said. "Miles, meet my wife, Nina."

Miles practically dropped his teeth. *"What?"*

"Wife," Aaro repeated. "You know, shared property, cohabitation, family values?" He glanced at Nina. "We haven't discussed surnames."

"Later for that," she said. "To be honest, I'm not exactly sure what your surname is."

"You've only known her for three days!" Miles's voice cracked.

Aaro shrugged. "So?"

"That's what I said, at first," Nina said. "But he's very . . . persuasive." She went pink, and Miles suddenly got hit with a faceful of that jittery energy that lustful couples generated when they started vibing at each other. Back to business. They could do hanky-panky on their own time. "So, uh, when did you guys tie the knot?"

"About a half an hour ago," Aaro said brusquely.

Miles looked from Nina to Aaro. "Is this some obscure joke?"

"Fucked if it is," Aaro said.

"What Aaro is trying to tell you is that we've already exchanged our vows," Nina explained.

Miles frowned. "So you're engaged?"

"No." Aaro's voice was hard. "Married. If we say we are, we are. Just because we haven't got a stamped document in triplicate registered at the right public offices means shit. Everything I've accomplished in my life, I did without permission. If you ask, they say no. So don't ask."

Miles grunted. "Bet you asked her." He jerked his chin at Nina.

"Uh . . . yeah," Aaro admitted.

"Yeah," Miles echoed bitterly. "Yeah. Nice work if you can get it, dude. Good on you. Congratulations and good luck and family values and all that great stuff. I wish you both the best. I really do."

"Shit," Aaro muttered. "Didn't mean to rub it in."

"Don't worry about it," Miles said wearily.

There was a pained silence. Nina piped up. "Excuse me?"

"Miles has women troubles," Aaro explained.

Miles looked at Nina. "My girlfriend ran off with a rock star."

She winced. "Oh. That sucks, Miles."

"It's OK," he said. "You guys are keeping me too busy to dwell on it. Speaking of which." He dragged forward the rolling luggage rack, and pulled off garment bags, tossing them onto one of the beds. "Here are the tuxes. Your dress, shoes, and whatnot, courtesy of Lily and Zia Rosa. And your swag from the Walgreens pharmacy." He hoisted a bag. "Hair clippers, shaving stuff, makeup, hairpins. Some rhinestone bling for you, and some guns for him." He hauled a hard-case suitcase off the rack, shoved the trolley out into the hall, and let the room door swing to. "Guess we should get ready for the party, right?"

Nina and Aaro gave each other significant looks. "There's something we need to talk about before we go," Nina said.

Her cautious tone tickled Miles's weirdness antennae. "Yeah?"

"You know how I was injected with this drug, right?" Nina asked.

"Of course," Miles replied. "You need the B dose, right?"

"Right," Nina said. "We haven't discussed the effects of the drug."

Miles blew out a breath. "Don't dole it out to me in dribs and drabs. That drives me bugfuck."

She nodded. "OK," she said. "It turned me into a telepath."

Miles was speechless for a minute. "And, uh . . . you haven't told anybody about this yet . . . exactly why?"

"I couldn't face seeing that look that's on your face right now," she said quietly. "Like I'm about to metamorphose into a giant housefly."

He held up his hands, defensive. "Hey. If you knew how much dumb, lame, X-rated crap goes on in a guy's head—"

"I do know," she assured him. "I do. And I don't care. Everybody's mind is full of dumb garbage, Miles. Mine, too. I don't judge."

"Besides, this isn't about you," Aaro said, his voice cutting. "Like we have time to care about the garbage in your head?"

"Ouch. Back off, man." Miles turned to Nina, who was at least being polite. "So how telepathic are you, anyway?"

"I don't have anything to compare myself to. Try me. Think of something specific, a visual image. And if you want to make it easy for me, make it one with a strong emotion attached."

That was when he fucked up. There were only two emotionally charged images on top of his mind, and once he'd nixed the mutilated body of Joseph Kirk, only one other thing popped up, like a jack-in-the-box. So poor, unsuspecting Nina got the full whammy. Not only high-definition sexual images, but all his existential angst on top of it. To say nothing of jealousy, anger, and hurt. The meaninglessness of his entire existence. How fucking stupid he felt.

She jerked back, with a gasp, like she'd been struck. "Ouch," she said. "Oh, Jesus, Miles."

"What did you show her?" Aaro turned to him, outraged.

"I'm sorry," Miles said. "I swear, I didn't mean to do that. I was just scrambling not to visualize Joseph Kirk, and this other thing was just, uh . . . just sitting there."

"What?" Aaro roared. "What other thing?"

"Cindy and her rock star," Miles confessed, abashed. "Sorry."

"Oh, Christ, Miles, did you have to inflict that on her? Was that necessary?" Aaro scolded. "You mean, them having sex?"

"That wasn't what bothered me," Nina said gently. "It was just very intense. Your feelings. I wasn't prepared."

"Sorry," Miles said again, miserably.

"Me, too," Nina whispered. "About all of it. Really."

Aaro paced between them. "Anyway, Miles. You have to process this fast. Get comfortable with it right now. Like, instantly."

Miles nodded. "OK. I'm good with weird. Hell. I hang out with McClouds. I've had full immersion training in weird. No problem."

"That's good," Nina said. "Because last night, the guys who caught up with us shot up Aaro with the same drug they gave me."

Miles turned to Aaro, his skin crawling. "Don't tell me you're a telepath, too, man. Because that would seriously creep me out."

Aaro looked betrayed. "You said you were good with weird!"

"Not that weird," he replied. "I have my limits."

"I'm not a telepath," Aaro snarled. "So chill out. In me, the stuff played out sort of, uh, differently."

"What?" Miles started to twitch. "Go on! Hit me! Stop being coy!"

"Coercion," Nina said. "He changes your mind for you. By force."

Miles gaped for a moment, and started to laugh.

"What's so goddamn funny?" Aaro demanded.

Miles shook his head, wheezing. "Coercion? You? Oh, man. That is just so fucking redundant, it kills me." He looked up at Nina. "I get it, now. So that's how you persuaded her to marry you."

"Shut up, Miles," Aaro said.

"Make me, dude," Miles said, wiping tears from his eyes. "You can, right? Show me how this works. Go on, I'm not scared."

"Don't tempt me," Aaro grated.

"Shut up!" Nina scolded. "We don't have time for this!"

Miles wrenched himself under control. "OK," he said. "Coercion. Telepathy. The attack of the mutant freak trio. The mind reader, the strong-arm, and the tech geek."

"But the people we're liable to meet in there?" Aaro said. "They can make your brains leak out your ears without even touching you."

Miles was sobered. "That is fucked up."

"Right," Nina agreed. "You need to learn to block them. So while we're getting ready, think of a shield image that works, as your personal analog. I use a wall of static, sort of like white noise. Aaro uses a bank vault. Come up with something that resonates for you. It's late, to try something like this, but it might give you more protection. If it works."

"OK," he said, bemused.

He set his brain to work on that problem. Aaro disappeared into the bathroom. They heard the snarl of hair clippers. Nina laid the outfit Lily had mandated upon the bed, and the underwear that came with it. Miles actually had to look away. Black, sheer, bustier, garters, wow.

The dress was slinky, stretchy, glittering red fabric with a deeply flared skirt that belled out into layered ripples like a flower. Strapless.

Nina held it up, dismayed. "How the hell will this thing stay on?"

"Cindy had one like that," Miles offered. "It stayed on fine, if you didn't, you know, mess with it." He started to blush, at her raised eyebrow. "It's true. And Cindy doesn't even have the, uh, assets to prop it up like you do." *Damn.* Dig himself in a little deeper, why didn't he.

"Where the hell do you get off gawking at my wife's assets?"

They turned at Aaro's voice, and gasped.

He'd shorn his hair off, military style. Miles would never have described anything about the guy as soft, but he realized now that the long hair had actually softened him. Without it, he looked hard, mean, seriously badass. Cheekbones that sliced, a nose like a scimitar, and those eyes, whoa. Miles hoped the tux would sweeten him up, or they weren't going to get through the door. Fifteen grand or no fifteen grand.

"Good God, Aaro," Nina murmured.

"What?" he snapped, defensive. "What else could I do? It looked like rats on crack have been chewing on the back of my head! It's that horrible? A lot of guys buzz their hair off!"

"Well, yes. But they don't look like you," Nina said. "I thought we were trying to be, er, unnoticeable. That haircut, well. It's memorable."

He glanced at her dress. "Well, once you prop your tits up in that bustier and put the red dress on, you can kiss unnoticeable good-bye."

"So what you're saying is, my tits can get us all killed?"

"Can't imagine dying for a finer cause," Aaro said nobly.

Nina did not appear to appreciate the sentiment. "Why couldn't it have been a basic black sheath?" she moaned.

"We can't fix it now," Aaro said. "We're already late. Get dressed." He fixed Miles with a slit-eyed gaze. "In the bathroom."

And he'd thought the guy had been tough to swallow before he found true love. Jeez.

He and Aaro got to work putting on their holsters and tuxes, and loading as much weaponry into them as the specially tailored garments would allow. Aaro seemed happy with the SIG Sauer Miles had brought for him, and the Ruger six-shot for backup. The bow tie civilized Aaro a little, but a dress military uniform would have looked more appropriate. And the bruises didn't help.

The bathroom door opened. The room got real quiet.

Nina looked amazing. She'd done some magic with her makeup that made the bruises vanish, and her face was a flawless ivory pale, eyes smoky, lips like berries. Wow. She'd put her glasses back on. Amazingly, they did not detract.

They sassed it up, like the lemon rind in the espresso, the wasabi on the sushi. She'd swept up her hair into a pouffy, femmy updo. Lily had included a glittery shrug, which covered the scratches on her shoulders and arms. The pendant and dangly earrings Miles had grabbed off the display kiosk at the Walgreens checkout counter looked like fucking Cartier. The gravity-defying tits should be registered as lethal weapons. And they held the dress up just fine.

Miles wrenched his gaze away before Aaro caught him slobbering, but he needn't have bothered. Aaro was in rapt contemplation of his bride. "What, should I go wait in the lobby?" he asked plaintively.

"No time." Nina looked them over with approval. "You gentlemen look wonderful. One last detail for you, Aaro." She came toward him clutching a handful of little bottles and makeup sponges. "Your face."

Aaro shrank back, horrified. "Me? No fucking way!"

"Don't be stupid. If there's one thing I learned at my mother's knee, it's how to cover bruises with makeup. Now sit, and don't move a muscle. I don't want to smear your tux."

He sat down, muttering, but he let her dab and sponge at him. She took her time, and when she was done, Miles was impressed. The bruises were gone, and it looked natural. "A person would only notice if she was going to tongue-kiss you," he told Aaro. "So you're good."

Aaro checked himself out in the room mirror, but his ferocious scowl smoothed out as he looked himself over.

Nina turned to him. "So, Miles? What's your analog?"

"An encrypted, password-protected computer," he said promptly.

Nina blinked. "Ah. And the password? If I need to contact you?"

Miles fidgeted nervously. "You can do that?"

"I have no idea. Won't know till I try, right?"

Miles shrugged. "The password is LARA all caps, hashtag, star, exclamation point, my great-aunt Barbara's zip code in California, hashtag, KIRK all caps, and two question marks."

"You have got to be kidding," Nina said, dismayed.

Aaro snickered. "The nerd's revenge."

"You said these guys can drain my brain out my ears!" Miles protested. "What did you want me to put? My dog's name?"

Nina sighed. "Could you write it down, at least?"

"It's lazy and dumb to write down passwords," Miles said.

"It's dumber to die screaming because you made up one too complicated to remember," Aaro commented.

Miles grabbed hotel stationery. He wrote his password along the top, tore it off, and handed it to Nina. She studied it, tucked it between her tits. Into that shadowy cleavage that looked oh, so velvety soft.

There was a moment of profound quiet.

"Uh . . . wow," Miles said, remembering that Nina read minds. The bodacious cleavage had made him totally forget that detail. *Shit.*

"Shut up, Miles," Aaro snapped.

"Could we just go, now?" Miles said plaintively. "Before I piss you off again?"

They made haste to do exactly that.

Dmitri was in a good mood by the time he cruised into Spruce Ridge. Playing with the new toy in his mind was more fun than he'd ever had. The applications became more vast with every use of his new trick. At the Outback Steakhouse, he'd had some fun with the blonde in the booth behind him. The bitch found a big shiny cockroach in her Caesar salad, trundling around on the romaine and the croutons. She'd run screaming out of the restaurant. He was still laughing. Uppity hag.

It had been fun to put one over on that doll-like cashier, too. She'd be getting it up the ass from her manager tonight when it came time to count her till, being as how he'd paid for his forty-dollar meal with a one-dollar bill. The cashier had seen a hundred, and given him a wad of change. Yeah, life was going to cost a lot less for him from now on. Not that he was hurting for money. But still. But still.

But the absolute best joke was on that long-haul trucker, the jowly asshole who'd flipped him off at the freeway exit. He'd followed the guy's rig for a half hour, waiting for his moment. The truck was going fifty-five, and Dmitri blocked the pass lane until the line of cars behind them was long, dense, and impatient. Then, with a surge of gas, he'd pulled up alongside and given the driver the finger before he jammed the image deep into the guy's mind . . .

. . . *four-year-old blond girl in her nightgown, barefoot, forty feet ahead of the truck, right in his lane. Holding a teddy bear.*

A frantic bray of the horn, and Dmitri pulled smoothly ahead, watching in his rearview mirror at the swerving containers, spinning, flipping, with massive, leisurely grace. Cars flew over them, bouncing every which way, on their heads, sides, tails. A pall of smoke rose.

Dmitri shook his head. Shame. Those poor people. But the guy shouldn't have flipped him off. People needed to be more polite. At least to him. Starting with Sasha and his whore. He had something special planned for them. Rudd, too. Anabel. So arrogant, so unsuspecting. No idea that they would soon be on their knees, anxiously sucking his dick.

The fantasy had him in a bubbling ferment, like a champagne high, except that his wits were razor sharp. He drove through Spruce Ridge on the freeway, following the directions of the GPS, though he scarcely needed it. The Greaves Convention Center had its own exit off the freeway. The roads were crowded with luxury cars.

Dmitri eased out onto the shoulder and pulled on past the crowded front entrance with the valet parking. He kept on going, until he found an overflow lot, far from the action, and walked around the building, to the back.

The kitchen entrance was swarming with staff, and security, too. He took a moment, from the shadows, to observe the white uniform coat as some men offloaded boxes from a truck, and crafted a constant feed of that white uniform over his clothes as he went in. It was tricky and strenuous, projecting something constantly. But he wouldn't have to do it for long. Slipped right past the security guys.

He wandered around in the hubbub, scoping out the perfect spot to bait his trap. This was a banquet for hundreds, so there would be an army of ringers hired on for the night, scores of people who didn't know each other. In ten minutes, he'd found himself a likely subject, and latched on to the guy's mind, leafing through what lay around on top.

The guy was similar in height and build to Dmitri, though much younger, and had the same color and length of hair. His name was Leo, and he was twenty-four years old and gay, but had not yet told anyone. He had a deep-seated terror of large dogs. Dmitri managed to glean these two facts because the kid was obsessing about his next-door neighbor as he worked, upon whom he had a huge crush, but he could not approach the guy because of his enormous German shepherd. The beast made poor Leo shit himself. Dmitri could work with that.

He followed the guy as he scurried on some errand involving rolling carts of champagne flutes, and called out as soon as they had gotten near the unused conference room he'd chosen. "Leo!" he called.

Leo turned, puzzled. "Huh? Excuse me?"

"Come here for a second," Dmitri ordered.

Leo looked bewildered and put upon. "Look, man, I have

to hurry! Mike is going to rip me a new one if I don't get these glasses to the—"

"Forget Mike. This is more important. You've got to see this." Dmitri shoved open the door, and gestured for Leo to go inside.

Leo was a good-natured, agreeable, innocent guy who didn't like to get on anybody's bad side, so he followed Dmitri in, and looked around, his eyes full of anxious puzzlement. "What is it, man?"

Dmitri closed the door, preparing two images in his mind, and launched the first one. The dog's growl, deep, ferocious, mutating into a gaping jawed, full-throated snarl.

Leo's gaze darted around, panicked. "What? Where is it?"

"Did you bring that animal in here, Leo?" Dmitri yelled, pointing.

"No!" Leo shrieked. "No, no, I swear . . ." The huge phantom dog materialized and leaped for him, enormous slavering jaws gaping, eyes a demonic burning red. Leo shrieked, lunging for the open door—

Crack, his head smacked against the door, which was not, in fact, open at all. Leo had lunged, full speed, headfirst, toward the projected image of an open door. The kid thudded to the ground with a pathetic, creaking sigh. The door now had a large, bloody splotch on it.

Dmitri knelt down. Leo was not going to be getting up anytime soon, perhaps not ever, if no one noticed him for a while. Even if he lived, he was unlikely to remember what had happened. That blow was hard enough to bruise his brain. Cause bleeding, swelling.

He was pleased with himself. He was good in a fight, proficient with guns, knives, bare hands when the occasion warranted it, but this new skill was so much better, so much smoother. The beauty of it, the simplicity, the lack of accountability. Who could link him to this?

He unbuttoned Leo's white jacket, with the latex gloves he'd picked up earlier that day. His biggest challenge now was to get Leo's catering uniform off without getting any blood on it.

The rest was cake.

29

Miles gazed uneasily at the bejeweled people bottle-necked at the entrance, wondering which were brain melters. He wasn't surprised at the heavy security. No party crashers allowed at a shindig with a fifteen-thousand-dollar ticket price. *Ouch.* That price tag still hurt him.

They'd scoped out every entrance before reluctantly coming back to the front. Security personnel were teeming at every single one, even the kitchen. So, full-on frontal attack, then. Hiding in plain sight.

Nobody liked it, but what the fuck.

Speaking of security, cameras were trained on them from all directions. Nina and Aaro did kissy face. Miles visualized his encrypted computer, and tried not to sweat. He'd picked up nerdy glasses for Aaro at the Walgreens, and they gave the guy's severity a geekier flavor. Still, nobody in his right mind would mistake Aaro for a nerd. His body was too dense.

"Burns my ass that I figured out how coercion worked after you laid out the cash," Aaro bitched beneath his breath.

"Could have just jabbed the guy who has the guest list. Saved us forty-five thousand."

"No, you could not," Nina whispered back. "You can use this ability to save a person, or a kitten in a goddamn tree. But not to save money, or time, or effort. Or else you're no better than them!"

"You're such a hard-ass. That's the cost of a nice new car!"

"And your point is?"

Aaro looked rebellious, but suddenly, his face went hard. "Miles," he said. "Ten o'clock, directly in front of the fake waterfall, talking to the lady in gold. See him? Fake tan, brow lift?"

"Brain-melt dude?"

"Yeah," Aaro murmured. "The bombshell in the gray dress, she's the telepath. Also badass. Also enjoys inflicting pain. The only way through the main hall is right past the two of them."

"Yeah?" Miles said. "Meaning?"

"Meaning, you go distract him and the blonde while Nina and I slither in like eels."

"Oh, God. Why couldn't we have just knocked out the six big security guys at one of the back entrances instead?"

"Too many," Aaro replied. "If it was two, or maybe even four, maybe. But we couldn't take out all six without somebody getting in a call on their com device first. And then we'd be toast."

"Behold, my first task," Miles muttered. "Schmooze the guy who melts brains, who is guarded by the hot nymph who reads minds."

"I'd do it for you if I could," Aaro said.

"Stop condescending to me," Miles snapped. "Let me bitch and moan and be sarcastic if I want, OK? It helps me!"

"Bitch and moan all you want while you get into position."

"Fine. I'll see you in hell, or whatever Han Solo says." He launched himself before he could get stalled out by his own good sense. Muscling ahead of an elderly couple who were also waiting to be admitted. Clearly, the old couple weren't used to waiting for anything.

He pretended not to hear their pointed comments about rude young people these days, about how it was all me, me, me.

Right. If he were thinking about me, me, me, he'd beat hell out of here. What was up with him, anyway? Always trying to show the world what a brave and righteous dude he was. Who was he trying to prove it to? Himself? The McClouds? Or worse, to she who could not be named who had ruined his life? He hoped not, since his noble gesture was wasted on her. She was too busy blowing her rock star to notice.

The image of Lara Kirk popped into his mind, complete with her streaming banner of dark hair and her nipple hardon as the guy with the list turned to him. "Your name, sir?"

"Miles Davenport," he supplied, banishing names and images from his brain. He was a blank plastic case, a keyboard, a blank screen with a dialog box and a blinking cursor, like a taunt. *Just try and get into my mental space, you evil brain-melting motherfuckers. Just try.*

The security guy's face did not change, nor did he attempt to melt Miles's brain. He located Miles on the list, checked him off with an electronic pen, smiled politely, and waved him on.

There was a thick crush at the meet and greet, so Miles took his time, oozing slowly in Rudd's direction. He was grateful to have spent last night reading up on Rudd. Business history, gubernatorial campaign, the blogs he had written.

He glimpsed the blonde. It was like getting kicked by a horse. He lost a few seconds, staring at her. Scary gorgeous, dressed in is-it-gray-or-is-it-black taffeta, shot through with iridescent gleams of rainbow, tits pressed cruelly flat by the front placket of her bodice, but still plumping up over the top, undaunted. Gold hair slicked back into a Japanese-looking topknot, a scary-sharp beaded hairstick stabbed through it.

The closer he got, the more her beauty scared him. Her soft-focus shimmer confused and destabilized him, crowding even what's-her-name out of his mind. He jerked his brain into line. Plastic computer case. Bland, impenetrable. The glowing fairy princess was a mind-raping sociopath, so keep that bad dog chained up *waaay* out there in the back, where nobody could hear him howl.

The press behind him was shoving him to the point of no return. Rudd was inches away. Into the jaws of death and all that good shit.

He stuck out his hand. "Mr. Rudd, I'm so honored to meet you," he gushed. "I've been your biggest fan, since you were CFO of Scion! We studied your company in my econ class, and you're, like, my hero! I read your business blog every week, and when I did exactly what you said, I made money! Like, when you warned everybody about Sylvan Industries? I got out just in time! Brillant, sir, absolutely brilliant. I paid for my graduate degree with money I earned because of you!"

Rudd continued to shake Miles's hand, since Miles did not let go. "Thank you," he said. "You hardly look old enough to have been reading stodgy investment advice six years ago."

"I'm older than I look." Miles grinned like a fool, presenting his body so that the people crowding in nudged him around, forcing the other man to turn . . . turn . . . and they no longer faced the front entrance, but stood at an angle to it.

"That's very gratifying," Rudd said. He turned his gaze over Miles's shoulder, getting ready to schmooze the next guy—

Miles grabbed his hand again and yanked him back that

crucial quarter turn. "Sir, I hope you don't mind, but I already sent my CV to your campaign manager. I wanted to urge you to look it over personally. I can't say I've been involved in a political campaign before, but I'm writing my thesis on the world's new emerging economic models, and I have an economic vision that dovetails perfectly with yours. Your administration will really need my kind of vision to—"

"This is all extremely flattering, Mr. . . . ?" Rudd's teeth flashed.

"Davenport," Miles supplied. "Please. Call me Miles."

The blonde had noticed her boss's plight, and was moving closer.

"Ah, yes," Rudd said. "As I said, I'm flattered, but this is not the time for us to conduct a job interview."

"Of course it's not, sir, I understand!" A flash of glittering red swept by, tickling his peripheral vision. Rudd did not react. "I need you to know how strongly I support your candidacy, sir. We need leaders who understand how money works, and can't be jerked around by advisors with their own personal agendas! You're the reason I'm here, sir. You're why I can donate fifteen grand to the Greaves Foundation. If I hadn't studied your blog, I'd still be working at the electronics store. So thank you. Really." He wagged Rudd's hand again. "Really."

"You're most welcome." Rudd gave him a big smile, and that was when Miles felt it. A breathless, anxious, eye-popping pressure. An urge to get away, as fast as possible.

Just another couple of seconds. Let them get ten meters away.

The feeling got more intense. It was sickening fear, now. But he'd been feeling queasy and frantic ever since what's-her-name defected with the rock star. Queasy and frantic was normal for him. He ate it with his morning cornflakes. He hung on tight to his shit, and persisted. "Could I set up a meeting with you, sir?" he begged. "It would mean so much to me. I'm sure you won't regret it."

"Anabel," Rudd called. "Come here a moment, my dear."

Oh, man. Thrown to the dogs. The bombshell drifted over, eyeing him. He began to sweat. Like she had a direct line attached to his glands. She yanked a pull chain, and *squirt squirt,* they went nuts.

"This is Miles Davenport," Rudd told her. "Miles, this is Anabel Marshall, my assistant. Anabel, this extremely force-ful and intense young man is a great admirer of my work, and I have reason to think he might be . . . special. Would you take down his vital stats? I want all his contact info in our files." He turned to Miles. "We vet our staff with ex-treme care. I count on Anabel's infallible instincts. Tell her all about yourself. As if she were me."

"Um, OK. Thanks," he said, as the blonde towed him away.

To God alone knew what.

"Aaro! Do you mind? I was just shaking his hand!" Nina hissed, as Aaro dragged her behind him through the tables.

"Did you see the way that guy was looking at you?"

"Ah, yeah," she said, with dry irony. "I thought that was the whole point of tight, sexy dresses. Isn't it?"

"Up to a certain point, Nina. Up to a certain point."

"I would have had to go a little beyond that point to read him! That was Thaddeus Greaves! He is the reason this party is happening! He's the name on the Institute, the name on the Convention Center, the only name Helga mentioned! If there's anyone I need to read here, it's him! And you yanked me away! You were *rude* to him!"

"He's a dick," Aaro muttered.

"Why do you say that? Because he liked my cleavage?"

His mouth tightened. "He looks fake. He's hiding something."

Nina snorted. "Yeah! Maybe the key to our survival!"

She was right, of course, and he had no good immediate excuse. "We had to get out of there before Rudd turned around," he muttered, and pulled her toward the decorative columns that lined the room. He ducked behind one of them, into relative quiet and shadow.

Nina glanced back anxiously over her shoulder. "And Miles?"

"He left with Anabel."

"He did *what?*" she gasped, craning her neck. "He went where? You're sure? You saw them?"

"He's six foot five. He's easy to spot," Aaro said. "He was glad-handing Rudd. Rudd got tired of it and sicced Anabel on him."

"Maybe Rudd tried to coerce him, and it didn't work," Nina fretted. "Anabel's rough. A new shield won't hold up to her."

Aaro shrugged. "Don't know."

"Aren't you the least bit worried? He's a sweet guy. And incredibly brave. That crazy bitch will eat him alive!"

"The worst that can happen is she breaches his security," Aaro said. "She will or she won't. If she does, Miles will have to deal with her. But he's tough, and armed. Who knows, maybe she'll even fuck him."

Nina jerked. "Eewww! That is a disgusting idea!"

"He'd survive," Aaro said. "There are more horrible fates than getting your bone kissed by the evil temptress from the dark side. Might do him good. Take his mind off that brainless slut he's so hung up on."

"He deserves better," Nina said tightly.

"Of course he does. But it's not like it would kill him, Nina."

"Let's not have this argument. Your sexist attitude is bugging me."

Aaro sighed. "Oh, for God's sake—"

"What if it was you who had to go off into some dark room with her? Would you feel justified in having sex with her, just for the cause? Would you expect me to think it didn't mean anything? Hey, just the evil temptress from the dark side kissing your bone, right? No biggie!"

He forced his voice to stay low and even. "We can't do this now."

"I forgot, in my impromptu marriage ceremony, to mention that detail about forsaking all others! I should have been more specific. Maybe we're not exactly on the same page. You think?"

His jaw throbbed with tension. "You're being irrational. This has nothing to do with what's between us."

"Suppose it was me!" she raged on. "Suppose I was the one who had to go provide a diversion, and Anabel was a man who dragged me out of the room to God knows where! Would you feel the same way?"

"No," he growled. "And you goddamn well know it."

She was on a roll, and couldn't stop. "Oh, it won't hurt her to get nailed by the evil emperor from the dark side. What's the worst that can happen? A dick's a dick, right? They go in, they go out, badda boom, badda bim. She'll be fine, she's not made out of soap!"

"Shut up, Nina," he said.

She sucked in air, so he kissed her. The first two seconds, it was just to shut her up, but a kiss with Nina always had its own agenda, apart from what his own personal agenda might have been.

She felt so soft and fragile in his arms. Trembling with emotion. He felt powerless to protect her. The enemy was everywhere. Inside her body. All around them. Diffused into the very air they breathed.

It clutched at his heart. He just held her and kissed her until he knew she felt it, too, relaxing with a long, rippling shudder.

He lifted his head, wiping her lipstick off his face. Her eyes shone with tears. "We cannot have this fight," he told her. "Not tonight."

Her mouth trembled. "I know. It just . . . pushed all my buttons."

"I'm sorry, too," he told her.

She dabbed her mascara. "Miles is kind and brave and smart. He deserves love. And Anabel's a polluted thing from a festering swamp. It would hurt him, to get close to that . . . thing. He's suffered enough."

"Uh . . . OK," he said. Not totally getting it, but whatever. She didn't need to know right now just how superficial a guy could be, depending on the context. Just as well if she never knew.

"And don't think that it's OK just because she's beautiful. That's not beauty. It's just an empty trick. Less than nothing. Understand?"

"Sure," he agreed hastily. "Of course."

She dug in her little beaded red purse for a tissue. "You want to know something kind of horrible?"

Oh, Christ, no, he really didn't, but that response was not on the list of permissible answers, so he braced himself, hard. "Go on."

"Stan was really handsome. Women fell all over him."

He took the purse, found a tissue. "Yeah?" was all he could say.

She blew her nose. "You can guess just how much of a difference his good looks made when he started feeling me up. When I was twelve."

He pulled her close to him again. "I'm sorry," he said helplessly. "I wish the bastard were still alive so I could kill him for you."

She nodded, against his chest.

"It's different for Miles, though," he said. "He's not a child, he's not helpless. He's big, and strong, and armed, and he's, ah—"

"He's a man," she finished bitterly. "I know. Go ahead, say it. He's a man, and that makes it different. I don't know why that bugs me so much, but it does. It makes me sick. And angry."

"Don't be mad," he said helplessly.

"I'm not," she muttered. "Not at you."

"We can't go looking for him now," he said. "We have to just do our thing, as best we can, and trust him to do his."

She nodded. Sniffling.

"I love you," he said. "And I'm adding an addendum to our wedding vows. Do you, Nina Louisa Christie, promise to never have sex with anyone but me, ever again? Not even the evil emperor?"

That earned him a soggy giggle. She blew her nose again before answering. "I do," she whispered. "Do you promise it, too?"

"Forever," he said fervently. "I swear. No one but you."

They swayed together for a silent, stolen moment, but it was time to make their last bid for survival, snooping in the heads of the crowd. Or Nina would, anyway. She had to do all the heavy lifting tonight.

"Remember to do the invisible trick, like I showed you," she said. "It won't work as well, because you're so big, and you look really hot in that tux. But it might help."

"You, too," he said. "Let's go."

30

"Um, where are we going?" Miles asked.

The weird emptiness in her eyes turned into a glittering smile. "Someplace quiet and private."

He felt hypnotized by the *tic-tic-tic* of her heels. Her fingernails dug into his arm. Checking out his muscle tone? Jesus.

"Flex," she ordered him.

He did so, an automatic reflex. Her fingers tightened on the bulge of his bicep. "You must work out a lot."

"Some." He darted a nervous glance at her starkly perfect profile. No clue if his shield would work, and he had to beta test it on a psycho sadist. He kept his visualization steady. Thoughts, feelings, hidden deep inside the encrypted structure. Wondering if he was trotting meekly to his own death by brain melt. He could ask, maybe. *Excuse me, miss, but are you planning on melting my brain?* Sounded like a line from a goofy British comedy flick.

She leaned closer, tilting her head so that the scary hairstick jabbed at his shoulder. "What are you scared of?" she purred.

Miles gulped back a hoot of nervous laughter. "Ah . . . you."

"Me?" She laughed. "I'm not scary."

"Yes, you are," he said grimly.

She stopped by a door, looking up at him through insanely long eyelashes. "But you're brave, Miles, aren't you?" She pulled him inside.

The light from the grounds outside barely illuminated an administrative office. Reception desk, partition, and behind it, cubicles, tables, file cabinets. "Shall we, ah, turn on the lights?" he asked.

Her pale shoulders lifted. She glowed in the darkness, like moonlight on snow. "Aren't we supposed to get to know each other? Sometimes that happens faster in the dark. Dark is license to reveal."

"It also can let you hide," he said.

She pulled him deeper into the room. "You're not going to hide anything, Miles." She stopped at one of the desks, swept off the surface. Things thudded to the floor. Something broke. A coffee mug bounced and rolled, piles of papers from an in-box scattered and slid, fluttering to the floor. "Come here." She yanked.

"This is really weird," Miles said nervously, his voice strangling into a squeak as she grabbed his crotch, squeezed. "Oh. My. *God*."

"Weird, yes." She stroked him, exploring his dimensions. "Weird is my life now, Miles. But weird can be fun. Wow. So it's true, what they say, about big noses and big cocks."

"Ah . . . I wouldn't know," he gasped out. "I, uh, have never done any statistical analysis." His voice choked off as she cupped his balls.

"Statistical analysis," she echoed. "Is that how econ nerds talk? I've never done an econ nerd. Never wanted to, until now."

Her attack was so sudden. He yelled as the pain gripped

his head, weirdly muscular, like a strangling snake squeezing, with a questing tendril of awareness like a flicking tongue, searching for entry points. Prodding, poking, licking. It felt sexual, in a nasty, dirty, prurient way.

He couldn't breathe. Didn't dare move, it hurt so bad. All he could do was hang on to the image. Data locked. Password box blinking.

The data was safe. It was his head that was about to implode.

The pressure released. He gulped in air.

"You lying son of a bitch," she said. "You're one of us, aren't you?"

He took a moment to remember how to speak. "One of who?"

"Don't play dumb." She slapped him. "You blocked me. You're not surprised. You're not confused. You knew exactly what you were doing."

Oh, shit. The jig was so very up, and he hadn't even come up with a coherent plan B. He had to just wing it.

"You're enhanced, right?" she yelled. "No one has ever blocked me but another user! Where did you get your stash? What's your talent?"

He shook his head. "I'm not enhanced."

"You're lying!" Her voice was shrill. "Who gave you the drug? Where did they get it? Who's producing? Where'd they get the formula?"

"Nobody," he insisted. "I'm not taking any drug."

"Then let . . . me . . . *see!*" The squeezing pain was back, harder than before. He struggled not to cry out. "Let me in! *Now!*"

Fucked if he would. He shook his splitting head. "No."

The pressure eased off, to his intense relief. "Want to know something about me, Miles?" Her voice was a caress. "A fun fact?"

He shrugged. "Whatever."

"I don't wear underwear. Not on my pussy. Other lingerie is fun, but not there. I like it to be bare. Accessible."

"Oh," he said stupidly, still struggling to breathe.

"Want to see?" She perched on the edge of the desk, and hauled up her rustling taffeta skirts. There was enough light from outside to see that she was telling the truth. She had a wax job, too, just a delicate swatch of curly fuzz at the end of her slit, like a decorative flourish. Her eyes glowed at him, hot and feral. She put her hand on her pussy, slid her fingers inside, diddled herself, as she stared into his eyes. The little wet sounds seemed extremely loud in the silence, the darkness.

She lifted up her glistening fingers, and wiped them on his cheek. "Don't you want to fuck me?" she purred. "Everyone else does."

"You mean, everyone wants to, or everyone fucks you?" he asked.

Her laughter sounded bitter. "Does it matter? Do you only fuck good girls, Miles? You kind of have that stink to you. Have you ever wondered what it would be like to do it with a bad, dirty girl? A girl who was up for anything you wanted?"

There she went again, with the python mind squeeze, oh, *shit*...

Miles dragged in as much air as he could before it got unbearable, but his hard-on had not abated. On the contrary, it intensifed, as if the stranglehold on his mind was on his cock as well.

He clenched his teeth and endured it. It was easier this time, without the element of surprise. She meant to lure him into sex, and then pounce. There was very little chance he could keep up the shield if he was fucking her, and if he came, no chance in hell. He simply was not that cool of a customer. He tried, but he wasn't.

"Of course I want to fuck you," he said.

She grabbed his hand, pressed it against her pussy. "Do it, then," she whispered. "Come on, whip that big, fat fellow out for me to play with. I'm so turned on, Miles. You have to. Now. Or I'll kill you."

Her pussy was silky, the folds of her labia so delicate, tightly furled. Her pussy hair was springy ringlets, totally different from—

"Cindy," Anabel sang out. "Is she your wife?"

He practically yelped, he was so startled, and whipped his shield back up. "None of your business."

She seized his hand, thrust it inside her, so hard his fingernails must have hurt her. He felt that squeeze around his mind and cock again, the questing snake tongue. "Cindy," she taunted, as she slid his fingers in and out like a dildo. "Tell me what you like that Cindy won't do for you. Does Cindy give good head? Does she take it up the ass?"

He hung on to his analog with every fiber of his being. "She hates doing it from behind," he said. "Says it makes her feel like an animal."

"Oh, does it? Well, guess what? I *am* an animal. We all are. Poor uptight Cindy doesn't know that. That's why her man has his hand up my snatch, and not hers." She turned, hoisting her skirts up. Braced herself against the desk, arching her back. He'd never seen an ass that perfect, not even in glossy, retouched magazine photographs.

"Are you animal enough for me, Miles?" she crooned.

"I'll try," he said, coming closer, to stroke the smooth globes of her ass cheeks. Taut, round, perfect. She wiggled, parting wider.

"Fuck me hard, Miles," she ordered him. "Now."

He yanked the plastic cuffs out of his sock. Shoved her facedown against the desk. She squawked as he snagged her hands behind her back, fastening them, ratcheting them tight.

She shrieked, flopped. "No!" she shrieked. "No, I don't

like it that way, you bastard! What the fuck do you think you're doing? *No!"*

She was very strong, but he gritted his teeth, hanging on to his mind shield with grim desperation as he bore her down to the floor. He planted his weight on top of her while he cuffed her feet, and hooked her hands and feet together. It was as uncomfortable as hell, and he hated doing it, but he had to immobilize her. Buy them some time.

She twisted, shrieking obscenities. Attacked with her mind, too. The strangling snake squeezed, and he thought his eyes would pop out of his head from the pressure by the time he'd dragged her across the floor and fastened her to the radiator. She sobbed, wailing incoherently. Her hair had come loose, spread like a bright fan across the floor.

It was the most distasteful, horrifying thing he had ever done, and when he stumbled to his feet, his legs shook beneath him. He groped in his other sock for the knife, and knelt, as far from her as he could, hacking two long strips of taffeta off the bottom of her skirt.

"What the fuck are you doing?" she spat.

He wadded up the piece of cloth, stared at it, stared at her, and decided, what the hell. Nothing to lose by not asking, at this point.

"Where's the B dose?" he asked.

The blankness on her face made his heart sink. She stared at him with her mouth open. "My God! If I knew that, would I be here, peddling my mind and my tail for these pig-fuckers? If I knew that, I'd be the queen of the fucking world! You ignorant jackass! Who are you, anyway? Are you with Arbatov? With that Christie bitch?"

So much for that. "Never mind. Where is Lara Kirk?"

"Lara? Why are you asking about her? What does she have to do with anything? Who the fuck cares?"

"I do," he blurted incautiously, and instantly cursed himself for it. He could get the poor chick killed with his big mouth. Better shut her up fast, and himself as well. He was making things worse.

"I'm sorry," he said, and tried to stuff the gag into her mouth.

She jerked away. "I'm going to tell everyone how you cuffed me, and beat me, and raped me! After they find me here like this, they will believe me! You will go to jail and rot there, you sick piece of *shit!*"

"I don't think so," he said.

"No? Miles, honey, do you see that hair stick? On the carpet?"

He looked, saw it. "What of it?"

"When I get loose, I will hunt you down, and fuck you with it."

"That's nice." That sentiment gave him the oomph he needed to jam the gag in, but she still writhed away. Just not done with him yet.

"You won't be able to stop me, and you know why? Because you're a pussy! I smell it, see? Nicey nice guy! No balls at all! I bet Cindy's out somewhere this very night, on her knees, taking it hard from behind from a guy who has what she really needs!"

"Huh," he said drily. "Yeah, probably."

"You don't even have the balls to kill me like a man, do you?"

"Nope, I sure don't. Shut up." He pinched her cheeks until her jaw yielded, stuffed the fabric in, tied the other piece over it, as tightly as he could stand to tie it. Fucking awful. He surveyed the results, uneasily. He'd heard horror stories, of people dying accidentally in stupid sex games from gags. Big suffocation hazard. Her wrists were bleeding. That sickened him. He didn't want to hurt her, not even if she meant to bugger him with a sharp stick when he least expected it. Hmm, tasty thought to ponder as he drifted off to sleep. Perfect for taking his mind off his love troubles. Along with the maddening question of whether or not he had balls. But she seemed to be breathing OK.

He was done here. He could not do any better or any worse than this. He backed away, staring at the blazing hatred in her eyes.

He shut the door, listened at it for a moment. Could not stand to stay there one more second. Or even walk down the corridor like a normal person. He kept breaking into a shaky, stumbling, panicked run. His legs so shaky, they threatened to dump him onto his face.

He spied a restroom and bolted for it, hanging over the sink for ten minutes, washing his hands and his face, over and over.

It was true, what she'd said. He was a fucking pussy. Toughen up, lamebrain. He could not fall apart like this. Could. Not.

He lifted his head, stared into his own face in the mirror. Dead grayish pale, dripping with water from his obsessive washing. Eyes haunted, like he'd seen the shambling horrors of the crypt.

Which, in effect, he had.

It occurred to him, some grasping instinct for self-comfort, that the only possible experience more disgusting and soul-killing than tying and gagging a screaming, weeping, unarmed woman—if you didn't count the mind-raping—would be tying and gagging a screaming, weeping, unarmed woman after having fucked her. But he hadn't. At least that.

Still, he had to wash about twelve more times before he could bear to leave the bathroom.

. . . cow should know when to lay off the Botox . . . plastic doll . . .

. . . was looking at me, oh, God, he was really looking at me. . . .

Nina strolled through the room while speeches droned on. She brushed everyone as she passed, the lightest mind touch she could manage, but her head still pounded, after letting a stampeding herd of smug philanthropists trample through it. Or maybe it was the specter of imminent death that was making her neck muscles stiff. She must have tapped everyone in the place, but she must have missed someone. There had to be someone here who knew something. Had to be.

. . . like to drag that dress down until those titties popped right out into my hands, and then bend her over the table . . .

That lascivious thought had been aimed at her. She recognized her red dress, though she herself was unrecognizable through the man's eyes. She glanced back, caught a hot-eyed guy chugging a glass of whiskey, eyeing her boobs. So exhausting. Didn't they have anything else to think about? Being invisible had been simpler. She missed it.

She'd have thought that the minds of the super-rich would feel different from the minds on the New York subway, but it was all the same obsessions, desperations. Sex, sex, more sex. Stress about money. Larger amounts, but the anxiety was the same. They worried about cheating spouses, or they were the cheaters worrying about getting caught. They were angry about failing marriages, terrified their kids were doing drugs, scared of their medical diagnoses. Some felt smug. Some trapped. Some numb. Most felt scared.

And she was in a daze, forgetting what she was trying to accomplish. Her eyes snagged upon Thaddeus Greaves, shaking the hand of the guy who'd just fawned all over him at the podium, going on and on about Greaves's amazing awesomeness. She studied his smiling face. Helga had mentioned his name, but she had not said to go to him for help.

But for God's sake, why not? What did she have to lose, at this point? She reached out again with her mind, feeling at random.

. . . how long until they find out about the money I took . . . got to make more money we're a family now . . . can't go to jail . . .

She pinpointed the balding guy, smiling as he poured a glass of something for his pregnant wife. She touched the wife's mind.

. . . can't tell him the baby isn't his . . . would break his heart . . .

Ouch. She moved away from those two, quickly. The speeches were over. The band began to play. She pulled away, scanning for Rudd or Anabel or Roy. Dug the strip of paper out of her bosom, visualized Miles's dialog box. She visualized typing the password in.

The screen in her mind changed, and a printed message scrolled swiftly down before her astonished mind's eye.

> Third column behind bandstand.
> Hurry.
> Been waiting 4fuckingever.

Wow. Miles's system worked. She hurried, casting out for Aaro. She sensed him, but could not read his thoughts beyond a certain distance. When she caught sight of him, she jerked her chin toward Miles's column, and made a beeline through the dance floor.

Aaro caught up with her as she slid behind the column, and pulled her into a tight hug. "No luck?"

She shook her head. Miles leaned on the wall, looking exhausted.

"You OK?" she whispered. "Where have you been?"

"Hiding from Rudd. I'm persona non grata now."

"Did she breach your shield?" Aaro asked.

"Only insofar as she knew I was up to no good. She thinks I'm drug enhanced, too."

Nina studied his face, his haunted eyes. "Where is she?"

"Cuffed and gagged in an administrative office upstairs," he said wearily. "Freaking awful. She didn't seem to know about the B dose. Although I'm no telepath, so she could have been lying. I'm sorry I didn't find any answers for you. I got squat."

Nina patted his arm. "It's OK," she murmured. She faced Aaro, bracing herself for a fight. "I'm going to go chat up Greaves now."

"No, you're not." His response was automatic, and predictable.

"I have to try to read that guy, Aaro," she said.

"I told you." His voice was low and savage. "He wants to fuck you."

Big whoop. Him and about a hundred and fifty other guys out there. She bit back the unwise retort. "He's not likely to do so in the banquet hall in front of a thousand donors to the Greaves Institute Fund." She adjusted her bosom, propping and fluffing for maximum bulge. "You said today my tits could get us killed. Let's see if they can save the day."

"What about your promise? What about our addendum?"

"I'm not going to have sex with the guy!" she said tartly. "And I did not solemnly swear never to flaunt my boobs to another man with an ulterior motive as long as we both shall live! Lighten up a little!"

"Hah," he said grimly. "Looks like I need to get a little more specific with the language in the vows."

"Sure, if you like, but not until after I talk to Greaves. OK, here goes. I've never done anything like this in my life, so wish me luck."

"Luck?" His voice cracked with outrage. "What the fuck constitutes luck in a scenario like this? Attempted rape?"

"Calm down, Aaro," she soothed. She scurried out into the room before he could organize his resistance.

Serendipitously, Greaves had left the dais, and was strolling through the banquet hall on a trajectory she could easily intersect. She felt Aaro's anger and unease blazing behind her, a silent shout of protest. She forged stubbornly on. She was doing this for them both. He just had to swallow it.

She tilted her head back, stood as straight and tall as she could, imagining the gray fuzz shield falling down off her like a cloak. It felt counterintuitive, to seek attention with Rudd on the prowl out there, but she'd had no luck so far just slinking around.

Greaves eyeballed her, and changed his course, his face lighting up. "Hello! I saw you at the meet and greet, and I've been looking for you ever since," he said. "I'm sorry, but I didn't catch your name."

"Moro," Nina told him. "Leslie Moro."

"Ms. Moro." He lifted her hand and kissed it, and stared for a moment at the network of scabs that covered the back of it. "Wow," he said. "Did you have a fight with a thorn-bush?"

"I like mountain climbing," she explained. "Had a fall this weekend. I'm lucky it went the way it did. Just scrapes and bruises."

"So you're a daredevil type?"

"When I need to be," she said demurely.

"We all need to be, sometimes." He crooked his arm, and she took it, as if some outside force had nudged her closer to him.

Wow. She was, in fact, *very* close, closer than she wanted to be, but pulling away didn't seem polite right now. Aaro probably had steam shooting out of his ears. Couldn't be helped. "Amazing event," she said. "The Institute is going to be wonderful. You're very ambitious."

"Yes, that word pretty much describes me," he admitted.

"We're thirty-eight million dollars closer to our funding goal. I don't think I've seen you at other parties around here, Ms. Moro. Are you local?"

"No, I'm visiting from New York City." She'd decided to keep it as true as possible. She was so tired right now, a lie could trip her up.

"Ah. And what do you do there?"

"Fund-raising." It was true, as far as it went. She'd done a good bit of grantwriting, back in her after-college days. Been good at it, too.

"Really? Well, perhaps you should send me your CV. I always need smart, talented people to scare up more money."

"I specialize in raising funds for women's and children's emergency health care. Campaigns to raise awareness about domestic violence, that kind of thing," she said. "I suppose I could say, I specialize in desperate straits."

"The Greaves Foundation is very eclectic in its giving, Ms. Moro."

"That's admirable," she murmured.

"We're not looking for admiration. We want to make the world a better place. That also means helping those in desperate straits."

"Well, then," she murmured. "Perhaps I'll send you my CV."

"I look forward to seeing it." He lifted her hand to kiss again.

She tried to make contact. Oh, so very delicately.

Nothing. Absolutely nothing. She could not get near his mind. It was like he had an invisible force field. The man was untouchable.

He smiled. She smiled nervously back. So he did have secrets to hide. And the skill and means to keep them hidden, too.

"Could I ask you a question, Mr. Greaves?" she blurted.

"Of course. And call me Thad. Ask away. May I call you Leslie?"

"Yes, of course. I'd love that," she said. "I was overhearing some people talk about the Wycleff Library. Wycleff is one of your major donors to the Foundation, right? I just wondered if that building is here, in Spruce Ridge, or is it somewhere else?"

Greaves laughed, throwing his head back as if she'd said something witty. "Let me show you the Wycleff Library."

Her heart started to thud. "So it's here? Physically here? In the Convention Center, you mean?"

"Actually, the Wycleff Library does not exist yet." He led her over to the model of the proposed Greaves Institute that dominated the center of the banquet hall. The detail was amazing, the perfect miniature buildings, the carefully sculpted rugged natural features of the hillside campus. There was even water from a spring, leaping and rushing down the hill in a constant gurgling flow. The light from the chandelier above blazed, illuminating every detail.

"Now, I'm going to ask you to use your imagination," Greaves said. "It's a beautiful spring day, and there's a bracing wind coming down off the mountains. It's, oh . . . let's be conservative, and say, 2017. The way things go, it will be at least that long. You and I are strolling here"—he pointed at a walking path—"right outside the Payne Whitthom Building, which will hold the classrooms and seminar rooms for the humanities courses. We'll stop . . . here." He pointed. "The Shay Cafeteria. Grab something in the multicultural food court, an ice cream cone, a calzone, a shish kebab, a skewer of Thai chicken, a hot crepe filled with crème Chantilly, an espresso drink. With our snack, arm in arm, we'll make our way up . . . here." He pointed again, tracing the path as it wended through a rocky natural park. "The botanists and landscape architects will work with natural indigenous vegetation. So in the spring, we might see lupine, Indian paintbrush, columbine. Wild flora is unpredictable, but if we're blessed by luck . . ." He lifted her hand again, kissed her scraped knuckles. "We might be graced with a glimpse of alpine wildflowers."

"Let's assume that we're lucky," she murmured. "And then?"

"Then, the bridge over this torrent, which the artist has recreated with unbelievable detail. He must have hand-sculpted it while studying aerial photographs. In the spring, the brook should be full, making a beautiful chattering loud noise. We circle the Meineke Braun Science Building, and over here, at the top of the hill, the Bauer Observatory, with its state-of-the-art telescope."

"Incredible," Nina said, since admiring noises were called for.

"It will be. This place will eventually be on par with Stanford and MIT, and offer comparable excellence in arts and humanities. It will be the go-to place for physics, astronomy, computer science, engineering, biotechnology. Everything to face our brave new world."

His choice of words made her shiver. "Brave new world? Is that what you're making here?"

"I don't presume so far." He gave her a modest shrug. "But for humanity to continue, we will have to evolve, adapt. Everyone will have to try a little bit harder. Don't you think?"

"I hesitate to agree until I know exactly what we're talking about."

He let out that laugh, like she'd gotten in a clever quip.

"Cautiously said. But back to our stroll. We stop at the lookout point here, to admire the view. Clear sky, valley before us, majestic mountains in the distance. Around the curve, and behold. The Wycleff Rare Book Library, with its climate- and humidity-controlled vaults that will house the Greaves Collection of rare books and manuscripts."

"Wow." Nina's heart, which had sunk at the news that the library did not exist, began to thud. Greaves pointed at a building on the second highest of the two hills, made of what was meant to be marble.

The tower on that model was big enough to tuck syringes inside.

"The exterior will be made of slabs of translucent white marble," Greaves said. "Look how the artist used those squares of translucent rubber to get the perfect matte finish. The building is translucent. It will glow like a lamp at night, and during the day, the sun will shine through it. It will be constantly flooded with light. Beautiful, isn't it?"

"Incredible." Nina shook with excitement. The little model was too far up and in to touch, far out of any normal human's reach. To get to it, a person would have to crush and trample the rest of the display underfoot. And she was oh, so totally up for that.

"Where did you get this amazing model?" she asked.

"It was a gift from one of my colleagues, Harold Rudd. We worked at the same company together years ago, though he's abandoned the world of business now for politics. I'm not sure how sound that decision is, but I'm sure he'll go far. All the way to the top, in fact."

"How long have you had it?" she asked.

He chuckled. "About four hours. Rudd brought it this afternoon, so my staff had to scramble to get it put together in time for the gala."

Helga could have gotten access to this. Smuggled the B doses into the model, knowing it would be transported here. Maybe they could hide, and check out the model after hours. "Is this going to be its permanent location?" she asked. "It looks gorgeous here."

"No, we can't leave it here. The Convention Center is hosting a medical conference tomorrow, and they are using this banquet hall. The model is too precious to leave out. I believe it cost Harold upward of a hundred and fifty thousand dollars. Human nature being what it is, the pieces would soon start to disappear. No, we'll dismantle it as soon as the party's over, and take it to my residence. We'll display it under glass in the entry hall of the Wycleff Library eventually. The light there will be perfect. A constant glow, changing with the angle of the sun."

"Amazing," she said.

"Oh, yes. And that's even before you see the collection," Greaves said. "In the entrance hall alone, we will be displaying a stunning Book of Hours made for the king of France, in 1342. A truly marvelous collection of St. John's apocalyptic visions, and my collection of medieval tapestries, as well. I think they would look well there."

She put on a look of dazzlement. "I love looking at antique manuscripts and tapestries. I can hardly wait to see them."

"Interesting that you should say that," Greaves said. "Because you don't have to wait."

She blinked at him. "Ah . . ."

"I've had quite enough of this party. I'll take you to my residence, where I keep the most precious pieces of the Greaves Collection. I'll show them to you, and my chef can serve us a light supper. In the conservatory. Under the stars."

"You have an appetite, after that meal?"

"You don't mean to tell me you actually ate that swill?"

She had not, in fact, being far too nervous to eat, but certainly not because she had disdained the food. "In my universe, if you pay fifteen thousand dollars for a meal, you're inclined to let yourself be pleased by it," she said drily. "Just to avoid the cognitive dissonance."

He looked charmed. "Clever. What a funny universe you live in. But I don't suffer from any cognitive dissonance, and I did not enjoy tonight's meal. In fact, my staff is going to hear about that tomorrow, at some length. I can call my chef right now. Do you like duck?"

"Ah, isn't it a bit late to call your chef?" she hedged. "It's after midnight already."

"For what I pay him, my chef would prepare a meal for me hanging upside down and naked. Not that I would recommend that. So, duck, then? An apple-and-roasted-walnut-and-goat-cheese salad? I'm thinking light. Some cured meats and cheeses, or a brie-and-artichoke tart? My chef does that divinely, with a golden puff pastry that just melts in your mouth. I'll call him right now." He lifted a questioning eyebrow. "Unless you'd rather eat something else. Say the word. I need, say, forty minutes to thank all the donors on the short list."

"Short list? Who makes the short list?"

"A million and up," he said.

She blew out a tight, nervous breath. "This is incredibly gratifying. But perhaps you didn't notice, when I came in. I'm here with my husband, so I cannot come up to, ah . . . look at your etchings."

He gazed down for an unnerving moment, and lifted her left hand. "I saw the gentleman you came in with. But I did not see a ring on this hand. Not any of the many times that you allowed me to kiss it."

"If I sent mixed messages, I apologize," she said. "I don't have a ring, but I am very married."

"Don't apologize. Life is like that. Mixed. Messy. But it's a cruel joke on me. Because we have something very important in common."

She was acutely aware of how prominently displayed they were. Greaves was an eye magnet, being tall, handsome, and a billionaire. And she was hanging on his arm, lingering in the floodlights, like she had a death wish. "Yes?" she forced herself to ask. "And what's that?"

"Something very intimate," he said. "Very special."

And you are so very full of shit. She bit the words back. "And what is that?"

He lifted his hand, pointing at the rhinestone pendant gleaming at her collarbone. "Let me illustrate. That pendant. Pretty. I estimate that it cost, at most, sixteen dollars at a drugstore, perhaps three or four dollars more, if it was bought at a department store."

She lifted an eyebrow. So much for his oozing charm. The presumptuous blowhard. "And your point is, Thad?"

"No point, really. Just trying to put all the pieces together. There's a piece in my private collection that I would have showed to you this evening, had things been different. A necklace that I got at an auction in London, from the collection of the Duchess of Creighton. Passed down from a French great-great-great-grandmother, guillotined in the French Revolution. The necklace was given to her by an aristocratic married lover in the French court. An object lesson, to remind us that violence lurks all around us. And that passion knows no rules."

"Oh, really," she murmured. "Is that what it reminds us?"

A flicker in his eyes showed that he had registered her sarcasm.

"Anyway, the pendant," he went on smoothly. "It is a magnificent square-cut ruby, surrounded by diamonds and seed pearls, with a silver-gray teardrop pearl dangling from it. I can't help but picture how it would look with that dress. The pearl would nestle right . . . there." His finger touched the top of her cleavage. She moved hastily back.

"Perfect," he murmured. "The way the pearl would echo the perfect, gleaming, luminous roundness of its new home."

She felt pulled, as if by some massive magnet. She swayed toward him, trying to brace herself. "Thad," she said. "Are you trying to buy me? Because I'm not for sale."

"I know you're not. I can feel it; I can see it. You cannot

be bought. I am an extremely wealthy man, Leslie, and no one better than I can know just how rare that is, and how precious. Which is why I am tormented by the urge to drape you with priceless gemstones."

Oh, please. "I sympathize with your torment, I guess."

"Please don't be facetious," he begged. "I'm not trying to buy you. But certain things about you only I can understand, you see."

Enough of this crap. "Well, I'm afraid I'll have to pass on the—"

"Look down, Leslie," he said. "At your pendant."

She looked, and her breath stopped. The rhinestone had floated up, by itself. It hung in midair.

She didn't dare move, or breathe. She met his eyes. "You?"

"Yes, Leslie," he whispered. "If that is really your name. Me."

"Ah . . . ah . . . did you . . ." She stopped, swallowing. Oh, God.

"Did you notice your telepathic probe?" He laughed. "Certainly. But it is the most delicate, subtle mental probe I have ever felt. Or barely felt, I suppose I should say. More a caress than a probe. Lovely. Intriguing. My compliments."

"Why compliment me?" she asked bluntly. "I failed to read you."

"And you will always fail, unless I choose to open to you. I can be reasonable about that. With the right incentives."

"Ah." She licked her trembling lips, thinking at a frantic pace.

"Based on that experience of your mental probe, I really need you to work for me," he said. "Name your price. I'll meet it."

She was terrified of messing up. No idea how to call it. One would think being a telepath would give a person more of a clue, when it came to things like this, but no. The higher the stakes got, the lower her confidence fell. "I guess, um . . . we do have quite a lot to talk about."

"My conservatory, tonight? Over duck, and artichoke puff pastry? Can you make it happen?"

She swallowed. "I'll, ah, make it happen. Forty minutes?"

He nodded. "A silver Porsche will be waiting out front."

The necklace drifted down to rest on her collarbone, as delicately as a kiss, and he strode away.

31

"You told him you would meet him *where?*" Aaro gripped Nina's upper arms, so angry he barely heard her speak. Her crimson lips were moving, but his mind was melted down into a red, seething hole after watching that self-important asshole billionaire slobber all over his bride's hand, grope at her tits. Whisper in her ear. *Prick.*

Nina was patting his cheek, and the pats were getting sharper. He dragged himself into line, just enough to understand. ". . . bonehead! Hello? Earth to Aaro? Just because I told him I would meet him doesn't mean I will! I lied to him, Aaro! OK? You got that? You connecting?"

He processed that. Lied? OK. So she'd lied. Good. But he was still agitated, scared to death, his balls still zinging nastily. "That guy is the evil emperor," he said. "He is bad news, Nina. Serious bad news."

"Sure he is, but you're focusing on him and missing the point, you idiot! Didn't you hear me? The Wycleff Library, Aaro! Right here!"

His jaw sagged. "Here? You mean, like, in this building?"

"No, I mean, in the ballroom! See the architectural model?

That's the Greaves Institute. The two hills? On the tallest is the observatory, and on the other is the Wycleff Rare Book Library!" Her face shone with excitement. "Who do you think donated the model? Take a guess!"

"No way," Miles breathed out.

Aaro lunged to peer around the column. His heart had begun to skip and stutter. He'd been steeling himself so hard for failure and disaster, the dizzying surge of hope scared him. The stronger the hope, the higher up it yanked him into the air. And the farther he had to fall again, if it all went to shit. He felt so brittle, now. Like glass.

The model was illuminated by the enormous chandelier, barely visible from so far away. "So we wait 'til everyone goes?"

"They're not leaving it here," Nina said. "His staff will dismantle it right after the gala. They'll take it to Greaves's residence afterward."

Aaro struggled to reason through the feelings that were jerking him around, but he could not reason with the constant *now! now! now!* thrumming inside him. So many reasons to wait. A thousand witnesses, for instance, and Rudd out among them somewhere.

But Nina couldn't wait. Better to grab it fast, inject the drug into her before anyone figured out what was happening, and apologize for the mess afterward. A thousand witnesses gave them a shield against Rudd, if they managed to stay out in public. The guy couldn't melt their brains in the banquet hall. Maybe the police would take them away, lock them up in the relative blessed safety of the local jail.

He turned to Nina. "You can't wait," he said. "We can't ask permission. We take it. Fast and hard. Shock and awe."

She looked worried. "You don't think . . . after the party, fewer people . . . ?"

He shook his head. "Rudd's not going anywhere until he pins down Miles, now that Anabel's gone missing. If he finds her, he'll be looking even harder. Greaves is going to be sniffing around for you, so lurking until after will only fuck the element of surprise that we have if we snatch it right now, while people are dancing and drinking."

"But what if we just called the cops? Explained to them?" Nina faltered. "We're in the right, after all."

Aaro shook his head. "It's day three," he said. "In the best of circumstances, they'd seize the syringes as evidence, and sit on them. Bureaucracies move slowly. Like continental drift."

"So it's another distraction you need," Miles piped up. "A strip tease on the central table, maybe?"

"That might work," Aaro said thoughtfully. "You've got the meat for it. At least the ladies and gay guys would get a decent floor show."

Miles looked vaguely alarmed. "I was joking, man."

"Better yet. A big fight. I'm a jealous husband. I fling you up onto the model, crunch, smash. As you struggle to get away, you grasp for something to defend yourself, and snap, you grab the library."

Miles frowned. "Might work. But if you're the aggressor, the security dudes will nab you and drag you away, and Rudd will have your sorry ass in his clutches. Then you die screaming in a little room somewhere with your brain running out your ears."

Aaro shrugged. "And if you're the aggressor, you get dragged away. You'd rather have your own brains run out your ears?"

Miles looked stoic. "He has less reason to melt mine than yours. At least until he finds Anabel. And you have a better chance of coercing your way out of the crowd so you guys can go shoot up with whatever that shit is in those syringes. Before you get stopped."

Aaro shook his head. "I can't let you do that."

"What, you don't think it's credible, me attacking you?"

Miles flung at him. "You don't think I could throw you around? Don't think I could take you?" Miles put up his fists. "I think I could, man."

"You think so, buddy?" Aaro said softly. "You really think so?"

"Shut up." Nina's voice was chilly. "We don't have time for a pissing contest. Why does it have to be one of you? Why can't it be me?"

Miles and Aaro exchanged eloquent looks.

"Um, yeah," Miles said, totally deadpan. "So, uh, Aaro had a gay fling with me, so you're beating the shit out of him, all super-buff two-thirty of him, and tossing him up onto the model? Ooh, ouch. You go, girl. That is a scene I would love to see."

"Oh, shut up, Miles," she snapped.

Miles crossed his arms over his chest. "It has to be you who gets thrown, and me who throws," he said, staring directly into Aaro's eyes. "Your chances of getting away clean with the syringes are a whole lot better than mine."

Aaro opened his mouth to protest, but stopped, staring at Nina. The guy was right. But he hated it. "It's fucking dangerous for you."

"Like everything else we've done isn't?"

He gazed at the younger man with new respect. "Do you have some kind of a death wish?"

"I don't fucking know," Miles said glumly. "I definitely need my head examined. But if we're going to do this, we'd better do it fast, before I lose my nerve."

Aaro looked at Nina. "Go outside and wait for us."

Her eyes widened. "And miss this floor show? Are you crazy?"

"No, I'm practical. Go out onto the terrace, and take it to the left, down to the very end of the building. There's a terrace on that side that juts out over the bluffs and the river.

That's far enough away from the balcony that it should be pretty empty. We'll join you there."

"*He'll* join you there, rather," Miles said. "I'll be well on my way to being incarcerated, I expect."

"Greaves did say the model cost upward of a hundred and fifty thousand dollars," Nina said.

Miles winced. "Oh, fuck me."

"I'll cover it," Aaro said. "Any financial damages. If I survive."

"That's not comforting me," Miles growled. "Let's just go for it. Some things you shouldn't think too hard about, man."

"Go, then," Aaro said. "A roundhouse is your signal to throw."

"You first," Miles told him. "I'm chasing you. You're running scared, you cowardly bastard, and I'm driving you. You prick. You sick, lying, cheating son of a *bitch*." Miles advanced on him, his eyes hot.

"Whoa!" Aaro took a step back, unnerved by the fierce intensity in Miles's voice. "Easy, man. This is playacting, remember?"

"Easy, my ass." Miles's voice was unrecognizable. "The time for easy is over, scumbag. Was it easy for you, fucking my wife? Move, you shit for brains. Get your ass out there! *Move!*"

Aaro fled.

Nina watched Miles herd Aaro out into the ballroom, and darted down the corridor of space between the columns and the far wall, trying to keep them in sight. Miles was terrifying, once he got worked up. The wisecracking, sarcastic nerd was a thin façade. Beneath it, he seethed. He was convincing as a jealous husband. He'd actually scared her.

She reached the far exit to the terrace, and peered around

the columns, craning on tiptoe, trying to see if she could catch a glimpse—

A hot, damp hand clamped over her mouth. "Hi, Nina."

Terror throbbed through her as his mind stabbed deep. He'd taken her so completely by surprise, he'd breached her shield, and he was unexpectedly powerful. He held her against him, covering nose and mouth until she was smothering, and rooted roughly inside her mind.

"Just as I thought," he whispered. "The B doses. And Sasha's gone to retrieve them. Meeting on the terrace over the bluff? Good girl."

She tried to reestablish her shield, but with him already inside, she could not dislodge him. Her head pounded as his probe continued. He laughed. "Wycleff Library, in the model? Clever of you, to figure it out!"

He dragged her along. To a casual observer, of which there were several, they looked like lovers, who clung together and tottered along because they could not bear to stop kissing. His mind was so horribly *strong*. Crushing her. Suffocating her. She wobbled, faint.

Aaro. Oh, Aaro. But he had just charged off to do something perilous and public. Now she expected him to rescue her, too?

She'd rescued herself from Dmitri before. But before the thought could even form, Dmitri bit her ear, hard enough to draw blood.

She let out a smothered yelp of pain, and he licked the wound he had made with relish, his slimy tongue hot and wet and revolting.

"Ah, ah, ah! Don't even think it," he whispered. "I am on to you."

He shoved her out the big double doors. It had begun to sprinkle outside, and it was chilly at this altitude, so most people who had been strolling outside had gone in. He pushed her against the railing.

"Beautiful," he said. "No one to be shocked and raise the alarm if I do *this*." He grabbed her strapless dress, along with the bustier, and jerked them both down to her waist, baring her to the wind and the rain, and his hot, lustful eyes. "Nice dress."

He bent her over the railing, until splinters of wood dug into her bare back and her spine felt like it would crack, and thrust his hot, slimy tongue deep into her mouth. She couldn't pull air into her lungs. Her bile rose. Memories she'd striven for years to leave behind her surged up, from their secret place, and the feelings that went with them. Being small, feeling helpless, overwhelmed. Worthless.

And the fiend saw it all and felt it all. He grubbed through her most painful memories and started to laugh, which liberated her mouth enough to almost, sort of breathe.

"Stan, eh? Oh, ho, ho! So you're one of those girls! The dirty stepdad. Such a cliché. Still turns me on, though. Feel, here. See?" He prodded the bulge of his erection against her thigh. "Does Sasha know about Stan? Does it excite him, too?"

Disgust sharpened her focus, just enough to give him a hard mental *thwack*. He rocked back, startled, but lunged for her again, and his monstrous force penetrated her shield once again.

"Check this out," he said. "I learned this trick from you, Nina, and I've been practicing it all day, on everyone I met. I have something special for you. Open your eyes, Nina. Look at this."

She shook her head, squeezing her eyes shut. So he'd learned to project. She didn't dare look. There was nothing his mind could create that she wanted to see.

But something was happening to her. The shoes Lily had sent with her dress were gone. Her bare feet pressed the rain-slicked wood of the terrace. Her legs were bare. How . . . ? She was wearing an evening gown. But her arms were bare, too, now, the wind and rain chilling them. What had happened to her shrug? What on earth . . . ?

She opened her eyes, peeked. Saw the pink lace-trimmed summer nightgown she'd worn when she was twelve. Her feet were bare, toenails painted pink. Her mother had used to paint them, back in the old days. Before things got really bad. The rain plastered the pink nightgown to her body. Her shorter, twelve-year-old body. Her budding twelve-year-old breasts showed through the wet fabric. Her twelve-year-old self cowered there, small and shrinking and terrified. Oh, God, no.

"Yeah," the monster said, his voice thick with lust. "Yeah, that's how I like you. Open your eyes, baby doll. Come to papa."

She looked up, unable to stop herself. It was no longer Dmitri standing there, leering at her, trapping her against the railing.

It was Stan.

When Miles was in college he'd had lots of girlfriends, or rather, friends who were girls, who told him all manner of intimate stuff about their lives. One had been a girl studying acting. She'd gone to a New York acting studio, and told him she had been taught to use real-life experiences. So the emotions portrayed on stage were not fake, but just as real and as potentially painful as the original emotions had been.

He'd been much struck by that. That a sane person would willingly jerk themselves off, and feel angry or abandoned or hurt, or whatever, and have it be real. And out there, for everyone's viewing enjoyment. Like, why? Why would anyone do that to themselves?

That question had just been definitively answered for him. He'd hauled out Cindy and her rock star lover, Aengus, and used them like a pitchfork as he went after Aaro. Who loped in front of him, half backward, half forward, stumbling over tables, knocking over chairs before Miles's furious charge with a look of absolutely genuine shock and alarm on his face. But it wasn't Aaro, it was that prick Aengus Mc-Gowan, with his fucking pasty Irish skin and his fucking nose ring and his fucking chest hair, sticking out of his fucking affected black silk poet's shirt, and fuck him and his whole fucking stupid alternative rock band, Raven Run, along with him. He aimed a kick at Aengus/Aaro's ass, sent him sprawling into some dowager's lap, amid shrieks and gasps. He smashed into a table, ignoring cries and yelps, the smash of breaking crystal. "Had a good time with her, huh?" he yelled. "Did you do it in my house, prick?" He hauled off with a savage side kick. Aaro jerked back barely in time. Almost to the model. Circling it. He threw another punch. Aaro blocked, stumbling into the model, making the low table shudder and rock.

"Hey, man, take it easy!" Aaro pleaded. "Calm down! I didn't—"

"Did you do it in my bed? Those nights when I called at two A.M., and she was all kissy kissy on the phone, were you in bed with her? Inside her? Did that get you off, you pervert? Hearing her lie to me while she fucked you? You twisted piece of *shit!*"

Aaro threw the signal roundhouse. Miles blocked, grabbed him, twisted him, and flung, accompanying him up and forward as Aaro sailed, headfirst . . . right onto the Greaves Institute model.

Crash. The underlying structure crumpled under Aaro's weight, and the guy scrambled frantically back on the table to get away from him, smashing miniature buildings to splinters. Miles flung himself onto Aaro, bellowing incoherently, punching and screaming. Aaro tried to block, knocking Miles off, lurching onto his knees. Tottering, falling back right between the two tallest hills, knocking a gaping hole between them. His arm reached, desperately groping. Snapped off the tower of the library just as Miles yanked the observatory building off the other hill and brought the telescope dome down right above Aaro's head.

It splintered. Suddenly, hands grabbed him, trying to drag him off the table, but he couldn't calm down. He kept screaming, flailing. Wanting it to be Aengus in the rubble, blood running from his nose.

People reached in to help Aaro out as they dragged Miles away. Aaro sat up, panting, wiping blood from his face, and looked at Miles, patting his tux jacket as if checking for broken ribs.

The crowd of civic-minded guys who'd subdued him dragged him down, getting themselves kicked and slugged in the process, but they knocked him to the ground at last, and sat on him, en masse.

Success. Aaro had signaled success. He'd done the job he set out to do. So why the fuck was he crying? Six guys on top of him, no way to wipe his nose as he hitched and sobbed. Horrified people in evening wear, staring down at him as if he were a threat to their way of life.

The security guys arrived. They jerked him into a painful hammer lock and hauled him through the ballroom with grim dispatch. Down a hallway. Into what looked like a security office. Full of big guys, all looking at him with unfriendly eyes. Yep, he was in for a rough night.

The door burst open, and Miles's stomach thudded down, like two ton of cold, hard lead punching through rotten floorboards. Harold Rudd stormed into the room. "Where's the asshole who destroyed . . ." He stopped, and stared blankly at Miles, for a long moment.

"You," he said, with vicious emphasis.

"Yeah," Miles said, swallowing hard. "Me."

* * *

Aaro allowed himself to be helped out of the wreckage, holding his prize tight against his body under his arm. He accepted a napkin from somebody, to mop up the blood from his nose.

He was genuinely shaken. Who knew? He'd seen Miles practice, had even sparred with him a few times. He was strong and fast and gifted, sure. But he had not known that the guy could flip a switch and go flat-out fucking insane. And it had been absolutely believable. He was practically feeling guilty for having boned Miles's nonexistent wife.

He shook off offers of help, using a few jabs of delicate coercion to intimidate away the most insistent ones, and limped through the crowd. The library tower dug painfully into his armpit. Every step he took felt like swimming through tar. He wanted to run, sprint, fly to Nina.

Stay normal, dickhead. Invisible. Neat trick, with blood streaming down his chin. He got out on the terrace. The people who were watching him melted away, with a sudden, overwhelming desire to be elsewhere.

The terrace was deserted. It was raining, with gusts of chilly wind. Nina would be cold in nothing but that skimpy wrap. He'd been an idiot to send her out here alone. He picked up the pace, turned the corner. And stopped, very suddenly.

"Hey, Sasha," said Dmitri.

"You're sure, sir? The guy has definitely had combat training," the security guy said doubtfully. "He had two firearms on him, and he might even be hopped up on some performance-enhancing drug. God knows what he was planning. I strongly suggest that you let me—"

"I'm sure," Rudd said. "I can handle him myself. For God's sake, he's handcuffed, right?"

"But, sir, ah, I strongly recommend—"

"I need to be alone with him." The edge in Rudd's voice made the hairs in Miles's neck prickle up, like nails on a chalkboard.

The security guy blinked, and started backing away. "Uh, yeah. Yeah, sure. Let us, uh, know if you need us, sir."

"Of course." Rudd smiled thinly. "Good-bye."

The man practically stumbled over his feet to get out the door fast enough. The click of the door closing was the knell of doom. Miles tasted blood in his mouth, and licked it away. It wouldn't be the last.

Rudd walked over to him. "Where is Anabel?"

"I didn't hurt her," Miles said.

Thwack. The guy backhanded him. "That wasn't my question."

Miles licked away more blood. "I left her upstairs."

Rudd went to the door, yanked it open, bawled for the security guy. Ordered them to search the place until they found Anabel.

"We shall see what she has to say when they find her," he said. "I'm sure she will enjoy helping me interrogate you, don't you think?"

Miles's tender places recoiled. Anabel and her sharp stick were going to catch up with him a lot quicker than he'd dreamed.

"I imagine she fucked you, hmm?" Rudd said. Miles shook his head, and Rudd rolled his eyes. "Of course she did. I know my Anabel."

"You don't know me," Miles said.

"Neither do you, you arrogant little shit," Rudd hissed. "You're going to know yourself a whole lot better by the time I'm through with you. So tell me, Miles, why you came after me here. Tell me all of it."

Miles grabbed onto his encrypted computer image, and hung onto it. He had no clue if it would give him any protection against this guy, but it didn't matter. It was all he had. So whatever.

Rudd tilted his head slightly, as if he were pondering some deep philosophical question. The sensation grew slowly, like a drum roll. It almost felt like pounding rain at first, getting louder, growing pressure.

It stopped abruptly. Miles dragged in a breath.

"You're shielded," Rudd said. His soft voice had a tone of utter betrayal. "You son of a bitch. How dare you."

Holy cow. If that was how it felt when a person was shielded, he didn't even want to imagine what unshielded felt like.

"Where did you get the drug?" Rudd demanded.

Miles shook his head again.

Rudd slapped him. "Who's supplying you, goddamnit?"

"I'm not using any drug," Miles said. "Evidently, it's possible to block without using the drug."

"Who taught you?" Rudd thundered.

"I taught myself," Miles said.

"That's a lie!" The sensation swelled again, stronger. He could feel the pressure in his eyes building, like they were bulging out.

Rudd's voice faded out, and then blared. ". . . worries me. The fact that you know about the drug is troubling. That you can block against it even when not using, that's even more troubling. I do not want news to spread. Publicity would negate my edge, see?"

Miles nodded, not quite sure what he was agreeing with.

"You see, with your shield, I can't get close enough to the inside of your mind to actually control your thinking," Rudd said. "But there is one thing I still can do to you."

He snorted back some tears, some blood. "And what's that?"

"Hurt you," Rudd said.

Miles's chest jerked with mirthless laughter. "Oh, yeah? What have you been doing so far?"

"Warming up," Rudd said.

This time, it slammed down on him all at once. Vicious stress on every nerve, a pounding hell of noise, pressure . . .

When he came to, something was dripping from his mouth. Blood, drool, who knew. Couldn't focus his eyes to see. The pain in his head. Beyond all pain. It occurred to him that death might not really be so bad. Just cutting loose, drifting off to who knew where. Anywhere would be fine. As long as it wasn't here.

"Who taught you to shield? Who else knows?" Rudd shrilled.

Miles shook his head. The Mack truck of nerve-induced stress bore down on him again, making him arch and shriek.

Death, be my pal. Make this crazy motherfucker fade away, and I'll go anywhere with you. Trusting as a little lamb.

". . . important that you understand, Miles. That you co-operate. Let me in, Miles. We can help each other, see? It doesn't have to be like this. It doesn't have to hurt. Just relax. Let me in. . . ." The hypnotic pulse of the words beat against him. He almost gave in. He wanted to behave. Good dog. Sit, stay, roll over. He wanted to be forgiven. It hurt so much. But he opened his streaming eyes, and looked up at the guy. Made the word with his mouth, but could not push it out with air.

There was no air. He met the guy's eyes. *No.*

Rudd shook his head. The noise again, louder than any of the previous times. He felt things start to shatter. Bones snapping, hearts breaking. The dark wave crested, higher, higher . . .

Sweet relief, when it finally broke, and washed it all away.

32

Aaro took in the scene. Nina, dress torn down to her waist, perched on the high wooden railing, bare feet dangling. Dmitri lounged next to her, shoving a Beretta between her breasts.

Her eyes met his. He looked away. Hating to do it, but no tender messages now. He needed to be cold. Detached.

"Dmitri," he said. "You found us."

"Doesn't she look nice this way?" His cousin caressed Nina's tit with the gun barrel. "I like it, with the tits out and the shoulder covering still on. Sort of kinky. Like jeans with the ass cheeks cut out."

"What do you want, Dmitri?"

He caressed her breast again. "I sure would like some of this, but I'm afraid the usefulness of you two has come to an end."

Aaro took a step closer. Dmitri jabbed the gun against Nina's sternum. She gasped, rocked backward, teetering.

Dmitri caught her. "Careful. No closer. I know all about your coercion trick. You're just like Rudd, and your prick of a father. I might have known you'd go that way. You always were an overbearing dickhead. But you can't use it on me. I'm stronger than you."

"OK," Aaro said.

"You try any tricks, if I feel the slightest tickle, boom! Right through the heart! Over she goes."

"Yeah," he said. "Got it."

"So?" Dmitri looked expectant. "Whip it out."

"Whip what out?"

"Don't play dumb with a telepath, Sasha. Especially not when your girlfriend's sitting on the edge of a cliff. The B dose, asswipe."

"What do you care about the B dose?"

"I don't know. I guess I just care because you care. Pull it out."

Nina had tried to cross her arms over her chest, but Dmitri knocked them apart again with the barrel of the gun. "Don't hunch. Stick 'em out . . . yeah, that's it. Arch your back. Yeah. Better."

He slid his arm around, far enough to squeeze and grab and pinch. Nina's eyes were shut, her face dead pale, and stiff.

Rage grew in that pressure chamber. He struggled to stay cool.

"The B dose, Sasha." Dmitri prodded Nina's breast with the gun.

Aaro pulled the tower out from under his coat. Dried wads of glue at regular intervals were dotted around the base where it had been fastened down. Inside the tower was a roll of bubble wrap.

Aaro pried it out. The small squares of rubber popped out of their little frames, tumbling around his feet.

He unwound the bubble wrap. The wind whipped the plastic stuff from his hand, twisting it away and twirling it upward. Three syringes were inside, prepared and capped. Rubber banded together.

They looked so small and ordinary. And they were life. The future.

Dmitri shoved Nina forward off the railing. She stumbled to her knees as she hit. He pushed her before him, yanking back a handful of her hair and shoving her with the gun at the nape of her neck, which twisted her head back at a painful, contorted angle.

She lurched toward Aaro, her eyes fixed on his.

"Nina, take the syringes," Dmitri said. "If you don't want him to watch your face disappear. These things make a hell of an exit wound."

She reached out. He brushed his fingers over hers as he pressed them into her hand.

"Take off the rubber band," Dmitri said. She peeled it off.

"Now we're going to play a game. Nina, take one of those syringes, and throw it out over the railing."

"What?" Her voice cracked.

"You heard me, bitch. Throw it. Or I shoot."

Still, she hesitated. Dmitri whacked her on the shoulder with the pistol. Aaro flinched, as she stumbled forward with a grunt.

"Throw it!" Dmitri yelled. "Now! You stupid whore!"

"Throw it, Nina, for God's sake," Aaro said softly.

She screamed as she threw the thing, a shrill, agonized sound.

They all watched its long arc, how it turned, end over end, until it vanished into the darkness below.

"That wasn't so hard, was it? Now take another one. Throw it, too."

Nina turned to Dmitri, and shook her head. "No."

"Not an acceptable answer." Dmitri hit her again with the pistol, this time her ribs. She was crying. Aaro did not watch. He could not get distracted. *Floating. Cold.*

"Were you planning to take the B dose together? One for him, one for her! Aw, that's so touching. Maybe I'll just give these last two syringes to you and let bygones be bygones, what do you think?" Laughter rang out, harsh and crazed. "Oh, wait! I forgot about you dropping spiders in my hair! And strangling me with the phone cord!" He yanked down his shirt, showed them the scabbed line across his throat. "I don't think so, bitch! Throw the fucking syringe, before I count to three. One. Two—"

"No!" she shrieked. "No, I won't! We'll die anyway, and the bullet is a better death, so *no!*"

Dmitri hooted. "It's not up to you. Give me those!" He groped around her body for the syringes, the gun barrel tangled in her hair. Nina screamed and writhed. A syringe flew, and bounced on the wooden floorboards. The other, Dmitri yanked away, and flung out over the railing. His howl of triumph blended with Nina's shriek of despair.

Everything that syringe had meant for them, gone.

Aaro put it aside. Floating . . . waiting . . . until the gun barrel angled away from her head . . . almost . . . almost . . . *now.*

He pounced, mentally.

Bam, the Beretta went off. Dmitri spun, yelling. His arm jerked upward, suddenly out of his control. He shot into the air, then at the side of the building. A bullet zinged off the railing, leaving a splintered gouge. *Bam. Bam.* Aaro had to struggle to control him. He wasn't very good at it yet. Lots of swerving, fishtailing. He drew the SIG.

Bam. Bam. One bullet caught Dmitri in the shoulder, one in the thigh. He fell against the railing, clutching the wounds.

Nina was huddled on the ground, her streaming eyes set off by a dark, dripping raccoon mask of makeup, hands clamped over her. He ascertained in an instant that she had not been hit, and put it aside to concentrate on the shaky hold he had on Dmitri's mind. The close contact felt foul, like wrestling a writhing venomous insect. But the bullets had cracked Dmitri's focus. He had the guy in his grip now.

He walked toward him, crouching to pull the ratchet cuffs from the stash in his ankle holster, never slackening his hold or releasing his gaze. "Put your gun down, and slide it across the deck to me," he said, punching all the coercive power he could into the words.

Dmitri's movements were shaky, jerky, but he extended the Beretta, and tossed it. It slid a few inches out of his immediate reach.

Rain pounded down now, mixing with the blood spilling through Dmitri's fingers. "You're going to kill me now, Sasha? Now that you're a heavyweight mind wrestler like your fucking father, you can crush everyone beneath your feet, just like him. Does that make you happy?"

"I'm not going to kill you," Aaro said. "Unless you make me."

Dmitri laughed, spattering blood. "'Not unless you make me,'" he mocked, in a singsong voice. "Fucking changeling. Oleg's crown prince, and you didn't even want the crown. You never gave a shit, did you? About any of it? The money, the power?"

"No," Aaro admitted. "I didn't want any part of it."

"I did." Dmitri coughed, his breath rapid and shallow. "It should have been me. I would have done anything he wanted. But he only wanted you. Poor, dumb Oleg." The laughter clearly hurt him, but he could not seem to stop. "But I got back at you, and good. And you never knew. Asshole."

"What do you mean, got back at me?" It was a stupid question, but it burst out before he could detach from it.

"Julie," Dmitri said triumphantly, licking pinkish foam from his lips. "I got Julie, you asshole. Started having my fun with her soon as she started looking like a girl and not a broomstick. Mmm. Yum."

Aaro stared, dumbstruck. "No," he whispered.

Dmitri laughed harder, but soundlessly, tears of pain streamed down his face. "For two whole years! I knew you and Oleg would kill me if she told you, but she never told! Too embarrassed, I expect. Mostly in the summertime. First time, the poolhouse on Long Island. You were at the beach, no one but Julie, reading her book by the pool. Man, she was so fine. It was just so easy, to drag her into the poolhouse and—"

Crack, the heel of Aaro's boot connected with Dmitri's jaw, smashing it. Blood flowed down over the guy's chin, but he just wouldn't stop laughing. Aaro hauled off to kick him again—

"Watch out, Aaro," Nina called, her voice sharp. "Watch out!"

"Yes, Sasha. Watch out." It was another soft female voice, one he knew, behind his back. He jerked his head around.

Julie stood on the deck. Her skin as gray and deathly pale as when they had found her. Wearing the drenched night-gown she had worn when she swam out to sea. Her long hair snarled with seaweed.

She gave him a sad little smile. "Yes, Sasha," she said. "It's me."

One stunned, blank moment was all Dmitri needed to lunge for his gun. Nina shrieked a desperate warning.

Bam, Dmitri's gun went off.

Aaro had been shot before, but it was always pretty damn special. That nasty thump, followed by the heat, dropping blood pressure, and the frantic feeling of *oh, fuck* . . .

The deck swung up, slammed into him. Rain hit his face at a new, more intimate angle. Nina was screaming. A bullet whinged off the wood about two inches from his face, re-leasing a shrapnel of splinters. He jerked around, yanked the Ruger from the ankle holster.

Bam.

Dmitri sagged back again, silent.

Nina knelt next to him, frantically talking, but he just jerked her down behind him. "Get down!"

"But you're shot! Aaro, let me at least—"

"Get *down!*" He rolled over onto his belly. Blood pooled beneath him, leaving a dark trail as he slithered into position, sighted . . .

Dmitri was not moving. The pistol lay inches away from his slack hand. Aaro stared, waiting. Wary of a trick.

"I'll get it!" Nina sang out, and before he could muster the breath to tell her to get the fuck back down, she was bounding like a gazelle over the deck, snatching up the pistol. The gun dangled from her fingers as if she were holding a dead mouse by the tail. She stopped to scoop up the syringe, lay the Beretta down on the floorboards next to him.

"You got the syringe," he said. "Take the drug. Now. Before anyone can stop you. *Now!*" He put all his coercive force behind the word. And she didn't even blink. True to form. The chick was cast iron.

"There's only one of them," she said stubbornly.

She tried to rip her skirt for a bandage, but the fabric was stretchy, yielding too easily to rip, so she peeled off her shrug. Leaving her topless torso gleaming with rain. Heart-stoppingly beautiful. She knocked him out. Not that he had far to go, but—

"Fuck," he gasped out, as she pressed the fabric against his wound. "Goddamnit, Nina!"

"Apply direct pressure," she said, her voice quivering. "That's all I know. So that's damn well what I'll do."

"The syringe, first! Take it! Now, goddamnit!"

"But there's only one," she insisted.

He grasped her arm, and his blood made pinkish trails sluice down her arm. "So there's only one. Tough shit! It's day three for you! End of the line! We'll figure out something else for me."

She shook her head. "There is nothing else, and you goddamn well know it, Aaro! So don't play hero with me!"

"Nina," he said. "Please."

She shook her head. "No. I might have a tiny margin beyond the three days, like Helga did. We'll get the stuff ana-
lyzed, duplicated, maybe. Or we'll split the dose evenly
between us, and face whatever happens together. Or we'll—"

"Take it, Nina. Take it now."

"I won't!" Her voice wobbled. "You can't bully me into it.
You're shot. Don't bother fighting me. I have to go get help
for you now, so you just press this thing down, as hard as you
can stand, and I'll—"

"Oh, for God's sake," said a sharp, disapproving voice.

Harold Rudd strode swiftly out of the shadows, and kicked
Dmitri's Beretta. It skittered across the floorboards, and flew
off the deck. "Just look at this godawful mess," he said fretfully.

Nina dropped the hypodermic beside Aaro's leg, and put
both her hands over the wad of bloody fabric, praying that
Rudd had not seen it. She dragged her shield up as the man
walked toward them, shaking his head in distaste at Dmitri's
still form, at Aaro staring up at him from the bloody floorboards, with his habitual coiled stillness. The kind of stillness that could spring into action in the fraction of a second.

Rudd concluded that Nina was the only one fit enough to
scold, so he focused on her. "Do you have any idea how bad
this looks?"

Nina could not believe her ears. "Excuse me? *Looks?*"

"I imagine it was you two who sent that irritating fellow
Miles to bother me, right? Am I right?"

New fear gripped her. "What did you do to him?"

Rudd's lip curled in ugly triumph. "Let's just say, he won't
be bothering anyone else," he said. "Not for a long, long time."

Oh, no, no, no. Nina met Aaro's gaze, horrified.

"All I ever wanted was a little discretion, a little re-
straint," the man raged. "And look what I get. Your Miles,

carrying on in the banquet hall, destroying my model. We'll probably have multiple lawsuits coming in from all the people that were kicked and punched. And now, a shootout on the terrace of the Convention Center! Greaves will kill me! You three just had to come to the highest profile event of the year, packed with the most influential people in America, to make trouble? And then proceed to make a bloody mess that I personally will have to explain away! Just . . . look at you!" He gestured at them.

Nina rose up, spine straightening. "What? What about us, Rudd?"

He gestured toward her bare torso. "People will be swarming out here any second. Do you suppose you could, ah, pull that dress up?"

"What? You're bothered by my tits?"

Rudd sniffed. "No need to be vulgar. It's just that with the blood and all, the bare breasts . . . things look lurid enough without you adding the element of orgiastic ritual sex to the mix. It's just . . . ugh."

She put her shoulders back. Stuck them out. "Fuck you, Rudd."

Suddenly, Aaro grabbed her arm, jerked her close to him, and plunged the hypodermic into her arm.

Nina jerked, screamed. The needle burned, and her body jerked and arched, but Aaro held her close, muscles trembling with strain until the thing was empty. He flung the syringe away and collapsed, a faint look of triumph in his eyes. "There," he said. "Done."

She stared at him, utterly betrayed. "You bastard!" she shrieked, and raised both hands to whale on him, but she couldn't hit him, damn it, he was shot, he was bleeding. She smacked her hands down onto the wet floorboards, again, and again. "Goddamn you, Aaro!"

"I love you, too," he whispered.

The strain of holding her struggling body had made his

bleeding worse. She jerked into action, pressing down on the cloth. He winced, but barely had the strength to react.

"It won't make any difference now." Rudd's voice was petulant. "She'll die anyway, you idiot. I'll see to that. And now you've wasted what I assume was the last of Helga's B doses on her. There were people who wanted to study the contents of that syringe! Powerful people! I have to answer to them! It's very awkward for me!"

"Your powerful people can blow me, Rudd," she snapped back at him. "He needs a doctor!"

Rudd shook his head. "No. I've had quite enough of you people. It's time to cut my losses." His eyes darted around the deck. "Let's see. Looks like a murder suicide. Lover's triangle. That works with the bare breasts. Caught by one lover while passionately involved with the other. The spurned one threw you over the edge, and then they shot each other to death. Is that squalid enough to suit you, my femme fatale extraordinaire?"

She pressed the cloth against Aaro's wound. He seemed to have fainted. "He's not going to die," she said, as if repeating it could make it more true. "He's not."

"He'll be dead by the time the medics get here." Rudd smiled thinly. "Count on it. On your feet, Nina. Walk."

The sensation began. Just like it had been in the cabin, but harder. The roaring pressure of his psi power, battering her shield.

It swelled, until it became an unbearable, head-splitting pain. He grabbed her arm, jerked her to her feet, and began frog-marching her toward the railing. She resisted, but the mental pressure increased. Every separate cell in her brain was going to explode. There was an enormous hive of gigantic wasps inside her skull.

When the noise and the pressure suddenly stopped, she was draped over the railing, splintery wood digging into her chest.

"Climb," he said.

She put her foot on the first two-by-four riveted to the logs, and climbed onto it. The wind gusted, making her skirts flap and whip around her knees. The darkness beyond the railing was a sea of endless nothingness. Wind whistled and howled. The voices of the damned.

"Another. Keep climbing," Rudd said.

"Stop," someone else said, from behind.

It was a deep and rasping voice that she did not recognize, but the roaring pressure, the head-splitting agony suddenly ceased. She stared out into the void. Afraid to move, to even think. The wind lifted her hair. Rain gusted in her face. She swayed, precariously, as Rudd let go of her. She heard him suck in a sharp breath. Almost a squeak.

She turned to look. Rudd clutched his throat. His eyes were wide, panicked. Gasping for breath, but he could not seem to get any.

"I'm not allowing his lungs to expand, you see," a voice said. That croaking rasp she'd heard before. She turned, swaying dangerously in the wind. Her knees were locked. She couldn't feel her legs.

"Careful, my dear. Here, let me help you." A large hand seized hers. She placed one wobbly bare foot on the lower slat, then the other, and then she was standing on the boards again, staring at a burly, stooped old man in a tuxedo, with a cane. He had a broad face, sunken eyes, pitted skin, but fierce intelligence burned in his slanted green—

Green eyes. Those eyes. Those cheekbones. Of course.

"Hello, Oleg," she said.

"Nina, isn't it?" He kept hold of her hand, pulling her to where Aaro lay. "My Sasha's brave and lovely bride."

Nina dropped to her knees at Aaro's side, fumbling for the cloth to press against his wound again.

Rudd finally sucked in some air. "Who are you?"

The old man's head whipped around. He fixed Rudd with a cold stare. "You," he said. "You did this"—he pointed at Aaro—"to my Sasha? You beat and terrorized and abused his bride? You have hunted and harassed him, and for what? For a stupid, fucking drug? You will soon see who I am, turd. And it will be the last thing you ever see."

Rudd's face tightened into a grimace of concentration.

Oleg began to laugh. "Oh, no, no, no. You are one of those junkie scum who think that power can be swallowed in a pill, ey? Power is a gift of God. You don't even know what power feels like." Oleg turned to her. "I am about to call the crowds, my dear, so you might consider—"

"Crowds?"

"Of course. We want witnesses for what is about to happen. But as I was saying, people will soon be flooding out here, so you might want to pull your dress up, my dear, before—"

"What is it about my dress?" she shrieked. "Like I give a flying fuck about my dress! Aaro needs a goddamn trauma surgeon, right now! This instant! So if you're going to call a crowd, *do* it!"

"As you wish," Oleg said mildly. "Be as bare-breasted as the angel of liberty, if you prefer. I'm sure no one will complain."

He straightened up, squaring off his body so he was staring at Rudd, still transfixed by the railing.

Soon, Rudd began to move. Stiffly at first, but then smoothly, as if it were of his own volition, he began to climb the railing. Meanwhile, voices and the noise of running feet began to sound behind them. Shouting.

Nina turned to the people arriving. "Call an ambulance!" she yelled. "A man's been shot! Go ask if there's a trauma surgeon in the room! Or any doctor! Fast! Please! Now!"

Rudd held the top of the railing, placing one foot carefully on the top rail, and then the other. He balanced there, squatting. Perfectly poised, facing out. The shouts and pleas began.

"That man's going to jump!"

"Oh, my God! No! Please, no! Don't!"

"Stop him! Somebody grab him! Quick, he's about to—"

"Rudd? Oh shit, that's Harold Rudd! Harold, no! Don't jump!"

But Harold did. His bent knees straightened into a powerful spring, arms spread wide. He let out a loud, despairing wail as he leaped, legs flailing as if he were trying to run upon the air.

In the sudden and terrible silence, everyone heard the awful sound when he hit the ground.

Things got loud and chaotic for a while. Screaming, shouting. Noise, movement. Oleg yanked up one of the flounces of Nina's skirt and tore it off. He pushed aside the soggy, blood-soaked rag in her hand, and pressed the new, somewhat dryer wad of cloth against Aaro's wound. He placed her hand upon it, and then covered it with his own.

"Do you, ah, want another piece of the skirt for him?" she asked, jerking her chin in Dmitri's direction.

"No," Oleg said.

"No? Isn't he your nephew? Doesn't he work for you?"

"He did. Let him bleed. If he lives, I will deal with him later."

She grabbed Aaro's cold hand, feeling for his pulse. At first she could not find it, but there it was. Faint, but there. Hanging on.

She was crying, she realized. And she didn't care. She was so far beyond embarrassment now. Like the bare tits. Who gave a shit. About anything. Rain poured down, harder than ever. The sky wept. All of existence wept with her.

Presently, people showed up who seemed to know what they were doing. They gently pushed her away from Aaro and got to work on him.

Someone wrapped a jacket around her shoulders and tried to make her get up. She refused to move, just sat there on the boards, watching them minister to him. Her eyes focused on Aaro's gun, sticky with blood. It lay forgotten, half hidden beneath the bloody rags of her dress. Voices began to register. The first one she understood filled her with panic. Oleg, as they strapped Aaro onto the gurney.

". . . want him airlifted to Denver. I will not have my Sasha taken to your local hospital. He must have the very best."

"But, sir, it's an extra forty minutes, and he's lost so much blood."

"I've arranged for two liters of O negative to be waiting in the helicopter. It will be landing in the pad on top of the Convention Center, in ten minutes," Oleg said firmly. "You will accompany us."

"No!" Nina sprang to her feet. "No, you can't!"

Oleg's eyebrow twitch was so eerily similar to Aaro's, it was unnerving. "I most certainly can," he said. "My Sasha will not go to a substandard country hospital to be tended by dogs and pigs."

"My Sasha! My Sasha!" Her voice was quivering. "You always say that! That's your problem, Oleg! That's always been your problem!"

Both brows shot up, affronted. "Oh?"

"You think he's yours! That he belongs to you! But he doesn't! He belongs to himself! That's what makes him special, but you don't get it! You just keep trying to make him part of you! Give it up! Let him go!"

"Calm down, my dear," he said. "You're delirious."

"I won't let you take him!" She lunged toward the gurney. People grabbed her and held her back. "He's been trying his whole goddamned life to get away from you! I will not let you take him back!"

"You will have nothing to say about it," Oleg said, his voice steely. "I will do what is best for my son."

Nina lunged for Aaro's gun, grabbing it from beneath the folds of the bloody cloth on the ground. She swung it up, aiming at Oleg's chest. "No!" She stared around wildly. "Don't let him control you!" she yelled at them. "It's what he does! Don't let him decide!"

Panicked voices swelled around them, but Oleg did not flinch. He stared at her for a moment.

So different from Rudd's coercion. Oleg's felt like a quiet, smothering blanket of absolute authority. He stepped forward, his big, bloodstained hands seized hers, forcing the gun barrel down. He pried her hands loose, and took the gun, slipping it into his pocket. "No, my dear," he said gently. "He is mine, and I will take him."

She stood there, frozen with despair. Her head swam, her vision blurred.

". . . certainly I don't intend to press charges." Oleg's voice blared back into focus. "Anyone can see that the poor girl is out of her head. God knows what she's just been through. Just look at her. Poor thing."

Sure. They could look all they wanted. It didn't matter anymore. Nothing mattered. The jacket placed on her shoulders slipped to the ground as she watched them wheel Aaro away, with Oleg stumping along close behind. Aaro's face was so still. Beaded with rain.

Panic rose up inside her. This was it, her last glimpse of him. She wanted to run after him, to beg them to let her stay with him, but her muscles wouldn't move. She would not even have that bitter solace, of being with him at the end. If he died from his wound. If he died from the drug. Either way, she would not be there to hold his hand.

This was all she got.

She flung her head back and let the rain mix with the tears until someone came up to her, pulling her inside, out of the rain. Setting her down, who knew where. She didn't care. It didn't matter.

A sting in her arm, and it all faded blessedly away.

33

Aaro stared at the sunlight that streamed through sheer curtains. He looked around at the room, when it finally came into focus.

Too comfortable and luxurious to be a normal hospital room, but too bland and antiseptic to be an actual house. Telltale signs of a medical facility, like the grab bars and handicapped toilet that he could see through the bathroom door. He tried to get up onto his elbow, and thudded back down, with a whistling gasp of agony.

Ah, *fuck*. So that was how it was. Bummer.

He was pinned to an IV rack. There was a snarl of confused, bloody memories in his mind. Desperation. Hopelessness. The B doses, found, and then lost again. The loss meant death. But he was alive. Wasn't he? He looked down at himself. With this much pain, he had to be alive. Only life hurt this much.

Nina. Why wasn't Nina here? He could think of a bunch of reasons why Nina might not be there. None of them were good.

He tried getting up again, and sweet holy shit, it *hurt*. But he couldn't just lie here like a lump. He ripped the IV off, left the needle dripping, and choreographed movement to utilize gravity as much as possible, to spare his torn abdominal muscles. Finally, he was on his feet, blood seeping through the bandages. He was in a hospital gown, the kind that tied in back and let a guy's ass hang out. Great.

He took a step. The world did a big three-sixty, and went dark.

He came to on the floor, a frowning face hanging over him. He knew the face, but wished he didn't. Angry, harsh, pinched. Not flattered by being seen from below. Who . . . ?

Oh, Jesus. Rita, the hell-bitch. His stepmother, only nine years older than he, putting her in her late forties now. But she looked older. Once so beautiful, but now, she looked like she was pulled tight over angular bones that were too large for the shrunken bag of her skin.

She gazed down at him with distaste.

"I guess I'm not in heaven," he said to her. "Not if you're here. So this is just regular life, right? Or is it hell?"

Her frown line struggled to engage in her Botox-numbed brow. "Charming as you ever were, I see. Oleg!" she called. "Your offspring is showing his usual intelligence, lying on the floor, bleeding like a slaughtered goat. Come deal with him. Because I absolutely cannot."

She stalked out, and left him on the floor, bemused. Oleg?

The black rubber tip of the aluminum cane planted itself on the floor a couple of inches from his nose, with polished black shoes behind it. Perfectly pressed cuffs. He let his eyes slide on up to his father's face.

They stared at each other, in blatant fascination.

Son of a bitch. He wouldn't have been surprised at the barrel of a gun, or a knife's edge, or even poison from Oleg. But high-end medical care in a swank private clinic—that surprised him.

Oleg sat in a chair next to the bed, folding his hands over his cane. A pair of male nurses came in, hoisting Aaro up, getting him back into the bed, reinserting the IV.

"I thought you wanted me dead," Aaro finally said.

"Never that, my son. I wanted you with me, fulfilling your potential and the promise of your heritage."

Aaro suppressed the adolescent eye roll with some difficulty. "Where is Nina?" he asked. "Is she all right?"

"Nina is fine," Oleg said dismissively. "I do not wish to talk of Nina."

Like he gave a fuck what Oleg wanted to talk about. "How did she get away from Rudd? I know it wasn't thanks to me."

"Me," Oleg said modestly. "Rudd leaped off the terrace railing, onto the rocks below. Had delusions of grandeur. Thought he could fly."

"Oh," Aaro said. After a long, confused pause, he added, "Thank you. For saving her life."

"And yours," Oleg said pointedly.

Aaro nodded. "And mine. Of course."

"So stiff," Oleg said mournfully. "So formal."

"It has been a while," Aaro pointed out.

"Yes, it has," Oleg said. "Twenty-one years, four months, twenty-two days, and give or take eight hours."

"Ah, yeah. Long time. So, ah. Where is Nina, then?"

Irritation flashed across Oleg's face. "Causing trouble, no doubt. A more stubborn, irritating, persistent female I have yet to come across."

"You got that right. But you didn't answer my question."

"She's been hounding me." Oleg sounded aggrieved. "Phone calls, police, lawyers, what have you. She wanted to see you. But I was not obliged to tell her where we were keeping you. Not that anyone could have compelled me, of course, but still. The principle of the thing."

"Keeping me? I don't want to be kept." He struggled up against stabbing pain. "Why didn't you let her come to me?"

Oleg's face hardened. "She defied me. Openly, in public. She brandished a gun at me, Sasha. She dared to scold me. And you expect me to invite the bitch into our life?"

"Yeah, well. The scolding. You get used to that," Aaro said. "She should be here with me. She's my wife. Never call her a bitch again."

Oleg's eyebrow twitched, but he let it pass. "She said she was your wife, too. She had no documentation to that effect, however."

Aaro thudded back onto his pillow, sweating with the effort. "That's going to change real soon," he said. "I need to see her."

"What's the rush?" his father asked. "She seems like an exhausting personality. Very intense. Wouldn't you rather get stronger first? Relax a little, before you face her again?"

"No," Aaro said. "I want her now."

Oleg's eyes were hooded and inscrutable. "So it's like that."

"Oh, yeah," Aaro said. "It is *so* like that."

Honesty had never been a wise course of action around Oleg, who could twist anything to fit his own agenda, but Aaro didn't have it in him to be crafty, not when he was this desperate. "What day is it?"

"Thursday," Oleg said.

Aaro tried to crunch the numbers. The sun had the color of late afternoon. "What . . . you mean . . . but the fund-raising party was Saturday." He counted, and counted again. It didn't add up.

"That's right. You were unconscious, in and out. For five days."

What the hell? He should be dead, or dying, at least. It was day six. He felt like six kinds of shit, for sure, but he didn't feel like he was on his way out. He felt like clawing his way back to Nina. Through giant spiders or poisonous green slime or solid rock. He wanted to *move*.

"Nina's OK?" he insisted. "Everything is fine? With her health?"

"She certainly seems feisty enough," Oleg said. "Though she hasn't come around today or yesterday. Perhaps she's gotten bored and moved on. God save me from a troublesome woman."

"She thinks I'm dead," Aaro blurted. "That's why she stopped coming."

Oleg's eyes narrowed. "How's that?"

He explained swiftly, about Kasyanov's A and B doses of psi-max. Oleg scowled thoughtfully throughout the strange account.

"You've shown no such symptoms, my son," he said. "And you do not have the vibration of a person who has been altered by artificial chemicals. Dmitri had it, assuredly. That turd Rudd did, too. Not you."

"What happened to Dmitri?" he asked.

"Dead," Oleg said, waving his hand as if fanning away a bad odor. "Thank God. At first, he seemed to improve. Then the day before yesterday, he began raving. His speech became disordered. It became impossible to care for him. No one could stay in the same room with him."

"Why not?"

Oleg shrugged. "Strange things happened. Visions. People saw ghosts, snakes, monsters. He died of cerebral hemorrhaging, early yesterday morning. Everyone was relieved to have him gone."

"He wanted to be your heir," Aaro said.

Oleg's face hardened. "He was not good enough."

"No one ever was," Aaro said.

Oleg was silent for a heavy moment. "You would have been," he said. "If you had only behaved. If you had made the smallest effort."

"I couldn't," Aaro said. "That Sasha in your imagination who behaved, the one who agreed with you and was glad to take your orders, he was never me." He pressed against the pain in his belly. "If only I hadn't been me, I would have been just perfect."

"I have seen how you make your money," Oleg said. "You do well enough. An independent contractor, clearing a half a million a year. Not bad. Not a shameful level of prosperity. By some standards."

Aaro braced himself. He knew where this was going.

"With me, you could add two zeros to that figure," Oleg said softly. "At least, Sasha. More likely double that, or more. Per year."

Aaro sighed. "Why should I?"

Oleg pondered him, expressionless. "My son," he said. "If you have to ask, then the answer would be meaningless to you."

"Yes," Aaro said. "Yes, exactly. It was meaningless then. It still is."

"My son," Oleg said, in Ukrainian. "You are home at last. Let us put the past behind us. Take your place with me."

Aaro chose his words carefully. "No, Father," he said, in the same language. "I thank you, but I cannot. I have another destiny."

Finally, it began. The feeling he had been bracing himself for, from the instant he laid eyes upon his father's face. The familiar clutch of psi energy, fastening around his mind, slowly squeezing. To force agreement, compliance.

But the things he'd learned in the past few days, the ways in which he had changed and grown, made his response entirely different now. The vault doors in his mind were firmly closed, their contents guarded and secure. He was not frantic, angry, or desperate.

He was calm. Fixed and serene. As unmovable as a mountain.

His own power rose to counter his father's. It was just as strong, and very similar, like a mirror image. They engaged mentally like arm wrestlers. The light shifted outside, the dust motes danced, as the two men sat in absolute silence and stillness, locked in concentration.

It occurred to him, as the time passed, that this connection was the most intimate and honest that he had ever felt with his father.

And it was combat. Ironic, sad. But true.

When the clash finally eased off, Oleg's face was a grayish yellow, his forehead beaded with sweat. Aaro was exhasted, too, head thudding.

Oleg wiped his forehead with a handkerchief he took from his pocket. "I imagine you are pleased with yourself."

"No," Aaro said. "Just tired. And I miss my wife."

"Ah, yes. About your wife." Oleg smiled unpleasantly. "There is more than one way to persuade a wayward son to make the right decision. You want what is best for your wife, no? And your children?"

"I have no children," Aaro said.

"You will," Oleg said. "Tonya saw them. In a dream."

"Tonya. Is she still . . ." He saw the answer to his question in his father's eyes, and his voice stopped short.

"She died the day after you saw her," Oleg said. "But you are changing the subject. We were discussing the safety and health of your wife, and your eventual children."

Aaro looked him in the eye. "You might as well kill me now, while I'm lying in this bed," he said. "Now is your chance. My reflexes are slow. My guard is down. Finish me, if that's what you want."

His father's eyes burned with impotent rage. "I will do what I must. I always have."

"And lose all hope of grandchildren? Touch my wife, and your line ends here," Aaro said quietly. "And so does your life."

"Ah," Oleg grunted. "Finally, you are talking like a man."

"I'm glad something meets with your approval."

Oleg got heavily to his feet. "I grow weary of this conversation," he said. "You are as tiresome as you ever were, Sasha. What do you want, if not my fortune, my empire, and all the kingdoms of the world?"

"I want your people to bring me some clothes, and some shoes," Aaro said. "I want a car to take me to my wife. I want the two of us, and any children we may have, left in peace."

Oleg snorted, derisive. "You are ambitious, Sasha."

"I get that from you."

"Yes, I suppose you do." Oleg's voice was fretful. He paused in the doorway, and turned. "These are my terms," he said. "I want—"

"No terms," Aaro said. "I owe you nothing."

"Shut up, boy. I saved your life, and your woman's life five days ago. Your children, when you have them. I want to see them."

Aaro chewed on that, but could not swallow it. True, he would not be alive but for his father's actions, and neither would Nina. But with all the long, strange history between him and his father, the true size of the debt was hard to calculate. "We will see," he hedged.

"What does that mean?" Oleg snapped.

"I would not be the only parent. And my wife is very protective, and impossible to coerce. We will see. I can't promise more than that."

Oleg made an impatient sound. He rapped the door with his cane. It opened instantly. One of his men peered through. "Yes, Vor?"

"My son is leaving us," Oleg said peevishly. "He cannot soil his lily-white hands to work for his father, being too noble and pure of heart. Bring him some fucking clothes. And call him a car."

He got up, and stumped out, slamming the door behind him.

Things moved fast, after Oleg stormed out. One of his father's men, a guy with a jaw like an anvil, soon came in with an armful of clothes; a black sweatshirt, jeans, athletic shoes. They hadn't bothered with socks or underwear, but he wasn't fussy. The trick was getting the clothes onto his body. Bending over to put a pant leg onto his ankle hurt so much, he lost consciousness, the first time he tried.

He finally worked out a system, laying the pants out on the bed and slowly wiggling into them while lying flat on his back. He was soaked with sweat, his heart bumping dizzily by the time he got them over his ass. They were loose. He'd gotten thinner. Just as well. A tight waistband over a bullet hole would really rot.

He worked his bare feet into the shoes, pulled the sloppy sweatshirt over his torso, and that was it. Preparations complete. Considerable blood had soaked through his bandage, but that was his problem and his alone now. By turning his back on Oleg, he'd abdicated all help and comfort. He was used to being without help or comfort, but it was more daunting than usual, with a bleeding hole in one's guts.

He pushed open the door. Anvil Jaw waited outside. The man started down the hall, jerking his chin for Aaro to follow.

He couldn't keep up, but he tried, holding himself up against the wall, pressing his hand against the bandage as if his guts were about to fall out of the hole. Doctors and nurses watched him shuffle by, sweat dropping off the end of his nose. They looked troubled, but no one stopped him or spoke to him. No medical professional in his or her right mind would release a guy in his current shape from a medical facility. But when Oleg Arbatov spoke, no one contradicted him. Except his son.

And it was yet to be seen if Aaro would survive to tell the tale.

Outside, the air was warm, humid. A car waited in the roundabout. Anvil Jaw opened the back door for him.

Another challenge. Getting into the backseat. He angled himself in, trying not to bend, or make any whimpering, undignified noises.

The guy slammed the door after him, got into the driver's seat, and waited for his cue, like some sort of formal ritual.

"Take me to my wife," Aaro said. The car surged forward.

He couldn't tell how long the trip was. He drifted in and out of consciousness for a lot of it. He had no idea where he was coming from, or where the guy was taking him. The pain was very bad, fogging his mind. He couldn't concentrate on the road signs, or identify exits, or recognize landmarks or towns. He had no clue if the man was really driving him to Nina or not. He could be taking Aaro to a landfill, to put a bullet in his brain stem, bury him under a ton of garbage.

One thing was certain. He was in no condition to defend himself. He'd spent all his mental energy in that psychic bout with Oleg. If Anvil Jaw had been ordered to execute him, he would die. So why concern himself? It was more relaxing to just lie back and think of Nina.

They left the freeways behind, and got on a flat, straight road now, with the kind of scrubby vegetation that only grew on sandy soil, near beaches. The car slowed, and then stopped.

Aaro looked out, at a gray, shingled beach house, perched on short stilts. Dunes lay beyond it. Marsh grasses waved on one side. Potato fields were green and bushy on the other side of the road, behind him. A mailbox was attached to a crooked pole next to the wooden walkway that led over the tufts of sandgrass to the front door.

Anvil Jaw opened the back door, and waited, for the painful minutes that it took Aaro to extricate himself. He lunged for the mailbox post for support. Anvil Jaw didn't look at him as he got into the car and drove away. The message was clear. He no longer existed.

And yet, he lived. He stared at the house. He wanted to laugh, but just the thought made his guts hurt. So ironic. He, Aaro, so uptight, it practically gave him an ulcer to check his guns at the airport security checks, stood here, no weapon, no wallet, no money, no ID, no cell phone. No clue where he was. No underwear. Balls flying free. If this house was deserted, he would never make it to another one for help. He would die here, looking up at the sky. All he could do was hope that there was a friend in that house who would catch him when he fell.

He launched himself from the mailbox post, and went for it.

34

Edie Parrish stared out the window at the beach. The far-away figure was barely visible in the distance. "She's been out there for seven hours," she fretted. "She didn't eat anything today, or yesterday, either. Lily will kill me if I don't take good care of her. I should go out and—"

"No," Kev McCloud said. "Leave her." He stroked his wife's slender back. "She just has to get through it. Figure out how to keep existing."

Edie's face tightened. "He could have let her see him. What would it cost him, to let her be at his bedside at the end? A little compassion."

Kev pulled her into his arms. "Arbatov doesn't know about compassion. I always wondered why Aaro was so tense."

They swayed, in the kitchen of the house Bruno had found through a vacation rental agency. The two of them had volunteered to stay with Nina during her fight to be with Aaro, since Lily and Bruno were bound to the incubator in the neonatal intensive care unit, in which their small but fierce son Marco lived while his lungs matured.

Kev's head jerked up. His eyes had that bright, hyper-alert glint. "Did you hear that?"

She shook her head.

"Stay here." Kev drew the pistol from the back of his jeans. But Edie, not being all that great at doing what she was told, followed him, so she was there when the front door opened, and a guy she barely recognized fell through it, right into Kev's arms.

She rushed to help. Together they lowered him to the floor.

Aaro. Dear God, he looked different. Rendered down to stark essentials. Cheekbones carved in so deep, the angle of his jaw so sharp. His hair had been shorn to thick stubble.

His fingers were sticky with fresh blood, she was horrified to realize. "Aaro? Are you shot? Jesus, you're bleeding!"

"It's an old wound," he said, his voice faint. "I'm leaking through the bandage, that's all. Don't worry about it."

She laughed at him. "Lunatic! Don't worry about it? Hah!"

"Nina," Aaro croaked. "Where is Nina?"

"She's here," Kev said. "Outside, on the beach. We'll get her."

Aaro shook his head. "I'll go out and meet her."

"You're not going anywhere!" Kev snapped. "You belong in a hospital! Don't even think about moving!"

But Aaro was struggling up. "I am going out to meet her. Or crawl out on my own, and bleed all over your fucking floor while I'm at it."

Edie had seen that look often enough on her own man's face to know there was no point in arguing with him. They met each other's eyes over Aaro's head. He was being irrational, but they didn't want him to have a big freak-out. If it was some big, important, symbolic thing for him, so be it. The medics could retrieve him from the beach.

They hoisted him up, and hauled him outside, through the

door, across the deck, down the walkway over the dune. There, on the sand and grass, he finally consented to sink to the ground. Deathly pale.

"I'm calling an ambulance now," Kev said, and hurried inside.

Aaro searched desperately with his eyes. "Nina?"

Tears were fogging up Edie's eyes. She patted his stubbled cheek. "I'll go get her for you," she said. "Don't move. Really. Not one muscle."

She ran out onto the sand toward Nina's distant figure, waving her arms frantically over her head.

It hurt to breathe, but air kept on knifing in and rasping back out of her chest. Her ribs had been cracked in that final showdown.

Nina stared at the waves. It was twilight, and the evening star hung in the sky, solitary, achingly brilliant under an ethereal sliver of moon. Beautiful, but she couldn't feel it. The part of her that loved beauty was buried in the rubble. She couldn't eat, with her stomach crushed under all that broken masonry. Couldn't sleep. Could barely speak. But her lungs just stubbornly kept on expanding.

The first few days of her desperate campaign to compel Oleg Arbatov to let her see his son had been all frantic effort, which had availed her nothing. Not surprising. She'd been incredibly rude to the man, and Arbatov was so corrupted by his secret power, there was no way to successfully oppose him. She'd known that, but just having something impossible to do had helped. The flailing, the carrying on, the noise she'd made. She'd been terrified to stop. As if squawking at Oleg while Aaro was still alive was her last, tenuous link to her love.

But day three had gone by. Day four. Day five. And Aaro

couldn't still be alive on day six. Squawking at Oleg had lost all meaning.

If only the man would just tell her what happened. When Aaro had died. If he had asked for her. Maybe she could eventually find out where he was buried. Having a place to visit. It might help.

Or not. She felt hollowed out, brittle. Edie and Kev were kind and gentle, but they both knew there was nothing anyone could say. So for the most part, they stayed quiet. The great thing about Kev and Edie were their impervious mind shields. Both of them. What a relief.

She couldn't just give up. There was still work to be done. Lara was still languishing in captivity somewhere. But she would have to be brilliant and heroic to figure out how to help Lara, and she was fresh out of brilliance and heroism. The well had run dry.

Then something made her turn. A pull, like wind in her hair.

She looked over her shoulder. Edie was slogging through the sand, waving her arms. Her words were impossible to make out, but her shouting tone was full of excitement. Her belly clutched in dread. Good news was impossible at this point. And that left . . .

She took off at a dead run, staying on wet sand for speed, angling out onto the sliding, sun-warmed, dry sand when she was close enough.

Edie's face was wet with tears. Nina grabbed her arms. "What is it? Is he dead?"

Edie sniffed back tears, and shook her head. "No," she said, her voice quavering. "Oh, Nina. Come. Quick."

She grabbed Nina's hand, and they sprinted. Edie pulled her over the dune that separated the house from the beach. And Nina stumbled to her knees, then her hands, a cry of shock choked in her throat.

Aaro was sprawled on the sand. His face was so thin,

drawn with pain, but his eyes shone with joy. Nina clapped her hand to her mouth, losing her balance. Edie helped her to her feet. She didn't trust her own eyes. After all that had happened, it had to be a dirty trick, a cruel joke. Just a way to slap her down again, once and for all.

"Nina?" he whispered.

She saw the blood on the fingers pressed to his side, and ran to him, dropping to her knees. "What is this? What happened?"

"Nah. Just the bullet wound from before. It's leaking. No big deal."

She snorted. "Just a bullet wound. Only you, Aaro. You can't be a dream or a hallucination, then. My mind could not spontaneously come up with anything as irritating as you."

He grinned. "Nope. It sure couldn't."

"We see him, too," Edie assured her. "He's really here."

"What about the drug?" she asked anxiously.

"I never took the A dose," Aaro said. "It was a dummy. Dmitri must have switched it out, at the cabin. He took the A dose, not me. He must have found your purse in the bedroom while they were messing with us. And he took his opportunity."

"Oh, God," she whispered. "Oh, my God."

"So Dmitri was the one who died raving, two days ago. Not me."

"So . . . so you're not dying?" she asked. Still afraid to believe it.

He gave her a crooked smile. "I'm all fucked up, but not dying. You're stuck with me, babe. To the ends of the earth, the end of time, and all that good stuff."

Her jaw trembled so hard, her teeth chattered. She was going to fly apart, into a million pieces.

"Dmitri wanted the B dose for himself. That was why he followed us to Spruce Ridge," Aaro said.

"But what about your psi talent? How the hell did that happen?"

His eyebrow twitched. "Just lucky, I guess. Must be a genetic thing. Remember, how Tonya said I never let it out of its cage? I guess, when I thought they'd shot me up with psi-max . . ." He shrugged, and froze halfway through, wincing. "I let it out of the cage at last. Thinking I was drugged gave me permission. An excuse to be more like my father, I guess." He looked up at Kev. "How's Miles?"

"Not great." Kev's voice was grim. "He was in a coma for a few days. Bruising, bleeding on the brain. Almost bought it. Sean's in Denver with him now. This morning he regained consciousness for a while. He was talking a little, to his mom, and Sean. About Lara Kirk. He's obsessed with her now. But his vitals are better. So we're hoping."

"And Rudd?"

"Rudd's red paste," Edie said, her soft voice unusually hard. "He disintegrated on the rocks. Thank God."

Kev placed his hand on her shoulder. "We should go out front, and wait for the ambulance," he told her. "Leave these two alone."

"Oh. Um, yeah. Sure." Edie wiped her eyes, gave them a tremulous smile, and followed her husband back into the house.

The two of them gazed at each other, almost shy.

"I want to hug you," she whispered. "But I'm afraid I'll hurt you."

Aaro lowered himself carefully to the sand. "Lie down, and hug my good side. I want you to hug me 'til the ambulance gets here. And after."

She did as he directed, shocked at how hard and thin his body felt, like a hot tangle of wires. He'd always been lean, but God. The contact unleashed a storm of silent sobs, and she hid her face against his shoulder and let them flow. He kissed her forehead. Warm, real.

"You be sure to tell the EMTs when they come that I'm your wife," she said, her voice shaking. "I want them to hear it from you."

"Sure thing, sweetheart."

"It almost killed me. When your father wouldn't let me see you."

"I'm sorry." He kissed her tears away. "We'll get all the paperwork straight, first thing. It'll never happen again."

"And I'm staying with you," she said, still defensive. "In the hospital. Stuck to you. They'll have to chain me to a radiator to keep me away from you. I own your ass, Aaro. Remember?"

He sighed contentedly. "Feels good. To belong to you." He stared up at the crescent moon and its dangling star, and waved. "Hey, Aunt."

She jerked up onto her elbow. "About Tonya. Did she . . . ?"

"Yes." He kept his eyes fixed on the star. "The day after we saw her. She told me she'd be my star for me now. That I could go out and look into the sky, and say hello to her. Remember? You were there."

"Yes, I remember." Her throat fogged up.

"She stole us away from Oleg once. Me and Julie. A whole month, on the Jersey Shore, one winter. I was thirteen, Julie was ten. Best month of my life." He glanced over at her, smiling tenderly. "So far."

She nodded, her throat too tight to speak.

"We would look up at the stars with her, on clear nights," he said. "She told us to wish on the stars. For freedom."

"Freedom?"

"Yeah. You live in Oleg Arbatov's household for any length of time, and believe me, you start fantasizing about freedom. But ever since then, I had this idea that we'd been so happy because we were free." He spoke slowly, as if puzzling it out as he went. "I thought freedom was the thing to strive for. But it wasn't freedom that made us so happy." He turned away from the star, and gazed at her, and the look in his eyes made her heart swell. "It was love," he said. "I get that now."

She was so happy, she could barely speak. "So, um, now you'd wish on the star for love?"

He shook his head. "No," he said. "I don't have to wish anymore. I have it. I'm in it. Lost in it. I'm in so far, I'll never find my way back."

"Let's stay lost," she said. "Let's just live there together. Forever."

"Yeah." His lips met hers in a slow, reverent kiss. "Forever."

If you enjoyed *One Wrong Move*,
you won't want to miss *Fatal Strike*,
Shannon McKenna's thrilling
romantic-suspense novel featuring
the intrepid Miles Davenport,
friend and ally of the McCloud brothers.
Read on for a special preview!

On sale now.

PROLOGUE

"She's lost six pounds since last week, sir," Jason Hu said.

Thaddeus Greaves gazed through the small pane of one-way glass, at the young woman inside the cell. Lara Kirk stood with her back to him. Sharp shoulder blades pressed against her cotton jersey tank. Loose pants hung on her thin but still graceful form. Her slender back radiated dignity, conscious of being observed, though she could not see them. Full of psi talent, even without enhancement. He tasted it in the air, like smoke.

So much like Hugh. The similarities reverberated inside him, stirring up a storm of disturbing memories. Feelings. He tamped them down.

Her long, dark hair dangled as she sank slowly down into a perfect back-bend. Her tank slid down, too. He could count every rib. The top snagged on the curve of her breast. He waited, breathless, for it to slip down, show him her nipple. It did not. "Other changes?"

"She no longer cries, or talks to herself, or sings. That

stopped a month ago. She spends her time meditating, or doing gymnastics—"

"Yoga," Greaves corrected him. "She's doing yoga, Hu."

"Ah, yes, yoga. Blood samples show her iron is low, and vitamin D. I've supplemented her food, but she averages less than seven hundred calories a day at this point."

"That can't go on indefinitely," Greaves said.

"We could use a feeding tube. Or feed her intravenously." Greaves grimaced. "Any progress with the new formula?"

Hu hesitated. "Not since last week," he admitted. "Without the A component, we're still stabbing in the dark. We need new test subjects."

Lara Kirk kicked up one slender leg. The pant legs pooled around her thighs as she did a handstand. The shirt sagged lower. At last, her nipple was revealed. Taut, dark brown, lovely. Her slim arms trembled with strain. They did not look strong enough to bear her weight, and yet, they did. Her dark eyes were wide, intensely focused, the message as loud as if she screamed it. You have not broken me.

After a time, Lara Kirk slowly folded her body and stood. Greaves was stirred. Something steely and indomitable about her called to him.

"Has she manifested psi abilities?" he asked.

"We never dosed her," Hu said, defensive. "You never authorized—"

"I mean naturally," Greaves snapped.

Hu looked clouded. "Haven't noticed. Couldn't rule it out, I guess."

Beautiful, how she held herself. That remote dignity. Hugh had that quality. He'd been an artist and visionary, too. She was a very talented sculptor. He owned some of her early works. They called to his soul.

He made the decision. "Dose her," he ordered.

Hu blinked. "Sir? Are you sure we should risk—"

"I'm sure." He stared, as Lara sank into a deep lunge, and then arched her arms back, like a bow pulled taut. Greaves licked his lips.

"Do it now," he said. *"I want to watch."*

1

Stop thinking about her. Concentrate, damnit.

Miles stared up at volcanic granite above him, scanning for handholds, footholds. He channeled energy into his shield. Thinking about Lara Kirk was not useful. Dreaming of her was even worse.

But he'd never been that good at suppressing unwanted thoughts. Even before being reduced to this current suck-ass state.

As for the dreams, what was up with that? White hot thundering erotic dreams, every night. What kind of twisted up scumbag weirdo dreamed every night about nailing the girl he had *failed* to rescue? If he'd saved her, now. Then maybe he'd be halfway entitled to his horndog fantasies. But as it was, no. No fucking way.

He lectured himself every night. Tonight, he chose his behavior. People could. He'd read dozens of books on lucid dreaming. But whenever she came to him, his dream self did not give a fuck what his waking self wanted. He just seized her. And went at her, like a maniac.

He remembered every last detail of it when he woke, too, in laser sharp detail. No foggy dream lens, no fade-outs. Her sweet salty taste, her satiny thick hair, twisted into his fingers. Her body moving against his. Strong, slender. Hot. He could feel it right now. And, oh man, he'd done it to himself, again. He contemplated the hard-on, dismayed.

The guys with the white coats should just take him and his perpetual stiffie away before he hurt himself.

You tried to help her. Move on. Think about climbing the cliff. Don't think about Lara Kirk. Don't think at all. No think. Empty.

He stared up, calculating the best ascent. His calculations were cold and distant when his shield was up and running. Neutral data, crunched through algorithms. Conclusions organized into neat categories, rank and file. As long as his shield was strong, he was chill. He had errant thoughts, sure, but they did not play themselves out through his body. They flickered, like a TV he was barely following.

But if his shield wavered, man, it was blitzkrieg. Full on screaming stress flashbacks of Spruce Ridge, Rudd's attack. Bad news.

He'd gotten better at keeping the shield up, after weeks of practice alone in the mountains. He'd discovered rock climbing the second week. The tight mental focus it required pulled him together. Free climbing, of course. Climbing equipment hadn't been on his supply list.

He pulled off his boots. He needed monkey toes to climb that big bastard, but he'd make do with what God gave him. He studied the big overhang, the stretch where the basalt had formed long crystalline striations, as if a huge beast had clawed violently downwards. There were cracks and crannies, maybe big enough for fingertips, maybe not. He cataloged them, even at this distance. His eyes were sharper than before Spruce Ridge. Sharp, like all of him. Like broken glass.

And to counteract that dubious advantage, his usual headache throbbed nastily away. A lingering hangover from Spruce Ridge, plus sleep deprivation. He was so damn ambivalent about sleep now. Ever since those crazy wild erotic dream trysts with the ghost girl started up.

The dream always began with her creeping through a mechanical wall. A big, steam-punk thing, full of huge gears, ax-shaped pendulums swinging, a confusion of parts in constant motion. But somehow, she found Lara-shaped openings, and slithered through them. Sinuous, practiced. A choreography that she knew without even thinking.

His shield wavered, and so did he. *Ouch.* He frantically sought the frequency. Lara was a dangerous ghost. She shorted him out.

He squinted at the Fork, which towered against the dawn sky. If he shorted out and lost the shield partway up, he was meat.

He'd decided, arbitrarily, that if the odds of surviving the climb were less than fifty, he'd pass. Not that he was afraid of death. Not since Spruce Ridge. Rudd had driven him to a place where death would have been his best friend. He'd never be afraid of it again. But even so, he wasn't going looking for death. A guy had to really give a shit, to plan his own suicide. He just couldn't be bothered. Who had the energy.

His shield seemed solid, after some deep breathing. OK. That put him at fifty percent. Good to go. He cracked his knuckles, flexed his hands. The pine needles beneath his bare feet were fuzzed with frost. He focused his mind to a diamond sharp point . . .

. . . and the perception washed over him, mixing into the data feed. *Cougar.*

Where? He looked around, neck prickling, keeping his mind as blank as possible, to make space for the flash flood of sensory info constantly roaring through it. Another souvenir from Spruce Ridge. Psychopath Harold Rudd had mind-fucked him into a coma with his coercive psychic powers a couple months ago. Miles had survived the encounter—barely. But when he finally did wake up, his brain was wired all wrong. He existed in a state of constant sensory overload. The world blared at him from all sides, no filters, no rest, no downtime.

It knocked him flat on his ass. He had to jerry-rig himself back into functionality again, and learn how to at least fake normal. Not that he'd been so very normal before, but everything was relative.

She watched him from that stand of trees. How did he know it was a she? Smell? Like he'd ever sniffed a cougar to determine its sex.

Still, the summation of all the bits of information he sensed, each individually too small to perceive on its own, swirled up like a pixelated cloud, focusing into a potent, predatory *her*. Almost invisible in the trees, eyes gleaming with inscrutable feline calm. Her tail swished when she registered that he saw her. He loved seeing the animals. These were the moments he was trolling for. Fleeting instants when his hypersensitivity was actually a gift, not just a huge pain in the ass.

Neither wanted to move until the other one did, but Miles finally surrendered, lifting his hands. "I'm not breakfast," he told her.

Her tail swished. Her gaze was unwavering.

Miles took a swig of his water, stowed the flask and gave her a respectful nod. "Later, then," he told her, and began his climb.

It was long, slow, near impossible. Perfect. Silence and solitude helped maintain the shield, and so did muscle-bulging, sweat dripping, eye-popping effort. Dangling a millimeter away from death for hours at a time was genuinely restful to him, at this point. Go figure.

Since he woke up from the coma, he'd been faced with two possible modes of existence. Mode One: a shaking, sobbing nightmare screaming stress flashbacks, reliving Rudd's torture. Big barrel of laughs, that one. Mode Two, he kept up that mind shield, constantly. It damped down the stress flashbacks, but it also damped down his regular emotional response. Strange, how he'd originally created the shield to protect himself from Rudd and his pet telepath, Anabel, for all the good it had done him. They hadn't been able to read his mind, but Rudd had ground him into hamburger anyway.

The shield kept the stress flashbacks from clawing him to pieces. But it also flatlined him emotionally. He'd made that wall to keep attackers out, but what he'd ultimately created was a bunker to keep his own self in. Whatever. Cowering in a fortress worked for him.

Mode Two still won, whatever the price. It was a no-brainer.

It changed him, though, to the dismay of his family and friends. Nobody liked chill, flatlined Miles. He was too cold for them. No fun anymore. Tough shit. He was done rolling around like a puppy, panting for approval. He was doing his best, and anyone who cherished strong opinions about his coping mechanisms could go get stuffed.

Nothing moved him. Not maternal guilt, not the scolding of his friends; Aaro, Sean, or various other components of the McCloud crowd, an opinionated group if there ever was one. To a man, they considered Miles to be their own personal creation, and as such, their personal property. It took a traumatic brain injury to jolt him free of that.

He'd always wondered how those McCloud guys, most notably Davy, Connor, and Kev, managed the strong, silent routine. Now he understood. They must have shields in their heads. Just like him.

Too bad the shield didn't block out the sensory overload. But no, the info dump ran on a different channel. With his senses ratcheted to the max, normal life was torture. Perfume, cigarettes, and car exhaust made him gag. All the intimate data about the hormonal states of the bodies of the people he encountered was really embarrassing. Traffic was ear-splitting, electric lights, oh God. Worst of all, electromagnetic radiation of wi-fi generated a buzz in his head that turned the chronic pain into something approaching agony, and he was a computer geek by trade, for God's sake. This was a game-changing professional handicap, and after months, it showed no signs of improvement.

There were drugs, sure, but to make a dent in this, a problem this big, he needed a dose so high, it turned him puddle-of-drool stupid.

The doctors said it would ease off, but months had gone by, and if anything his nerves felt more raw than before. At least the shield made it easier to be stoic about the pain. He felt it, and it sucked, but he didn't panic. He just kept breathing, kept waiting for it to ebb.

It was easier, out in the woods. Sensory data still flooded in, but the data was cleaner, more balanced. Nothing made his head explode.

He'd sucked down some books on wilderness camping, taken all the macho gear the McClouds had equipped him with over the years: guns, ammo, all-purpose belt knife, etc. Part of the McClouds' ongoing quest to transform him from a basement dwelling geek freak into a kick-ass commando like them. They'd made some progress over the years, but those guys wouldn't be satisfied until he was prepared to sew up his own bullet wounds with dental floss. As fucking if.

Thinking too much. Cut that shit out. Concentrate.

The rock-face shifted back into focus. He felt the energetic pulse of every living thing near him. Lichen rasped beneath his fingertips. He sensed every bird, every bug. Felt the cougar, studying him from below. He didn't look down, just felt it on his back. She was staring up like she wanted something from him. Something he just couldn't give.

Made him think of Lara. Bad idea, dangling from a cliff face. He saw her in his head, even though his eyes were on the handholds.

But there she was, sliding through grinding gears, just like she did in his dreams. She was inside, now. Looking around, curious, expectant. Big dark eyes alight with fascination. He saw her so clearly.

Fear grew, vibrating in his stomach, through his limbs, because he wasn't guiding this image. It was unspooling on its own, but he wasn't dreaming, or even daydreaming. He was wide awake, fully conscious, hanging off a cliff. Like, what the *fuck?*

His shield flickered. A shock of raw screaming electricity blasted through him—

He came to sliding rapidly down the wall. Barely caught himself on a narrow chink with a bone-jarring *thud,* fingers clawed—

Focus. Don't look down. His feet dangled over nothing.

A few panicky moments, to find the frequency. He glommed onto it. Strong and steady. Better. Hard as ice. Chill. Empty. No think.

He looked down at the jagged boulders hundreds of feet below, toes wiggling in the foreground as they searched for purchase. Blood on the rocks in front of him. He'd scraped all the skin off his fingertips.

It took many long, shaking, straining minutes before he found a jut of rock with his foot, and could lift himself, recalculate a fresh route.

He made it to the top somehow, muscles hollow and quivering. He had named this rock formation "the Fork," today's destination being the top of the tallest, sharpest tine. He stood on the summit and took it in: deep green forest, snow dusted Cascades, shreds of moving clouds above and below.

Right now, he almost enjoyed the flash-flood info feed, when every single piece of data was harmonious with the rest. Except him. His fingertips oozed blood, and his cock was still hard, from that weird not-exactly-a-dream.

He pushed the thought of Lara away and gnawed some jerked elk meat Davy had given him, a relic from their hunting trip last year. A thinly disguised campaign to force Miles to learn to shoot a rifle properly; a necessary rite of passage, according to Davy. Davy himself was an awesome sniper. Mostly, Miles surmised, because the guy could shut down his emotions at will. Miles had not been great at it. Too twitchy. He couldn't find that still place between the thoughts, breaths.

He'd found it now. The new, chill Miles would be a good sniper. Technique, wind drop, it was just math. He was good at math. If he ever needed to waste somebody at two kilometers, he was all set.

No misadventures on the way down, but he was exhausted by the time he got back to his rough campsite, which consisted of a tarp tied over his sleeping roll, a small fire pit, and a tiny gas burner.

Too tired to cook. He built a fire for warmth, chomped a protein bar. He'd get scurvy if he went on like this, but foraging for edible plants did not engage his brain in the excellent way that rock climbing did. And all that chewing, Jesus. It made his jaw sore. Damn fiber.

He fed wood into the fire, enjoying his too-zonked-to-think state when he felt it again. That shivery tingle. He rose, scanning the trees.

Cat eyes caught the firelight, flashing eerily. The sounds of the night swelled as his perceptions amplified. He felt no sense of menace, just cautious awe, but he pulled the loaded Smith & Wesson out of his pack. Too small a caliber for a cougar, but it was better than nothing.

God forbid it come to that. She was so damn beautiful.

He fed twigs into the fire. Wind sighed and tossed the treetops. It was a clear night, wind blowing. The shifting swatches of velvety night sky were smeared with stars. His eyes wanted to close so badly, but the cougar's presence gave him that extra zing of adrenaline that kept them open. He'd shifted position to keep her in plain sight.

She seemed fascinated. She wanted to figure him out, make some sense out of him. *Good luck with that.* There was no sense to be made.

They'd told him depression was normal after a brain injury. And PTSD flashbacks would drive anybody half bonkers. He got it. Duh. But Christ, the sex dreams he had in his sleep were hard enough for him to justify. If Lara started haunting him while he was awake, too . . .

Yeah, that took him up to a whole new level of crazy.

He'd taken on Lara's rescue like a holy quest after Spruce Ridge. Lara was another victim of the psychic freak squad who had attacked Miles. Lara's mother Helga Kasyanov had developed psi-max, the psi-enhancing drug that augmented latent paranormal ability. Helga had been murdered by Rudd's people. Miles had been the one to find Lara's father's freshly mutilated body, too, chained in his own basement.

So Lara had been orphaned, as well as abducted. It made him angry, sick, and sad, which touched off a useless but uncontrollable urge to save the princess. Too many video games in his egghead youth.

He'd tried to find Lara harder than he'd ever tried at anything in his life. He'd found exactly squat. Lara Kirk stayed stubbornly lost.

It burned his ass. No one better than he knew what she'd been up against, what she might have suffered. How could a guy know that, and just take it easy, convalesce? *Sorry lady, I need some R&R to get my brain swelling down before I can rescue you from the slavering monsters.*

And why did he still give a shit at all, with his shield up? He managed not to care about anything or anyone else.

Because everyone else is outside your shield. She keeps sneaking inside. At which point you bone her brains out. Man. What a prince.

Stop. That train of thought stank of schizo delusions. Sleep was like a hand, pressing down on his head. He fought it, which left him less willpower to withstand the impulse to grope in his jacket for the plastic envelope. The envelope held a copy of the head shot on Lara's website. She was a sculptor. *Had been* a sculptor. He knew every last piece in her online catalog. He'd studied them. Pored over them.

He stared at her haunting dark eyes, for who knew how long, and then started cursing, low and long, picking up steam. His tantrum culminated in tossing the photo at the fire, but he choked it, of course. The picture fell short and landed at the edge of the embers, where the plastic edges began to melt and twist. He picked it up, defeated, and waved it until the plastic solidified. Stuck it back in his jacket.

So much for that little hissy fit. Why did he even try?

He was keeping his eyes open by brute force of will when the images started running in his head. Just like while he was climbing. Like a dream, but he was not asleep. He watched her, in some clear place in his head. Lara, moving through the guts of some big machine, but the machine was him. She wore that gauzy white thing, like a baby-doll nightdress, tattered and distressed, with a sexy Victorian poorhouse vibe. Her hair hung long, tousled. Long, slim legs.

The dress fluttered as she sidled through gnashing gears, arching here, bending there, ducking, leaping . . . and then she was inside.

Of him. While he watched. Holy shit. His muscles contracted, shaking with strain. Oh, man. This was weird. This was bad.